ROSAMUND LUPTON

AFTERWARDS

Complete and Unabridged

CHARNWOOD
Leicester

First published in Great Britain in 2011 by
Piatkus
An imprint of
Little, Brown Book Group, London

First Charnwood Edition
published 2012
by arrangement with
Little, Brown Book Group
An Hachette UK Company, London

British Library CIP Data

Lupton, Rosamund.
    Afterwards.
    1. Arson- -Fiction. 2. Mothers- -Fiction.
    3. Suspense fiction. 4. Large type books.
    I. Title
    823.9'2–dc23

ISBN 978–1–4448–0977–0

Published by
F. A. Thorpe (Publishing)
Anstey, Leicestershire

Set by Words & Graphics Ltd.
Anstey, Leicestershire
Printed and bound in Great Britain by
T. J. International Ltd., Padstow, Cornwall

This book is printed on acid-free paper

AFTERWARDS

Black smoke stains a summer blue sky. A school is on fire. One mother, Grace, sees the smoke and runs. She knows her teenage daughter Jenny is inside. Grace races along the tree-lined driveway, which Jenny had walked down only a few hours earlier. She goes into the burning building to rescue her child. Afterwards Grace must find the identity of the arsonist and protect her family from the person who's still intent on destroying them. Afterwards she must confront the face of evil and discover the limitlessness of love.

Books by Rosamund Lupton
Published by The House of Ulverscroft:

SISTER

To my sons
Cosmo and Joe

I couldn't be prouder.

To see a world in a grain of sand,
And a heaven in a wild flower,
Hold infinity in the palm of your hand,
And eternity in an hour.

William Blake — 'Auguries of Innocence'

PROLOGUE

I couldn't move, not even a little finger or a flicker of an eye. I couldn't open my mouth to scream.

I struggled, as *hard as I could*, to move the huge heavy hulk that my body had become but I was trapped under the hull of a vast ship wrecked on the ocean floor and moving was impossible.

My eyelids were welded shut. My eardrums broken. My vocal cords snapped off.

Pitch dark and silent and so heavy in there; a mile of black water above me.

Only one thing for it, I said to myself, thinking of you, and I slipped out of the wrecked ship of my body into the black ocean.

I swam upwards towards the daylight with all my strength.

Not a mile deep after all.

Because I was suddenly in a white room, brightly gleaming, smelling pungently of anti-septic. I heard voices and my name.

I saw the body part of 'I' was in a hospital bed. I watched a doctor holding my eyelids open and shining a light into my eyes; another was tipping my bed back, another putting drips into my arm.

You won't be able to believe this. You're a man who dams rivers and climbs mountains; a man who *knows* the laws of nature and physics. 'Hogwash!' you've said to the telly, when anyone

1

talks about anything paranormal. Although you'll be kinder to your wife, not consigning my words to be fed to pigs, you'll think it's impossible. But out-of-body experiences *do* happen. You read about it in the papers; hear people talking about it on Radio 4.

But if this was real, what should I do? Push my way through the doctors and elbow out the nurse who was shaving my head? 'Excuse me! Gangway! Sorry! My body, I think. I'm right here actually!'

Thinking ridiculous things because I was afraid.

Sick, goose-bumps, shivering afraid.

And as I felt afraid I remembered.

Blistering heat and raging flames and suffocating smoke.

The school was on fire.

1

You were in your important BBC meeting this afternoon, so you won't have felt the strong warm breeze — 'A godsend for sports day,' parents were saying to each other. I thought that even if a God existed he'd be a little tied up with starving people in Africa or abandoned orphans in Eastern Europe to worry about providing free air-conditioning for Sidley House's sack race.

The sun shone on the white lines painted on the grass; the whistles hanging around the teachers' necks glinted; the children's hair was shiny-bright. Touchingly too-big feet on small legs bounced on the grass as they did the one-hundred-metre dash, the sack race, the obstacle course. You can't really see the school in summer time, those huge pollarded oaks hide it from view, but I knew a reception class was still in there and I thought it was a shame the youngest children couldn't be out enjoying the summer afternoon too.

Adam was wearing his 'I am 8!' badge from our card this morning — just this morning. He came dashing up to me, that little face of his beaming, because he was off to get his cake from school *right now!* Rowena had to get the medals so was going with him; Rowena who was at Sidley House with Jenny all those moons ago.

As they left, I looked around to see if Jenny had arrived. I'd thought that after her A-level

3

disaster she should immediately start revision for her retakes, but she still wanted to work at Sidley House to pay for her planned trip to Canada. Strange to think I minded so much.

I'd thought her being a temporary teaching assistant at seventeen was challenge enough — and now she was school nurse for the afternoon. We'd gently crossed swords at breakfast.

★   ★   ★

'It's just a little young to have that much responsibility.'

'It's a primary school sports day, Mum, not a motorway crash.'

★   ★   ★

But now her shift was almost over — with no accidents at all — and soon she'd be out to join us. I was sure she'd be itching to leave that small stuffy medical room stuck at the top of the school.

I'd noticed at breakfast that she was wearing that red frou-frou skirt with a skimpy top and I'd told her it didn't really look very professional but when did Jenny ever listen to my advice on clothes?

★   ★   ★

'Just count your lucky stars I'm not in bumsters.'

'You mean the jeans that hang around boys' bottoms?'

4

'Yup.'

'I always want to go and give them a hitch up.'
She bursts out laughing.

And her long legs do look rather wonderful
under the too-short, gauzy skirt and despite
myself I feel a little proud. Though she got her
long legs from you.

*　*　*

On the playing field, Maisie arrived, her blue
eyes sparkling, her face one large smile. Some
people dismiss her as a jolly-hockey-sticks Sloane
in FUN shirts (long sleeves a different pattern to
the rest) but most of us love her.

'Gracie,' she said, giving me a hug. 'I've come
to give Rowena a lift home. She texted me a little
while ago, said the tubes were up the spout. So
Chauffeur-Mum to the fore!'

'She's getting the medals,' I told her. 'Adam's
gone with her to get his cake. They should be
back any minute.'

She smiled. 'What kind of cake this year?'

'An M&S chocolate tray-bake. Addie dug out
a trench with a teaspoon and we took off all the
Maltesers and replaced them with soldiers. It's a
World War One cake. Which is violent but fits
with key stage two, so I don't think anyone'll
mind.'

She laughed. 'Fantastic.'

'Not really, but he thinks so.'

*　*　*

'Is she your <u>best</u> friend, Mum?' Adam asked me recently.

'Probably, yes,' I said.

★ ★ ★

Maisie handed me a 'little something' for Adam, beautifully wrapped, which I knew would contain a spot-on present. She's brilliant at presents. It's one of the many things I love her for. Another is that she ran in the mothers' race every single year that Rowena was at Sidley House, and always came last by a mile but didn't give *a hoot!* She has never owned a piece of Lycra clothing and, unlike virtually every other mum at Sidley House, has never been inside a gym.

I know. I'm dawdling on that sunny playing field with Maisie. I'm sorry. But it's hard. What I'm getting to is just so bloody hard.

Maisie left to find Rowena in the school.

I checked my watch; it was almost three.

Still no sign of either Jenny or Adam.

The PE teacher blew his whistle for the last race — the relay — bellowing through his loudspeaker for teams to get in position. I worried that Addie would get into trouble for not being in his designated place.

I looked back towards the school, thinking surely I'd see them coming towards me any moment.

★ ★ ★

Smoke was coming from the school building. Thick black smoke like a bonfire. I remember the calm most of all. The absence of panic. But knowing it was accelerating towards me, like a juggernaut.

I had to hide. Quickly. No. I am not in danger. This terror isn't for me. My children are in danger.

It hit me in the chest, full on.

There is a fire and they are in there.

They are in there.

*   *   *

And then I was running at the velocity of a scream. Running so hard that I didn't have time to breathe.

*   *   *

A running scream that can't stop until I hold them both.

*   *   *

Darting across the road, I heard sirens blaring on the bridge. But the fire engines weren't moving. There were abandoned cars by the traffic lights blocking their path, and women were getting out of other cars just left in the middle of the road and were running across the bridge towards the school. But all the mothers were at the sports day. What were these women doing, kicking off their high-wedged shoes and tripping over

7

flip-flops and screaming as they ran, like me? I recognised one, the mother of a reception child. They were the mothers of the four-year-olds coming to do their usual pick-up. One had left a toddler in her abandoned SUV and the toddler was hitting the window as he watched his mother in this ghastly mothers' race.

★   ★   ★

And then I was there first, before the other mothers because they still had to cross the road and run down the drive.

And the four-year-olds were lined up outside the school with their teacher, a neat little crocodile; and Maisie was with the teacher, with her arm around her, and I saw how shaken the teacher looked. Behind them black smoke poured out of the school like a factory chimneystack, staining the summer-blue sky.

★   ★   ★

And Adam was outside — *outside!* — by that bronze statue — and he was sobbing against Rowena and she was holding him tightly. And in that moment of relief, love flooded out from me not only onto my boy but onto the girl who was comforting him.

I allowed myself a second, maybe two, to feel gut-wrenching relief for Adam and then I was looking for Jenny. Bobbed blonde hair, slender. No one like Jenny outside. From the bridge the sirens wailed.

8

And the four-year-olds were starting to cry as they saw their mothers, running full tilt towards them down the drive, tears streaming down their faces, arms outstretched, waiting for that moment to hold their child.

And I turned towards the burning building, black smoke billowing out of the classrooms on the second and third floors.

Jenny.

2

I ran up the main steps to the school and opened the door into the small vestibule and for a moment everything was normal. There was that framed photo on the wall of the first pupils at Sidley House, smiling their baby teeth smiles. (Rowena exceptionally pretty then, Jenny our gawky little duckling.) There was the day's lunch menu, with pictures as well as words; fish pie and peas. And I was overwhelmingly reassured. It was like coming into school every morning.

I tried to open the door from the vestibule into the school itself. For the first time I realised how heavy it was. A fire door. My hands were shaking too hard to get a grip on the handle properly. And it was hot. I'd had my shirtsleeves rolled high up. I unrolled them and tugged them over my hand. Then I pulled the door open.

⋆　⋆　⋆

I screamed her name. Over and over. And each time I screamed her name, smoke came into my mouth and throat and lungs until I couldn't scream any more.

The sound of burning, hissing and spitting; a giant serpent of fire coiling through the building.

Above me something collapsed. I heard and felt the thud.

10

And then a roar of rage as the fire discovered fresh oxygen.

The fire was above me.

Jenny was above me.

* * *

I could just see my way to the stairs. I started climbing them, the heat getting stronger, the smoke thicker.

I got to the first floor.

The heat punched me full in the body and face.

I couldn't see anything — blacker than hell.

I had to get to the third floor.

To Jenny.

* * *

The smoke went into my lungs and I was breathing barbed wire.

* * *

I dropped onto my hands and knees, remembering from some distant fire practice at my old school that this is where oxygen is found. By some small miracle I found I could breathe.

I crawled forwards, a blind person without a stick, fingers tapping in front of me, trying to find the next flight of stairs. I ought to have been crossing the reading area with the huge brightly coloured rug. I felt the rug under my fingers, the nylon melting and crinkling in the heat, and

11

my fingertips were burning. I was afraid my fingertips would soon be too burnt to feel. I was like the man in Adam's mythology book, holding onto Ariadne's thread to find his way out of the labyrinth; only my thread was a melting rug.

I reached the end of the rug and felt the texture change, and then I felt the first step.

I began to climb the stairs up to the second floor, on my hands and knees, keeping my face down to the oxygen.

And all the time I was refusing to believe it could really be happening. This place was soft-cheeked children and fidgeting on the stairs and washing lines strung up across classrooms with flying pennants of children's drawings. It was reading books and chapter books and beanbags and fruit cut up into slices at break-time.

It was safe.

Another step.

All around me I heard and felt chunks of Jenny and Adam's childhoods crashing down.

Another step.

I felt dizzy, poisoned by something in the smoke.

Another step.

It was a battle. Me against this living breathing fire that wanted to kill my child.

Another step.

I knew I'd never get to the third floor; that it would kill me before I could reach her.

★   ★   ★

I felt her at the top of the stairs. She had managed to get down one flight.

She was my little girl and I was here and everything was going to be alright. All alright now.

'Jenny?'

She didn't speak or move and the fire's roar was getting closer and I couldn't breathe much longer.

I tried to pick her up as if she was still tiny, but she was too heavy.

I dragged her down the stairs, trying to use my body to shield her from the heat and smoke. I wouldn't think how badly hurt she was. Not yet. Not till the bottom of the stairs. Not till she was safe.

I cried to you, silently, as if by telepathy I could summon you to help us.

And as I dragged her, step by step, down the stairs, trying to get away from burning heat and raging flames and smoke, I thought of love. I held onto it. And it was cool and clear and quiet.

Maybe there was telepathy between us, because at that moment you must have been in your meeting with the BBC commissioning editors about the follow-up to your 'Hostile Environments' series. You'd done hot, steamy jungles and blazing, arid deserts, and you want the next series to be in the contrasting frozen wilds of Antarctica. So maybe it was you who helped me envisage a silent, white acreage of love as I dragged Jenny down the stairs.

But before I reached the bottom, something hit me, throwing me forwards, and everything went dark.

As I lost consciousness I talked to you.

I said, '*An unborn baby doesn't need air at all, did you know that?*' I thought you probably didn't. When I was pregnant with Jenny I found out everything I could, but you were too impatient for her to arrive to bother with her prologue. So you don't know that an unborn baby, swimming around in amniotic fluid, can't take a breath or she would drown. There aren't any temporary gills so that she can swim, fish-like, until birth. No, the baby gets her oxygen from the umbilical cord attached to her mother. I felt like an oxygen supply attached to a tiny, intrepid diver.

But the moment she was born, the oxygen supply was cut off and she entered the new element of air. There was a moment of silence, a precipitous second, as if she stood on the edge of life, deciding. In the old days they used to slap the baby to hear the reassuring yell of lungs filled with air. Nowadays they look closely to see the minute rise of a baby-soft chest, and listen to the whispering — in and out — to know that life in the new medium of air has begun.

And then I cried and you cheered — actually cheered! — and the baby equipment trolley was wheeled out, no need for that now. A normal delivery. A healthy infant. To join all the billions of others on the planet who breathe, in and out, without thinking about it.

The next day your sister sent me a bouquet of roses with gypsophila, known as 'baby's breath', sprays of pretty white flowers. But a newborn baby's breath is finer than a single parachute from a blown dandelion clock.

You told me once that when you lose consciousness the last of the senses to go is hearing.

In the darkness I thought I heard Jenny take a dandelion-clock breath.

3

I told you already what happened when I woke up — that I was trapped under the hull of a vast ship wrecked on the ocean floor.

That I slipped out of the wrecked ship of my body into the inky black ocean and swam upwards towards the daylight.

That I saw the body part of 'me' in a hospital bed.

That I felt afraid and, as I felt fear, I remembered.

Blistering heat and raging flames and suffocating smoke.

Jenny.

* * *

I ran from the room to find her. Do you think I should have tried to go back into my body? But what if I was trapped, uselessly, inside again, but this time couldn't get out? How would I find her then?

In the burning school, I had searched for her in darkness and smoke. Now I was in brightly lit white corridors but the desperation to find her was the same. Panicking, I forgot about the me in the hospital bed and I went up to a doctor, asking where she was: *'Jennifer Covey. Seventeen years old. My daughter. She was in a fire.'* The doctor turned away. I went after him,

16

shouting, 'Where's my daughter?' He still walked away from me.

I interrupted two nurses. 'Where's my daughter? She was in a fire. Jenny Covey.'

They carried on talking to each other.

Again and again I was ignored.

I started screaming, loud as I could, screaming the house down, but everyone around me was deaf and blind.

Then I remembered that it was me who was mute and invisible.

No one would help me find her.

I ran down a corridor, away from the ward where my body was and into other wards, and then on again, frantically searching.

'I can't believe you've lost her!' said the nanny who lives in my head. She arrived just before I gave birth to Jenny, her critical voice replacing my teachers' praise. 'You're never going to find her like this, are you?'

She was right. Panic had turned me into a Brownian motion molecule, darting hither and thither, with no logic or clear direction.

I thought of you, what you would do, and made myself slow down.

You would start on the bottom floor, far left, like you do at home when something is lost for good, and then you'd work your way to the far right, then up to the next floor, methodically doing a sweep and finding the missing mobile phone/earring/Oyster card/number 8 Beast Quest book.

Thinking about Beast Quest books and missing earrings because the little details of our

17

lives helped to root me a little, calmed me a little.

So I went more slowly along the corridors, although desperate to run, trying to read signs rather than race past them. There were signs to lift banks, and oncology and outpatients and paediatrics — a mini-kingdom of wards and clinics and operating theatres and support services.

A sign to the mortuary tore into my vision and lodged there, but I wouldn't go to the mortuary. Wouldn't *even consider it.*

I saw a sign to Accident & Emergency. Maybe she hadn't been transferred to a ward yet.

I ran as fast as I could towards it.

I went in. A woman on a trolley was pushed past, bleeding. A doctor was running, his stethoscope flapping against his stomach; the doors to the ambulance bay swung open and a screeching siren filled the white corridor, panic bouncing off the walls. A place of urgency and tension and pain.

I looked into cubicle after cubicle, flimsy blue curtains dividing intense scenes from separate dramas. In one cubicle was Rowena, barely conscious. Maisie was sobbing next to her, but I only paused long enough to see that it wasn't Jenny and then I moved on.

★ ★ ★

At the end of the corridor was a room rather than a cubicle. I'd noticed doctors going in, and none coming out.

I went in.

18

There was someone appallingly hurt on the bed in the middle of the room, surrounded by doctors.

I didn't know it was her.

I had known her baby's cry from any other baby's almost the moment she was born; her calling for Mummy had sounded unique, unmistakable amongst other toddlers; I could find her face immediately, however crowded the stage. I knew her more intimately than I knew myself.

As a baby I knew every square centimetre of her; each hair in her eyebrows. I'd watched them being drawn, pencil stroke by pencil stroke, in the first days after birth. For months, I'd stared down at her for hour after hour, day after day, as I fed her from my breasts. It was dark the February she was born and as spring turned to summer it brought increased clarity in how I knew her.

For nine months, I'd had her heart beating inside my body; two heartbeats for every one of mine.

How could I not know it was her?

I turned to leave the room.

I saw sandals on the appallingly damaged person on the bed. The sandals with sparkly gems that I'd got her from Russell & Bromley as an absurdly early and out-of-season Christmas present.

Lots of people have those kind of sandals, lots and lots; they must manufacture thousands of them. It doesn't mean it's Jenny. It can't mean it's Jenny. Please.

19

Her blonde glinting hair was charred, her face swollen and horribly burnt. Two doctors were talking about percentage of BSA and I realised they were discussing the percentage of her body that was burnt. Twenty-five per cent.

'Jenny?' I shouted. But she didn't open her eyes. Was she deaf to me too? Or was she unconscious? I hoped that she was, because her pain would be unbearable.

I left the room, just for a moment. A drowning person coming up for one gulp of air before going back into that depth of compassion as I looked at her. I stood in the corridor and closed my eyes.

'Mum?'

I'd know her voice anywhere.

I looked down at a girl crouched in the corridor, her arms around her knees.

The girl I'd recognise among a thousand faces.

My second heartbeat.

I put my arms around her.

'What are we, Mum?'

'I don't know, sweetheart.'

It may seem strange, but I didn't even really wonder. The fire had burnt away everything I once thought of as normal. Nothing made sense any more.

A trolley with Jenny's body on it was wheeled past us; surrounded by medical staff. They'd covered her up using a sheet like a tent so the fabric wouldn't touch her burns.

Beside me I felt her flinch.

'Did you see your body?' I asked. 'Before they

covered it, I mean.'

I'd tried to let out the words delicately but they fell with a clump on the floor, forming a boorish, brutal question.

'Yeah, I did. 'Return of the living dead' kind of summarises it, doesn't it?'

'Jen, sweetheart — '

'This morning I was worried about blackheads on my nose. *Blackheads*. How ridiculous is that, Mum?'

I tried to comfort her, but she shook her head. She wanted me to ignore her tears and believe the act she was putting on. Needed me to. The one where she is still funny, lively, buoyant Jenny.

A doctor was talking to a nurse as they passed us.

'The dad's on his way, poor bloke.'

We hurried to find you.

4

The large hospital atrium was crowded with press. Your TV fame from presenting the 'Hostile Environments' series had attracted them. *'Not fame, Gracie,'* you'd corrected me once. *'Familiarity. Like a tin of baked beans.'*

A smartly dressed man arrived and the people who'd been buzzing around with cameras and microphones moved towards him. I wondered if Jenny also felt vulnerable and exposed in this swarm of people, but if she did, she gave no sign of it. She's always shared your courage.

'This will just be a brief statement,' the suited man said, looking annoyed at their presence. 'Grace and Jennifer Covey were admitted at four fifteen this afternoon with serious injuries. They are now being treated for those injuries in our specialist units. Rowena White was also admitted suffering from minor burns and smoke inhalation. At this point we have no further information. I'd be grateful if you would now wait outside the hospital rather than here.'

'How did the fire start?' a journalist asked the suited man.

'That's a question for the police, not us. Now if you'll excuse me.'

They carried on shouting out their questions, but we were looking out of the glass wall of the atrium for you. I'd been looking for our Prius and it was Jenny who spotted you first.

'He's here.'

You were getting out of an unfamiliar car. The BBC must have driven you in one of theirs.

Sometimes looking at your face is like looking in the mirror — so familiar it's become a part of me. But there was a mask of anxiety covering your usual face, making it strange. I hadn't realised that you are nearly always smiling.

You came into the hospital, and it was all wrong seeing you here in this hectic, frightening, sanitised place. You are in the kitchen getting a bottle of wine out of the fridge or in the garden waging a new offensive against snails, or driving out to dinner, me next to you, bemoaning traffic jams and praising sat-navs. You belong next to me on the sofa and on the right-hand side of our bed, moving slowly in the night towards mine. Even your appearances on TV in a jungle on the other side of the world are watched by me and the children on our family squashy sofa; the foreign mediated through the familiar.

You didn't belong here.

Jenny ran to you and put her arms around you, but you didn't know she was there and hurried on, half running up to the reception desk, your stride jerky with shock.

'My wife and daughter are here, Grace and Jenny Covey.'

For a moment the receptionist reacted, she must have seen you on the telly, and then she looked at you with sympathy.

'I'll bleep Dr Gawande, and he'll come to get you straight away.'

Your fingers drummed on the counter, your

eyes flicking around; a cornered animal.

The journalists hadn't yet spotted you. Maybe that mask over your old face had foxed them. Then Tara, my ghastly colleague at the *Richmond Post*, made a beeline towards you. As she reached you she smiled. *Smiled.*

'Tara Connor. I know your wife.'

You ignored her, scanning the room and seeing a young doctor hastening towards you.

'Dr Gawande?' you said.

'Yes.'

'How are they?' Your quiet voice was screaming.

Other journalists had seen you now and were coming towards you.

'The consultants will be able to give you a fuller picture,' Dr Gawande said. 'Your wife has been taken to have an MRI scan and will then return to our acute neurology ward. Your daughter has been taken to our burns unit.'

'I want to see them.'

'Of course. I'll take you to your daughter first. You can see your wife as soon as she's finished her MRI, which will be in about twenty minutes.'

As you left the foyer with the young doctor, journalists hung back a little, demonstrating unexpected compassion. But Tara brazenly followed.

'What do you think about Silas Hyman?' she asked you.

For one moment you turned to her, registering her question, and then you walked quickly on.

★ ★ ★

24

The young doctor accompanied you swiftly past outpatient clinics, which were deserted now, the lights off. But in one empty waiting room a television had been left on. You stopped for a moment.

On the screen, a BBC 'News 24' interviewer was standing in front of the gates to the school. I used to tell Addie that it was a seaside house which had grown too big for the seafront and had to move inland. Now its pastel blue stuccoed façade was blackened and charred; its cream window frames burnt away to reveal pictures of the destruction inside. That gentle old building, so intricately associated with Adam's warm hand holding mine at the beginning of the day and his running, relieved little face at the end of the day, had been brutally maimed.

You looked so shocked, and I knew what you were thinking because I'd felt the same when the rug was melting in my hands and masonry was falling around me — if fire can do this to bricks and plaster, what damage must it do to a living girl?

'How did we get out of there?' Jenny asked.

'I don't know.'

On the TV, a reporter was giving the facts but, shocked by the image on screen, I caught only fragments of what he was saying. I don't think you were listening at all, just staring at the school's cadaver.

' . . . private school in London . . . cause at the moment unknown. Fortunately most children were at sports day. Otherwise the injuries and death toll . . . Emergency services were prevented from reaching the scene as desperate

25

parents . . . One thing as yet to be explained is the arrival of press before the fire services . . . '

Then Mrs Healey came onto the screen, and the camera focused on her, mercifully blocking out most of the school in the background.

'An hour ago,' the reporter said, 'I spoke to Sally Healey, the headmistress of Sidley House Preparatory School.'

You went on with the young doctor, but Jenny and I stayed for a little while longer watching Sally Healey. She was immaculate in pink linen shirt and cream trousers with manicured nails occasionally coming into view. I noticed her make-up was flawless; she must have retouched it.

'Were there any children in the school when the fire started?' the reporter asked her.

'Yes. But not one child at the school was hurt. I'd like to emphasise that.'

'I can't believe she put on make-up,' Jenny said.

'She's like one of those French MPs,' I said. 'You know, with the lipgloss next to the state papers? Make-up in the face of adversity.'

Jenny smiled; sweet, brave girl.

'There was a reception class of twenty children in the school at the time of the fire,' Sally Healey continued. 'Their classroom is on the ground floor.'

She was using her assembly voice, commanding but approachable.

'Like all our children, our reception class had rehearsed an evacuation in the event of fire. They were evacuated in less than three minutes.

26

Fortunately, our other reception class were at an end-of-term outing to the zoo.'

'But there *were* serious casualties?' asked the interviewer.

'I cannot comment on that, I'm sorry.'

I was glad that she wasn't going to talk about Jenny and me. I wasn't sure if she honestly didn't know, if she was being discreet on our behalf, or if she was just trying to maintain a pink-linen façade that everything went according to plan.

'Have you any idea yet how the fire started?' the reporter asked.

'No. Not yet. But I can reassure you that we had *every* fire precaution in place. Our heat detectors and smoke detectors are connected directly to the fire station and — '

The reporter interrupted. 'But the fire engines couldn't get to the school?'

'I am not aware of the logistics of them getting to the school, I just know that the alarm went immediately through to the fire station. Two weeks ago some of the same firefighters came to give a talk to our year-one children and let them look at their fire engine. We never dreamt, any of us, that . . . '

She trailed off. The lipgloss and assembly voice wasn't working. Under that carefully put-together frontage she was starting to fall apart. I liked her for it. As the camera panned away from her and back to the blackened school it paused on the undamaged bronze statue of a child.

★   ★   ★

27

We caught up with you in the corridor that leads to the burns unit. I could see you tense, trying to ready yourself for this, but I knew nothing could prepare you for what you'd see inside. Next to me I felt Jenny draw back.

'I don't want to go in.'

'Of course. That's fine.'

You went through the swing doors into the burns unit with the young doctor.

'You should be with Dad,' Jenny said.

'But — '

'At some level he'll know you're with him.'

'I don't want to leave you on your own.'

'I don't need babysitting, really. *I* am a babysitter nowadays, remember? Besides, I need you to keep me updated on my progress. Or lack of.'

'Alright. But I won't be long. Don't go anywhere.'

I couldn't bear to have to search for her again.

'OK,' she said. 'And I won't talk to strangers. Promise.'

★ ★ ★

I joined you as you were taken into a small office, grateful that they were doing this by degrees. A doctor held out his hand to you. I thought he looked almost indecently healthy, his brown skin glowing against the white walls of his office, his dark eyes shining.

'My name's Dr Sandhu. I am the consultant in charge of your daughter's care.'

I noticed that as he shook your hand his other

28

hand patted your arm, and I knew he must be a parent too.

'Come in, please. Take a seat, take a seat . . . '

You didn't sit down, but stood, as you always do when you are tense. You'd told me once it's an atavistic, animal thing, meaning you are ready for immediate flight or fight. I hadn't understood until now. But where could we run to and who could we fight? Not Dr Sandhu with his shining eyes and softly authoritative voice.

'I'd like to start on the positives,' he said and you nodded in vehement agreement; the man was talking your kind of talk. '*However tough the environment*,' you say in the middle of some godforsaken place, '*you can always find strategies to survive.*'

You hadn't seen her yet, but I had, and I suspected that 'starting with the positives' was putting a few cushions at the bottom of the cliff before pushing us off it.

'Your daughter has achieved the hardest thing there is,' continued Dr Sandhu. 'Which is to come out of that intensity of fire alive. She must have huge strength of character and spirit.'

Your voice was proud. 'She does.'

'And that already puts her ahead of the game, as it were, because that fight in her is going to make all the difference now.'

I looked away from him to you. The smile lines around your eyes were still there; too deeply etched by past happiness to be rubbed out by what was happening now.

'I need to be frank with you about her condition. You won't be able to take in all the

29

medical speak now, so I'll just tell you simply. We can talk again — we most definitely will talk again.'

I saw a shake in your leg, as if you were fighting the instinct to pace the room, flee from it. But we had to listen.

'Jennifer has sustained significant burns to her body and face. Because of the burns, stress is being placed on her internal organs. She has also suffered inhalation injuries. This means that inside her body her airways, including part of her lungs, are burnt and not functioning.'

She was hurt inside as well.

As well.

'At the moment I'm afraid I have to tell you she has a less than fifty per cent chance of surviving.'

I screamed at Dr Sandhu: 'No!'

My scream didn't even ruffle the air.

I put my arms around you, needing to hold onto you. For a moment you half turned towards me as if you felt me.

'We are keeping her heavily sedated so that she won't feel any pain,' Dr Sandhu continued. 'And we are breathing for her with a ventilator. We have a highly specialist team here who will be doing everything possible for her.'

'I want to see her now,' you said in a voice I didn't recognise.

★   ★   ★

I stood close against you as we looked at her.

We used to do that when she was small, after

30

coming in from a party. We'd go to her room and stand and watch her as she slept — soft pink feet sticking out of her cotton nightie, silky hair across her stretched-out arms, which were yet to reach beyond her head. *We made her*, we'd think. Together we somehow created this amazing child. Chocolate moments, you called them, to make up for broken nights and exhaustion and battles over broccoli. Then we'd each separately give her a hug or a kiss, and feeling — I admit it — smugly proud, we'd go into our own room.

I was glad, for your sake, that her face was covered in dressings now. Just her swollen eyelids and damaged mouth visible. Her burnt limbs were encased in some kind of plastic.

As we looked at her, Dr Sandhu's sentence coiled inside us like a viper. '*She has a less than fifty per cent chance of surviving.*'

Then you made yourself stand tall and your voice was strong.

'Everything is going to be alright, Jen. I promise. You're *going to get better.*'

A pledge. Because as her father your job is to protect her; and when that's failed you make everything better.

Then Dr Sandhu explained about the intravenous lines and the monitors and the dressings and, although he didn't intend this, it quickly became clear that if she got better it would be because of him, not you.

But you don't take that lying down. You don't just hand over power over your daughter. So you asked questions. What did this tube do *exactly*?

31

That one? Why use this? You were learning the lingo, the techniques. This was your daughter's world now, so it was yours and you would learn its rules; master it. The man who stripped down a car engine at sixteen and then rebuilt it following a manual — a man who likes to know exactly what he's putting his trust in.

At sixteen I would have been reading George Eliot; as equally useless now as a car engine manual.

'How badly will she be scarred?' you asked.

And your optimism was glorious! Your courage in the face of it all was marvellous. I knew you didn't give a *monkey's arse* about how she looked compared to whether she lived. Your question was to show your belief that *she will live*; that the issue of scarring is a real one because one day she will — will — face the outside world again.

You've always been the optimist, me the pessimist (*pragmatist*, I'd correct). But now your optimism was a lifebuoy and I was clinging to it.

Dr Sandhu, a kind man, didn't mention your question's hopefulness when he replied.

'She has suffered second-degree partial thickness burns. This type of burn can be either superficial, which means the blood supply is intact and the skin will heal, or deep, which inevitably means scarring. Unfortunately it takes several days before the burns reveal which type they are.'

A nurse came up. 'We're arranging a family room for you to stay in tonight. Your wife has been brought back to the acute neurology ward,

32

which is just across the corridor.'

'Can I see my wife now?'

'I'll take you there.'

★ ★ ★

Jenny was waiting for me in the corridor. 'Well . . . ?'

'You're going to be fine. A long haul ahead, but you're going to be fine.'

Still holding tightly to your optimism. I couldn't bear to have told her what Dr Sandhu said.

'They don't yet know about scarring,' I continued. 'If they're the kind of burns that leave a scar.'

'But they might not?' she asked, her voice hopeful.

'No.'

'I thought I was going to look like that permanently.' She sounded almost euphoric. 'Well, maybe not *quite* as bad as that, like a Halloween mask, but something like that. But I really might not at all?'

'That's what the consultant said.'

Relief shone out of her face; made her luminous.

Looking at me, she didn't see you come out of the burns unit. You turned your face to the wall and then your hands slammed onto it, as if you could expel what you'd seen and heard. And I knew then how hard-won your hopefulness was; the bravery and effort it took. Jenny hadn't seen.

We heard footsteps pounding down the corridor.

Your sister was hurtling towards you, her police officer's radio hissing at her side.

I instantly felt inadequate. If Pavlov's dog had had a sister-in-law like Sarah it would be a recognised emotional reflex. I know. Unfair. But spiky emotion makes me feel a little more resilient. Besides, it's not that surprising, is it? The most important woman in your life from the age of ten till you met me; a sister-in-law/ mother-in-law rolled into one; little wonder I feel intimidated by her.

Her voice was breathless.

'I was in Barnes, doing a joint thing with their drugs — Oh for God's sake it doesn't matter where I was, does it? I'm so sorry, Mikey.'

That old childish name that she uses for you. But when was the last time?

She put her arm around you, held you tightly.

For a little while she didn't say anything. I saw her face stiffen, hardening herself to tell you.

'It was arson.'

5

Each of Sarah's words a razor blade to be swallowed.

Someone had deliberately done this. My God. *Deliberately*.

'But why?' Jenny asked.

At four years old we'd nicknamed her the 'Why-Why Bird'.

'But why doesn't the moon fall on top of us? But why am I a girl not a boy? But why does Mowgli eat ants? But why can't Grandpa get better? (Answers: Gravity; Genes; They are tangy and nutritious. By the end of the day, worn out: 'It's just the way it is, sweetie.' A tired kind of answer, but an answer.)

There was no answer to the why in this.

'Do you remember anything, Jen?' I asked.

'No. I remember Ivo texting at half past two. But that's it. I can't remember anything after that. Nothing.'

Sarah touched you lightly on the arm and you flinched towards her.

'Whoever did this, I'll kill them.'

I'd never seen you angry like that before, as if you were fighting for survival. But I was glad of your rage; an emotion that met this information head on and fought back.

'I need to see Grace now. And then I want you to tell me everything you know. After I've seen her. Everything.'

★ ★ ★

I hurried ahead to my ward, wanting to know before you did what state I was in, as if I could prepare you in some way.

There were tubes and monitors attached to my body now, but I was breathing without any equipment, and I thought that must be a good thing. I was unconscious, yes, but I really looked hardly injured apart from the neatly dressed wound on my head. Maybe it wasn't so bad.

'I'll be outside then,' Jenny said.

She's never given us privacy before; never seemed to even consider we might need it. It's Adam who dashes out of the kitchen when we have a hug and a kiss. '*Being mushy! Yuck!*' But Jenny's radar hasn't detected any embarrassing parental passion. Maybe like most teenagers, she thinks that's long gone, while they discover it and keep it all for themselves. So I was touched by her.

I waited for you; listening to the sound of trolleys and bleeping machines and the soft foot-fall of nurses in plimsolls; wanting to hear your footsteps, your voice.

The seconds ticked past and I had to be with you. Right now! Please.

And then you were running over the slippery linoleum towards my bed, a nurse pushing a trolley out of your way.

You put your strong arms around my body, holding me tightly against you; the softness of your linen important-meetings-shirt against my creased stiff hospital gown. And for a moment

36

the room smelt of Persil and you, not the hospital.

You kissed me: one kiss on my mouth and then one on each closed eyelid. For a moment, I thought that like a princess in one of Jenny's old storybooks your three kisses would break the spell and I'd wake up and I'd *feel* your kiss — your stubble scratchy on my skin by that time of day.

But thirty-nine's probably a little old to be a sleeping princess.

And maybe a bash on the head isn't as easy to reverse as a witch's curse.

Then I remembered — how could I have forgotten, even for three kisses — Jenny outside; waiting for me.

I knew that I mustn't wake up, mustn't even try, not yet, because I couldn't leave her on her own.

You understand that, don't you? Because if your job as a father is to protect your child, and mend her when she's broken, my job as a mother is to be there with her.

'My brave wife,' you said.

You called me that when I'd just given birth to Jenny. I'd felt so proud then — as if I'd stopped being the usual me and had instead abseiled down from the moon.

But I didn't deserve it.

'I didn't get to her in time,' I said to you, my voice loud with guilt. 'I should have realised something was wrong before; I should have got there *before*.'

But you couldn't hear me.

37

We were silent — when have we ever been silent together?

'What happened?' you asked me, and your voice cracked a little, as if you were winding back the years to your teenage self. 'What the hell happened?'

As if understanding could make it better.

I started with the strong, warm breeze at sports day.

★　★　★

Your eyes are closed now, as if you can join me if your eyes are shut too. And I've told you everything I know.

But of course you couldn't hear me.

'So why do it?' that bossy nanny voice says to me. 'Waste of time! Waste of breath!' A cognitive therapist would send her packing but I've got used to her and besides I think it's good for a mother to have someone bossing her around, so she knows what it's like.

And she has a point, doesn't she?

Why talk to you now when you can't hear me?

Because words are the spoken oxygen between us; the air a marriage breathes. Because we have been talking to each other for nineteen years. Because I would be so lonely if I didn't talk to you. So no therapist in the world, with whatever logic they brought to bear, could get me to stop.

A woman doctor is coming purposefully towards us. I'm reassured by her being in her fifties; by her air of tired professionalism. Beneath her sensible navy blue skirt she's wearing high, spiky red shoes. I know, a silly thing to notice. You're looking at her name badge and rank; the important things. 'Dr Anna-Maria Bailstrom. Neurologist. Consultant.'

Is it the Anna-Maria in her that wears the red shoes?

'I thought she would look worse,' you say to Dr Bailstrom. Neurologist. Consultant. 'But she's hardly hurt, is she? And she's breathing for herself, isn't she?'

The relief in your voice strings your words together.

'I'm afraid that her head injury is severe. A firefighter told us that a part of the ceiling had fallen on her.'

There's tension stringing Dr Bailstrom's words together.

'She has unequal pupil reflexes and isn't responding to stimuli,' she continues, her voice tight as wire. 'The MRI, which we will repeat, indicates significant brain damage.'

'She'll be alright.' Your voice is fierce. Your fingers tense around mine. 'You're going to be *fine*, my darling.'

Of course I am! I can quote medieval poetry and tell you about Fra Angelico or Obama's health reforms and the heroes in Beast Quest books — and how many people can do all that? Even my bossy nanny is still in place, in her element actually. The thinking me isn't in the body me, but I'm right here, my darling, my mind undamaged.

'We have to warn you that there's a likelihood she may never regain consciousness.'

You turn away from her, your body language saying, 'Bollocks!'

And I think you're right. I'm pretty sure that if I tried, I'd be able to get back into my body. And then — maybe not right away but soon — I'd wake up again. *Regain consciousness*, to put it into Dr Bailstrom language.

Dr Bailstrom is now leaving, precipitous on her red spiky heels on the slippery linoleum. She's probably letting you have some time for it to sink in. Dad, with his GP hat on, was a firm believer in sinking-in time.

I'm talking too much. The problem with being 'out of body' is that you don't need to take a breath for new sentences and so there are no natural physical pauses.

And you're so quiet. I think you have stopped talking to me altogether. And I am so afraid that I scream at you.

'Jenny's been badly hurt, darling,' you say. And my fear is swept away in compassion for you. You tell me that she'll get better. You tell me that I'll get better too. We'll be '*right as rain*,' again.

As you talk I look at your arms: strong arms that years ago carried three boxes of my books at a time from the bottom of the student house to my room at the top; that on Tuesday carried Jenny's new chest of drawers upstairs to her bedroom.

Is your character that strong too? Is it really possible to be as brave as you are now — this resiliently hopeful?

You talk about the holiday we're going to take when this is '*all over*'.

40

'Skye. And we'll camp. Adam'll love that. Making a fire and fishing for our supper. Jenny and I can climb the Cuillins. Addie can manage the smallest one now. You can take a whole stack of books and read by a loch. What do you think?'

I think it sounds like a paradise on earth that I never knew was there.

I think that while I have my head in the clouds, you climb a mountain to do it.

As I did earlier at Jenny's bedside, I cling onto your hope; let myself be carried by it.

I see that Sarah has arrived on the far side of the ward, on her phone. Busy, efficient Sarah. The first time you introduced us I felt I was being interviewed for something I'd inadvertently done wrong. But what? The crime of loving you and plotting to take you away from her? Or, worse, of being fraudulent in my affections and not loving you *enough?* Or maybe — the one I picked — not being *worthy* of you; not being as interesting and beautiful and downright *remarkable* as I should be if I was going to claim her brother and become a part of your clan.

Even before this, I saw myself paddling round a duck pond in a rubber dinghy, while she steered her life on a fast, direct course to a clearly mapped destination. And now here I am, unable to speak or see or move, let alone help you or Jenny or Adam, head partially shaved, in a hideous hospital nightgown — and she's sailed in, competent and capable, at the helm.

My nanny voice would be a lot happier if I were more like her. You reassured me, touchingly, that you wouldn't be.

41

A nurse is with her and I see they're debating the phone, with Sarah flashing her warrant card, but the nurse is clearly adamant and Sarah leaves again. You spot her as she leaves, but stay with me.

We return to that camping trip to Skye — to arching blue-grey skies and still blue-grey water and huge blue-grey mountains, their soft colours so alike that they are almost indistinguishable from one another; to Jenny and Adam and you and me, softly coloured, not separated from each other. A family.

★   ★   ★

We leave my ward and Skye, and I see Jenny waiting for me in the corridor.

'So, what's happening to you?' she asks me, her voice anxious.

'They're doing scans and what not,' I say.

She hasn't been giving us romantic privacy, I realise, but medical privacy; like me staying out of the room now when I take her to the GP's.

'And that's it?' she asks.

'So far, yes. Pretty much.'

She doesn't question me more closely — afraid, I think, to know any more.

'Aunt Sarah's in the family room,' she says. 'She's been talking to someone at the police station. It's funny, but I think she knows I'm here. I mean, she kept kind of glancing around at me. Like she'd caught a glimpse.'

It'll be sod's law if the only person who has

any real inkling of Jenny and me turns out to be your sister.

⋆ ⋆ ⋆

It must be late evening now and in the family room, someone — who? — has brought a toothbrush and pyjamas for you and put them neatly at one end of the single bed.

Sarah closes the phone as she sees you.

'Adam's at a school-friend's house,' Sarah says. 'Georgina's on her way from Oxfordshire and will pick him up. I thought it would be best if he was in his own bed tonight and he's particularly close to Grace's mum, isn't he?'

In all of this Sarah has found space and time to think about Adam. Has had the kindness to worry about him. I've never been grateful to her before.

But you can't take Adam on board, not with me and Jenny already weighing you down this heavily.

'Have you spoken to the police?' you ask her.

She nods and you wait for her to tell you.

'We're taking statements. They'll keep me fully informed. They know she's my niece. The fire investigation team are working at the scene of the fire.'

Her voice is police officer, but I see her reach out her hand and that you take it.

'They've said that the fire started in the Art room on the second floor. Because the building was old, it had ceiling, wall and roof voids — basically spaces connecting different rooms

43

and parts of the school — which means that smoke and fire could travel extremely fast. Fire doors and other precautions couldn't stop its spread. Which is one reason it could overwhelm the whole building as quickly as it did.'

'And the arson?' you ask, and I can hear the word cutting at your mouth.

'It is likely, more than likely, that an accelerant was used, probably white spirit, which causes a distinctive smoke recognised by a firefighter at the scene. As it's an Art room, you'd expect to have some white spirit, but they think it was a large quantity. The Art teacher says that she keeps the white spirit in a locked cupboard on the right-hand side of the Art room. We think the fire was started in the left-hand corner. A hydrocarbon vapour detector should give us more information tomorrow.'

'So there's no doubt?' you ask.

'I'm sorry, Mike.'

'What else?' you ask. You need to know *everything*. A man who has to be in full possession of the facts.

'The fire investigation team have established that the windows on the top floors were all wide open,' Sarah says. 'Which is another signifier for arson because it creates a draught, drawing the fire more quickly up through the school; especially given the strong breeze today. The head teacher told us that the windows are never left wide open because of the danger of children falling out.'

'What else?' you ask and she understands you need to know.

'We think that the Art room was deliberately chosen,' she continues. 'Not only because there was a chance that the arsonist could get away with it — the use of an accelerant being camouflaged as it were by Art supplies — but because it's the worst possible place for a fire. The Art teacher has inventoried what materials were kept.'

'There were stacks of paper and craft materials, which meant the fire could take hold easily and spread. There were also different paints and glues, which were toxic and flammable. She'd brought in old wallpaper samples for a collage, which we think were coated in a highly toxic varnish.'

As she describes an inferno of poisonous fumes and choking smoke I think of children making collages of hot air balloons and papier-mâché dinosaurs.

You nod at her to go on and she sturdily continues.

'There were also cans of spray mount in the room. When they are exposed to heat the pressure builds and they explode. Vapours from the spray mount can travel long distances along the ground to an ignition source and flash back. Next to the Art room was a small room, little more than a cupboard, where the cleaning materials are kept. They too would have contained combustible and toxic substances.'

She pauses, looking at you; sees how pale you are.

'Have you eaten anything yet?'

The question irritates you. 'No, but — '

45

'Let's talk more in the canteen. It's not far.'

It's not up for negotiation. When you were younger, did she bribe you to eat then too? A favourite TV programme if you finished your shepherd's pie?

'I'll tell them where you are, just in case,' she says, preempting any arguments.

I'm glad she's making you eat.

She goes to tell the staff in my acute neurology ward where you will be; you go to tell the burns unit.

Once you've gone, Jenny turns to me.

'It's true, what Mrs Healey said about the windows not being left open. Ever since that fire-escape accident, they're paranoid about children falling and hurting themselves. Mrs Healey goes round herself, checking them all the time.'

She pauses a moment, and I see that she is awkward. Embarrassed even.

'You know when I went to your bed?' she says. 'Before Dad got there?'

'Yes.'

'You looked so . . . ' She falters. But I know what she wants to ask. How come I am so undamaged compared with her?

'I wasn't in the building as long as you,' I say. 'And I wasn't so close to the fire. And I had more protection.'

I don't say that I was in a cotton shirt with sleeves I could pull down and thick denim jeans and socks with trainers, not a short, gauzy skirt and skimpy top and strappy sandals, but she guesses anyway.

46

'So I'm the ultimate fashion victim.'

'I'm not sure I can do gallows humour, Jen.'

'OK.'

'Positive and even silly,' I say. 'That's fine. That's great. And black humour, that's alright too. But when it becomes gallows — well, that's my line.'

'Point taken, Mum.'

We could almost be at our kitchen table.

★ ★ ★

We follow you into the absurdly named Palms Cafe; the Formica-topped tables reflecting the overhead striplights.

'Great atmosphere,' Jenny says and for a moment I can't work out if this statement is because of her relentlessly positive attitude, inherited from you, or her sense of humour, which she gets from me. Poor Jen, she can't be positive or funny without one of us taking the credit for it.

Sarah joins you with a plate of food, which you ignore.

'Who *did this*?' you ask her.

'We don't know yet, but we will find out. I promise.'

'But someone must have seen who it was, surely?' you say. '*Someone must have seen.*'

She puts her hand on your arm.

'You must know something,' you say.

'Not much.'

'Do you know what they were doing to Jenny, when I left her just now?' you ask.

'Jen, leave, please,' I say to her, but she doesn't budge.

'They were giving her an eye toilet, *an eye toilet*, for Christ's sake.'

I feel Jenny stiffen next to me. Sarah's eyes fill with tears. I've never seen her cry.

She hasn't yet asked how Jenny is. I see her brace herself. I will her not to do it.

'Have they told you the chances of . . . ?' she asks, her voice trailing off, unable to continue. Her life is spent questioning people, but she can't finish this one.

'She has a less than fifty per cent chance of surviving,' you say, repeating Dr Sandhu's words exactly; maybe it's easier than translating them into your own voice.

I see Sarah pale, literally turn white, and in the colour of her face I see how much she loves Jenny.

'Why didn't you tell me?' Sarah asks you, and her words could be Jenny's to me.

'Because she *will* be alright,' you say to Sarah, almost angrily. 'She will *get better*.'

'There were only two members of staff, apart from Jenny, who weren't at sports day,' she tells you. 'We think it highly unlikely it was one of them.

'The school has a gate, which is permanently locked with a code. The secretary buzzes people in via entry phone from her office. No parents or children are told the code; they all have to be buzzed in. Members of staff know it, but they were all out on the playing field at sports day. So we're probably looking at an outsider.'

'But how could they get in?' you ask. You'd wanted a culprit but now you don't want that person to have access; as if you can change what's happened if you prove it was impossible.

'He or she could have slipped in earlier in the day,' Sarah replies. 'Possibly behind a legitimate person who was buzzed in. Perhaps blended in somehow and not been noticed if parents thought they were a member of staff and vice versa. Schools are busy places, lots of people coming and going. Or the arsonist may have watched a member of staff key in the code and memorised it and come back while everyone was out at sports day.'

'Surely you can't just walk in, though? Surely . . . '

'Once someone is through the main gate there's no more security, the front door isn't locked and there's no CCTV or other security device.

'That's really all we've got so far, Mike. We haven't yet made it public that it's arson. But the investigation is urgent; they're allocating as many people as they can to it. Detective Inspector Baker is running the case. I'll see if he'll have a meeting with you but he's not the most sympathetic of people.'

'I just want the police to find the person who did this. And then I will hurt him. Hurt him like he's hurt my family.'

6

'Your definition of 'fine' is a more than fifty per cent chance of dying?' Jenny asks, and I hear a tone in her voice that sounds like teasing, but surely she can't be?

'I'm sorry.'

'I don't want to look at myself but I do want to know what's happening. I need the truth, OK? If I ask for it, it means I can take it.'

I nod and pause a moment, chastened.

'The scarring,' I say. 'What I told you about that, it was the truth.'

I see her relief.

'I will be alright,' she says. 'Like Dad said, I know I will. And so will you. We *will get better.*'

I used to worry about her optimism, thinking she hid behind it instead of facing things.

'*In a way it's a good thing, Mum,*' she'd said about flunking her A levels. '*Better to realise I'm not cut out for university now, than three years and a large overdraft too late.*'

'Of course we will get better,' I say to her.

Further along the corridor, we spot Tara coming towards you. I remember seeing her earlier, in the melee of press. Now she's tracked you here. Jenny has also noticed her.

'Isn't she the one who thinks the *Richmond Post* is the *Washington Post?*' Jenny asks, remembering our joke.

'That's the one.'

50

She reaches you, and you look at her, perplexed.

'Michael . . . ?' she says, using her purring voice.

Men are usually hoodwinked by Tara's girlish rosy face, slender body and pretty glossy hair, but not a man whose wife is unconscious and daughter critically ill. You shy away from her, trying to place her. Sarah joins you.

'She was asking me about Silas Hyman earlier,' you tell Sarah.

'Do you know her?'

'No.'

'I'm a friend of Grace's,' Tara calmly butts in.

'I doubt it,' you snap.

'Well, more a colleague. I work with Grace at the *Richmond Post*.'

'So a journalist,' Sarah says. 'Time to go.'

Tara's not going to budge. Sarah flashes her warrant card.

'*Detective Sergeant* McBride,' Tara reads, looking smug. 'So the police *are* involved. I presume that this teacher, Silas Hyman, is a line of enquiry you'll be taking?'

'Out. Now,' Sarah says in her uniform-and-truncheon voice.

Jenny and I watch as she virtually manhandles Tara towards the lifts.

'She's fantastic, isn't she?' Jenny says and I nod, not graciously.

'She was wrong though earlier,' Jenny says. 'Or at least Mrs Healey was when she told her about the code on the gate. You know, that people don't know it? Some of the parents do. I've seen them

51

letting themselves in when Annette takes too long answering the buzzer. And a few of the children know it too, though they're not meant to.'

I don't know the code, but then I'm not pally with the in-the-know kind of mothers.

'So a parent could have come in,' I say.

'All the parents were at sports day.'

'Perhaps someone left.'

I try to think back to this afternoon. Did I see something and not realise?

⋆   ⋆   ⋆

The first thing I remember is cheering on Adam in the opening sprint, his face anxious and intent, his spindly legs going as fast as he could make them, desperate not to let down the Green Team. I was worrying about him coming last and you not being there and Jen's retakes; not seeing the huge truth that we were all alive and healthy and undamaged. Because if I had, I'd have been sprinting around that field, cheering till my voice was hoarse at how fantastic and *miraculous* our lives were. A blue-skies and green-grass and white-lines life; expansive and ordered and complete.

But I must focus. *Focus.*

I can remember a group of parents from Adam's class asking me if I'd go in for the mothers' race.

'Oh go on, Grace! You're always a sport!'

'Yeah, a *slow* sport,' I replied.

I look again at their smiling faces. Did one of

them, shortly afterwards, leave for the school? Perhaps he or she had left a container of white spirit in the boot of their car. A lighter slipped into a pocket. But surely their smiles were just too relaxed and genuine to be hiding some wicked intention?

A little while later, and Adam hurried up to tell me he was going to get his cake *right now!* Rowena had to collect the medals from school so she was going with him. And as he left with her, I thought how grown-up she looked now in her linen trousers and crisp white blouse; that it hardly seemed a minute since she was a little elfin girl with Jenny.

I'm sorry, not relevant at all. I have to look harder.

I turn away from Adam and Rowena, swinging my focus to the right then to the left, but memory can't be replayed that way and nothing comes into focus.

But at the time I did check round the playing field, a broad sweep from one end to the other, looking for Jenny. Maybe if I concentrate on that memory I will see something significant.

She'll be so bored, I was thinking as I scanned the playing field. *Up in the sick-room on her own. Surely she'll leave her shift early.*

A figure at the edge of the playing field, half obscured by the border of chest-high azalea bushes.

The figure is still and its stillness has attracted my attention.

But I only looked long enough to know it wasn't Jenny. Now I try to go closer, but I can't

53

get any more detail. Just a shadowy figure on the edge of the field; the memory yielding nothing more.

The figure haunts me. I imagine him going into classrooms at the top of the school and opening windows wide; I imagine the children's drawings pegged onto strings across the classrooms flapping hard in the breeze.

Back on the playing field, Maisie came to find Rowena and I told her she was at school. I remember watching Maisie as she left the playing field. And something snags at my memory. Something else I saw on the outskirts of the playing field that I noted at the time; that means something. But it is slipping from my grasp and the harder I try and pull at it, the more it frays away.

But there's no point tugging at it. Because by this point the arsonist had already opened the windows and poured out the white spirit and positioned the cans of spray mount. And soon the strong godsent breeze will be sucking the fire up to the third floor.

The PE teacher blows his whistle and in a minute, not quite yet, but soon, I will see the black smoke, thick black smoke like a bonfire.

Soon I will start running.

★   ★   ★

'Mum?'

Jenny's worried voice brings me back into the brightly lit hospital corridor.

'I've been trying to remember,' she says. 'You

54

know, if I saw someone or something, but when I try and think about the fire I can't . . . '

She breaks off, shaking. I hold her hand.

'It's OK when I think about being in the medical room,' she continues. 'Ivo and I were texting each other. I told you that, didn't I? The last one I sent was at two thirty. I know the time then, because it was nine thirty in the morning in Barbados and he said he was just getting up. But then . . . it's like I can't think any more, I can only feel. Just feel.'

A judder of fear or pain goes through her.

'You don't need to think back,' I say to her. 'Aunty Sarah's crew will find out what happened.'

I don't tell her about my shadowy figure half glimpsed on the edge of the playing field, because he really doesn't amount to very much, does he?

'I was worried you'd be bored up there,' I say to her lightly. 'I should have known you and Ivo would be texting.'

Put together, they must have texted the equivalent of *War and Peace* by now.

When I was her age, boys didn't say much to girls, let alone write, but mobiles have upped their game. Some must find it pressurising, but I think it appeals to Ivo to send love sonnets and romantic haikus through the airwaves.

But it's only me who thinks Ivo's texted poetry a little bit effeminate; while you are — surprisingly to me — firmly on his side.

* * *

Jenny's gone off to be with you, while I *'pop to my ward to get an update on how I'm doing'* — as if I'm nipping down to Budgens for an *Evening Standard*.

Maisie is sitting by my bed, holding my hand, talking to me, and I'm moved that she thinks I can hear too.

'And Jen-Jen's going to be alright,' she says. 'Of course she is.'

Jen-Jen; that name we used for her when she was little, and sometimes slips out by accident even now.

'She's going to be just fine! You'll see. And so are you. Look at you, Gracie. You don't look too bad at all. You're all going to be *alright*.'

I feel her comforting warmth and another vivid memory of sports day flashes into my mind. Not a detective one, but one that comforts me and I'll allow myself to play it for a moment; a paracetamol for my aching mind.

★   ★   ★

Maisie was hurrying across the bright green grass, in her FUN shirt, stepping over the painted white lines, delphinium blue sky above.

'Gracie . . . ' she said, giving me a hug, a proper bearhug kind, none of this air-kissing.

'I've come to give Rowena a lift home,' she said, beaming. 'She texted me a little while ago, said the tubes were up the spout. So Chauffeur-Mum to the fore!'

I told her that Rowena had gone to get the medals from school and that Addie was getting

56

his cake; an M&S chocolate tray-bake we'd turned into a World War One trench scene.

'Fantastic!' she said, laughing.

Maisie, my surprising kindred spirit. Our daughters, those chalk-and-cheese little girls, never became friends but Maisie and I did. We'd meet on our own and share small details of our children's lives: Rowena's tears when she didn't make the netball team and Maisie offering Mr Cobin new team outfits or sex if he'd make Rowena wing attack — and having to explain the second offer was *a joke!* Rowena's horror when her big teeth came through and demanding the dentist give her small ones again; exchanged like a gift with my dentist story of Jenny refusing to eat or smile when she got a brace until we found a make that was bright blue.

And it was Maisie I turned to when I started my third miscarriage at Jenny's seventh birthday party, when you were away filming.

'Listen to me, kiddly-winks! Jenny's mummy has to go and visit Father Christmas now — yes, it is three months early! — but he needs advance warning of REALLY GOOD children — and because you've all been so FANTASTIC this afternoon she wants to make sure you'll all get an extra special present in your stocking.'

Aside to me. *'Materialism and Father Christmas, usually works.*

'So it'll be me now doing musical bumps, alright? Everyone ready?!'

And it was alright. And nobody knew. And she kept twenty children entertained while I went to hospital; had Jenny to stay that night.

Three years later, she waited for those twelve weeks with me till Adam was safely inside and likely to go to term. Like our family, she understood how deeply precious Adam is to us; our hard-won baby.

And now she's sitting next to me, my old friend, crying. She cries all the time — '*Stupidly soppy!*' she'd say at carol services — but these are painful tears. She tightens her grip on my hand.

'It's my fault,' she says. 'I was inside, going to the loo, when the fire alarm went off. But I didn't know Jenny was in the building. I didn't know to call for her. I just went looking for Rowena and Adam. But they were fine, outside in no time.'

At sports day I'd told her Adam and Rowena were at the school. If I'd said, '*And Jenny,*' she'd have called for her too, made sure she was out before the fire took hold.

Two words.

But instead I'd wittered on about Adam's cake.

Her voice is a whisper. 'Then I saw you running towards school. And I knew how relieved you were going to be when you saw that Addie was safe.'

I remember Maisie outside, comforting the reception teacher, Rowena comforting Adam by the bronze statue of a child, as black smoke was swirled by the wind, dirtying the blue sky.

'And then you shouted for Jenny and I realised she must be in there. And you ran inside.' She pauses for a moment, her face pale. 'But I didn't go to help you.' Her voice is staccato with guilt.

But how can she think I blame her? I'm just moved that she thought, even for one moment, of going into a burning building after me.

'I *knew* I should help you,' she continues. 'Of course I should. But I wasn't brave enough. So I ran to the fire engines that were still on the bridge instead. *Away* from the fire. I told them there were people inside. I thought if they knew they'd get there more quickly, that it would be more urgent. And they did. I mean, as soon as I told them, one of the fire engines drove at a parked car and shoved it off the road onto the pavement. And then people parked behind them realised what was happening and got out of their cars and the firemen were shouting that there were people in the school and then we were all pushing cars out of the way. Everyone pushing the cars out of the way so they could get through.'

I can see that her memory is over-spilling into her present, so that it's happening now in front of her, and she can smell it and hear it — diesel fumes, I imagine, and people shouting and horns going and the smell of fire reaching the bridge.

I want to interrupt her from her reverie, rescue her from it. I want to ask her if Rowena's alright because I remember seeing her in A&E when I was searching for Jenny. And I remember the suited man talking to the journalists and saying Rowena was in hospital too. But I hadn't paused to think about her since; anxiety for my own child selfishly pushing out space for anybody else.

59

But why is Rowena hurt when I saw her safely outside next to the statue with Adam?

Dr Bailstrom arrives on her precipitous red heels and Maisie has to go. I think she leaves reluctantly as if there's something more she wants to tell me.

★   ★   ★

It's late now and the pull of home is unbearably strong. Own bed. Own house. Own life back again to be lived as usual tomorrow.

You are on the phone to Adam and for a few moments I hang back, as if it'll be my turn in a minute to speak to him. Then I hurry close to you, listening for his voice.

'I'm going to spend the night with Mum and Jenny here. But I'll see you as soon as I can, OK?'

I can just hear him breathing. Short, hurried breaths.

'OK, Ads?'

Still just breathing, terrified breathing.

'I need you to be a soldier right now, Addie, please?'

Still he doesn't speak. And I hear the gap between you, the one that used to make me sad and now frightens me.

'Good night then. Sleep tight, and send my love to Granny G.'

I have to hug him, *right this moment*; feel his warm little body and ruffle his soft hair and tell him how much I love him.

'I'm sure Granny G will bring him to see you

tomorrow,' Jenny says to me, as if reading my thoughts. 'I'd probably scare him too much, but you look alright.'

★   ★   ★

You want to spend the night next to me and next to Jenny — splitting yourself in two, to keep watch over both of us.

A nurse tries to persuade you to go to the bed they've sorted out for you. She tells you that I am unconscious and therefore unaware of whether you're with me or not, and that Jenny's too deeply drugged to be aware of anything either. As the nurse says this, Jenny pulls a silly face at her and I laugh. There's really a lot of opportunity for bedroom-farce-style comedy here and I think Jenny will try and beat me to it.

The nurse promises you that if my condition or Jenny's 'worsens' they'll get you immediately.

She's telling you that neither of us will die without you.

Perhaps I jumped the gun a bit in the potential for comedy.

You still refuse to go to bed.

'It's late, Mike,' your sister says firmly. 'You're exhausted. And you need to function properly tomorrow for Jenny's sake. And for Grace's.'

I think it's her advice that you need to function properly *tomorrow* that decides you — it's optimistic to go to bed, demonstrating your belief that we will still be alive in the morning.

★   ★   ★

61

Jenny and I stay with you next to the single bed they've given you in the family room, just by the burns unit. We watch you as you fitfully sleep, your hands tightly tensed.

I think of Adam in his bunk bed.

'He has several lions among his soft toy menagerie,' I tell you. 'But his favourite is Aslan and he needs Aslan to get to sleep. If he's fallen off the bunk, you have to find him. Sometimes you have to pull the whole bed out because he falls down the side.'

'Mum?' Jenny says. 'Dad's *asleep*.'

As if when you're awake you can hear me. I am touched by this distinction.

'Anyway,' she continues. 'He must know about Aslan.'

'D'you think?'

'Of course.'

But I'm not sure you do. Anyway, you think it would be better if Adam grew out of soft toys, now he's eight. But he's only *just* eight.

'You'll be able to put Adam to bed yourself soon,' Jenny says. 'Find Aslan. All of that.'

I think of holding Adam's hand in mine as he drifts into sleep. All of that.

'Yes.'

Because *of course* I'll be at home again. *I have to be.*

'Is it alright if I go for a walk?' she asks. 'I'm feeling a little stir-crazy.'

'Fine.'

Poor Jenny; an outdoorsy person like you, it's terrible for her to be cooped up in a hospital.

We're alone and I look at your sleeping face.

I remember watching you as you slept not long after we'd started going out together and I'd thought of that passage in *Middlemarch* — I know, not fair! I can quote to you now and there's not a thing you can do about it! Anyway it's when the poor heroine realises that in her elderly husband's head there are just dusty corridors and musty old attics. But in yours I imagined there to be mountains and rivers and prairies — wide-open spaces with wind and sky.

You haven't yet said you love me. But it's a given, isn't it? A taken-as-read thing, as it has been for the last few years. In our early days you'd write it in the steamed-up mirror in the bathroom after you'd shaved, for me to find when I came in later to clean my teeth. You'd phone me, just to tell me. I'd sit down at my computer and you'd have changed the screen saver so that 'I love you!' marched across it. You'd never done this to anyone before, and it was as if you needed to keep practising.

I know hearts don't really store emotion. But there must be some place in us that does. I think it's a jagged and anxiously spiky place until someone loves you. And then, like pilgrims touching a rough stone with their fingertips, nineteen years of practising wears it smooth.

Someone has just passed the family room. I saw a glimpse in the glass panel in the door; a shadow fleetingly under it. I better just check.

A figure is hurrying along the burns unit corridor. For some reason, I think of that shadowy figure on the edge of the playing field.

He's going towards Jenny's side-ward.

He goes in and through the half-open doorway I see his shape bending over her.

I scream, making no sound.

I can see a nurse walking towards Jenny's room. Her plimsolls squeaking on the linoleum alert the figure to her presence and he slips away.

The nurse is checking Jenny now. I can't see anything different at all, not that I'd know what all the monitors are telling us, but to me it looks no different. But the nurse in the squeaky plimsolls is checking a piece of Jenny's equipment.

Out in the corridor, the figure has disappeared.

I didn't get close enough to see his face, just an outline in a long, dark blue coat. But the door to the burns unit is locked, so he must have been authorised to be in here. He must be a doctor, perhaps a nurse, probably going off shift, which is why he wasn't wearing a white coat or nurse's uniform, but an overcoat. Maybe he just wanted to check on Jenny before going home.

I see Jenny returning and I smile at her.

But I feel afraid.

Because who wears a long dark overcoat in the middle of July?

7

Garish artificial lights snapping on; doctors already alert and moving in packs; loud crashings of trolleys and nurses briskly whipping away breakfast trays and pulling out drugs charts. Christ, I think, you have to feel robust to face morning in a hospital. But at least all this noisy bright aggressive busyness turns my glimpsed figure last night into a quiet nothing.

When I arrive at my ward, I see that Mum's already here and in an office with Dr Bailstrom. She's aged years in a day; hard lines of misery are scraped across her face.

'Grace chattered all the time when she was a little girl, such a bright button,' Mum says, her voice quicker than usual. 'I always knew that she'd grow up to be really bright, and she did. She got three As at A level and a scholarship to Cambridge to read Art History, with an option to switch to English, because they wanted her to come to their university.'

'Mum, *please!*' I say to no avail. Presumably she wants them to know what kind of brain I had — *a top-notch one!* as Dad used to say — so they'll know what to aim for. The before photo.

'She got pregnant before finals,' Mum continues. 'So she had to leave. She was a little disappointed, we all were, but she was happy too. About the baby. Jenny.'

I've never heard my life history potted before

65

and it's a little alarming. Is it really that simple?

'That makes her sound like a brainbox, but she's not really like that at all,' Mum continues. 'She's a lovely girl. I know she's nearly forty now, but she's still a girl to me. And she'd do anything for anyone. *Too good for her own good*, that's what I used to say to her. But when my husband died, I realised then that nobody can be too good for their own good, not when it's you they're helping.'

Mum never speaks in a rush. And hardly ever speaks more than two or three sentences at a time. Now she's haring along in paragraphs as if she's on a timer. And I wish there *was* a timer, because listening to this is terrible.

'I don't know what I'd have done without her; juggling her whole life around for me. I don't mean that she has to get better for me, though. You mustn't think that. I mean I love her more than you can possibly know but it's her children who really need her, and Mike. You think it's Mike who's the strong one, he looks it, but really it's Gracie. She's the heart of the family.'

She stops for a moment, and Dr Bailstrom pounces in.

'We'll do everything we possibly can. I can absolutely assure you of that. But sometimes, with a severe head injury, there's not a great deal that we can do.'

Mum looks at her.

And for a moment Dr Bailstrom is the doctor who told Mum and Dad that he had Kahler's disease.

'*But there must be a cure!*' she'd said then.

66

She doesn't say that now. Because when Dad died, the impossible, *unthinkable* happened to her and nothing would ever be unthinkable again.

I look away from her face to Dr Bailstrom's same-as-yesterday high red shoes. I bet from time to time Dr Bailstrom looks at them too.

'We'll let you know what we find out when we've done the next set of tests,' Dr Bailstrom says. 'We are having a specialists' meeting about your daughter later today.'

Once Mum would have told them Dad was a doctor. Once she'd have thought it would make a difference.

She thanks Dr Bailstrom — too nicely brought up not to always thank people properly.

★ ★ ★

Adam is hunched by my bed.

Mum rushes over to him.

'Addie, poppet? I thought you were going to wait with the nurses for five minutes?'

He's lying with his face against mine, holding my hand, and he's crying. A desperate, terrible sound.

I put my arms around him and I tell him not to cry, I tell him I'm alright. But he can't hear me.

As he cries I stroke his soft silky hair and I tell him over and over and over that it's alright, that I love him, not to cry. But he still can't hear me and I can't bear it a moment longer and I have to wake up for him.

I fight my way into my body, through layers of

67

flesh and muscle and bone. And suddenly I'm here. Inside.

I struggle to move this heavy hulk of a body, but I'm again trapped under the hull of a ship wrecked on the ocean floor and moving is impossible.

But Adam is out there crying for me and I have to open my eyes for him. *Have to.* But my eyelids are locked shut and rusting over.

A fragment of a poem echoes in the darkness.

A soul hung up, as 'twere, in chains
Of nerves, and arteries, and veins,

I've left Jenny on her own. Oh God. What if I can't get out again?

I hear the panic in my heartbeat.

Deaf with the drumming of an ear.

But I can escape my body easily, just slipping out into the dark ocean and then struggling upwards towards the light.

Mum is putting her arm around Adam, magicking a smile onto her face for him, making her voice sound cheerful.

'We'll come back later, alright, my little man? We'll go home now, then when you've had a bit of a rest, we can come back.'

And she's mothering me by mothering my child.

She leads him away.

★ ★ ★

A few minutes later Jenny joins me.

'Have you tried getting back into your body?' I ask her.

She shakes her head. I'm an *idiot*. She can't

68

even *look* at her body let alone try to get into it. I want to say sorry but I think that would just make it worse. *Klutz!* A Jenny word.

She doesn't ask me if I've tried getting back in. I think it's because she's afraid of the answer — either that I couldn't; or that I could, but it made no difference.

No difference at all.

That ghastly poem I'd once thought so clever echoes still in our silence.

. . . *with bolts of bones, that fettered stand*
In feet, and manacled in hands.

'Mum?'

'I was thinking about the metaphysical poets.'

'God, you *really* still want me to do retakes?'

I smile at her. 'Absolutely.'

★ ★ ★

You're having a meeting with Sarah's boss in an office downstairs. We go to join you.

'Aunt Sarah's normal boss is on maternity leave,' Jenny says. 'Rosemary, remember, the really quirky one?'

I don't remember Rosemary-the-really-quirky-one. I've never heard of a Rosemary.

'Aunt Sarah loathes this guy, Baker. Thinks he's an idiot,' Jenny continues. She's been fascinated by the flashing-lights-and-sirens side of Sarah's police life since she was six years old. And I get that. How can my part-time job writing an arts review page in the *Richmond Post* compete with being a detective sergeant in the Met? What film, book or exhibition is going

69

to out-cool directing a helicopter during a drugs bust? Bust. You may as well throw in the towel at the start on that one. But joking about fellow workers, that's what Jenny and I do. OK, so Sarah didn't *joke* to Jenny about quirky-Rosemary and Baker, whoever he is, but she clearly tells her the gossip.

We reach the office they've allocated for this meeting at the same time as you and Sarah.

Why on earth are you holding a newspaper? I know that I have a go at you at the weekends for reading the papers rather than *engaging with the family*, and we've done the whole 'It's the caveman looking into the fire to have time to let the week settle' thing. But now? Here?

We follow you and Sarah in. The ceiling is too low, trapping the heat. There's no window. Not even a fan to shift the stale heavy air around.

★   ★   ★

Detective Inspector Baker introduces himself to you without getting up from the chair. His sweaty, doughy face is unreadable.

'I want to fill you in on a little of the background to our investigation,' DI Baker says, his voice as stodgy as his physique. 'Arson in schools is extremely common. Sixteen cases a week in the UK. But people getting hurt in arson attacks on schools is not common. Nor is it common for fires to be started during the daytime.'

You're getting irritated — *get to the point, man*.

70

'The arsonist may have thought that the school would be empty because it was sports day,' DI Baker continues. 'Or it may have been a *deliberate* attempt to hurt one of the occupants.'

He leans forward, his sweaty polyester shirt sticking slightly to the back of his plastic chair.

'Do you know of anyone who may have wished to harm Jennifer?'

'Of course not,' you snap.

'That's ridiculous,' Jenny says to me, a shake in her voice. 'It was just a fluke I was in there, Mum. Pure *chance*, that's all.'

I think of that figure last night, going into her room, leaning over her.

'She's a seventeen-year-old girl, for fuck's sake,' you say.

Your sister tightens her hand on yours.

'For fuck's sake!' you repeat. You never use that word in your sister's hearing, or your children's.

'She was the victim of a hate-mail campaign, wasn't she?' DI Baker asks you, an edge now to his bland voice.

'But that stopped,' you said. '*Months ago*. It's not connected. It has *nothing to do with the fire.*'

Beside me, Jenny has become rigid.

She never told us how she felt when she was called slut, tart, jailbait and worse. Or when dog mess and used condoms were posted through our letterbox addressed to her. Instead she turned to Ivo and her friends, excluding us.

'*She's seventeen now, darling, of course she turns to them.*'

You were so infuriatingly understanding, so 'I've-read-the-manuals-on-teenagers' rational.

'*But we're her parents*,' I said. Because parents out-rank everyone else.

'There's been nothing for almost five months,' you tell DI Baker. 'It's all over.'

DI Baker flicks through some notes in front of him as if finding evidence to disagree with you.

I remember how desperate we were for it to be over. Those awful things that were said to her. It was shocking. Grotesque. The ugly, vicious world had come crashing through our letterbox and into our daughter's life. And, this I think is key, *you hadn't kept it at bay.* You thought you hadn't done your job as her father and protected her.

Those hours you spent looking at the pieces of A4 lined paper, trying to trace the origin of the cut-out letters — which newspaper? Which magazine? Studying postmarks on the ones that had been posted, agonising over the meaning of the ones that had been hand-delivered — he'd been here, *right outside our door*, for God's sake, and you hadn't got him.

I'd understood after a little while that *you* wanted to be the person who caught him and made him stop. To make amends to Jenny or to prove something to yourself? I thought it was both enmeshed together.

Then two weeks after — *two weeks* Mike — the day the hand-delivered envelope with the used condom arrived, you told Sarah. As you'd predicted, she told us we must go to the police — and why the hell hadn't we done that to start with? We duly did as she said but, as you'd also

72

predicted, the police — apart from Sarah — didn't consider it important. Well, not as important as it was to you and me. Not *life-stoppingly* important. And they didn't find out anything. It wasn't as if we could help them; we had no idea who might target Jenny like that or why.

Poor Jen. So furious and mortified when the police interviewed her friends and boyfriend. The teenage paranoia that adults disapprove of their choices taken to an extreme.

But you'd already interrogated most of them, grabbing them as Jenny tried to hurry them past us and up to her room. Those long-limbed, long-haired, silly girls seemed unlikely hate-mailers. But what about one of the boys who were friends with her? Did one harbour hatred? Unreturned love turning acrid and spreading across venomous letters?

And Ivo. I've always been suspicious of him — not as a hate-mailer but as a man. Boy. Maybe because he's so different to you, with his slight frame and fine features and his preference at seventeen for Auden over car engine manuals. I think he lacks *substance*. But you disagree. You think he's *a fine fella; a great lad*. Possibly because you don't want to be a clichéd possessive father? Because you don't want to alienate Jenny? But whatever our reasons, you support Jenny over Ivo, while I jibe.

Though even with my prejudices against him, I don't think he'd send her hate mail. Besides, he's her boyfriend, and she adores him, so why would he?

'When, exactly, was the last incident?' DI Baker asks you.

'February the fourteenth,' you reply. '*Months ago.*'

Valentine's day. A Wednesday. Adam worried about his times-tables challenge; Jenny late down to breakfast as usual. But we'd been up for an hour already, waiting for the sound of the letterbox. Just the click of metal shutting made me feel physically sick.

It was the letter with the C word across it. I can't say that word in connection with her. I just can't.

But the day after that letter there was nothing. Then a whole week went by with no hate mail. Then a fortnight. Until over four months had passed, so that yesterday I picked up the post hardly bothering to check.

'You're sure there's been nothing since the fourteenth of February?' DI Baker asks.

'Yes. I told you — '

He interrupts you. 'Could she have hidden something from you?'

'No, of course not,' you say, frustrated. 'The fire is nothing to do with the hate-mailer. Presumably you haven't seen this yet?'

You slap the newspaper you're holding in front of DI Baker. The *Richmond Post*. The headline shouts out: '**Arsonist Sets Fire to Local Primary School!**'

The by-line is Tara's.

DI Baker ignores your newspaper.

'Were there any other forms of hate mail that you didn't tell us about?' he continues. 'Texts on

74

her mobile, for example, or emails, or postings on a social networking site?'

You glare at him.

'I asked Jenny and there was nothing like that,' Sarah says.

You're pacing the office now; five paces from one wall to the other, as if you can outpace whatever is hunting you down.

'Would she have told you?' asks DI Baker.

'She would have told me, or her parents, yes,' Sarah replies.

But we hadn't just taken her word for it. We searched; you breaking every rule in the bringing-up-teenagers book, me being a normal mother.

'MySpace? Facebook?' DI Baker asks as if we don't know what 'social networking site' means, but you interrupt.

'The hate-mailer *had nothing to do with it.* Christ, how many more times?' You jab at the newspaper. 'It's this teacher, Silas Hyman, you should be investigating.'

'We haven't read the paper, Mike,' Sarah says. 'We'll read it if you'll give us a minute.'

She must be humouring you, I think. After all, what on earth could Tara know about the fire that she — a policewoman and your sister — doesn't?

★ ★ ★

The picture of the burnt-out school dominates the front page, the oddly undamaged bronze statue of a child in the foreground. Under it is a picture of Jenny.

75

'It's from my Facebook page,' Jenny says, looking at her photo. 'The one Ivo took at Easter, when we did that canoeing course. I *can't believe* she's done that. She must have gone onto my site and then just printed it off, or scanned it. Isn't that theft?'

I love her outrage. Out of all of this, to mind about her photo being used.

But the contrast between our daughter in the burns unit and that outdoorsy, healthy, beautiful girl in the photo is cuttingly painful.

Maybe Jenny feels it too. She goes to the door. 'The hate-mailer didn't do it and Dad's idea that Silas Hyman did it is completely ridiculous and I'm going for a walk.'

'OK.'

'I wasn't asking permission!' she snaps. And then she leaves. Just the word 'hate-mailer' pushing those old buttons again.

★   ★   ★

Just after she's gone, Sarah opens the paper out to show a double-page spread, with a banner headline across both pages.

'**Jinxed School**.'

On the left-hand page is the sub-headline, '**Fire Started Deliberately**', and another photograph of this '**popular and beautiful**' girl.

Tara has turned Jenny's torment into private entertainment. '**Beautiful seventeen-year-old . . . fighting for her life . . . horribly burnt . . . severely mutilated**.' Not news, but prurient news-as-porn; titillating garbage.

76

Tara makes me out as a kind of superhero-mum racing into the flames. But a rather tardy superhero, arriving too late in the day to save the beautiful heroine.

Tara finishes with a flourish.

'The police are continuing their urgent hunt for the person responsible for arson, and possibly a double murder.'

Jenny and my deaths would add more cachet to her story.

★ ★ ★

Directly opposite, on page 2, Tara's just rehashed an article she'd written in March, adding a new intro.

Only four months ago, the Richmond Post reported on Silas Hyman, 30, a teacher at Sidley House Preparatory School who was fired after a child was seriously injured. The seven-year-old boy broke both his legs after plunging from an outside metal fire escape onto the playground below in an alleged 'accident'.

Just as she had the first time, she doesn't say that Mr Hyman was *nowhere near the playground* at the time. And those quotation marks around the word 'accident' — saying that it wasn't. But who's going to sue her over quotation marks? Slippery as her patent leather Miu Miu bag.

And still her bid for journalistic glory, measured in column inches, continues.

Situated in a leafy London suburb, the exclusive £12,500-a-year school, founded thirteen years ago, is marketed as a nurturing environment where 'every child is celebrated and valued'. But even four months ago questions were being asked about its safety.

I interviewed parents at the time.

A mother of an eight-year-old girl told me, 'This is supposed to be a caring school, but this man clearly didn't look after the children. We are thinking about taking our daughter away.'

Another parent told me, 'I am very angry. An accident like this just shouldn't be allowed to happen. It's totally unacceptable.'

In March Tara had titled her article 'Playground Plunge!' but now she's changed it to 'Teacher Fired!'

So on the right-hand side of the newspaper is **'Teacher Fired'** and on the left-hand side is **'Fire Started Deliberately'**. And the connection crackles between them, an invisible circuit of blame — the fired teacher exacting his fiery revenge.

DI Baker's mobile goes and he answers it.

The *Richmond Post* lies on the table, like a challenge thrown into the ring — your Silas Hyman contender for arsonist versus DI Baker's hate-mailer.

I know that you've never liked Mr Hyman. Before he was fired we'd had weeks of sniping

78

over him. You thought I *totally over-exaggerated* Mr Hyman's effect on Addie.

'"Exaggerated' doesn't need 'totally' and 'over' added to it,' I said frostily.

'Not all of us did an English degree,' you replied, stung.

'Only <u>half of one</u>, remember?'

Mr Hyman made us fight. And we don't normally fight.

'Before Mr Hyman, Addie was miserable,' I said. 'Don't you remember?'

He was picked on, couldn't do the work, had virtually no self-esteem.

'So he's come through that,' you said.

'Yes, because of Mr Hyman. He's sorted out who he sits next to, worked out the boys who are likely to become his friends, and they are now. They're asking him on playdates. He's got a sleepover this weekend. When's he ever had one of those? And he organises who the children sit next to on the coach when they go on trips. Addie used to dread no one sitting next to him. And he's got him confident in Maths and English.'

'He's just doing his job.'

'He calls Addie 'Sir Covey'. That's lovely, isn't it? A knight's name?'

'It'll probably make the other kids tease him.'

'No, he's got pet names for all of them.'

Why didn't you appreciate him more?

⋆　⋆　⋆

An attractive young teacher with a sparkle in his eyes, I'd wondered if your antagonism towards him was because he'd kissed me on the cheek when we went to parents' evening in the first term. '*Totally inappropriate!*' you'd said, not realising that Mr Hyman is just very physical — tousling the children's hair as he passes them at their desks, a quick warm hug at going-home time. And yes, us mothers did smile a little about him, but not in a serious way.

Then when Mr Hyman was fired and I came home that day and was outraged on his behalf, you just seemed irritated. You said you paid the school fees, worked *bloody hard* to do that, and before you set off for a gruelling trip the next day you didn't want to hear about *some inadequate teacher who'd got himself the sack.*

Until yesterday afternoon I'd have argued with you for suspecting him. Like Jenny, I'd have said it was *completely ridiculous!* But all my old certainties are burnt to the ground. Nothing is like yesterday any more. So I don't trust anyone. Not even Mr Hyman. No one at all.

★   ★   ★

DI Baker stops his phone call and glances at the *Richmond Post*.

'One peculiar thing,' he says to Sarah, 'is how quickly the press were on the scene of the fire. Before the fire engines even. We'll need to know who told them, or how they found out. In case that's relevant.'

You are infuriated by his anodyne off-the-point remark.

'It's not only the article,' you say, but DI

80

Baker's radio interrupts. He answers it but you continue.

'I *saw him* acting violently a few weeks after he was fired. It was at the school prize-giving. He gatecrashed it and made threats. *Violent* threats.'

8

'*Do you think I'll win a prize, Mum?*' Adam said. '*For anything?*'

It was the morning of the prize-giving. Adam, still seven then, was eating Coco Pops and watching *Tom and Jerry*.

Mr Hyman had been fired three and a half weeks before and already he hated going to school, so I was trying to compensate. You were away filming and I'd allowed myself to spoil him a little. Your man-to-man talk could come later. My excitement about your homecoming was cloaked by anxiety for him.

'You should win a prize,' I said to him, fairly certain that he wouldn't. 'But if you don't, you mustn't be disappointed. Remember what Mrs Healey said at assembly? Everyone will get a prize in the end, even if it's not your turn this year.'

'That's such bollocks,' Jenny said, still in her dressing-gown although we were meant to leave in ten minutes. 'I mean, think about the maths,' she continued. 'Number of children, number of prizes, number of prize-givings. It doesn't compute, does it?'

'And the same people always win them,' Adam said.

'I'm sure that's not — '

Adam interrupted me, hotly frustrated. 'It is *true*.'

'He's right,' Jenny said. 'I know they *say* every

82

child is equally valued, blah blah blah, but it's rubbish.'

'Jen, you're not helping.'

'She is, actually,' Adam said.

'The school has to get a few of its pupils into a top secondary school like Westminster for boys or St Paul's Girls,' Jenny continued, pouring out cereal. 'Otherwise new parents aren't going to truck up with their four-year-olds next year. So it's the brightest kids that get the prizes, so it'll help them get into the top secondary schools.'

'Antony's already won it for best in the class,' Adam said, miserably. 'And for Maths and for leadership.'

'He's eight. Who's he meant to be leading, exactly?' Jenny asked with derision, making Adam smile. Thank you, Jen.

'It was Rowena White when I was at school,' Jenny continued. 'She cleaned up.' She stood up, her movements languid. 'Is it still at St Swithun's church?' she asked.

'Yup.'

'Nightmare. I always got stuck behind a pillar. Why can't they use that perfectly good modern church right next to the school?'

Adam saw the clock and panicked. 'We're going to be late!' He raced to get his bookbag, his fear of being late temporarily outweighing his fear of school.

'I'll be super-quick,' Jenny said. 'I'll eat my Shreddies in the car, if Mum can drive a little more smoothly than last time.' She paused as she left the room. 'Oh, and you know all those silver cups and shields? They make the school seem older and more established than it really is. So the current parents are kept happy too.'

'I think you're being a little cynical,' I said.

'I've worked there, remember,' Jenny said. 'So I *know* to be cynical. It's a business. And prize-giving is a part of that.'

'You were only there for three weeks. And there's a prize for improvement,' I said a little lamely.

Adam glanced up from fastening his bookbag. His look identical to Jenny's. 'That doesn't mean anything, Mum. Everyone knows that.'

'But you'd like to win it anyway?' Jenny asked him.

He nodded, a little embarrassed. 'But I won't. I never win anything.'

She smiled at him. 'Me neither.'

★ ★ ★

Eight minutes later, we were in the car. Adam is the only person Jenny will hurry for.

We were going to arrive at school early, as we did every morning. I know you think we shouldn't *buy into his anxiety* but arriving five minutes earlier than necessary is something you have to factor in when you're looking after him. It just is.

'How long till you're working at school again?' Adam asked Jenny as we neared Sidley House.

He'd been so proud of her being a teaching assistant there last summer, even though she wasn't in his class.

'After A levels,' Jenny replied. 'So just a couple more months.'

'That's really soon,' I said, panicked by the proximity of A levels. 'You must get that revision timetable sorted out this evening.'

'I'm going to Daphne's.'

'But Dad's coming home,' Adam said.

'He'll be at the prize-giving evening with you, won't he?' Jenny replied.

'S'pose so,' Adam agreed, not fully trusting that you'll turn up. That's not a criticism; he worries about anyone actually turning up.

'You should cancel,' I said to Jenny. 'At least do the timetable this evening, even if not any actual revision.'

'Mum . . .'

She was putting on mascara in the sun-visor mirror.

'Working hard now means you'll have so many more choices in the future.'

'I'd rather live my life now than revise for a future one, alright?'

No, I thought, it's not alright. And if only she could put the mental agility used in that rejoinder into her A-level work.

We walked the last bit, as we always do, along the oak-lined driveway. Adam was gripping my hand.

'OK, Ads?'

Tears were starting, and he was trying not to let them out.

'Does he really have to go?' Jenny asked. I was thinking the same. But Adam stoically let go of my hand and went to the gate. He pressed the buzzer on the gate and the secretary let him in.

You'd been away filming since the day after Mr Hyman was fired, so you hadn't been there to see the consequences. In our brief, badly-connected phone calls you'd been more worried about Jenny, checking up that no more hate mail had arrived — which it hadn't, thank God — but it didn't leave much space for Adam. And I hadn't told you; perhaps fearful of igniting a flashpoint between us. So you still didn't know that for Adam it was almost like a grief. Not only had he lost a teacher he adored, but the adult world had proved itself cruel and unjust and nothing like the stories he read. Beast Quest books and Harry Potter and Arthurian legends and Percy Jackson — his whole literary culture up to this point — didn't end like this. He was prepared for unhappy endings, but not unjust ones. His teacher was sacked. For something he didn't do.

And school was already mutating back into the hostile place it had been before Mr Hyman was his teacher.

★ ★ ★

At quarter to six, after a *'lightning-quick supper, Ads!'* and a change into clean uniform, we arrived early at the prize-giving with his shoes polished and his blazer brushed so he wouldn't get into trouble. I was in faded jeans with a genuine rip as a protest, which he liked. *'Cool, Mum!'* There's a subversive streak lurking in Adam somewhere.

Other mothers would be in their designer Net-a-Porter uniforms and expensive sleek boots.

We were fifteen minutes early, partly because Adam is in the choir so had to get there in good time, but also because of his anxiety about being late, which had got so much worse in the last three weeks.

I spotted Maisie waving to me from a pew near the front, even earlier than us. Adam went to the side-room to wait for the rest of choir and I joined her.

'Bagged you and Mike a good spot,' she said, budging up to make a space for me. 'Rowena was sorry not to be here, but it's just too close to their exams now, isn't it?'

So Rowena was revising, even though she'd already been offered a conditional-but-virtually-guaranteed place at Oxford to read Science. While Jenny, who most definitely hadn't been offered a place by anyone, was at a friend's house. As small girls, Jenny used to gripe about Rowena being too competitive and needing to be *the best* at everything. I'd wished she shared a little of those traits. I still did.

'Is Addie in the choir again this year?' Maisie asked. 'I do love hearing him sing.'

She's so tactfully sensitive, never asking, 'So do you think Adam will win a prize?' but instead celebrating his small contribution.

I saw Maisie smoothing her brown cotton dress over her tummy, trying to tug it flat, and tears starting in her eyes.

'Do you think I look like a bulimic hog in

this?' she asked me quietly, almost furtively. It was such un-Maisie language that for a moment I didn't think I'd heard her properly.

'Of course not, my honey!' I said. 'You look gorgeous. Sex-on-a-stick lollipop-gorgeous.'

She giggled. 'Like a Shiny-Mum?'

The name we have for the mothers in the shiny slinky boots and expensive silky clothes and shiny hair professionally salon-blow-dried this afternoon.

'Shinier,' I said.

I stuck out my scruffy jeans and indicated the rip. Should I ask her about the bulimic hog?

'You are the kindest woman in the world, Gracie.'

Then Donald arrived, holding the cup that he'd give out later.

'Just polishing up the silverware,' he said, his avuncular face beaming.

When Jenny first went to the school we were both left of centre, embarrassed our child went to a private school, and thinking 'Donald-and-his-cup' absurd and funny. But less critical and hypocritical now, I find it touching that he still wants this link to the school. I never got to know Donald well, Maisie and I usually meet in the daytime when he's at work and Rowena's at school, but I know from Maisie how much he adores his wife and daughter.

I watched Donald take Maisie's hand, sit a little closer to her than he needed to, and felt jealous that you weren't there.

★　★　★

88

In the small, sweaty office, DI Baker has finally stopped his hissing radio conversation.

'The prize-giving was held in St Swithun's, a mile or so from the school,' you say. 'My flight was delayed so I arrived late, at about six fifteen. They didn't even have someone on the door. I just walked straight in. The school's policy on security was negligently bad.'

You don't say anything about lightning-quick suppers and brushed clothes; nothing domestic in your memory.

'I noticed that the headmistress seemed tense,' you continue. 'Even before Hyman came into the church.'

I agree with you. Mrs Healey did seem more than usually uptight, but surely it was because the school was on parade that evening and she wanted it all to go like clockwork?

'It was as though she was *expecting* something to happen,' you say.

DI Baker's radio hisses again and he answers it. You're outraged, but what can you do?

★ ★ ★

I saw you standing at the back with a group of fathers, who'd also got there late. You caught my eye but the bustle of an airport and a busy important career was still hanging about you and your smile wasn't yet fully engaged with me.

Mrs Healey was about halfway through handing out the cups, interspersed with short musical performances. The school was meant to be '*Fostering Self-Confidence in Every Child*'

— but I'd noticed that all the important cups were again going to the ablest children.

Perhaps Jenny was right after all. Perhaps the cups were there to add a silver gleam to future eleven-plus papers and help the top students into the top schools. An investment of silver, which would be paid off in new children joining the school. I didn't like to think that we were part of a business model rather than a prize-giving that spring evening.

I searched for Adam amidst the rows of identically dressed children, trying to work out what I'd say to him later, at bedtime, when he again felt a failure. I spotted other mothers like me — Sebastian's mother, Greg's — sitting a little too upright, hands tight around their programmes, also wondering how they'd persuade their child that prizes don't matter; that they matter. But the mothers of the school heroes — the children who are in the top sets, and captain the teams and already own the sports-player-of-the-week shield and the musician-of-the-week trophy — met each other's eyes over the pews, beaming faces locating other beaming faces, never guessing at the thoughts in our upright-seated brigade.

The fathers of those children were always there on time.

No, that wasn't a dig. Your plane was late. I'm sorry.

★ ★ ★

DI Baker has finally stopped his hissing radio conversation.

'At about six forty,' you say, 'Silas Hyman barged through the door. He shoved his way past the parents.'

The church door clanged behind him, silencing a wobbly solo clarinet. We all turned and stared as he pushed his way through the parents at the back. I saw that his suit was pressed, his shoes were polished, his boyish face clean-shaven. But he was unsteady as he walked up the aisle and was sweating profusely.

The silence around him sounded so lonely.

'He went up to the headmistress at the front,' you continue. 'And he *yelled* at her. Called her a '*bitch*'. He said she'd made him a '*fucking scapegoat*'.

'And then he said, and I remember it very clearly, he said, '*You can't do this to someone, you hear me? Out there?*' and he was jabbing with his hand, gesticulating around all the pews. '*All of you, at the back? Have you got this? You won't fucking well get away with it.*''

He sounded desperate, I'd thought, on the edge of despair; choosing to rage instead of weep.

'Two fathers went and grabbed him,' you continue. 'And pulled him away from the headmistress.'

All you could hear was the scuffle as they tried to get him out of the church. Even the children — all two hundred and eighty of them — were silent.

Then, in the silence, I heard a child's voice. 'Let go of him.'

Adam's voice.

I turned to see Adam — Adam of all people! — standing up, amongst the sea of seated pupils and teachers. His voice was louder now.

'Leave him alone!'

The whole church was quiet, all staring at Adam. He was terrified, I could see that, but he continued, looking all the time at Mr Hyman.

'It's not fair! He didn't do anything wrong. It's not fair to fire him. It wasn't Mr Hyman's fault.'

It was extraordinary. Heroic. A shy little boy, standing up in front of the dark-suited fathers at the back, all the teachers, the headmistress who terrifies him; in front of all of them. The boy who's afraid of getting into trouble if his homework isn't done, scared of being five minutes late, this boy was — literally — standing up for his beloved teacher. I'd always known he was good — not a goody-goody but *good* — but it still astounded me.

And then it was as if Adam connected to something in Mr Hyman. As if he made Mr Hyman aware for the first time of what he was doing. Mr Hyman shrugged off the two fathers and started walking towards the door. As he passed Adam he smiled at him tenderly, and it was a signal to sit down.

I couldn't see Adam any more, but I knew that the enormity of what he'd done would be hitting him like a steam train. But nearly all his classmates loved Mr Hyman too, so surely they'd support him?

At the door Mr Hyman turned. 'I didn't hurt anyone.'

On the pew beside me I saw that Maisie's face was pale with an expression I'd never seen before.

'That man should never have been allowed near our children,' she said vehemently. And I saw that she loathed him, hated him even — gentle Maisie who's usually so quick to be kind.

*   *   *

'It was a clear threat,' you say to DI Baker. 'A violent one. You could see how much he hated the headmistress. All of us.'

'But at the time you didn't think it worrying enough to report it?' asks DI Baker, his tone blandly scornful.

'At the time I underestimated his capacity for violence. We all did. Otherwise this never would have happened. So you'll arrest him?'

More a statement than a question.

'We already spoke to Mr Hyman, last night,' DI Baker retorts, sounding irritated.

'So you were suspicious enough to question him already?' you ask.

'We would have spoken to anyone who may have had a grudge against the school straight away,' Sarah says. 'As a matter of course.'

DI Baker glares at her, not wanting her to give away state secrets. But Sarah continues, 'The headmistress or a governor would have given us the information that he'd been fired, straight off the bat.'

'Mr Hyman didn't ask for a lawyer to be present. And he was happy to volunteer a sample of his DNA,' DI Baker says. 'In my experience, that is not the response of a guilty man.'

'But surely — '

DI Baker interrupts you. 'There is no reason to think Mr Hyman had anything to do with the fire. A scurrilous piece of inaccurate journalism doesn't change that. And your account of his behaviour at prize-giving is interpretative rather than fact.

'However, I do appreciate your anxiety, Mr Covey. And given what you are going through, and to put your mind at rest, I will get an update on our enquiry from one of my officers.'

He ostentatiously gets out his radio again, suggesting, without saying so, that you are putting him to unnecessary trouble.

'I'll be with my daughter,' you say, standing up. 'You can 'update' me there.'

You leave the office, the cheap thin door banging shut behind you.

★　★　★

I follow you along the corridor. As I look at your broad back, I long for you to hold me; and I remember how excited I'd been about seeing you that evening at prize-giving — how long those three and a half weeks had felt.

When you first came into the church, and didn't properly meet my eye, I'd hurriedly tried to remember if there were any of those bright, attractive BBC girls on your filming trip. I'd done that before, over the weeks you'd been gone. But I was pretty sure it was an all-male crew.

No, I didn't *suspect* you. I just felt a little insecure, that's all. I'd never have asked you or even articulated the niggling little concern. 'Back in your box and stay there!' bossy Nanny Voice said. Sometimes she has her uses.

When I came out of the church, I scanned the large group of parents, trying to find you. The father-crowd at the back had been first out of the church, most of them on their mobiles now, but in the dusk I couldn't see you. The children weren't out yet.

I was worried Adam had got into trouble, and how much he'd mind. I wanted to tell him how *proud* I was of him; that what he did took great courage. All around me was the hiss of gossip as the incident turned into anecdote.

Donald and Maisie were a few feet away. I thought for a moment that they were arguing, but their voices were low and quiet, so I realised I must be mistaken. Besides, Maisie says they never argue. '*Sometimes I think we need a jolly good row, blow some cobwebs away, but Donald's just too good-natured.*'

Donald had a cigarette, dragging hard on it, making a fiery tip in the gloomy light. Maisie had never told me he smoked. He dropped the butt onto the ground, stubbing it out with his shoe, grinding it down.

I saw Adam coming towards me. His small face looked zoned out, trying to disconnect from the world around him. As he got closer, he passed Donald lighting another cigarette and flinched from the lighter's flame.

'It's OK, young sir,' Donald said. He clicked his lighter shut.

'Are you alright, Ads?' Maisie asked him.

He nodded and I put my arm around him. 'Let's find Dad.'

I was no longer looking for my husband but Adam's father — our identity as parents always usurping the one of husband or wife.

I finally saw you standing away from the main group of parents. You took my hand and your other arm gave Adam a hug. 'Hello, young cub.'

No mention of what he'd done. You saw that facial signal between parents over the head of their child when one isn't doing something right.

'You two go on home,' you said, ignoring my sign. 'I'll catch up with you later.'

We hadn't even kissed hello and our disagreement about Adam exacerbated my frisson of insecurity at your homecoming.

'I'll be home as soon as I can,' you said in a masculine, commanding way. I was glad you hadn't had any pretty-bright-young-women filming with you, but the downside was that you'd been too long in an all-male environment; it usually takes you about the same amount of time to recover from sexism as jet-lag.

★   ★   ★

I was cooking a late supper when you arrived home. Adam had fallen asleep half an hour before.

96

You came up behind me and kissed me and I smelt beer on your breath. For a moment we met as a couple.

'Jenny not here?' you asked.

'Daphne's dad is driving her home now. He just called.'

'Decent of him.'

You put your arms around me. 'Sorry that took a while, but I wanted to do some damage limitation. Been in that wine bar by the church, schmoozing the teachers. Mrs Healey especially. I really could have done without that this evening.'

You didn't see my face.

'I asked her not to discipline him, but to let us handle it and she agreed.'

I turned and then we argued.

You thought Adam standing up for Mr Hyman wasn't from loyalty and courage, but because of 'some *kind of brain-washing by* that man.' You thought Silas Hyman had an *unnatural hold* over Adam.

Then Jenny came into the kitchen, ending our row. We've never argued in front of the children, have we? Not when it matters. They are our cease-fire treaty.

'*Scrap the UN*,' you'd said once. '*Warring countries should just get a teenage daughter in the room.*'

* * *

We've arrived at the burns unit and you're scrupulously washing your hands, following the

97

diagrammed instructions to the letter. Sarah does the same. Then a nurse lets you in through the locked door.

As we reach Jenny's side-ward I brace myself. You turn to Sarah.

'It's not the hate-mailer who did this to her.'

Your voice is furious and it startles her.

A nurse is taking the last of the dressings off Jenny's face.

Her face is blistered beyond recognition, far worse than in A&E. I quickly turn away. Because I can't bear to look at her. And because I'll have to tell Jenny what I've seen, rather than just glimpsed, because surely you can withhold your knowledge of something if you've only just glimpsed it? And not *made sure of it* by looking again?

But you don't look away.

The nurse sees your distress.

'Blistering the day afterwards is quite normal,' she says. 'It doesn't mean that her burns have got any worse.'

You lean towards Jenny, your face close to hers, and then you kiss the air above her as if it will float down on top of her.

And in that kiss I know why you're adamant that it *can't be the hate-mailer*.

Because if it is the hate-mailer, you haven't protected Jenny. You haven't stopped him from doing this. And that would mean it's your fault. You'd be responsible for her eyes and mouth needing to be sluiced, for her blistered face; for her limbs wrapped up in God-knows-what; for her decimated airways.

For her possible death.

A burden you can't pick up.

'It's not your fault,' I say, going to you, putting my arms around you. 'Really, my darling, whoever did this, *it's not your fault.*'

I understand now why you haven't just been *suspicious* of Mr Hyman but grabbed onto him, *certain* that it's him. Anyone but the hate-mailer.

And maybe you are right.

I remember again Maisie saying, '*That man should never have been allowed near our children,*' and seeing that she hated him. Maisie, who always thinks the best of everyone and is kind to a fault.

Maisie must have seen something bad in him too.

'You've always been naive,' Nanny Voice says.

Perhaps I've just been blind.

9

As we wait at Jenny's bedside for DI Baker, I think back to the rest of that prize-giving/homecoming evening. I don't think there'll be anything useful but I need to escape from here back into the sanctuary of our old life; memory as respite care.

★ ★ ★

Jenny was on the downstairs computer with Facebook open. She'd had her long hair cut while you were away and it no longer shielded her face when she leant forward.

'Rowena's revising this evening,' I said as I passed her.

'I thought her place at Oxford was a cert,' Jenny replied, not hearing my subtext of criticism.

'She still wants to get the best A-level grades she can. They are really important for your CV as well as university.'

'Well, bully for her, Mum,' she said. 'Night,' she called, as you went upstairs.

'Night, sweet prince,' you called back, as you have done since she was about five. Only now it's you who was going to bed before her.

I joined you in our room.

'It would be nice if she knew where that quotation came from. She's got her English A

100

level in about seven weeks and she doesn't have a clue.'

'I thought her set text was *Othello*.'

'That's not the point. She should know her tragedies.'

You started laughing.

'I just want her to do well. So at least she has a shot at university.'

'Yes, I know,' you said affectionately. You kissed me. And the sum of our marriage was bigger than our differences.

Our argument about Adam was still there, as present as his warm sleeping body in the bedroom next to ours; just as my anxiety about Jenny hovered somewhere in the house, as she played on her social networking site rather than open a book. But I was just so pleased you were home.

You told me about your trip and I told you about small details while you'd been away, omitting Mr Hyman and Adam, which had pretty much dominated, but wanting this time with you for myself.

A little later on, while you went to have '*a hot shower that isn't from a bucket*', the latent anxiety stalking the house tracked me down. I thought about Rowena. At Sidley House, she had been top of every subject, in almost every team, star of the assemblies, and now she was off to Oxford to read Science while our daughter would be lucky to pass a single A level.

My anxiety fanned outwards into jealousy. I knew from Maisie how much Donald adored his family. I was sure that if it had been Rowena bravely standing up in the church, Donald would have supported her and been *proud*. The perfect family.

I took off my make-up, which I'd put on so carefully earlier. Your face has got more famous over the years, but mine has just got older, and I'm always conscious of this when you've been away and we re-meet each other.

I remembered Maisie's peculiar remark about her appearance. Perhaps it was because I was looking in the mirror. Or maybe it was because I was searching for a flaw in the perfect family. Anyhow, for whatever reason, I remembered again her '*bulimic hog*' comment and it burrowed away until it connected with other apparently innocuous incidents — the way she checked herself in our hall mirror on the way out, and then hurriedly looked away. '*God, what a crone,*' she'd *say. 'Beyond Botox!*' The bruise on her cheek from a '*trip against the garden shed — that's the problem with two left feet!*' The cracked wrist: '*Went dashing out on the icy pavement, in <u>court shoes</u>. My own silly fault. Just went flying, <u>what a twit!</u>*'

One by one none of these incidents had seemed worrying, but put together at my dressing-table mirror they became a dense murky network of something sinister.

But I made myself stop. I'd been looking for flaws but my imagination had conjured up something so much worse. Because surely it *was* imaginary.

So, enough, I said to myself, sternly. Ugly jealousy makes for ugly imagery. Enough.

* * *

I'd hoped thinking back would be a little respite, but it hasn't worked out that way. Because that uncomfortable memory about Maisie is still with me now, as if my mind won't let me fold it flat and put it away. And it's pulling at another — the memory I couldn't retrieve earlier, the one that frayed before when I'd tried to hold it.

It's Maisie leaving the sports-day playing field, but then stopping *to check her face in her handbag mirror*. A gesture that I've come unknowingly to associate with her. The gesture that made me realise how unconfident she is now compared with the flamboyant mothers'-race Maisie in her *not giving a hoot!* days.

Such a small thing; not the important memory I'd hoped for. So I wonder why it won't leave me.

* * *

DI Baker arrives, and flinches when he sees Jenny. Is that why you wanted him to come here? To *make him realise?*

If so, you were right. I want Baker to know what this is about too.

'I hope you will be reassured to know,' he says in his bland, irritating voice, 'that Mr Hyman's alibi has been checked by one of my officers. He couldn't have been at the school at the time the fire started.'

A red flush of anger creeps down your neck. 'Who gave him the alibi?'

'It would be inappropriate for me to tell you that. I will assign a family liaison officer to keep you informed of any new information.'

'I don't want an FLO,' you say, and I notice he doesn't like you using police lingo. 'I just want to know when you've arrested Hyman.'

DI Baker pauses a moment and turns his back on Jenny.

'We will be pursuing the hate-mail enquiry urgently,' he says. 'And treating the arson as the attempted murder of your daughter.'

Sarah puts her hand on your arm, but you shrug her off.

'I have a meeting to go to,' you say.

You murmur something to Jenny, too quietly for anyone but her to hear, then leave the room.

DI Baker turns to Sarah.

'I gather we interviewed her friends, but didn't do any forensic tests, except for the DNA test on the used condom? You presumably know the case well, having a personal interest.'

'Yes. But we didn't find a match.'

'No samples were taken from a boyfriend or friends?' DI Baker asks.

'No, we didn't have — '

'We'll do it now. What about the locations of the postmarks?'

'Random,' Sarah replies. 'But all within London. One of the letterboxes has a CCTV camera in the street. There's a slim chance the hate-mailer was filmed posting the letter, but at the time we didn't have the resources to — '

'I'll put someone onto it.'

★ ★ ★

I find Jenny in the corridor, back from her wanderings.

'I saw Tara,' Jenny says, choosing, for the moment, a neutral kind of subject. 'She was hanging around on the ground floor.'

'The lazy journalist's way to ambulance-chase,' I say. 'Wait for them to come to you.'

'Does Aunt Sarah think it's the hate-mailer?' she asks, ending our decoy conversation.

'I think she'll be considering everything. About the hate-mailer, was there anything you — '

'No, *don't start*. Please. It was bad enough you and Dad doing it at the time.'

'I just — '

'No one I know would do this to me,' she says, just as she did at the kitchen table during the hate-mailer days.

'I'm not suggesting for one minute that it's one of your friends. Really. I just want to know if there was anything you didn't tell us.'

She looks away from me and I can't read her expression.

'You got pretty fed up with us always wanting to know your movements,' I say.

'You *policed* me,' she corrects. 'Dad *tailed* me, for heaven's sake. I used to see him.'

'He just wanted to make sure you were safe. That's all. And when you refused his offer of driving you to — '

'I'm *seventeen*.'

Yes, only seventeen. And so pretty. And so unaware.

'Then Maria's party, you wouldn't let me go,' she continues. 'Because it didn't start till nine. *Nine*. Everyone else went but you grounded me because of something I didn't even do.'

Jenny made me a dictionary a couple of years ago, as a kind of joke, so I could understand her vocabulary. (I had to promise I wouldn't actually *use* any of the words myself.) 'Grounded' was one word I already knew.

She's right though. It wasn't fair, was it? She hadn't done anything to deserve what she saw as punishment and we saw as protection. And our increased need to keep her safe just fuelled her desire to pull away from us. Thinking about it now, 'hate mail' is the right term for it, not just because of what the messages said and the awful things that were posted — but because while it was happening it sapped so much happiness out of our family.

'I went,' Jenny confides, 'to Maria's party. It was the night I was staying over at Audrey's house after the squash tournament. She'd been invited too.'

Why has she felt the need to come clean about this?

Did something happen at that party? I wait, but she doesn't say anything more.

'Was there *anything* you didn't tell us about the hate mail?' I ask her again. 'In case we 'policed' you even more?'

She turns a little away from me.

'Sometimes, I'm back there, inside the school,' she says quietly. 'I can't escape. Can't get out. I can't see anything. I mean, it's not like a memory. Not like that. Just pain. And fear.'

She's shrinking into herself, making herself as small as she can.

I put my arms around her. 'Hey, it's over. All over.'

There must be something she didn't tell us. Because asking her made her think deeply about the fire, made her *feel* it again, as if she connected the two. But she's trembling and I can't ask her again. I can't. Not yet.

I think that she will tell me though, in time.

When I used to pick her up from school she'd tell me, as Adam does now, that school was 'fine, Mum'. But an anxiety was often tucked into a uniform pocket, a problem slipped up a sleeve, fears hidden under a jumper. You had to wait patiently for the pocket to be emptied as you drove home; a rumpled problem pulled out during homework; the fear finally revealed from under the jumper on the sofa at TV time. You had to wait till bath-time to hear if there was anything really big; I suppose there was nowhere for it to hide any more.

She gestures towards the burns unit.

'So how am I?' she asks.

I've been preparing my answer.

'I didn't see you properly. But the nurse says you're doing everything they'd expect. It's still another few days until they'll know about the scarring.'

That much is true at least.

'Is Dad there?' she asks.

'No, he's had to go to a doctors' meeting,' I say.

107

It's the meeting with my doctors about me. They'll have the results of my brain scans now. I decide to use the decoy conversation again.

'Shall we go and see what Tara is doing?' I suggest.

'Shouldn't we be with Dad?'

'He'll be alright on his own for a little while.'

I don't want Jenny to hear what the doctors say to you.

I don't want to hear.

Not yet.

Not yet.

'D'you remember when I got the dog mess?' she asks.

'It was in a box, like the ones you get to post a book,' I say, surprised that she wants to think about this.

'Remember Addie?'

★ ★ ★

'I think it's a terrier's poo,' he said, peering into the box.

I was horrified he'd seen. 'Adam, really, I don't think you —— '

'I mean, if you look at its size it's from a small dog's bottom.'

Jenny started to smile.

'Maybe a Yorkie?' he hazarded.

'Or a Scottie?' suggested Jenny, smiling more.

'No. I know!' Adam shrieked. 'It's a poodle's poo*!'*

And for a few minutes their giggling filled the house.

10

Tara is by the hospital shop, multitasking flicking her hair with texting.

'D'you think she's waiting to collar Dad again?' Jenny asks.

'Probably.'

She's like a glossy, pretty vulture waiting for more news carrion.

Through the glass wall of the shop, next to the old fruit and teddies, is a pile of *Richmond Posts*. I imagine people reading the paper and then discarding it in their recycling box on Tuesday; Jenny's laughing face looking up at the refuse collectors before they empty the boxes into the back of their truck.

'It's not fair that she can print this about Silas,' Jenny says. 'And there's fuck all he can do about it. Sorry.'

I find it endearing that she still apologises for swearing. Maybe we should come clean now and tell her we do it behind her back all the time.

She met Mr Hyman when she was working at Sidley House last summer but didn't get to know him well. After all, she was just a lowly teaching assistant. Her loyalty towards him is because of what he did for Addie. I think she flourishes 'Silas' as proof she crossed from the pupil to the teacher side of the school. Although us mothers, like our children, always call him Mr Hyman.

Is she naïve to still be loyal to him? But I don't

want to taint her view of the world with my ugly universal suspicion. Not unless I have to.

I never told Jenny or you about confronting Tara in March when she printed her first 'Playground Plunge!' piece.

Tara just teased me for calling him Mr Hyman.

'Jesus, where are you living, Grace? In a Jane Austen novel?'

'Caught the TV adaptation then?' I jibed back. In my head. Ten minutes later.

When I went to the editor, Tara dismissed my defence of *Mr Hyman* as being about me, rather than him. More specifically, me being jealous of her. I was *thirty-nine years old*, with a *part-time* job writing a review page. What wouldn't I give to be a twenty-three-year-old Tara with her talent as a *real journalist* and her soon-to-be-meteoric career when mine had hit the bumpers so many years before?

Of course she didn't say that directly; she didn't need to. Like her prose, she could say what she wanted to, without ever being caught articulating it directly.

And her article was printed.

How could I tell Jenny — or you — that I was such a pushover? Sarah wouldn't have stood for it for a second. It was around then that my nanny voice became particularly strident.

Because Tara did have a point, of sorts. I did fall into the job at the *Richmond Post*, and never climbed out again. I used to pretend to everyone, pretty much, apart from Maisie, that childcare costs meant it wasn't worth me going for a full-time, career-style job. I'd tell myself, and

110

you, that given it was an either/or choice, I chose to be with Jenny and Adam. But my nanny voice would butt in and tell me that it was me who was creating the either/or scenario. '*Plenty of other women juggle careers and children and keep different plates spinning.*'

'*My life isn't a circus performance,*' I'd retort, admirably fast, to myself.

But the nanny voice always won by using the list attack. You lack, she told me:

Aspiration;

Ambition;

Focus;

Talent;

Energy.

It's the energy one that clinched it. I'd hold my hands up. Yes! You're right! Now I need to go and help Adam with his homework and check Jenny isn't still on Facebook.

★ ★ ★

Tara is reading a text on her mobile. She sets off down the corridor, a sashay to her stride. Jenny and I follow her.

Jenny smiles. 'Starsky and Hutch or Cagney and Lacey?'

But actually there is something a tiny bit thrilling about following someone.

★ ★ ★

In the cafeteria Tara meets a man at a table. Older than her, a little paunchy. I recognise him.

111

'Paul Prezzner,' I tell Jenny. 'He's a freelance journalist. Not a bad one actually. He mainly gets his stuff into the *Telegraph*, has done for years.'

'She's got a *broadsheet* onto this now?'

Both of us worry that it's because you are a known face on TV; that your fame will attract more 'press interest'.

I see him leer at Tara and feel relieved rather than repulsed. So that's the reason he's here.

We go closer to eavesdrop.

'The fact it's a school is irrelevant,' Prezzner is saying. 'The point is that it's a *business*. A *multi-million-pound business*. And it's gone up in smoke. That's what you should be investigating. That's the angle.'

Next to me, Jenny is listening intently.

'The *angle* is that it's a *school*,' Tara says, taking a teaspoon of cappuccino froth into her rosy mouth. 'OK, so no children got hurt, but a seventeen-year-old girl did. A pretty, popular, seventeen-year-old girl. And that's what people want to read about, Paul. Human drama. So much more interesting than balance sheets.'

'You're being deliberately naïve.'

'I simply understand what readers want to know about. Even the ones who buy the *Telegraph*.'

He leans closer to her. 'So you're just supplying their need?'

She doesn't back away from him.

'It'll be about the money in the end, Tara, it always is.'

'Columbine? Texas High? Virginia Tech? No financial motive in any of those, was there? Do

112

you know how many schools in the last decade have been subject to violent attacks?'

'They were gun attacks, not arson.'

'Same difference. It's violence in our schools.'

'*Our* schools? Pap. And totally inaccurate. Your examples are all in America.'

'There have been attacks in Germany, Finland, Canada.'

'But not here.'

'Dunblane?'

'A one-off. Fifteen years ago.'

'Maybe school violence is a new import. An unwelcome immigrant into our leafy suburbs.'

'Your next piece?'

'It may be the start of a new trend.'

'This guy you're fingering, he's not a deranged student or ex-student but a teacher.'

'*Fingering?* You've been watching too many cop shows. And it's ex-teacher. That's the point.'

'Well, you've got yourself a good story, I'll say that for you. Fake, concocted and utterly libellous if you weren't so sneaky with your layout, but a good story.'

He smiles at her. I can't take much more of this sickening flirtation.

'And I like the pics. Bronze statue of a child as foreground when you couldn't get any real ones to pose for you, and a photo of Jennifer, all on the same page.'

'Let's go and find Dad?' Jenny asks.

We leave the cafeteria and I remember DI Baker asking how the press knew to get to the school so quickly. Did Tara have something to do with it? But if so, what?

'He's right,' Jenny says. 'About the school being a business. I already told you that, didn't I?'

For a moment I see the flash of silver cups at the prizegiving; remember again the uncomfortable feeling that we were part of a successful business model.

'But even if it is a business,' I say, 'I don't see why anyone would want to burn it down.'

'Some kind of insurance fraud?' she asks.

'I don't see why. The school is full. And they keep on putting up the fees. In business terms it must be doing really well. So there'd be no point burning it down.'

'Perhaps there's something we don't know about,' Jenny says, and I realise that she's grabbing onto this as you grabbed onto Silas Hyman. Anything or anyone but the hate-mailer; for this not to be an attack on her.

* * *

As we arrive at my acute neurology ward, I hear Dr Bailstrom's high heels clicking quickly across the linoleum. She turns to a senior nurse.

'The case meeting on Grace Covey?'

'Dr Rhodes's office. The whole crew.'

'Waiting long?'

'Fifteen minutes.'

'Damn.'

She hurries towards an office as fast as her shoes will let her.

'Shall we wait for Dad here?' I ask Jenny.

114

She doesn't reply.

'Jen . . . ?'

Nothing. I turn to look at her.

Something is wrong. Terribly wrong. Her eyes glitter and she's shimmering with light; too bright; too vividly colourful; heat pulsating out of her.

I am mute with terror. I cannot move.

'Find out what's happening to me,' Jenny says and her voice is so quiet I can hardly hear it, and her face is iridescent now, so dazzling I can barely look at her.

You're leaving the meeting room and running full tilt down the corridor, doors swinging back behind you, people getting out of your way.

I'm running after you, trying to keep up.

You reach the burns unit and bang on the door but a nurse is expecting you and opens it hurriedly. She says Jenny's heart has arrested. They're trying to restart it.

But it's criminals who are arrested, not a heart. Not Jenny's heart. Because it isn't meant to stop, it's meant to keep beating, every second, every minute, every hour of every day, long after yours and mine have stopped. Long after. I think of that Sylvia Plath poem, *'love set you going like a fat gold watch'*, and I think love *did* set our daughter's heart going, but it isn't a *bloody watch* that needs winding up, or sending to the mender's. Thoughts about words, things, poetry to keep thoughts about Jenny's body away. A useless semantic screen. Ripped away the moment I catch up with you by her bed.

There are too many people, their actions

speeded up, and machines are bleeping and flashing and in the middle of it all is Jenny. You can't reach her; the people around her bed block your path. I feel your frustrated anguish, wanting to barge your way through to her. But if she's to be saved it's these people who'll do it, not you.

And I know that Jenny is outside in the corridor, blindingly bright, as if formed by light, and I start to scream.

On the heart monitor is a flat line. A depiction of death.

Is she still there, outside in the corridor?

She can't be dead. *She can't.*

They're trying *so hard* to bring her back to us again, speaking quickly to one another with words we don't understand; their actions deft and practised; a modern pagan ritual with high-tech magic that might summon her back from the dead.

A spike on her heart monitor.

Her heart is *beating!* Not a fat gold watch but a girl's heart.

She's alive.

Elation buoys me up and everyone around me so that for a moment we are all outside the normal, contained, pragmatic world.

Jenny arrives next to me; no longer too bright.

'Still here,' she says and smiles at me.

She can't see her body, screened by the doctors and nurses.

Dr Sandhu turns to you. His brown face no longer looks indecently healthy, but exhausted. What must it be like to hold someone's life in your hands? How heavy Jenny's must be for him, weighted with our love for her.

'We'll be taking her directly to our intensive care unit,' he tells you. 'I'm afraid we think her heart is likely to have suffered damage. Possibly very severe damage. We'll be running tests straight away.'

I try to usher Jenny away, but she doesn't budge.

'You'll get through this,' you say to Jenny's unconscious body. 'You *will get better*.'

As if you know that Jenny can hear you.

'I'm Miss Logan, Jennifer's consultant cardiologist,' a young woman says, who was at the forefront of the resuscitation. 'Let's talk when we have her test results back. But I have to warn you that if the findings are as we predict, then — '

But you leave the room, refusing to hear the end of her sentence.

Jenny goes too. Because medical staff are leaving her bedside and she can't bear to see her face and body.

★   ★   ★

Sarah's waiting outside.

'She's alive,' you say.

Sarah hugs you. She's shaking.

I join Jenny further down the corridor.

'It was amazing, Mum,' she says.

'Amazing?' I ask. Will this be the one adjective Jenny uses to describe her near-death experience? The same adjective she and her friends use to describe ice cream. I used to worry that the subtlety of verbal adjectives had been vandalised

117

by TV and computer screens; I used to lecture her about it sometimes.

'It was as if all the light and colour and warmth and love in my body was leaving it and being put into me,' she says. 'It was beautiful. The feeling. And what I was. Beautiful.' She searches a moment for the right words. 'And I think, what was happening, was that my soul was being born.'

I am stunned by her description. Not just by the content but by the way she describes it; our daughter who has previously never used more than one adjectival phrase in a sentence.

'But it's not going to happen again,' I say. 'Not till you're an old lady, OK?'

★　★　★

Dr Sandhu joins you and Sarah.

'One of our nurses has told us that a piece of equipment we're using to help Jenny, the endotracheal tube which connects to her ventilator, came loose last night. There's a chance that it was tampered with. She should have reported this last night but I'm afraid it hasn't been brought to light until this emergency.'

My anxiety for Jenny last night expands to terror.

'Was that why her heart stopped?' Sarah asks.

'There's no way to be sure,' Dr Sandhu replies. 'We were already concerned about organ failure.'

I saw him. The figure in the coat. *I saw him*.

'Someone did this to her?' you ask, incredulous.

'Pieces of equipment can occasionally be faulty,' Dr Sandhu says. 'It's rare, but it happens. And it's very hard to see how tampering could have occurred. We are one of the few units in the hospital with a low turnover of staff. Most of us have worked here for a long time. And nothing like that has ever happened.'

'What about someone coming in?' Sarah asks.

'The door to the burns unit is kept locked, with a code keypad. Only members of staff know the code and visitors have to be let in.'

Just like the school. Why hadn't I realised that before? *Just like the school.*

I see anxiety pinching at Sarah's face.

'Thank you,' she says quietly. 'One of my colleagues will need to talk to you.'

'Of course. In fact, we have already followed protocol and the clinical director has just spoken to the police. But I wanted to tell you myself.'

Next to me Jenny has gone rigid, her face afraid.

'You heard him, Mum. Equipment can be faulty.'

She doesn't want to believe this.

'Yes,' I say, because how can I tell her what I saw last night? How can I frighten her more now?

You walk away down the corridor, and I'm worried you're walking away from what you've been told. Even the suggestion of it. I go after you, away from Jenny.

'Someone's trying to kill her, Mike,' I say to you.

But you can't hear me.

119

'I'll stay with Jenny,' you say to Sarah. 'Twenty-four seven. Make sure the bastard can't get to her.'

I love you.

★ ★ ★

An hour or so later and Jenny has gone for a wander round the hospital, which worries me, but: *'I'm seventeen, for heaven's sake, Mum. Besides, what more can go wrong now?'*

I'm with you, next to Jenny's bed. The world of the intensive care unit is so alien, so utterly foreign to anything in our previous life, that having a policeman next to Jenny now is no more peculiar than the banks of monitors that surround her. I think you are grateful to have a *uniformed presence*, but hover close to Jenny, still wanting to protect her yourself.

Although Jenny's description of almost-dying — her birth of a soul — amazed me, it's not totally accurate. Love can't leave your body as it's not there in the first place. Because I know as I look at you, and at Jenny's damaged body, that love is held in whatever I am now.

'Mr Covey?'

Miss Logan, that young consultant cardiologist, has come up to you.

'We have the results of Jennifer's tests back now,' she says. 'Shall we go into my office?'

But how can this pretty Miss Logan, this *slip of a thing*, as Dad would have said, possibly know what's going on in the complex intricacies of Jenny's heart? Surely she's too young to be a proper consultant; to really know what she's talking about. And even as I think this, I know I'm trying to invalidate what she might say before the words are spoken.

★ ★ ★

I follow you into a doctor's office, the air dense with heat.

Dr Sandhu is waiting. He takes your hand in his and pats your arm and I try not to think that he's giving you sympathy in advance.

Nobody sits down.

And I *hate* this hot institutional room with its depressing carpet-tiles and plastic stacking chairs and drug company calendar. I want to be in the kitchen with Adam and Jenny, just back from school, the French windows wide open, making Jenny tea and squash for Adam and listening to gripes about homework. For a moment I imagine myself there so clearly that I almost hear the thump of Jen's bag on the table and Adam asking if there are chocolate minirolls left. Surely there's a wormhole you can step into, taking you into a parallel universe where your old life, your real life, is going on the same if only you can find your way back to it.

It's Dr Sandhu who speaks first, taking responsibility for breaking the news; like an eggshell, I think as he speaks, the contents poisonous and corrosive, destroying the way home.

'We've run extensive tests on Jenny. And I'm afraid that, as we feared, her heart has suffered catastrophic damage.'

I look at Dr Sandhu's face and quickly turn away, but it's too late. In his expression I've seen there's a moment when a doctor realises that the life he holds in his hands is too fragile for the medicine he knows.

'Her heart will only be able to function for a few weeks,' he says.

'How many weeks?' you ask, each syllable a physical strain, tongue forced against the palate of your mouth; sounds bitter as wormwood.

'It's impossible to be accurate,' he says, *hating* having to do this.

'How many?' you ask again.

'Our guess would be three weeks,' replies Miss Logan.

★ ★ ★

'This time in three weeks we'll be in Italy! Only three weeks till Christmas, Ads! Just three weeks to A levels, don't you realise how <u>soon</u> that is?'

When Jenny was born her life was measured first in hours, then days, then weeks. At about sixteen weeks it turned to months — four months, five months, eighteen months — until two, when you measure your child's age in half years. Then gradually the measurement of her life became whole years. Now they're measuring what's left of it in weeks again.

I won't let it happen.

I have got her from two cells to a five-foot-five-inches-tall teenager and she's still growing, for crying out loud, and she can't stop now. She *can't.*

'There must be something you can do,' you say, as always, even now, certain there must be a solution.

'Her only option is a transplant,' said Miss Logan. 'But I'm afraid — '

'Then she'll get a transplant,' you interrupt.

'It's highly unlikely that a donor whose tissue matches Jennifer's will be found in time,' she says. Her youth gives her an edge, which separates her from the information she's giving. 'I have to tell you that the chance of her receiving a donor heart in time is extremely remote.'

'Then I'll do it,' you say. 'I'll go to that place in Switzerland, Dignitas or whatever it's called. They let you die if you want to. There must be a way of doing it so that my heart can be donated to her.'

I look at their faces, not yours; I can't bear to look at yours. I see compassion rather than astonishment. You can't be the first parent to suggest this.

'I'm afraid there are many reasons why you can't do that,' Dr Sandhu says. 'Primarily legal ones.'

'I heard that your wife is still unconscious — ' tough Miss Logan begins but you interrupt her again.

'What the hell are you suggesting? That I donate *her* heart?'

I feel a leap of hope inside me. Can *I* do this? Is it possible?

'I just want to offer my sympathy,' Miss Logan says. 'It must be particularly hard for you with Jennifer.' Almost as if she has to spell it out to

123

herself. 'In any case,' she says, 'even if your wife is found to have extremely limited brain function, she is breathing for herself so — '

'She can also hear me,' you interrupt, vigorously. 'And she's thinking and she's feeling. She can't show it yet. But she will. Because she will get better. And Jenny will too. They'll both recover.'

And I admire you so much because in the face of 'catastrophic' and 'three weeks' and 'extremely remote' and your suicide bid proving futile, you refuse to admit defeat for Jenny or for me.

Inside your head now, on those wide-open prairies, I see a one-man stockade of hope, built by your strength of spirit.

Dr Sandhu and the young cardiologist say nothing.

An honest, ghastly quietness in place of agreement or reassurance.

You leave the mute room. Shortly afterwards Miss Logan also leaves.

I want to bolt to your one-man stockade of hope, but I can't, Mike. I just can't get there.

I can't move at all.

Because I am surrounded by sharp spikes of information and a step in any direction will mean I am pierced through. So if I don't move, I can stop it from being true.

Dr Sandhu thinks he's alone. He brusquely wipes his tears away. What has led him to this room? I imagine a Science teacher noticing his intelligence and suggesting medical school; and his parents being proudly encouraging, and then a career path, with a right turn here and a

124

straight ahead there, ending up here, now.

But the Dr Sandhu career-path distraction is useless. The spikes are coming towards me and they have a sound; the sound they've had since the words 'three weeks' were spoken — a tick tick tick over every thought, every action, every word until they are used up.

Jenny's heart has become a watch after all.

Beating or ticking into an ending of silence.

11

Jenny is waiting for me as I come out of ICU.

'Well?' she asks.

'You're going to be alright,' I say. A brazen, bare-faced lie. A deceit. A shawl woven of untruths in which a mother wraps her child.

She looks so relieved.

'But they can't be *totally* sure?' she asks me.

'Not *totally*.'

As close as I will get to the truth.

We see you coming out of ICU and going towards my ward. Sarah must be with Jenny.

★   ★   ★

You sit next to my comatose body and you tell me what the doctors have said. You tell me that she will get a transplant. She will be alright. *Of course she will!*

I press against you and I can *feel* your courageous hope for Jenny.

I hold onto it as I hold onto you.

For now, at least, I can believe in your hope for her and the ghastly ticking down of Jenny's life is paused.

★   ★   ★

Jenny is in the corridor.

'Shall we go to the garden?' she suggests. She

must see my surprise because she smiles with a note of triumph. 'I found one.'

She takes me to a corridor with a glass wall. Still holding tightly to your hope, I look through the glass to see a courtyard garden. It's in the heart of the hospital, walls rising up on all four sides. It must have been designed to be seen from the many overlooking windows, rather than be used. The entrance on the ground floor is a nondescript, unmarked door, presumably only used by whoever looks after it.

Through the glass, the garden looks so pretty with its profusion of English flowers: tissue-paper pink roses and frilly white jasmine and velvet peonies. There's a wrought-iron seat and a fountain; a stone bird-bath.

I go outside with Jen, thinking the garden will be a gentle place to be.

The walls surrounding this garden have trapped the heat, funnelling it down. The water in the bird-bath has evaporated. The edges of the tissue-paper roses have curled and dried; the peony is dropping with the weighted humid air.

Summer boxed in.

'At least it's sort of outside,' she says.

Through the glass wall, which abuts one side of the garden, you can see through to rooms and corridors. We watch people walking along. And I know why she likes it now, because even though it's not outside *proper*, we are separate from the hospital.

As I sit with her, the lie I told digs into me like razor wire.

We carry on watching people through the glass

wall. For a long time. Jen seems soothed by it and it is quite soporific, like watching tropical fish in a tank.

'That's Rowena's dad, isn't it?' Jenny asks.

Amongst the melee of fish-people I spot Donald.

'Yes.'

'But why's he here?'

'Rowena's in the hospital,' I say.

'Why?'

'I don't know. I saw her with Adam outside the school and she looked fine then.'

After Maisie's visit, I'd again forgotten about Rowena; my anxiety for Jenny still making me too selfish to have room for her as well.

'Maisie will be with her,' Jenny says. 'Shall we go and visit?'

It's sweet of her to think I'd like to be with my old friend.

'It gets kind of boring here after a while,' she says.

★   ★   ★

We're near the burns unit now and are catching up with Donald. A nurse is with him. As we follow him, I'm glad that for a little while at least Jenny and I have a focus that is not on her injuries or mine.

Donald is wearing a dark suit, jacket still on despite the hotly humid day, and is carrying a briefcase.

I can smell cigarettes on his clothes. I've never noticed that before, but my sense of smell has become so much more acute now, overpoweringly so.

We're now close enough to hear the nurse talking to him. Her voice is briskly competent.

' . . . and when someone has been in an enclosed space in a fire, we have to monitor them extremely carefully in case there have been any inhalation injuries. It can sometimes take a little while before there are any symptoms, so it's wise to be on the safe side.'

Donald's face looks severe, barely recognisable from the smiling, avuncular man I last saw at the prize-giving. It's probably these horrible, glaring striplights partitioning the corridor ceiling, which gouge out shadows in people's faces, making them look harsher.

The nurse presses a keypad on the door to the burns unit and holds the door for him.

'Your daughter's bed is this way,' she says.

But surely he's been to see her before? He wouldn't have waited a day before coming to her bedside. Maisie has told me how protective he is of his family countless times. *'He'd kill crocodiles for us with his bare hands! Good job there aren't that many crocs in Chiswick!'*

Jenny and I reach Rowena's side-room a little before Donald and look through the glass panel in the door. Rowena has a drip in her arm and her hands are bandaged. But her face is undamaged. How could I not have thought her face beautiful before? Next to her is Maisie.

I wait for Donald to arrive and take Rowena in his arms and for the three of them to be reunited.

I brace myself against the stinging contrast.

Donald goes into the room, passing Jenny in the doorway. I notice she's very pale.

'Jen?'

She turns to me, as if snapping out of a reverie.

'I know it's mad but for a moment, well, it was like I was back in the school, really back there, and — ' she pauses — 'I heard the fire alarm going off. *I heard it*, Mum.'

I put my arm around her.

'Has it gone now?'

'Yeah.' She smiles at me. 'Maybe it's mad person's tinnitus.'

We look through the glass in the door to Rowena's room.

Donald is going towards Rowena and I think she looks panicked. But that can't be right, surely? His back is towards me, and I can't see the expression on his face.

Maisie is hurriedly pulling down her sleeves to cover large livid bruises on her arms.

'I told you he'd be here soon,' she says to Rowena in a too-bright, nervy voice.

Donald has reached Rowena. He grabs hold of her bandaged burnt hands; she gives a sharp scream of pain.

'Quite the little heroine, aren't you?'

There's hatred in his voice. Ugly and raw and shocking.

Maisie tries to pull him away. 'You're hurting her, Donald, please. Stop.'

I'm in the room now, wanting to help, but there's nothing I can do but watch. Still he holds

Rowena's bandaged hands, and she's trying not to cry out.

I think of Adam flinching from Donald's lighter as he lit a cigarette after the prize-giving; his foot grinding the stub into the ground.

He lets go of Rowena's hands and turns to leave.

Rowena is crying.

'Daddy . . . '

She gets out of bed and walks shakily towards him. She looks fragile and slight in the cotton hospital gown, so much smaller than Donald in his hard dark suit.

'You disgust me,' he says as she reaches him.

Maisie puts her hand on him, trying to stop him from leaving.

'Your bruises,' he says to her. 'Have you shown anyone?'

Maisie drops her head, not looking at him. Her FUN sleeves cover her bruises now; the same long-sleeved shirt she'd been wearing at sports day, despite the heat.

'It was an accident,' Maisie says to him. 'Just an accident. Of course it was. And you can hardly see any more. Really.'

Donald abruptly leaves the room.

'He didn't mean it, sweetheart,' Maisie says to Rowena.

Rowena is silent.

I turn away from them and leave the room too, as if they're too naked for me to watch; the bones of the family exposed.

I reach Jenny who's been watching through the glass in the door.

'I never knew,' she says to me, shocked.

'No.'

But I think again about Maisie's 'bulimic hog' comment, her bruised cheek, her cracked wrist, her lack of self-confidence. I again see the image I'd glimpsed as I looked into my dressing-table mirror the night of the prize-giving — that dense murky network of something sinister.

I'd dismissed it as an illusion at the time. But a little later, going to sleep that night when thoughts slip out from being censored, I'd wondered.

But I didn't ask Maisie about Donald; didn't even give her an opening to a conversation. Not just because in daylight it seemed an absurd suspicion, but because I thought it was a territory beyond our friendship. I didn't want to — didn't know how to — step outside our customary domestic landscape in which we were both so comfortable and sure-footed.

But she doesn't constrain our friendship that way; isn't cowardly that way. She thinks she should have gone *into a burning building* for me. And I didn't even ask her if she was OK. If there was anything she'd like to tell me; talk about.

And Rowena.

Even if I'd managed not to see what was happening to Maisie, I should have seen what was happening to her. A child. Because when Donald grabbed hold of her burnt hands that surely wasn't the first time he'd hurt her.

I remember her in reception and year one at Sidley House; that elfin beautiful child. Was it happening then? Later, perhaps; year three or four?

132

'I thought she was a spoilt little princess,' I say to Jenny, guilt making my words taste sour.

'Me too.'

Maybe she's also remembering the hand-embroidered pillow-cases, and hand-painted rocking chair and fairytale bed and princess party-dresses. I used to worry that when the little princess grew up her adult life could only be a disappointment to her.

Never once guessing at this.

'She always had to be the best,' Jenny says. 'At everything. It used to freak me.'

She's remembering her a little older, nine or ten maybe.

I'd wished Jenny had a little more ambition, yes, but I'd found Rowena's need to excel repellent at times. It wasn't just the scholarship to St Paul's Girls, it was being two grades ahead of anyone else on the violin as well as captain of the swimming team and lead in any play or assembly.

'She was trying to make him love her, wasn't she?' Jenny says.

Surely it can't be so simple. Can a seventeen-year-old really be able to see through years of abuse to such a simple reason for a child's behaviour?

But I think it is that brutally in-your-face obvious.

'Yes,' I say to Jenny.

And I'd condemned her for being overly competitive. Not once seeing an abused child trying to win her father's love.

Was that why she worked so hard to get into

Oxford? Was she still trying to make him love her?

'*You disgust me.*'

Rowena is lying in bed again now, her face turned to the wall. Maisie has a hand on her, but Rowena doesn't turn to her.

Maisie. *My friend.* Why didn't she leave Donald? For Rowena's sake if not her own. It must kill her to see Rowena being hurt. Why has she kept up this elaborate charade, protecting him?

Jenny and I walk away from Rowena's room.

'I used to avoid her,' Jenny says. 'When we were children. I mean, it was more than just not liking her. She gave me the creeps. God, in retrospect . . . I mean, I thought she was weird, but she was just different because of what was happening to her at home. And it's hardly surprising if she was cruel.'

'Was she cruel?' I asked.

'Cruel's too strong. She was just . . . well, as I said, weird. There was this one time, she cut off Tania's ponytail. For Tania it was like the main thing about her, having this long hair. We were all jealous of it, used to spend break-time plaiting it. So cutting it off, well, it's like violence. When you're nine.'

'I'd forgotten that.'

'I think she must have been lashing out at someone else for a change and that was as near physical violence as she could get.'

'Yes.'

'I avoided her after that. We all did. God, if I'd known.'

'And recently? While you've been teaching assistants at Sidley House?'

I'm hoping that Rowena's been one of the gang, happy and popular, that she's breaking free of Donald.

'I barely saw her. During lessons we were in separate classrooms and at lunch time she goes to the park.'

'Don't you?'

'Well, the pub has a really nice outside bit, most of us go there.'

★　★　★

Jenny waits outside ICU and I go in to join you.

You're sitting at Jenny's bedside. The other side of her is a uniformed policeman, who's pretending not to be there as you talk quietly to her.

Your gentleness and loyalty and love are such a contrast to Donald.

Why didn't I see through his disguise of overly indulgent father? And was it there, not just to throw outsiders off the scent, but also to confuse Rowena? Because how can a daddy who buys princess party-dresses and over-the-top birthday gifts and a hand-painted rocking chair with hearts on it also be cruel to you?

At Sidley House, I'd thought Maisie too soft on Rowena. Rowena talked back to her and her tongue could be sharp and she rarely did what Maisie gently asked of her. But how could Maisie discipline her for small instances of bad behaviour when Donald was abusing her? When his abuse was probably the reason for Rowena's 'bad behaviour' in the first place?

When I was safely pregnant with Adam, Maisie had confided in me that she was desperate for another baby. She'd been putting it off for *various reasons* but she was nearly forty so it was *'now-or-never time!'* Six months later, not pregnant, she told me that Rowena had *'absolutely forbidden!'* her to have another baby. I'd thought it another instance of spoilt-princess-Rowena bullying tender-hearted Maisie to get her own way. I thought it terrible that a child of nine could dictate to an adult in that way.

But I think now Rowena may have been trying to protect another child, not yet born.

The PC gets a hissing message on his radio. He tells you that Detective Inspector Baker wants a meeting with you and is waiting in the office on the ground floor. He's barely more than a boy but he sees your anxiety plain as day.

'It's alright, sir. I'll be here with her.'

*   *   *

Jenny and I go with you to your meeting with DI Baker (it no longer seems like following you).

'Do you think they've found something?' Jenny sounds anxious.

'I don't know, sweetheart. But there must be something.'

I'm anxious too — that at this meeting with DI Baker she'll find out what the doctors have said about her heart.

I don't think you'll tell anyone because saying

136

the words will make the facts more solid. I think you'll justify this as waiting until you can tell everyone that a donor heart has been found; that *everything will be alright. No need to worry.* You always tell me of potential calamities after you've sorted out a solution. Calamities. As if walking out of an A-level exam early or pranging the car get any rating on a calamity scale.

But I still believe in your hope for her; I'm still clinging onto it.

★ ★ ★

As we reach the office on the ground floor, Jenny stops.

'Do you think it could be Donald who started the fire?' she asks.

'No', I say immediately.

'Maisie and Rowena were almost the only people in the school at the time,' she says. 'Maybe it was aimed at them.'

'He couldn't possibly have known that,' I counter.

I'm not arguing with logic but from emotion. I cannot bear to think a father and a husband can be that evil. And surely there's a world of difference between bruises and trying to burn someone alive.

But I remember that figure I saw yesterday afternoon on the periphery of the playing field: an innocent bystander, most probably, but just conceivably Donald.

And earlier with the nurse. Could he have been pretending that this was the first time he'd been to the burns unit? Could he have come last night in a long dark coat? Though God knows why he'd want to hurt Jenny.

It was only eight weeks ago that I looked into my dressing-table mirror and saw connections between instances of possible abuse, connecting underground in a dense mass. Just eight weeks.

Would anything be different if I hadn't turned away?

★ ★ ★

We go into the office, which is oppressively hot and airless. Like the family rooms and the doctors' offices it has peeling institutional green paint and ugly carpet-tiles and a clock. Always a clock.

DI Baker doesn't get up from his chair when you come in.

'I know you don't want to go far from your daughter and wife,' he says to you. 'Which is why we're having our meeting here.'

You nod your thanks, surprised by his demonstration of thoughtfulness. Like me, you think we may have misjudged him.

'A new witness came forward shortly after we met,' he continues.

Sarah barges into the room, uncharacteristically flustered. No, flustered is wrong. She's angry and she's been running. Her blouse has dark patches under the arms, her forehead filmed with sweat.

'I've just come from the station,' she says to DI Baker. 'They told me — '

'No one should be telling you anything,' he says curtly. 'I've given you a week of compassionate leave, so take it.'

'It's a mistake,' she says to DI Baker. 'Or deliberate misinformation.'

'The witness is entirely credible.'

'So why wait till now to report it?' she asks.

'Because this person knows how much the Covey family are dealing with and didn't want to add to their distress. But with the press accusations felt it was their duty to come forward.'

Sarah is more emotional than I've ever seen her.

'Who is 'this person'?' she asks.

He looks at her with silent rebuke, and then he continues.

'They have asked for their identity not to be revealed, which is a request I granted. There will be no trial so no need for identification. Neither we nor the school will be pressing charges.'

You look stunned. But also, I think, relieved. As I am. This wasn't done maliciously. It can't be, if there aren't going to be any charges. It's no longer necessary to have this ghastly hostile suspicion to the world. It isn't the hate-mailer or Silas Hyman or Donald. Thank God.

But why is Sarah so upset?

DI Baker's face shows no emotion. He pauses a moment, before he speaks to you.

'Your son was seen leaving the school Art room moments before the automatic smoke detector went off. He was holding matches. There is no doubt in our mind that it was Adam who started the fire.'

Adam? For God's sake, how can he say that? *How?*

'Is this some kind of sick joke?' you ask.

'Whoever told you that is lying,' Sarah says. 'I've known Adam all his life and he's the most gentle, kind child imaginable. There's not an iota of violence in him.'

DI Baker looks irritated. 'Sarah . . . '

'He likes reading,' Sarah continues. 'He plays with his knights and he has two guinea pigs. They are the parameters of Adam's world. He doesn't play truant, he doesn't graffiti, he doesn't get into trouble. Reading, knights, two guinea pigs. Have you got that?'

Our gentle boy accused of this.

Madness.

'It was Hyman, not a child,' you say.

'Mr Covey — '

'How the hell did he persuade you?'

'The witness is nothing to do with Mr Hyman.'

'You're saying that *a child* took white spirit into the Art room?'

'I think we were too hasty to see certain occurrences as significant. The Art teacher may well have been mistaken about the quantity of white spirit kept in the Art room. After all, if she wasn't following the regulations to the letter she was hardly going to tell us that, was she? I had a brief talk with her earlier and she admitted it was possible she'd been mistaken. She's not one hundred per cent certain at all.'

I think of Miss Pearcy, sensitive, artistic Miss

Pearcy, who'd be so easily intimidated by DI Baker.

'Of course she's not *one hundred per cent certain*,' Sarah says. 'Are you *one hundred per cent certain* when you go on holiday that you didn't leave the oven on? Or when there's a crash are you *one hundred per cent certain* you checked your mirror first before turning? It just means that this Art teacher has a conscience and the courage to admit to her fallibility. Especially when a policeman tells her she might have done something wrong.'

'I understand your loyalty to your nephew but — '

She interrupts, sparks flying off her words.

'You can't think *a child* had the knowledge of fires and the premeditation to open the windows at the top of the school?'

'It was a hot day,' DI Baker replies. 'A teacher or child could easily have opened the windows to let in the breeze, despite it being against the rules.'

You have been stunned into silence and stillness, but now you move towards DI Baker and I think you're going to hit him.

'Have you ever seen Adam?' you ask, then gesture to beneath DI Baker's breast pocket. 'He'd come up to about here on you. He's *eight*, for fuck's sake, just eight. His birthday was yesterday. A little boy.'

'Yes, we're aware of his birthday.'

His words sounded menacing, but why?

'Hyman's lied about him,' you say.

Sarah turns to you. 'Silas Hyman can't be the

witness, Mike. It would look too strange if he was in the school at the time.'

'So he must have had an accomplice and — '

'I appreciate it's hard to believe an eight-year-old child could do this,' DI Baker interrupts. 'But according to fire-brigade records, children were responsible for ninety-three per cent of all intentionally started school-time school fires. Just over a quarter were started by children younger than seven years old.'

But what have statistics to do with Adam?

'We think it was most likely a prank, a bit of fooling around that went wrong,' DI Baker says, as if this will appease you.

'But Adam *knows* lighting a fire is wrong,' Sarah says. 'He'd *think* about the terrible consequences that may happen. For a child that age he's extremely mature and thoughtful.'

I didn't realise how well Sarah knows Adam. I've always thought she was critical of him, seeing him as wet, not like her tall, athletic sons.

'And he knew Jenny was in the school,' Sarah continues, desperately trying to convince him. 'His own sister was in there, for God's sake.'

'Is there any animosity between the siblings?' DI Baker asks.

'What are you suggesting?' you ask and there's violence in your voice.

'I'm sure he didn't intend the fire to do the terrible damage — '

'He didn't do it.' Yours and Sarah's voices overlap with the same certainty.

'What about the intruder?' you ask. 'The one who tampered with Jenny's oxygen. You think

142

that was a little boy too, do you?'

'There is absolutely no evidence that there ever was an intruder,' DI Baker responds impassively. 'We have talked to the medical director and connections sometimes become faulty. It's not significant.'

'There was an intruder! I *saw him*!' I shout, but no one hears me.

'Jenny must have seen Hyman at the school,' you say. 'Maybe his accomplice. Something that implicated him. That's why he came here, to — '

DI Baker interrupts you. 'It really isn't helpful to indulge in unsubstantiated theories.'

'Adam wouldn't do it,' Sarah says again, with controlled fury. 'Which means that someone else did.'

'So you believe your brother's theory now too?' His tone is mocking her.

'I think we should look at every possibility.'

His face shows contempt.

'You told us Silas Hyman voluntarily gave a sample of his DNA?' Sarah says and Baker looks irritated. 'But have we actually *got* any DNA evidence from the scene of the fire?'

'It's really not productive to — '

'I thought not. And now we won't be looking for it, will we?'

'Sarah — '

'If it was Hyman behind this, he'd happily volunteer his DNA if he knew that within twenty-four hours his accomplice would nail a child for it, and the forensic search would stop. He could well have banked on nothing being found for the first twenty-four hours.'

143

DI Baker looks at her with doughy immovability.

'The truth of the matter is that we have a reliable witness who saw Adam Covey coming out of the Art room, where we know the fire was started, holding matches. Just moments later the automatic heat detector and smoke detectors went off.

'But as I said we won't be pursuing it any further. We are satisfied that he didn't intend the terrible consequences of his actions and that he's been punished enough as it is. So we'll just interview him and — '

'No,' you say vehemently.

They are not going to interview Adam. They can't do that to him.

'You can't accuse him of this,' Sarah says. 'He can't know people thought him capable of this.'

'He doesn't need to go to the police station to be interviewed. We can do it here. So that his father can be present. You too, if you want. But I do need to interview him. You know that, Sarah.'

'What I know is that a totally innocent and vulnerable child has been set up.'

'I have asked a police constable to bring Adam and his grandmother to the hospital. They should be here in half an hour. I suggest we reconvene then.'

*   *   *

Baker leaves the room and I hurry after him.

'You don't know Adam,' I say to him. 'Haven't met him. So it's not your fault that you don't

144

understand why he couldn't have done this. He's *good*, you see. Not in a goody-goody way but a moral way.'

'Mum, please, he can't hear you,' Jenny says.

'He likes reading Arthurian legends,' I continue. 'His favourite is 'Sir Gawain and the Green Knight'. And that's what he wants to be. Not a pop star or a footballer or whatever it is other boys want to be, but a knight like Sir Gawain, and he's trying to find a modern equivalent. And you might think that quaint or funny, but it's not for him; it's a moral code that he wants to live by.'

'Even if he could hear you,' Jenny says, 'I don't think he knows about Gawain.'

She's right, this man wouldn't have a clue.

'He also likes history programmes,' I continue. 'And asks not only why people are wicked and do wicked things, but why people allow themselves to be led by such people. He *thinks* about these things.'

How can you make someone understand a boy like Adam?

DI Baker seems to be hurrying now, speeding his pace; I keep up.

'You probably think that all mothers say these things about their sons, but they don't. Really. They boast about how fantastic their boy is at sport and doing outdoorsy things and being fearless — breaking an arm as he was *determined to climb it!* That kind of thing. Not being good and kind. Not being like Adam.

'You might think it's me boasting now, but it isn't. Because we don't live in an age of chivalry,

145

do we? We don't live in a time when Adam's virtues are valuable.

'And all I really want is for him to be happy. Just happy. And if it would make him happy I'd swap his kindness for being in the football team in a blink and trade decency for popular. But he doesn't have the choice and so I don't either. Because that's how he is.

'And even though it makes him unhappy and I want him to have less lonely characteristics, I am so *proud* of him.'

'He's afraid of fire,' Jenny says to DI Baker, joining me. 'He won't even hold a sparkler,' she continues to his back. 'He got burnt by a spark from the fire when he was a toddler, and ever since he's been afraid.'

If she could make herself heard she'd give DI Baker logical reasons for why Adam couldn't have started the fire.

And she's right. He is afraid of fire. I remember, again, him flinching from Donald's lighter.

DI Baker reaches the exit of the hospital and I yell at him.

'Don't do this to him! Please! Don't do this to him!'

And for a moment he feels my presence. For a second I am a draught on his back, a tingling in his scalp, something touching his thoughts. A mother. A guardian angel. A ghost.

12

You're at Jenny's bedside. There's no longer a police officer as it's *no longer deemed necessary*.

You deem it necessary.

Sarah arrives. 'Ads is on his way,' she says.

'I can't leave Jenny on her own, now that Baker's taken away her protection.'

'There's lots of medical staff here, Mike. Far more than the burns unit.'

Doesn't she think there's a real risk?

'Tell Baker why I can't leave Jen.'

'I think he'll get it.'

Because in protecting Jenny you're showing your belief that the real criminal is still out there and a threat. And the criminal isn't an eight-year-old boy. It's a bodily demonstration that DI Baker is wrong and Adam is innocent.

I know you want to be with him; that you feel torn in two. I've felt it countless times in minor ways over the years. With just Jenny it had been so simple, but with two children the seamless narrative of our lives became disjointed. 'For goodness sakes,' Nanny Voice snaps at me. 'This is hardly helping Jenny with her homework against taking Adam to cubs; having a water-sports holiday for Jenny against a Welsh-castles one for Adam.' But I think it's the same thing, translated onto a huge scale.

And this need to be with both of them feels like a physical tearing.

'Look after him,' you say to Sarah.

As she leaves, I go after her, desperate to tell her that *I saw the attacker*.

Before Adam was accused, the police were on the case and I was sure they'd find him. But now the police have abandoned us and this piece of information is crucial and is turning corrosive the longer it stays, untold, inside me.

★   ★   ★

In the goldfish-bowl atrium, Sarah's on her BlackBerry while Jenny and I wait for Addie.

The young PC, who was previously guarding Jenny, comes in through the main doors. Mum and Adam are just behind him.

Sarah gives Adam a kiss, and gently pushes his fringe out of his eyes. I should have trimmed it on Sunday as I'd meant to, but we'd watched the history channel together instead.

He looks thin and pale and bemused.

Sarah turns to Mum; her voice is quiet. 'Has he said anything yet?' she asks.

'Nothing. I've tried, but he still can't. Not a word since it happened.'

Addie didn't speak to you on the phone last night; nor when he came to my bedside. But can he really not speak *at all*? Like me, you don't know about this. You haven't even seen him yet because, unbelievably, the fire was only yesterday afternoon.

'Does he know what this is about?' Sarah asks Mum.

'Yes. Can you stop it? Please.'

Sarah turns to the young PC.

'Give me five minutes.' Speaking as his boss, not a member of Adam's family.

Jenny and I follow her.

'Why isn't Dad here?' Jenny asks. 'He should be with Addie.'

'He wants to be with you.'

'But I don't *need* him.'

I think she looks scared but is determined to hide it.

'Dad knows that Addie will have Aunty Sarah with him,' I say to her, surprised that I find this reassuring.

'Yes.'

★ ★ ★

We follow Sarah back into the oppressively hot office. DI Baker is sitting on a plastic chair that's too small for him. Sarah stands far back as if she finds him physically repellent.

'This interview is pointless,' she says. 'Adam can't talk.'

'Or won't,' asks DI Baker.

'He is suffering post-traumatic stress. Sufferers can become mute and — '

'He has a diagnosis for that?' interrupts DI Baker.

'I'm sure we could get one,' Sarah responds. She must see the undisguised scepticism on DI Baker's face.

'I spent six months on secondment to a charity which works with torture victims. Trauma can — '

'I hardly think this is a comparable situation.'

'I've talked to many parents who were at the school,' Sarah says.

'You've no business — '

'As Adam and Jenny's *aunt*, and Grace's *sister-in-law*, in that capacity. God, I've had half the school on the phone asking how they are.

'Adam saw his mother running into the burning school, screaming for his sister. And he waited. Watching the burning building. Lots of parents tried to get him away, but he wouldn't leave. Then he saw firefighters bringing his mum and sister out. Both of them were unconscious. He thought they were dead. I think that qualifies as trauma, don't you? And you can't put him through an interview. You just *can't*.'

'Where's your brother?'

'With Jenny. As there's no longer a police guard.'

DI Baker looks irritated. He knows the point you're making. 'Are they here?'

Sarah's hostile silence annoys him.

'If you are willing to cooperate in this you can stay with him, but if — '

She cuts off his threat. 'He's outside.'

Sarah goes into the corridor.

★   ★   ★

'You need to come with us now, Ads,' she says to him. 'I want you to know that apart from my idiot boss, none of us think you did this. Not for one minute.'

The PC looks astonished by her. She turns to

150

my mother, who is shaking.

'Why don't you go and see Grace for a little while? I'll take care of him.'

Maybe she's afraid of my mother not holding it together.

She gives Mum a quick unexpected hug, then accompanies Adam into the office.

★   ★   ★

'Sit down, Adam,' DI Baker said. 'I need to ask you some questions, alright?'

Adam is silent.

'I asked if that was alright, Adam. If you find it hard to speak, then you can nod.'

Adam is totally still.

'I'd like to talk to you about the fire.'

The word 'fire' makes Addie crumple into himself.

I put my arms around him but he can't feel my touch. And then Sarah pulls him onto her knee. Small for eight, he's still able to sit on knees. She clasps her hands in front of her, encircling him.

'Let's start with yesterday morning,' DI Baker says. 'It was your birthday, wasn't it?'

Maybe this is his attempt to put Adam at his ease.

'Sorry, Ads,' Sarah says. 'Useless aunt. I always forget, don't I?'

I used to think it was because she couldn't be bothered with our children.

'I always open my presents at breakfast,' DI Baker says to Adam. 'Did you do that?'

151

★ ★ ★

I'd piled up his presents in the middle of the kitchen table, trying to make them look as many as possible; ours done up with a blue satin bow, to make it look extra present-like. Inside, a 'play-space enclosure' for his guinea pigs. '*Looks like the bloody Hilton,*' you'd said on Tuesday evening as I'd wrapped it up. '*Alton Towers for guinea pigs,*' I'd corrected.

I'd got him a card with an 'I am 8!' badge so he could wear it to school, because it's important that everyone knows it's your birthday. It was a rocket card, even though he's not into space, but by the time you get to eight, the age cards have almost petered out and there's virtually no choice.

The smell of coffee and toast and pain au chocolat in the oven because it's a birthday.

Adam came down the stairs hurriedly, two at a time. He did almost a comic-book double-take when he saw the presents. 'All for me? *Really?*'

Calling up to Jenny and you that the birthday boy was here and knowing he liked being called that and thinking that next year he probably wouldn't.

Jenny came downstairs, far earlier than usual, and — amazingly — dressed already. She hugged Adam and gave him her present.

'Aren't teaching assistants meant to be smartly dressed?' I said. 'Professional looking?'

She was wearing her short, gauzy skirt and skimpy top.

'It'll be fine, Mum, really. Besides, my outfit

152

goes with the shoes.'

She stuck out her suntanned bare legs and the jewels in her sandals glinted in the morning summer sunshine.

'I just think you should be a little more . . . '

'Yeah, I know,' she said and teased me about bumsters.

Then you came into the kitchen, singing 'Happy Birthday' loudly and out of key. Really loudly. And Adam laughed. You said we'd do something special that evening.

His voice was quiet. 'I hate going to school on my birthday.'

'But your friends will be there,' you said. 'And it's sports day, isn't it? So not all work today.'

'I'd rather have work.'

A flash of annoyance on your face — or was it sadness — covered because it was his birthday. You turned to Jenny.

'Don't kill anyone, Nurse Jen,' you said.

'Being school nurse is a serious thing, not something to joke about,' I said, snappish.

'It's just for the afternoon, Mum.'

But what if there's a head injury? I'd thought. And she doesn't know to watch out for sleepiness and sickness when a child has an internal bleed in the brain. Aloud, I said, 'Seventeen is just too young to have that much responsibility.'

'It's a primary school sports day, Mum, not a motorway crash.'

She was teasing me, but I didn't catch the ball she threw me.

'Children can be severely injured if they fall

153

wrong. All sorts of unforeseen accidents can happen.'

'Then I'll dial 999 and call in the pros, OK?'

I didn't argue with her any more. There was no point. Because I'd be there at sports day, with the watertight alibi of cheering Adam on, to keep an eye on things — any signs of sleepiness in injured children and I'd be on it.

She doled out the pain au chocolat hot from the oven, bought from Waitrose two weeks ago and waiting in the freezer for this morning.

'I have done a St John Ambulance training, Mum,' she said to me. 'I'm not *totally* incompetent?'

A rise at the end of her sentence, like all teenage girls, as if life is one long question.

You took a hot pain au chocolat, juggling it from hand to hand to cool it, going to the door.

'Run super-fast,' you said to Adam. 'And I'll see you tonight.' Turning to me: 'Bye. Have fun.'

I don't think we kissed goodbye. Not in a pointed way, but in a kiss-taken-as-read way. We thought we had a never-ending supply of kisses and had become careless with the ones we didn't use.

★ ★ ★

'And did your mum make you a cake?' DI Baker asks Adam.

Silence.

'Adam?'

But he doesn't move or speak.

'It was a brilliant cake,' Jenny says to me. She

154

puts her arm around me. 'They'll find out it's a mistake.'

*   *   *

I remember Jenny and Adam searching the house for Adam's tiny Lego skeleton man to put on the cake's no-man's-land and me saying I thought this was going a little far, but secretly being glad that he was doing something boyish.

I remember counting out eight blue candles (three would go into the artillery guns) and thinking it hadn't felt long since I'd had to take just two candles out of the full packet, and it had felt extravagant and touching. How could he need a *whole fistful* of them? The cake bristling like some pastel blue foreboding of stubble.

*   *   *

'Right, let's move on then,' DI Baker says to Adam. 'Did you take your cake to school?'

Adam doesn't reply. Can't reply.

'I spoke to your form teacher, Miss Madden,' DI Baker says, and it seems strange that he's talked to the insipid and mean Miss Madden.

'She told me that children are always allowed to bring a cake in on their birthdays?'

I remember putting the cake tin into the jute bag with the square base, which is perfect for cake tins as they don't fall on their sides. And then —

'Oh God.'

'Mum?' Jenny asks but DI Baker is talking again.

155

'She told me that parents supply the candles and also the matches.'

A slight stress on 'matches' but Sarah reacts as if scalded.

'Your headmistress has corroborated this,' DI Baker continues.

I plead with Sarah to stop this Sherman tank of an interview before it reaches its destination. But she can't hear me.

'Miss Madden told us that she keeps the cake, with the candles and matches, in a cupboard next to her desk. Usually she would get it out at the end of the day, just before the children go home. But yesterday was sports day, wasn't it?'

Adam is silent and still.

'She said that if it's sports day, the birthday child can take it out to the playing field to have at the end?'

Adam is motionless.

I remember how anxious he'd been that his birthday cake would be forgotten and he'd miss that once-a-year singing to him; all the children clustering around him.

'She told us that you went to get your cake from your classroom?'

⋆   ⋆   ⋆

He dashed up to me, his face one big smile. He was going to get his cake *right now!*

⋆   ⋆   ⋆

156

'So you went to your classroom, which was empty?' DI Baker asks, not waiting for a reply any more. 'And then did you take the matches to the Art room?'

Adam is mute.

'Did you use your birthday cake matches to start a fire, Adam?'

The silence in the room is so loud that I think my eardrums will burst with the force of it.

'You just have to say yes or no, lad.'

But he's stock still; frozen.

* * *

He's standing by the statue of the bronze child, watching me running into the burning school, smoke pouring out and I'm shouting and screaming for Jenny.

* * *

'We don't think you *meant* to hurt anyone, Adam,' DI Baker says.

* * *

But how can Addie speak with the noise of sirens and shouting and his own screams? How can he make himself heard above that din?

* * *

'How about if you just nod or shake your head?'

157

* * *

He doesn't hear Adam screaming. Just as he can't hear me as I yell at him to leave my child alone.

* * *

'Adam?'

* * *

But Addie is staring at the school, waiting for me and Jenny. The smoke and the sirens and the waiting. A child turned to stone.

* * *

'I am giving you a caution, Adam,' he says to him. 'Which is a serious thing. If you ever do anything like this again we will not be so lenient. Do you understand?'

* * *

But Adam is watching us being carried out by firefighters. He thinks we are dead. He sees Jenny's charred hair, her sandals. He sees a firefighter shaking.

* * *

Sarah's arms are locked around Addie.
'That's the evidence? That he brought in

matches? And that someone saw him?'

'Sarah — '

She interrupts him, coldly furious. 'Someone's made him the perfect patsy.'

13

Adam comes out of the office, looking dazed.

In the corridor, he retches and then he runs, trying to find a loo, but he can't find one and he's sick on the floor. I hold him but he can't feel me.

Mum is coming down the corridor. As she sees Addie she magicks that smile onto her face.

'Poor old you,' she says, giving him a hug.

Sarah has come out of the office now. She wipes his face with a Kleenex from her pocket, then bends down so that her face is level with his.

'I'm really sorry the policeman said those things to you. Someone has lied to him and we are going to find out who, I promise. And then I expect he'll want to come and apologise to you in person. I would, in his shoes. I'm going to talk to him right now.'

Mum takes Adam's hand. 'Let's go outside and get some fresh air, shall we?'

She takes him towards the exit of the hospital and Jenny goes with them.

As I watch them leave I remember watching a history series with Addie while you were away. (It had that flirty 'snogging-the-bloody-camera!' presenter who irritates you.) During the ad breaks, they showed a trailer for a crime programme. It gave Addie a nightmare, so afterwards Jenny or I would grab the remote to turn it over until it was finished. It's a little bit mad, I know, but I feel as if our old safe life is on the other channel, and we've been sucked into a violent and frightening one that we can't escape.

★ ★ ★

I go with Sarah back into that hot, vile office.

DI Baker is writing notes on a form; a done-and-dusted form, I imagine, naming Adam and a caution and a job finished.

He's irritated to see her.

'I need to know who said they saw Adam,' she says.

'No. You don't. You're not a part of this investigation.'

'Whoever told you was lying.'

'I think I'm the best judge of that. Believe me, it gives me no pleasure to have to caution a child, let alone a police officer's nephew.'

'You said that on sports day the birthday child takes his or her cake, with matches, out to the playing field?'

DI Baker leans forward; his shirt is untucked, a droplet of sweat on his back glistens.

'There is no point to this conversation.'

'So the child would have to return to the school to get his or her cake.'

'Where, exactly, are you going with this?'

'I think the arsonist wanted to set fire to the school on sports day — maybe because the school would be virtually deserted. He chose the child who had a birthday that day, knowing that the child would go back to school to get their cake and matches — and could be made a scapegoat.'

'This story you're cooking up — '

'No story. The school PTA make a calendar every year with a photo of the children who have birthdays that month.'

Adam gave her one for Christmas. All the relatives got one.

'So this month has a photo of Adam and three other children with July birthdays,' she continues. 'Yesterday's date has 'Sports Day' written in large type and 'Adam Covey is 8' in small type. It's on the wall of my kitchen. I saw it last week then forgot about it.'

DI Baker is tucking his shirt back in, hiding the sweat.

'Anyone with a calendar would know it was Adam's birthday on sports day,' Sarah continues. 'Including the arsonist. He *planned* for the blame to fall on him.'

DI Baker turns, crossly uncomfortable.

'Let's suppose, for just one moment, that you're right. Let's go with that. So why didn't Adam *deny it*? They're guilty when they're silent, aren't they? In your experience?'

He's enjoying taunting her.

' 'They' are adult criminals, not an eight-year-old child.'

'All he had to do was shake his head. I even suggested it to him. But he didn't.'

'I think he could well be suffering from amnesia.'

'Oh, come on.'

'It is another recognised symptom of PTS.'

162

'You clearly learnt a lot on that secondment.'

'Memories of the trauma, and often a little while before or afterwards, are blanked out by the brain as a means of self-preservation.'

'So he's conveniently wiped the whole thing?' he asks, enjoying his sarcasm now.

'No, the memory is there. But his self-defence mechanisms have blocked access to it.'

DI Baker goes to the door, his back to her.

'It explains why he doesn't respond to your questions,' Sarah continues. 'He can't. Because he simply doesn't remember. And he's an honest child, so he wouldn't deny something he can't remember. I just hope he doesn't believe your verdict on him.'

DI Baker turns.

'The only time I've seen genuine amnesia is when someone is drugged up to the eyeballs or has had a bash on the head. This is claptrap and you know it.'

'Dissociative amnesia is a recognised psychological condition.'

'Mumbo-jumbo reserved for slippery defence lawyers, not police officers.'

'It's called retrograde amnesia following a traumatic event.'

Being Sarah, she probably knows all this. But she must have brushed up on her knowledge to have the terms at her fingertips. That must be why she was on her BlackBerry as she waited for Adam to arrive. I used to get annoyed at the amount of time *she spent on that thing*.

But I don't think Adam is suffering from amnesia but the opposite. I think he hasn't

163

forgotten the traumatic event but is locked into it and that's why he can't speak.

I have to find him.

I leave the office, remembering Mum saying she was going to take him outside for fresh air, her cure for most ailments. *'If it was up to you, Georgie,'* Dad had teased, *'I'd be prescribing half a kilometre of a healthy walk.'*

★ ★ ★

Jenny is in the large goldfish-bowl atrium at the entrance to the hospital, looking through the glass wall.

'He's with Granny G and Aunt Sarah,' she says, and gestures to a municipal patch of grass a little distance away, where I can just see them.

'I tried to go with them,' she continues. 'But it hurts to be outside. Really hurts.'

I long to go to him, but Jenny has no one with her and I can feel her unhappiness.

We watch Addie, the glass separating us from him.

'Maybe it won't be so bad,' Jenny says, and I think of her at six bringing me tepid tea when I had flu; sweetly, uselessly, trying to make me feel better.

'You and Dad and me and Aunt Sarah and Granny G, we all know that Adam didn't do it,' she continues. 'If his family believe in him then — '

'He'll have to grow up with this,' I say, interrupting her without meaning to. 'He'll be the boy who tried to kill his sister and mother.

School. University. Wherever he goes, it will go first. This terrible thing that's being said about him.'

She's silent for a little while, watching Addie.

'There's something I didn't tell you,' she says. 'About the hate-mailer. He threw a can of paint at me.'

My God. He was *following* her.

'Did you see who it was?' I ask, trying to sound calm.

'No. He threw it from behind. I don't remember anything useful at all. Nothing that will help Addie. I just remember this woman screaming and screaming. It was red gloss, the paint. She thought it was blood. It covered the back of my coat. And all down my hair.'

Was the paint meant to look like blood? A hideous warning of the violence to come?

'It was on the tenth of May,' she says.

That was just a few weeks ago. Just *a few weeks*. It hadn't stopped at all. *It had got worse.* Not just posting her vicious letters, but following her and throwing paint at her. Is he still stalking her now? Attacking her for real?

'If I'd told the police, they might have found him,' she says. 'Stopped him in time. And Addie . . . '

Guilt crumples her face; she looks more like ten right now than seventeen.

I put my hand on her, but she shakes me off as if sympathy just makes it all worse.

'I tried to convince myself it wasn't the hate-mailer who set fire to the school. But now with Adam being accused, I can't . . . '

165

She's admitting this awful possibility out of love for Adam.

'Why didn't you tell us, Jen?'

'I thought it was the right thing to do,' she says quietly.

Before the fire, I'd have told her that the right thing was to be *responsible* and tell us and the police. I'd have become my nanny voice and got up onto my washing-powder box and told her this wasn't about her being 'grounded' or 'policed' but about keeping her *safe*, and unless she told us she was putting herself at risk.

'Who else knows?' I ask.

'Just Ivo,' she replies. 'I made him promise me he wouldn't tell anyone.'

You'll think it's unfair of me to hate Ivo now, but he *should have told us*.

'When's he coming home?' I ask.

'Ten days. But he's bound to find out about this and come back sooner.'

I nod. But I doubt he'll fly back to be at her side. And you think my doubt is unfair on him too.

As I stare out of the window, a man brushes past me.

Mr Hyman.

I feel jolted by shock. Shivery with it. What is he doing here?

He's in shorts and T-shirt, looking so suntanned in this white place. At school he had to wear a formal jacket and trousers and I find his bare arms and legs too intimate.

He's by some kind of vending machine now, taking a ticket.

166

He goes through a door I hadn't noticed before.

I follow him.

'Mum?'

'I want to know what he's up to.'

'I'm sure he's not up to anything.'

But she comes with me anyway.

The door leads onto steep concrete steps. It closes behind us.

We follow him down to a basement car park. After the bright sunshine of the atrium, the basement is oppressively dark. The heat smells of petrol fumes and exhausts. The concrete is stained, the roof too low. I automatically look for exits.

There's only us down here and Mr Hyman.

'I don't like this,' I say.

'It's just a car park. He was getting a ticket for it.'

'You're invisible,' my nanny voice snaps, so much harsher than Jenny. 'And probably *half dead already*. So what can possibly happen to you?'

Mr Hyman reaches an old yellow Fiat and sticks the ticket from the vending machine on the windscreen. There are three children's seats crammed into the car.

'What's he doing here?' I say.

'He's probably come to have it out with Tara,' Jenny says. 'She deserves it.'

'But how would he know that she hangs around here?'

'Maybe he's a good guesser,' Jenny says. 'I don't know. Or he's just trying to get away from his wife. He used to pretend to run the after-school scrapbook-making club so he could get more time away from her.'

She smiles as if it's funny but I don't.

'You can't blame him, really. She's horrible to him,' Jenny continues. 'Told him he was a loser, and that was when he still had a job. Said she was embarrassed by him. But she won't get divorced. Says if he leaves her, he'll never see the kids.'

I look at the three car seats in the car, a discarded teddy, a Postman Pat comic.

'He *told you* that?' I ask.

'So?'

So, you were sixteen last summer and he's thirty, I want to say, but don't.

'Perhaps he's come to see one of us,' Jenny continues. 'Bring flowers or something. He's really kind, remember, Mum? You do remember that, don't you?'

A challenge to remember him, as I used to think him.

We follow him back up the basement steps, me staring at his back, as if I can X-ray through his body to see the inner man. He's hot and sweating, his T-shirt sticking to him, and I see how muscular he is.

I am relieved to be back in the goldfish-bowl atrium of daylight and people and noise.

I spot Adam coming in with Mum and Sarah. As I look at him, I lose sight of Mr Hyman.

Mum has her arm around Adam.

'Mummy will still be having a few bits and bobs sorted out,' she says to him, reducing MRIs and CT scans and God knows what else to bits and bobs and I love her for it. 'So let's get a drink to settle your tummy and then we can see her later.'

When Dad died I'd found out that my parents were the roof which had been sheltering me. Icy winds of grief blew through what had once been warm and safe; terror clawing its way in. Now Mum is putting up a canopy for Adam and I so admire her strength as she tries to shelter him.

I go up to Sarah, desperate to talk to her. Because I have information that will surely exonerate Addie.

I now know that the hate-mailer attacked Jenny with red paint. It didn't stop in February as everyone thinks, but in May, just a few weeks ago. And maybe he's attacking her now, not symbolically with red paint, but trying to kill her.

Because I know that a man sabotaged Jenny's ventilator — I saw him.

But I also think you're right to be suspicious of Silas Hyman because what the hell was a thirty-year-old man doing bad-mouthing his wife to a sixteen-year-old? And what's he doing here? Now?

And I've seen Donald being vicious to Rowena and I think he's probably been violent to Rowena and Maisie for years. Both of them were in the school at the time of the fire. But they won't tell anyone about him, not when they haven't done so in the past.

I feel like I've become the keeper of the keys and one of them, surely, will unlock the truth.

It's my job now to find out everything I can.

Then I will make sure that Adam is proved innocent.

I have to.

That is all there is to it.

14

You're at Jenny's bedside, staring at the monitors around her. You barely glance at Sarah as she arrives.

'Baker's going to get the bastard now?' you say to her.

'He still thinks it's Adam.'

It's as if she's slapped you.

'I don't understand.'

'He didn't speak, Mike. He *can't speak.*'

'But surely he shook his head or . . . '

'No. Nothing. There was nothing I could do. I'm so sorry.'

'Oh Christ. Poor Ads.' You stand up. 'How the hell can Baker believe Hyman's lies?'

'It can't have been Silas Hyman who said he saw Adam,' Sarah says. 'He'd have no business being in the school in the first place.'

'You said already. So he got someone to lie for him.'

'Mike . . . '

'And who the fuck gave him an alibi?'

Sarah doesn't answer.

'You know, don't you?'

You look at her and she finally meets your eye.

'It was his wife.'

'I'm going to see them.'

'I really don't think — '

'I don't give a monkey's arse what anyone thinks.'

I've never heard you snap at her before. She's upset by it but you don't notice.

'Will you stay here? Look after her?'

'I don't think you'll achieve much, Mike.'

You are silent.

'A friend brought your car from the BBC to the hospital car park,' she says. 'The one outside. They've paid for an extended stay. Here.'

She hands you a parking chit. As I look at it, I glimpse people standing on the shore of our old life, waving at us with new toothbrushes and parking chits and nightdresses for me and meals left on the doorstep for Mum and Adam.

She takes your seat next to Jenny.

'There's been no change since this morning,' you say. 'Stable, they said, for the time being.'

When Jenny told me it had hurt her to go outside, I'd worried it had affected her body in some way, but thank God it clearly didn't.

'Let me know if there's anything, right away, anything,' you say.

'Of course.'

You leave ICU and I want to tell you that Silas Hyman is right here in the hospital. But maybe seeing his wife without him will be an advantage. Maybe you'll find out more that way.

And Sarah is with Jenny. Mum is with Adam. Both our children are safe.

★   ★   ★

Jenny is outside ICU.

'Where's Dad going?'

'Silas Hyman's house.'

172

She turns away from me, so that I can't see her face.

'Jen?'

'If I could remember more about that afternoon then maybe the police wouldn't blame Addie; you and Dad wouldn't blame Silas. But I can't. *I can't remember!*'

'It's not your fault, sweetheart.'

I touch her on the shoulder but she shakes me off, as if angry with herself for needing comfort.

'It could be the drugs they've given you,' I say. 'DI Baker told Aunt Sarah that drugs can affect memory.'

What he'd actually said was, '*The only time I've seen genuine amnesia is when someone is drugged up to the eyeballs . . .*'

'But the drugs aren't affecting anything else,' Jenny says. 'I can think clearly now, can't I? I can talk to you.'

'Who knows what effect they have? And if it's not the drugs, then there might be another reason. There's something called retrograde amnesia. At least I think it's called that.'

I want her not to blame herself; to have a reason she can understand. So I continue, 'It's when your brain blocks off access to a traumatic memory so you can't get it. It can affect the time before and afterwards too.'

Although I'm pretty sure this doesn't apply to Adam, it might be true of Jen.

'So it's like a protective thing?' she asks.

'Yes.'

'But the memory *is* still there?'

'I think so, yes.'

'Then I'll just have to be braver.'

I remember the judder of fear going through her when she tried to think back to yesterday afternoon.

'Not yet, sweetheart, alright? Maybe Aunt Sarah and Dad will find out what happened, without you needing to remember.'

She looks relieved.

'Is it OK if I go with Dad?' I ask her.

'Course. But won't it hurt you to go outside?'

'Oh, I'm a tough old bird,' I say to her; one of Mum's expressions.

'Yeah, right. From the person who goes to bed with a cold.'

★ ★ ★

I leave the hospital with you. My skin is scalded by the warm air and the gravel is shards of glass under my feet, as if the hospital building with its white walls and cool slippery linoleum has been giving me protection and now it's ripped away.

I grip hold of your hand and although you don't feel me, you give me comfort.

We reach our car and I see Adam's books stuffed into the pouch behind the driver's seat, a lipstick of Jenny's in the bit meant for a mug, a pair of my boots that need re-heeling on the back seat, like archaeological finds of a long-ago life; shockingly evocative.

We drive away from the hospital.

The pain hits me like blows, so I must focus on something else. But what?

It's silent in the car. It's never silent in the car.

Either we are chatting, or there's music playing (blaring if it's Jenny in charge). Radio 4 if it's me on my own and I've spent too long with eight-year-old boys or teenage girls.

I look at you as you drive. People always warm to you. I wonder about this sometimes. Not that tall, not that handsome, not handsome at all really, what is it that causes this warming thing? When I've asked you, you say they've just seen you on the telly, they think they know you already.

But I've always thought it's a charismatic, self-assured thing. After all, I didn't see you on the telly before I fell for you.

You involuntarily reach your left hand across towards the passenger seat to hold mine, as you always do when you drive. '*One of the advantages of an automatic.*' And for a moment we are driving out to friends for dinner, with you praising sat-navs because we can talk instead of map-read, our bottle of wine rolling around in the boot. Then you move your hand away.

In our silent car, I remember your old familiar voice, warm and deep and confident. The voice you had until yesterday morning.

Until now you've always been so happy, in that easygoing, masculine way; sometimes infuriatingly so. *It'll be fine, relax!* will be written on your headstone, I've sniped. But it's attractive, that happiness with yourself and the world; looking confidently outwards not anxiously inwards.

'Always been happy?' Nanny Voice chides, reminding me that your parents' car crash was when you were only a little older than Adam is now.

'*Little orphan Annie*,' you said, when you first told me about it. '*Only I don't have the ringlets.*'

You've suffered terrible terrible things before, even if you don't bear the scars now. '*I had Sarah, so I survived it*,' you told me when we knew each other better. '*A person version of a Swiss army knife.*'

★ ★ ★

You take our turning off the main road.

Pain makes a noise, like a loud, high-pitched vibration, breaking down barriers around thoughts I've been trying to keep at bay.

I think back to Jenny being attacked with red paint. I imagine a man going into a DIY superstore, a few days before; a huge place where no one will remember him. I think of him walking along an aisle lined with paint tins, passing the gentler water-based paints until he finds the oil-based polyurethane glosses. In my head he walks quickly past the plentifully stocked whites and creams until he reaches the colours; not many of those because who wants to gloss their window frames and skirting boards in a colour? He chooses crimson.

I imagine a girl on the checkout not finding it strange that he's bought red paint and white spirit. Because the only way of getting out gloss paint is with white spirit and, yes, there is a large quantity, but there's a queue building behind him now and her break's in a minute.

176

Did Jen go to a friend's house to wash her hair? Not knowing that gloss can be impossible to wash out. Did she then go to a hairdresser or did a friend or Ivo snip snip snip the evidence?

Did she scrub at her coat before taking it to a dry cleaner's? They would have tutted and shaken their head and told her they couldn't promise it would come out.

Why didn't she come to me?

★ ★ ★

You're turning into a street, three away from ours. Mr Hyman's road.

I didn't know you'd listened to me when I said we often passed Mr Hyman on the way to school.

You're pulling over, not bothering to park.

You slam the driver's door so hard the car rocks.

I think that to survive loving Jenny, this terrible compassion, you need to feel counter-balancing rage.

From the car, I watch you as you ring doorbell after doorbell asking which number Silas Hyman lives at. The pain is getting worse the longer we are away from the hospital. I try to visualise it, as I did during childbirth, turning it into crashing waves and dancing lights. I'd thought it was bodies that feel pain, but maybe skin and flesh and bones are protecting something exquisitely tender inside.

I join you as you press Mr Hyman's doorbell, keeping your thumb hard down on it.

His wife answers the door. I recognise her and remember she's called Natalia. I met her at the school 'soirée' two years ago (you refused to go to anything called a '*soirée-for-God's-sake*'). She'd looked like something out of a Tolstoy novel then and I'd wondered if she'd changed her name from Natalie to something more appropriately exotic. But Natalia's striking beauty has become subtly coarsened since then; something — anxiety? tiredness? — slackening the skin on her face, causing her green cat-eyes to lose their perfectly outlined shape; foreshadowing her ageing, when her feline beauty will be covered over without trace.

Looking at her face, imagining it in the future, because I don't want to look at yours. You're no longer a man people would warm to.

'Where's your husband?' you ask.

Natalia looks at you; feline features stiffening, sensing threat.

'You are . . . ?'

'Michael Covey. Jenny Covey's father.'

★   ★   ★

Adam whips off a plastic helmet with a flourish as he pretends to be a Roman gladiator as played by Russell Crowe.

'*My name is Maximus Decimus . . .* '

'*Meridius,' prompts Jenny.*

'*Maximus Decimus Meridius. Commander of the armies of the north. General of the* — '

'*Blah, blah.*'

'*Armies aren't blah blah.*'

'It's the next bit that's good.'

'OK, OK. I am Maximus Decimus Meridius. Skip armies bit. Father to a murdered son, husband to a murdered wife. And I will have my vengeance, in this life or the next.'

'It gives me shivers,' Jenny says. 'Every time.'

Adam, holding his helmet, nods solemnly in agreement. You are trying desperately not to laugh and I daren't catch your eye.

We haven't let him watch the film yet. Much too violent. But Jen's taught him all the punch lines.

Yes, I know, your situation is nothing like Maximus Decimus Meridius', because your child and wife are still alive.

★ ★ ★

'My husband isn't here,' Natalia says with a slight emphasis on the word 'my'; a stressing of loyalty.

'Where is he?' you ask.

'A building site.'

He's lied to her. I feel a flash of anxiety for Jenny and Adam. But Sarah is with Jenny, Mum is with Adam. Neither of them would desert their posts.

'Where is the building site?' you ask.

'I don't know. It's different every day. Unskilled labourers don't have the luxury of regular work.' She sounds upset for him.

'I read about your wife and daughter,' she continues. I wait for her to offer sympathy but she doesn't.

179

Instead she turns her back on you, leaving the door open behind her, and walks away. I follow her into the hotly oppressive house. There are three small children, looking grubby and out of control; two of them fighting.

Their house is almost identical to ours, just a few streets away, but a door blocks off the entrance to the first floor. It's a flat, not a house. I've never really thought of the financial discrepancy between the teachers and parents at Sidley House before.

She goes into the small kitchen. The school calendar is hanging on the wall, with three children's photos for July. On 11 July is 'Sports Day' in large type, 'Adam Covey is 8' in small type.

The date is ringed in red.

Adam had been so pleased that Mr Hyman had sent him a birthday card.

I remember Sarah talking to DI Baker.

'Anyone with a calendar would know it was Adam's birthday on sports day. Including the arsonist. He planned for the blame to fall on him.'

Natalia picks up a copy of the *Richmond Post*. She comes back to you, holding the paper. Her fingers are over the picture of Jenny.

'Is this why you're here?' she asks. 'Because of this fucking load of crap?'

I'm shocked that she uses language like this in front of her children. I know, absurd. If a paper had said that about you I'd be swearing too.

'It's lies,' she says. 'All of it.'

'The alibi you gave him,' you say to her. 'What was it?'

'How about I tell you what I know,' she says. 'Then I will answer your questions.'

You are wrong-footed, I can see that. You are Maximus Decimus Meridius looking for vengeance with Mr Hyman. You're not sure what to do with a BBC-style debate presented to you, with the option of having your say in a minute.

'Silas is the most gentle man you could meet,' she says, taking advantage of your hesitation. 'To be honest, it annoys me sometimes that he's so gentle. Our boys could do with a little discipline. But he won't. Doesn't even raise his voice to them. So the idea that he could set light to a school, well, it's just ridiculous.'

'At prize-giving?' you say. 'He was hardly 'gentle' then. I saw him myself.'

'He wanted to tell everyone it wasn't his fault,' Natalia replies. 'Can you blame him for that? For wanting his chance to tell the truth? You didn't give him one before firing him, did you?'

I feel her hostility now; crouching behind her words.

'He dressed up for it,' she continues. 'Put on a tie and a jacket, so he'd look smart, so that people might listen. But it's not surprising he went to the pub first, is it? Had a few drinks to find the courage. He's passionate. And he even gets a little drunk sometimes, but he'd never destroy something, set fire to something, let alone risk hurting anyone.'

Her northern accent at the school soirée had been barely noticeable, but now it's pronounced. Did she disguise it before, or is she deliberately accentuating it now, to show how different she is

181

from you — a Sidley House parent?

'It doesn't tell you in here that he only went into teaching to give himself time to write a book. All those holidays and half-terms teachers get — and in private schools they're longer — that's why he went into teaching, so he'd have time to write.'

You try to interrupt, but she continues. 'Doesn't say he didn't actually write his book, the whole *point* of it all, but spent his free time doing teaching plans and researching new ways of inspiring his class in History, English, even bloody Geography; finding field trips and teaching resources, even what kind of music helped kids concentrate best. He still talks about them all. He still calls them 'his' class.'

Her fingers are sweating; smudging Jenny's face.

'And here our kids are, not likely to see the inside of a private school unless they're lucky enough to teach in it, or more likely clean it, with our eldest starting in September at the local thirty-in-a-class failing primary. But even so, I'm still really proud of him. For being the best bloody teacher that school could have.'

Aggression is pressing up against her words.

'His friends from Oxford are all having these high-flying, highly paid careers in media and law,' she continues. 'While he is — was — just a primary school teacher. Not that he ever got any credit for that. It's a private school, so not even considered worthy. You think it's any wonder he went and sounded off at your prize-giving?'

A child has come to join her. She holds the

little boy's hand. 'That's where I met him,' she says. 'At Oxford. I was just working as a secretary there. I was so proud to be with him. I couldn't believe it when he chose *me*; married *me*; made those vows to *me*.'

Is that what this is about? For richer for poorer; to lie for and cover for.

Such undeserved and unreturned loyalty.

'He's a good man,' she continues. 'Loving. And decent. There's not many you can say that about.'

Does she believe her version of her husband? Or is she, like Maisie, presenting an image to the outside world, no matter the cost to herself?

'It wasn't Silas's fault, what happened to that boy in the playground. It was — '

You interrupt; you've had enough. 'Where was he yesterday afternoon?'

'I haven't finished telling you — '

'Where was he?' Your voice angry, loud; frightening the child.

'I need to tell you the truth. You need to hear it,' she says.

'Just tell me.'

'With me and the kids,' she says, after a moment. 'All afternoon.'

'You said he works on building sites,' and your tone implies she's a liar.

'When there's work, yes, he does, but there wasn't any work for him yesterday. So we went to the park for a picnic. He said we might as well make the most of him not being in work. And it was so hot indoors. Left here together about eleven, got back around five.'

183

'A long time.' Your disbelief is clear.

'Nothing to come back for. And Silas likes playing with them outside, giving them rides on his back, playing footie, he's devoted to them.'

Jenny said he'd pretended to be running an after-school club so he could avoid coming home. This picture of a family man that Natalia is painting doesn't exist.

'Did he ask you to say this, or did you come up with it yourself?' you ask and I am relieved you're challenging her.

'Is it so hard for you to believe that a family like ours could have an afternoon out together?'

I think by 'like ours' she means a family in a flat not a house with no money and the dad working on a building site. And no, of course, it's not hard to believe a family like that could enjoy an afternoon in the park. But she's keeping something from you, I'm sure of it. She has been from the moment she opened the door to you.

'Did anyone see you in the park?' you ask her.

'Loads of people, it was packed.'

'Anyone who'd remember?'

'There was an ice-cream van, maybe that guy would remember.'

A hot July afternoon in a park, how many families with small children did he see yesterday? How likely is it he'd remember?

'Who did your husband get to lie for him?' you ask. 'To say they'd seen Adam?'

'Sir Covey?'

That pet name infuriates you but I think her surprise looks genuine.

'Who did he get to blame my son?' Your anger

184

hurling the words at her.

'I've no idea what you're on about,' she says.

'Tell him I want to speak to him,' you say. You turn to go.

'Wait. I haven't finished! I told you, you need to hear the truth.'

'I have to get back to my daughter.'

You start to leave but she comes after you. 'The accident in the playground was Robert Fleming's fault, nothing to do with Silas.'

You hurry on, not listening. But for a moment I think of eight-year-old Robert Fleming, who bullied Adam so horribly.

You open the car door and one of Adam's knight figures slips out of the door pocket.

'Children can be little bastards,' she says, catching up with you. 'Evil.' She holds the car door so that you can't close it. 'You made Mrs Healey fire Silas for not supervising the playground properly, didn't you? You wanted him out.'

'I don't have time for this. Have a go at other parents if you need to, but not me. Not now.'

I can smell her hostility, like a strong cheap perfume around her.

'You got the *Richmond Post* to print that crap about him, to make sure he was pushed out.'

You yank the car door out of her grasp and slam it shut.

You're driving away and she's running after the car. She bangs her fist on the boot and then we turn from the street.

Maybe she should seem more like a victim to me. After all, in return for her love and loyalty

185

Silas lies to her and bad-mouths her to teenagers. But her spikiness and aggression means she can't be pigeon-holed so neatly. Is her rage because she genuinely thinks that Silas has been wronged? Or is it the anguish of a woman who knows she made a terrible mistake in the man she married?

15

The pain has gone. It stopped the moment I stepped into the hospital; as if this white-walled building offers me its own skin.

My mother is sitting next to Jenny. I know she won't have left Addie on his own; a friend or a nurse must be with him. Amidst the shiny hard equipment she looks so gentle in her cotton skirt and Liberty-print blouse. Her hand hovers over Jenny, as yours often does, unable to touch her.

You go up to Sarah, who's standing a little distance away — giving Mum time with Jen while still fulfilling her obligation to you to protect Jenny. I'm still not sure if she thinks it's necessary or if she's just doing it to make you feel better.

'Hyman wasn't there,' you say to her. 'And his wife would do whatever the bastard asked.'

Then Mum sees you. 'Is there any more news on Gracie?' she asks.

'Not yet,' you reply. 'I was meant to have a meeting with her doctors earlier, but I got called away.' You don't say you were called away because Jenny's heart stopped. You haven't told Mum about the three weeks.

'They've said they might not have time now today,' you continue.

'But surely they could *make the time*?' Mum says, as if time was one of her tapestries, minutes stitched onto canvas in flower-coloured yarns.

'Apparently there's been some awful coach crash, so it's all hands to the pumps.'

And for one moment this hospital isn't all about us. There are others too, God knows how many; all that anguish and anxiety compressed into the bricks and glass walls of this one building. I wonder if it leaks out of the windows and roof; if birds fly a little higher overhead as they pass.

Trying to think this to avoid ugly, awful thoughts.

But I suspect you're thinking them too.

Will any of the coach casualties die? Will any of them be a match for Jenny? How strange that selfless love can make you morally ugly. Wicked even.

'I'm sure they'll have the meeting as soon as they can,' you say.

She nods.

'Adam's in the relatives' room,' she tells you.

'I'll go and see him in a minute. I'd just like a little time with Jen first.'

★ ★ ★

I go to the relatives' room. A fan whirrs the heated air.

Addie is huddled close to Mr Hyman, who has his arm around him, reading him a story.

I go cold.

Jenny is on the other side of the room. 'He saw Granny G and Adam in the café,' she says calmly. 'He offered to look after Adam, so that Granny G could be with me.'

188

And Mum would never suspect anything. She's heard me and Addie praise Mr Hyman countless times.

Over the whirr of the fan, I listen to him reading. At his feet is a bunch of flowers.

'He told his wife he was going to work on a building site,' I tell Jenny.

'Poor bloke. Is that all the work he can get?'

'He lied to his wife, Jen.'

'Probably to get away from her.'

She looks at me, and must catch my expression because I see exasperation in hers.

'I've told you about the hate-mailer now. The red paint. You can't still think it's Silas.'

'Could there be a connection?' I ask, more thinking aloud.

'No. There is *no way* that he is anything to do with the hate mail. Quite apart from the fact that he's just not that kind of person, why would he?'

I also think it's very unlikely that Silas Hyman is the hate-mailer turned stalker. Even if he had a reason for hate mail, which he doesn't, an Oxford-educated, highly articulate man doesn't fit with hate mail and red paint. I simply can't imagine him cutting out words from a newspaper or a magazine and sticking them onto A4. He's far too subtle and intelligent for that.

But the fire might be nothing at all to do with the hatemailer. It could be, as you are so certain, simply revenge by Silas Hyman.

'He tried talking to Addie,' Jenny says. 'But Addie couldn't say anything back. That's when he started reading him the Percy Jackson story. Perfect choice, isn't it?'

189

'Yes.'

You missed most of Addie's Percy Jackson phase, but he's a schoolboy who can vanquish evil monsters against impossible odds. Mr Hyman knows that Adam loves Arthurian legends but knights would be too adult, lacking any childlike vulnerability, for him to relate to them now. They wouldn't offer him any fantasy escape from what is happening. This is a better choice.

I'm disturbed by how well he knows Addie.

Once I liked his physicality, but now I don't want his arm around our son, and I want him in smart trousers and a jacket, not shorts and a clinging T-shirt.

Mr Hyman. Silas.

Two names. Two men.

★　★　★

Jenny and I were in the sitting room, the night before her English A-level paper. Jenny was in her pyjamas, her hair still wet from the shower.

'So do you know what Dryden called Shakespeare?' I asked her.

She shook her head and water flecked the paper I was holding.

'A Janus poet,' I told her. 'Because . . . ?'

'He was two-faced?'

'Wore two faces,' I corrected as she dangled a slipper on one toe. 'Janus was also the god of gates and doors, beginnings and endings. January is from Janus, because it's the month which begins the New Year.'

'I don't have to be that informed, Mum, really.'

'But it's interesting, isn't it?'

She smiled at me. 'I can see why it should be,' she said. 'And why you went to Cambridge and I'll be lucky to scrape into anywhere.'

★ ★ ★

I watch Silas's Janus face, so close to Adam's.

I remember again Maisie's words at the prize-giving: 'That man should never have been allowed near our children.'

And I want him to get away from my children. *Get away!*

Then Mum comes in. She's again, somehow, forced colour into her cheeks and energy into her voice, that magic smile appearing on her face.

'Have you had a good story, Addie?' She turns to Silas Hyman. 'Thank you for giving me time with my granddaughter.'

'Of course. It was great to be with Addie.' He gets up. 'I'd better be going now.'

Adam looks as if he'll follow.

'Daddy will be here in a minute,' Mum says. 'So let's wait here for him, shall we?'

Silas picks up the bunch of flowers and leaves the room. I follow him. The flowers are yellow roses — mean buds that will never open, plastic-wrapped and scentless. He must have got them from the hospital shop because he didn't have them when Jenny and I followed him earlier.

He presses the button on the door of the ICU

ward. A pretty blonde nurse comes to answer it. I see her notice his attractiveness. Or maybe it's just his vigorous health, which stands out in this place.

The nurse opens the door and explains to him that flowers aren't allowed because they are an infection risk. There's a flirtatious tone to her voice but flirting isn't an infection risk, is it? However inappropriate it seems.

'For you then,' he says, smiling at her. She takes the flowers and lets him into ICU.

A smile and flowers.

That simple.

I follow him.

To be fair to the pretty nurse, she's accompanying him all the time, making him wait while she puts the flowers in the nurses' station, away from the patients. But are all nurses so cautious?

He follows her towards the section that has Jenny's bed.

Through the glass wall I see you sitting next to her; Sarah a little distance away.

Silas Hyman doesn't recognise her. The pretty nurse has to point.

'That's Jennifer Covey, there,' she says.

He no longer looks healthy or handsome, but pale as if he's about to vomit, his forehead sweaty; stricken by what he sees.

I think I hear him whisper, 'Oh God.'

He turns away and shakes his head at the nurse. He isn't going closer.

Or is he pretending this is the first time he's seen her since the fire? A brilliant performance so that nobody will suspect him of being the person who tampered with her oxygen tube?

Perhaps he feels watched.

Through the glass wall, you see him turning away. You hurry out after him. The ICU doors close behind him and you follow.

You catch up with him in the corridor, your anger skidding on the slippery linoleum and bouncing off the walls.

'What the hell are you doing here?'

'I saw Adam and his grandmother earlier and — '

'Your wife said you were at a building site.'

For a moment he is speechless; caught out.

'A load of crap, wasn't it? Like your alibi. Lying bastard!'

Yelling now, sound tumbling through the open door of the relatives' room where Adam is waiting for you.

He and my mother come out, but you don't see them, rage-focused on Silas Hyman.

'Who lied for you about my son?'

'What do you mean?'

My mother tries to be appeasing. 'Someone lied and said they saw Addie starting the fire,' she tells him.

'But that's ridiculous,' Mr Hyman says. 'For goodness sake, of all people to accuse.' He turns to Adam. 'I know you wouldn't do that, Sir Covey.'

He bends towards Adam, perhaps to stroke his hair or give him a hug.

'Keep away from him!' you roar, moving towards him, going to hit him.

And then Adam is standing between you and he's pushing you away from Silas Hyman; protective of him; furious with you. All his strength in those small hands as he pushes you away.

I see the terrible hurt on your face.

It's the first time you've seen Adam since the fire.

Silas turns and walks away.

Mum takes Adam's hand in hers. 'Come on, sweetheart, time to go home.' She leads him away.

'Go after him!' I say to you. 'You've got to tell him you know he didn't start the fire.'

Silas Hyman said that straight away. *'I know you wouldn't do that, Sir Covey.'*

But you turn away.

You think that he must know you think he's innocent. I hope to God that he does.

* * *

You return to Jenny's bedside. Sarah doesn't know what has just happened in the corridor.

'Can you stay here?' you ask.

Something in your voice sounds a warning and she doesn't automatically agree.

'Why?'

'Hyman told his wife he was on a building site,' you say. 'But all the time the bastard was *right here*, with Adam.'

'Is Addie OK?'

'Yeah.'

You hesitate a moment, but don't confide in

Sarah about Addie pushing you away.

'I need to find out who Hyman got to lie about Adam,' you say. 'I need to do that for him.'

But what Addie needs from you is to be with him. For you to make a testudo for him. It makes me so sad you don't know this.

'Finding out who this witness is — and the arsonist — should be *my* job,' Sarah says. 'I'm a police officer; it's what I do.'

'I thought Baker had made you take compassionate leave?'

'He has.' She pauses a moment. 'OK, we know there were only two members of staff, apart from Jenny, who weren't at sports day — a reception teacher and a secretary. We need to speak to both of them, but especially the secretary because it's her job to buzz people in and out of the school.'

'I'll go now,' you say, standing up.

She puts a hand on your arm.

'He's my son.'

'Exactly. And what if she recognises you? Do you think that'll help if she is involved in this?'

You are silenced and frustrated by her logic.

'The most useful thing for you to do is to stay here and guard Jenny,' she continues, and I'm not sure if she really thinks Jen needs guarding with so many medical staff around, or if she sees you as a loose cannon and wants to tether you at Jenny's bedside.

'Here's how it's going to work,' she says, using one of your expressions — or perhaps it was hers first, which you adopted as you grew up. 'I will share everything with you, brief you, update you on everything.'

I don't think you believe her. You've had years of her only giving you small pieces of information, no more than was allowed to the press, and only hints at the bigger and more dramatic picture. Such a rule-abiding police officer; such a frustrating older sister.

'You think the arsonist is Silas Hyman, with an accomplice who lied about Adam, and we'll come back to him, but we also have to look at the hate-mailer.'

She waits for you to argue. Like me, she heard your categorical denial of the hate-mailer being responsible to DI Baker and maybe, like me, guessed it was because if it *was* him you'd feel it was your fault.

But you don't contradict her. For Addie's sake you want the truth so will keep an open mind; your love for Adam so much fiercer than your terror of being to blame.

'The hate-mailer has a track record for aggression in the form of malicious mail,' Sarah goes on. 'And a motive for arson, which was to hurt Jenny for some reason.'

And he attacked her with red paint, I silently add. Just a few weeks ago.

'Because hate mail is a crime under the Malicious Communications Act,' Sarah goes on, 'it can be fully investigated by the police.'

'They didn't get far last time,' you say.

'DI Baker's asked for a much wider investigation.'

'You think he'll still do that?'

'My colleagues won't give him a choice. They'll want to do something to help our family,

196

whether they believe Adam guilty or not. There'll
be a lot more welly in the investigation than last
time: looking at CCTV footage; wider DNA
testing. The works.'

'And Hyman?'

'With the arson investigation closed, there's no
reason for the police to investigate him further.'

'But you will?'

She hesitates a moment.

'Every interview I do now is illegal,' she says.
'So we have to weigh up very carefully what we
want to achieve because I'll be treading on thin
ice and it *will* give way; it's just a question of
how much I can find out before it does.'

'You're saying you won't talk to him?'

'No. I'm saying I need to be well informed
before I do. Before I talk to anyone — including
Silas Hyman — I need to read the witness
statements and interviews taken straight after
the fire. We need to be armed with as much
information as possible before going after any
suspects.'

I'm stunned by how many rules Sarah will be
breaking.

'Silas Hyman was Addie's form teacher,
wasn't he?' Sarah asks. 'Aren't they very close?'

'Adam wouldn't set fire to anything, however
much he loves someone,' you say.

I hear the word 'loves' crying out.

I remember the terrible hurt on your face as
he pushed you away from Silas Hyman and only
now see that you're jealous.

That's why you thought he had an unnatural
hold over Addie; why you loathed him, even

before the fire. No wonder you resented working *bloody hard* to pay the fees so that another man could be with your son all day. No wonder you weren't upset when he was fired.

But I didn't see it.

I'm so sorry.

'Did you come into contact with Silas Hyman before the prize-giving?' Sarah asks. 'Is there anything else that makes you so hostile towards him?'

'Isn't what I told you enough?'

She doesn't reply.

And I'd do anything to be able to tell Sarah that the man Silas Hyman pretends to be is a fraud. That the man Adam loves, if he does love him, doesn't exist.

I again think of him as a Janus — not only two-faced like that god but also, like him, the beginning and the ending. Because if Silas Hyman started this horror then he'll also be there at its conclusion.

The clicking of high heels, an incongruous sound in ICU. I turn to see Dr Bailstrom in her red shoes — maybe she wears them as a warning device for patients and their relatives.

A meeting with my doctors has been arranged in an hour's time.

16

Your familiar long stride has become short steps, as if you're in unknown, hostile territory.

But when you near my bed you hurry towards me.

You reach my bed and sit down next to me, but you don't speak.

You *don't speak*.

I hurry towards you — *talk to me!*

'Grace, my darling,' you say as I reach you; as if you know when I am really there. Or is it just a coincidence?

You could run a florist's shop from my bedside table. Only one vaseful is ugly — odourless, thornless, last-minute-shop-bought roses. 'To Mrs Covey, with all best wishes, from Mr Hyman.'

But you don't see the flowers, looking only at me.

'There's still no news on Jenny's heart,' you say. I think I'm the only person you've confided in about her lifespan of three weeks. 'But they'll find one for her. I know they will.'

'Lifespan.' Jesus. How could I use that word? It makes her sound like a tadpole or a mayfly. A punnet of ripen-at-home peaches. Children don't have a bloody *lifespan*.

Thinking panicky loud thoughts, loud as I can, to try and drown out the ticking that has started again — faint but audible; a ghastly unstoppable rhythm.

'Sarah said she'd told you about Addie,' you say.

I remember Sarah at my bedside.

'You have the right to know, Grace. You must hate the police for this. I understand that. But I promise you we'll get it put right.'

She was so awkward with me, not realising how much I like her now.

You were worried that telling me this, *on top of Jenny*, would sap the remaining life force I have. But Sarah understands that for a mother, when your children are threatened, your life force isn't sapped but galvanised.

You stand up. *Don't go!* But you're just pulling the flimsy ugly curtains around us, blocking out the bustle of the ward, and somehow, although it contradicts even key-stage-two Science, the noise of the ward seems blocked out too.

You hold my hand.

'Ads doesn't want me near him,' you say.

'That's *not true*. And you need to go to him right now and tell him you know he didn't do this and be with him. Sarah can stay with Jen for a bit. The detective stuff can wait for a little while, surely.'

You are silent.

'You're his *father* and no one else can be that to him.'

But you can't hear me, nor can you guess now at what I am saying to you.

You stare at my face, as if staring at it will make my eyes open.

'We always do this, don't we, Gracie?' you say. 'Talk about Addie or Jen. But I'd like to talk

200

about you and me, just for a few minutes, alright? I'd really like to do that.'

I'm touched. And yes, I'd really like to do that too — change the subject onto us — just for a few minutes.

'Remember our first date?' you ask.

Not so much a change of subject as a rewind of twenty years to a safe past. Leaving this white-walled London hospital far behind for a tea shop in Cambridge.

For a little while I'll let myself join you there.

Pouring with rain outside; inside, fuggy with talk and damp anoraks.

You told me later you thought it would be romantic but some milk must have been spilt and not cleaned up and the rancid smell permeated the fug. The chintzy curtains were designed for tourists. Your hands looked absurdly big around a silly little china cup.

It was your first 'first date'.

'The only girl I'd ever asked on a date,' you say.

You came clean about this amongst the chintz and the china.

Later I found out that usually you just went home with a girl after a party and sometimes would find her still there the next morning under your hideous duvet — I think Sarah chose the cover in the hope of it acting as a contraceptive device. If you liked the girl it stayed that way for a while. Nice things just happened to you — pretty girls ending up under your ugly duvet.

'I courted you,' you say.

We talked about attraction.

You, a scientist (what was I doing with a *Nat Sci?*), were all pheromones and biological imperatives while I was all coy mistresses and eyebeams threading on a double string. 'You thought Marvell was a comic.'

'You quoted something about a man spending a century admiring each bosom and I got the hint.'

In that prim little tea shop you told me that you were desperate to be away from the confines of university and '*out there doing stuff*'.

I didn't know anyone who used the word 'stuff'. I'd done a year of Art History and then a term of an English degree and had never once used the word. My friends were all black-clothed, earnest arts students with a thesaurus for a vocabulary.

I liked the word 'stuff'. And I liked it that you weren't pale with cheekbones studying Kant but were muscular and robust and wanted to be mountaineering and canoeing and white-water rafting and abseiling and bivouacking the world rather than reading and philosophising about it.

'I liked the climbing-a-volcano thing,' I say. 'Mad, but kind of mad in an attractive way.'

'I wanted to impress you. You were so fucking beautiful.'

'Thanks so much.'

'Sorry. *Are* so fucking beautiful.'

As if you'd heard me but it's just a verbal fluke, isn't it?

'You had two Chelsea buns,' you say. You *remember* that? 'And I liked it that you ate so much.'

202

I didn't want you to guess that I was nervous so I ate to prove that I was cool about this.

'It rained.'

Lashing against the ditzy little windowpanes, and the sound was wonderful.

'I'd brought an umbrella.'

You asked if you could walk me home.

'I knew we'd have to get close.'

I spotted your bike and you looked annoyed that I noticed it.

'That bloody bike. Should have locked it round the corner.'

You walked me back to Newnham through the rain, pushing your bicycle on the road with one hand, but staying on the pavement next to me with your other hand holding the umbrella.

'I couldn't touch you at all.'

The first night we spent together — two weeks later, me not being a coy mistress — we re-ran our first date, creating our own mythology. But that was years and years ago and we should be talking about our children now. And we both know that. And we will, in a few moments. They are with us all the time. But there is a tiny glimmer of happiness here in the time before them, and we want to hold it a little while longer. Just a little while longer. So I carry on walking next to you through the bitterly cold Fen rain, your stride so much longer than mine, wondering what will happen when we reach Newnham.

But of course I know what happened.

You wanted a second date that very evening, ignoring Marvell completely, and I danced

— *danced!*, an absurd robotic thing that made people stare — the entire way down the second longest corridor in Europe.

The memory pulls me towards you until I reach you right here and now in this room; somehow closer than before. This close to you, I can *feel* your brave optimism for Jenny go into me; making love with courageous hope.

And as you hold me tightly, I too believe that Jenny will get better.

She will get better.

The curtains are abruptly pulled back and Dr Bailstrom is there.

'Can you come for the meeting now?' she asks you.

'I'll be back a little later, my darling,' you say to me; telling Dr Bailstrom that I can hear and understand.

★   ★   ★

I get to the door of the Dr Bailstrom's office where the medical staff are waiting and imagine her putting on a black hat before reading out my fate. I think she'd like the dressing-up aspect. But if I have the language to form a sarky sentence about Dr Bailstrom then I'm clearly not a cabbage — why did a cabbage get chosen? — so no need for her to have a black hat.

I am on the ball, switched on, marbles still there, compos mentis. The same Grace I was yesterday. But somehow I've become split from myself.

In our conversation when this is over, you'll

tell me that this splitting in two idea is '*total bollocks, Gracie!*' But that's because you abseil and bivouac through life rather than learn about it second-hand. Because if you'd read more and climbed up mountains less, you'd know about Cartesian dualism, and ids and egos, and body versus soul. You'd know about a whole strand of literature called 'the divided self'. Really. So I'll remind you, as you scoff, of the fairy tales you read Jenny when she was little — princesses dancing in the fairy world every night and frogs really being princes and girls turning into swans. If you're really unlucky, I'll start quoting *Hamlet*: 'There are more things in heaven and earth, Horatio, than are dreamt of in our philosophy.'

You'll hold your hands up, *enough!* But I'll ignore you.

The visible world isn't the only world and the writers of fairy tales and ghost stories, mystics and philosophers, have known that for centuries. Jenny unconscious in her bed and me in mine isn't who we really are; the only way that it is.

I should join you now.

Instead of imagining a black hat on Dr Bailstrom's head, I will look at her feet and think of Dorothy's ruby shoes. You never know, Dr Bailstrom might click hers together and I'll return to the real world again.

I'm sorry, that was flippant. You know I tend to take the air out of big moments. The thing is, I *will be with you and Addie again*. Because Jenny is going to get better, so I'll be free to get back into my body and wake up.

But when I was inside my body I couldn't do

205

anything. Nothing at all. 'Banish that thought this minute!' Nanny Voice says. 'No houseroom for negativity in here!' And she's right. I just wasn't ready. But I *will join you again*.

★ ★ ★

I've never seen you look slight before. But in here, outnumbered by doctors, you look hollowed out. Dr Bailstrom doesn't fully look at you as she speaks.

'We have run a series of tests, Mike. Many of them are repeats of the ones we did yesterday.'

Is she using your first name to be friendly, or because 'Mr Covey' would underline your connection to me, 'Mrs Covey', and she'd rather not major on that right now?

'I'm afraid you're going to have to start preparing yourself for Grace never regaining consciousness.'

'No, you're wrong,' you say.

Of course she's *wrong*! The very fact I know that demonstrates it. And the thinking, feeling part of me will rejoin my body and *I will wake up*.

'I know it's a lot to take in right now,' Dr Bailstrom continues. 'But she shows only the basic responses of gagging and breathing. And we don't think there will be any improvement.'

You shake your head, refusing to allow the information entry.

'What my colleague is saying,' interjects an older doctor, 'is that the damage to your wife's brain means that she can't speak or see or hear.

Nor can she think or feel. That is what is meant by cognitive function. And she won't get better. She won't wake up.'

He's obviously a graduate from the sock-it-to-them-straight school of medicine. And *totally-bloody-wrong* school of medicine.

'What about those new scans?' you say. 'People who'd been written off as cabbages were told to imagine playing tennis for yes, and the brain scan then picked it up.'

I'd heard it in one of my Radio 4 car journeys and told you about it as a snippet of interesting information. I'd liked the idea of imagining playing tennis for yes. A smash, I'd imagined, or an ace serve. Such a positive and vigorous yes. I'd wondered if it mattered if you're useless at tennis and can, in all honesty, only visualise hitting the ball into the net, or pathetically limping it over. Will they think that's a 'don't know' answer?

'We will try all the tests there are,' the doctor says, irked. 'We have already put her through many. But I need to be honest with you here. The bottom line is that she isn't going to get better.'

'You just don't get it, do you?' I say. 'The mother thing.'

'In simple terms, all our scans show massive and irreparable trauma to her brain.'

'My son needs me. It's not just the big stuff; the proving that he's innocent. In the mornings, I help him design an imaginary shield to put over his heart so it won't hurt so much if people are mean to him.'

207

'Her brain tissue is too damaged to mend.'

'And some evenings he'll only be able to get to sleep if he holds my hand.'

'There's nothing we can do. I'm sorry.'

'But all of that could be bullshit, right?' says a voice in the doorway. For a second I think it's my nanny voice bossing someone else for a change, though she's never said bullshit. I turn to see Sarah. I've never heard her say bullshit either.

She comes into the room. Behind her is my mother. Both of them have clearly heard the doctors.

'Dr Sandhu is with Jenny,' Sarah says to you. 'He's promised not to leave her for a second.'

And you no longer look slight because Sarah is with you.

'Sarah Covey. Mike's sister,' Sarah announces. 'This is Grace's mother, Georgina Jestopheson. There have been patients who have woken up from comas after years, haven't there? With 'cognitive function'?'

The sock-it-to-them doctor is unabashed. 'Yes, there are occasionally stories in the press about such cases, but on closer scrutiny you'll see they are different medically.'

'And what about stem-cell therapy?' you ask. 'Growing new neurons or what-have-you?'

You're still grabbing at information half heard on the news driving home or skimmed over in the Sunday papers.

But I'm holding onto it too — imagining heavy lifting equipment heaving that wrecked ship of a body off the ocean floor; the rust being scraped from my eyes.

'There's no proof that any of these therapies will work. They've mainly been used on patients suffering from degenerative disease, such as Parkinson's and Alzheimer's, rather than on massive trauma.'

He turns from Sarah to you. 'You must want to know how long her state will continue this way. The answer is that it can last a very long time. There's no reason why your wife should die. She's breathing for herself and we are feeding her through a tube, which we will continue to do. So this state can go on indefinitely. But I'm not sure that it qualifies as *living* in the way we think of it. And although now it seems a relief that she's not going to die, it can have its own particular problems for the family.'

Now that I am a long-term burden I'm 'your wife', underscoring your onerous responsibility.

'Are you talking about a court order for withdrawing food and fluid?' Sarah asks, and I think if a tiger was reincarnated as a police officer she would look like Sarah.

'Of course not,' Dr Bailstrom says. 'It's early days and would be premature to — '

'But that's where you're headed?' Sarah interrupts; prowling around her, growling.

'A lawyer?' she asks.

'A police officer.'

'A tigress protecting her brother who she's been a mother to,' I add, to try and clarify the situation for him, and loving Sarah for this.

'We simply want to be straightforward with you,' the sock-it-to-them doctor continues. 'In time, yes, there may be a conversation about whether it's in Grace's best interests — '

Sarah interrupts again. 'Enough of this. I agree with my brother that Grace can think and hear. But that's not the point.' She pauses then drops a word at a time into the silent pool that this room has become.

'She. Is. ALIVE.'

Realising he's met more than his match in Sarah, the doctor turns back to you. I see that Jenny has slipped in.

'Mr Covey, I think — '

'She's more intelligent than the lot of you,' you say, interrupting while I cringe — they are consultant neurologists, darling, *brain surgeons*. You take no notice. 'Knows about books, paintings, all sorts of stuff; interested in everything. She doesn't see how clever she is but she's the brightest person I've ever met.'

'*What goes on in that head of yours?*' you'd asked me, a year into our romance, with admiration and affection. While you had wide open prairies in your head, I had libraries and galleries, stuffed full.

'It doesn't all just disappear,' you continue. 'All those thoughts she has and feelings and knowledge; all that kindness and warmth and funniness. It can't just *go*.'

'Mr Covey, as neurologists, we — '

'You're scientists. Yes. Did you know that four billion years ago it rained for thousands of years, making the oceans?'

They are listening politely; they'll allow you this time to go mentally AWOL after devastating

210

news. But I know where you're going with this. You'd told Addie about it a few months ago; livening up his water-cycle homework.

'The water that rained down four billion years ago is exactly the same water we have today,' you continue. 'It might be frozen into glaciers, or in the clouds, or in rivers or raining. But it's the same water. And exactly the same amount. No more, *but no less*. It didn't go anywhere. It couldn't.'

Dr Bailstrom taps an impatient red heel, either not getting it or not wanting to try. But I like the idea that I'm a melted bit of glacier joining the ocean; the same but outwardly changed. Or, optimistically, part of a cloud, which will be rained down again, back to where I came from.

'We will continue to do tests,' Dr Bailstrom says to you. 'But there really is no chance that your wife will ever regain consciousness.'

'You said that she could live for years,' you say to her. 'So one day there'll be a cure. And we'll just have to wait, for as long as it takes.'

Had we but worlds enough and time.

In time, a cloud rejoins the ocean.

Wait long enough and a dull piece of grit becomes a luminous pearl. I feel it in my hand, round and smooth until it became warm; Adam's hand in mine as he falls asleep.

17

A little while later Mum arrives at my bedside. Unlike you and Sarah, she didn't argue with the doctors, and I'd seen each medical fact — *supposed* medical fact — hitting her face like flying glass, cutting new lines.

'A nurse is with Addie,' she says. 'Just for a little while. I can't leave him long. But I had to talk to you on my own.' She pauses a moment. 'Someone's going to have to tell him that you're not going to wake up.'

'For fuck's sake, Mum, you can't do that!'

I have never, ever, said fuck to my mother before.

'I just want what's best for him,' Mum says quietly.

'How can this be best for Ads? Jesus!'

It's been years since we argued, and even then it was more of a disagreement. Of all times and places we shouldn't start now, here.

'I know that you can hear me, Gracie, angel. Wherever you are.'

'I'm right here, Mum. *Right here*. And soon their tests will pick it up. I'm going to be Roger fucking Federer, smashing the ball at a hundred miles an hour over the net for a 'YES I CAN UNDERSTAND YOU!' And once they know that I can still think, then they'll try and find a way of getting me well again.'

'I'd better get back to Addie.'

She pulls the curtain back. Jenny is outside and has clearly overheard; the curtains obey the laws of science after all.

She looks so anxious.

'Granny G is wrong,' I say to her. 'And so are the doctors. I can think and feel, can't I? Talk to you now? Their scans aren't sophisticated enough, that's all. So one day, hopefully soon, I'll give them a great big surprise.'

'Roger fucking Federer?' she says.

'Absolutely. Venus Williams, if I don't fancy a sex change. Honestly, sweetheart, once they give me the right scans, they'll know I'm OK.'

But she's still anxious; her head bent down and her narrow shoulders hunched together.

'You were so brave. Going into the school for me.'

'Dad said that too, and it's really nice of you both, but it's not in the least accurate and makes me feel a fraud.'

She half smiles. 'Oh right. So what *does* qualify as brave? If you're not allowed running into a burning building to rescue someone?'

'It was just instinct, that's all. Really. Something any mother would do for their child.'

But I'm not being totally honest. Most mothers — maybe *all* apart from me — would instinctively risk her life to rescue her child. And to start with I ran without thinking too. I just saw the school on fire and knew Jenny was inside and ran. But once I was inside.

Inside.

Every moment in that heat and choking smoke, my love for Jenny had to fight against my overwhelming urge to run away. A riptide of self-ishness, which was trying to pull me out of the building. I was ashamed to tell you before.

'You said you could get back into your body?' she asks.

'Yes. That's right.'

'I think that if you can get back into your body,' she continues, 'it means you're not going to die. When my heart stopped, and I was technically dead, I suppose, it was warmth and light *leaving* my body and coming into me, not the other way around. I think it's living that's the other way around.'

'Absolutely.'

Because surely she *is* right.

We are interrupted by Sarah arriving, with a ramrod-straight woman with steel-grey hair in her late sixties, who I know but can't quite place.

'Mrs Fisher,' Jenny says, surprised.

The old secretary at Sidley House.

She's brought me a fat bunch of sweet-peas wrapped in newspaper and the scent is glorious, temporarily overpowering the sanitised smell of the ward.

Sarah looks along my vases of flowers, then deftly bins Silas Hyman's ugly yellow roses. She smiles at Mrs Fisher.

'I think in the race for space here, yours win,' she says lightly, but I see her notice Mr Hyman's card and pocket it.

'I didn't think I'd actually see her,' Mrs Fisher says to Sarah. 'I just wanted to bring her flowers. We used to talk about gardening sometimes. But I hardly know her.'

I remember now that Mrs Fisher is the only person on her stretch of allotments to grow sweet-peas rather than their edible cousins. She told me about it on Jenny's first day at school, distracting me with flowers, and by the end of our horticultural conversation Jenny had stopped crying and was on the reading rug.

'Would you mind having a chat with me?' Sarah asks. 'I'm a police officer and Grace's sister-in-law.'

Sisters-in-law. I've never before properly considered that we have our own separate and connecting thread in the matrix of the family.

'Of course,' Mrs Fisher replies. 'But I really don't think I'll be of any help.'

Sarah escorts her into the relatives' room.

'Before you ask me anything,' Mrs Fisher says, 'I have a police record.'

Jenny and I are both startled. *Mrs Fisher?*

'I was an activist for CND and Greenpeace. I still am, but I don't tend to get arrested nowadays.'

Sarah looks a little judgmental, but I know not to misinterpret that now.

'You said you were the secretary at Sidley House?'

'For almost thirteen years. I had to leave in April.'

'Why was that?'

'Apparently I was too old to do the job. The head teacher told me that if I looked at my contract I'd see that there was 'a policy of non-voluntary retirement for all support staff at sixty'. I'm sixty-seven. She'd waited seven years

215

before enforcing the clause.'

'And were you too old for the job?'

'No. I was still bloody good at it. Everyone knew it, including Sally Healey.'

'So do you know why she got rid of you?'

'You don't mince your words. No. I've no idea.'

Sarah took out a notebook, an incongruous Paperchase one with little owls on it, and wrote something down.

'Can I have your details?' Sarah asks. 'Your full name is Mrs . . . ?'

'Elizabeth Fisher. And it's Ms, however you pronounce it. My husband left me six months ago and I think it's customary to drop the 'Mrs' at that point. The ring won't come off. I have to get it cut, apparently. The symbolism is a little brutal for me at the moment.'

Sarah looks sympathetic but I feel cold. Mrs Healey sent all the parents a letter saying Mrs Fisher's husband was terminally ill and that was the reason she'd had to leave the school. I'd organised a card and Maisie had traipsed off to some super-snazzy flower place in Richmond for a bouquet for her and, at my suggestion, bulbs.

'Can you write down your address?'

As Elizabeth writes down her details, I want to tell Sarah about the lie Mrs Healey told the parents. Why did she do that?

'Do you know Silas Hyman?' Sarah asks her — a logical question but not the one I hoped for.

'Yes. He was a teacher at Sidley House. He was fired for something he didn't do. A month before me. We've spoken on the phone once or

216

twice since then. Kindred spirits and all that.'

'Why was he fired?'

'In a nutshell? An eight-year-old boy called Robert Fleming wanted him out.'

'And the longer version?'

'Robert Fleming loathed Silas because he was the first teacher to stand up to him. Silas called Fleming's parents in, during the first week he had him in his class, and used the word 'wicked' about their son; not suffering from some attention deficit disorder or a problem with socialisation. Wicked. But unfortunately that's not the form with fee-paying parents.

'In March, when Silas was on playground duty, Fleming told him that an eleven-year-old boy had locked himself in the toilets with a five-year-old little girl, and she was screaming. Fleming said he couldn't find any other teacher. So Silas went to the little girl's aid. For all his faults, he's very kind like that. And Robert Fleming knew that.

'When he'd got Silas out of the playground, Fleming forced a boy called Daniel up the fire escape and then managed to get him over the edge. God knows what he must have said to the little chap to have got him to climb over. Then Fleming pushed him. He was badly injured. Broke both his legs. It was lucky it wasn't his neck.

'Part of my job was school nurse. I looked after him until the ambulance arrived. Poor little mite was in such terrible pain.'

I'd had only Adam's version of events, and adult rumours, distorted as time went by. It became a terrible accident, not deliberate, and the blame was targeted on Mr Hyman for not supervising the playground rather than Robert Fleming. Because who wants to believe an eight-year-old child can be that disturbingly manipulative, that vicious, that malevolent?

But we already knew that he was from Adam, who lived in physical fear of him. We knew this wasn't like regular teasing and bullying. I think it was when he pulled Adam's tie around his neck, leaving a red welt for a week afterwards, saying he'd kill him if he didn't 'kiss his butt'. Or the skipping rope that he wound around Adam, tying him up, while he drew swastikas on his body.

Jenny called him psycho-child and you agreed.

'Those aren't things that a boy should be doing,' you said. *'If it was an adult, we'd say he was sociopathic. Psychopathic, even.'*

It was after the swastika incident, just before this last half-term, that you demanded a meeting and got a guarantee from Mrs Healey that Robert Fleming wouldn't be coming back to Sidley House in September.

'Mrs Healey knew that a playground accident like that should never have happened in a primary school,' Mrs Fisher continues. 'She needed someone to blame, so she blamed Silas Hyman. I don't think she wanted to fire him for it. She's not stupid. She could recognise a gifted teacher, as a business asset if nothing else. But then there was that scurrilous article in the *Richmond Post* and the phone didn't stop ringing with parents wanting action. So she had no choice as she saw it. Parents have a great deal

218

of power in a private school, especially a new one.

'The really appalling thing is if that wicked boy *had* been blamed and hauled over the coals, there might have been a fighting chance of stopping him before it was too late.'

He wasn't hauled over the coals, was he? Mrs Healey gave him a quiet exit.

'You think he'll do something again?' Sarah asks.

'Of course he will. If he can plan and execute *at eight* breaking a boy's legs, what will he do at eighteen?'

Did Robert Fleming leave the playing field during sports day? No. I can't believe that. I know we were told that almost all school-time fires are started by children, but not fires which injure people so badly. Not fires like this one. I refuse to be like DI Baker and think a child capable of that.

'You said that after the *Richmond Post* article the phone didn't stop ringing?' Sarah asks.

'That's right. And Sally Healey was forced to fire Silas.'

'Do you know who told the press?'

'No. I don't.'

'Does Silas Hyman have any enemies?'

'None that I know of.'

'You said earlier, 'for all his faults'. What do you mean by that?'

'I shouldn't have said it.'

'But there is a reason?'

'I just mean that he was arrogant. Male teachers in a primary school are a rare species.

219

He was a cockerel in the hen-house.'

She pauses a moment and I can see she's fighting off tears.

'How are they,' she asks. 'Jenny and Mrs Covey?'

'Both of them are critically injured.'

Elizabeth Fisher's ramrod-straight posture bends a little and she turns her face from Sarah, as if embarrassed by her emotion.

'I was there at the start, and so was Jenny. Reception children would come to my office to show me the work they'd done. Jenny Covey would come in and give me a hug and then walk out again. That was what she'd come to show me. In year one she got into Hama-beads. Other children would do meticulous geometric patterns and she'd do something completely random, no design or maths to it — and it was wonderful. All those coloured beads just put together any old how. Just so . . . energetic and unworried.'

Sarah smiles. Does she remember Jenny's Hama-bead phase? She probably got an anarchic mat for a Christmas present.

'And Adam's a lovely little boy,' she continues. 'A credit to Mrs Covey. I wish I'd told her that, but I didn't. Not that it would have made any difference, what I thought, but I wish I'd said it anyway.'

Sarah looks moved by her, and Elizabeth Fisher has the encouragement she needs to continue.

'Some of them, they hardly bother to say hello to their mothers at the end of the day, and the mothers are too busy gossiping to each other to really focus on their child. But Adam runs out there like a plane coming in to land, with his arms out to Mrs Covey, and she looks like there's no one else in the entire place but him. I used to watch them out of my office window.'

She hasn't got anyone to talk to about us, I realise, not with her husband gone. And she can hardly contact anyone at school after the excruciatingly embarrassing flowers-for-a-dying-husband.

'Do you have any idea who might have set fire to the school?' Sarah asks.

'No. But if I were you, I'd look for someone like Robert Fleming as an adult — because no one intervened early enough.'

★ ★ ★

As Jenny and I return to my ward, I remember that meeting you had with Mrs Healey about Robert Fleming. I'd been annoyed she'd listened to you when she hadn't listened to me all those times I'd gone into school and complained. I'd thought it was because you're a man and I was just another mum with Kit Kat crumbs in my pocket and spare PE socks in my handbag. You said it was because of your celebrity status: 'I can kick up a smellier stink.'

Maisie is arriving next to my bed. She pulls the ugly flimsy curtains around it.

'Another visitor,' I say to Jen. 'It's like a seventeenth-century salon in here this evening, isn't it?'

'A salon was in *France*, Mum.' She gestures to

the brown geometric curtains around my bed. 'And it had *walls*. With oil paintings and ornate mirrors.'

We'd spoken about salons a few months ago. I'm touched she listened.

'Nit-picky. It had a bed, didn't it? And there was a woman at the centre of the attention. *N'est ce pas?*' Alright, so she was meant to be a glittering witty intellectual . . .

Jen smiles.

Maisie sits down on the side of my bed, rather than the visitor's chair, and takes my hand. I now know that the confidant, exuberant, *not-giving-a-hoot!* Maisie doesn't exist. But she did once. I'm sure of that. I don't know when Maisie started imitating herself as she used to be; the person she still should be.

But her kindness and warmth are genuine.

'You're looking lots better,' she says to me, smiling at me as if I can see her as well as hear her. 'Roses in your cheeks! And you don't even use blusher, do you? Not like me. I have to slap on the stuff, but you look that way naturally.'

Instead of a French salon, I imagine myself now in her Aga-warm kitchen.

When she came to see me last time, I was sure she was going to tell me something but was interrupted. Maybe she'll confide in me now about Donald. I hope so. One of the things about all this I find so hard is that she didn't, or couldn't, turn to me.

She's fumbling in the pocket of her cardigan. She takes out Jenny's mobile, with the little charm on it that Adam gave her for Christmas.

'Tilly, the reception teacher, gave it to me,' Maisie says.

Jen is staring at her phone in silence. Inside are texts of parties and travel plans and everyday chat with her friends; a teenage life in eight centimetres of plastic. It is shiny and undamaged.

'Tilly found it on the gravel outside the school,' Maisie continues. 'Gave it to me as I got in the ambulance with Rowena. Wanted to make sure I gave it to Jenny. Like it was important. I suppose she just wanted to be doing something to help. Well, we all did. Then I just forgot about it. I'm sorry.'

'How could she just *forget?*' Jenny asks.

'There was a lot going on,' I say, marvelling at my understatement.

'Should have returned it before, sorry,' Maisie says, as if she's heard Jenny. 'Complete *scatterbrain.*'

Maisie finds a space between the vases of flowers for the phone.

'They've gone overboard with the air-conditioning in Ro's room,' she says. 'So I put on my cardi. Found it in the pocket and wanted her to have it back. You know girls and their mobiles.'

'But how could I have dropped it?' Jenny asks. 'Ivo and I were texting each other while I was up in the medical room. And then it was the fire and I was still inside. So how come she found this *outside?*'

'I don't know, sweetheart.'

'Maybe the arsonist stole it from me and then

dropped it by mistake?'

'But why would he steal it?'

'If it was the hate-mailer,' Jenny says slowly, 'perhaps he wanted some kind of trophy?'

The idea sickens me.

'Or maybe you went outside for some reason,' I say. 'And then returned.'

'But why would I do that?'

I have no idea. We're both silent.

Maisie sits down on my bed again, chattering on in her sweet voice, trying to make this as normal as she can, as if she wants to pretend we're in her kitchen together — and that it's as cosy as it seems. A deception within a deception.

Until today I'd thought Maisie's babbling way of speaking was from a surfeit of things to say, a friendly warm outpouring, but maybe it's more of a nervous habit, a flow of chat to swirl over underlying jagged unhappiness.

Like the baggy, soft cardigan now covering her bruises.

'They wouldn't let Jenny have her phone in the intensive care unit,' she continues. 'In case it interfered with the machinery and what-have-you. I said it would be off, just by her for when she wakes up. But even if it's switched off it's still no good because they said it might carry bugs and of course we don't want that!

'So I'll leave it next to you and tell Mike it's here because maybe he'll want to keep it safe for her at home.'

Jenny is staring at her phone.

'I still can't bloody remember. If I could . . . '

She trails off, furious with herself.

224

Maisie has turned slightly away from me.

'There's something I have to tell you, Gracie. I don't want you to hate me for it. Please.'

The curtains are swirled open around my bed and two doctors come in to do their usual frequent checks. One of them turns to Maisie.

'Please don't pull the curtains round her bed. We have to be able to visually monitor her all the time.'

'Oh yes, of course, I'm sorry.'

The doctors leave but the noise and urgency of the ward is all around us; not even a pretence at a salon or kitchen now.

'Donald came to visit Rowena earlier,' Maisie says. Finally, she'll confide in me. And I want her to. Maybe it will unburden her a little.

'He's so proud of her.'

'Oh for God's sake,' Jenny says — her frustration and anxiety so near the surface now. But I try to understand. Perhaps Maisie needs to keep that film of a happy family playing to someone who's been watching it for years, maintaining the illusion, because the reality — Donald hurting her already injured child — is just too hard.

'You know I'd do anything for Rowena,' she says quietly. 'Don't you, Gracie?'

'Except leave your husband so that he can't hurt her any more,' Jenny snaps.

'It's not that simple, Jen.'

'Oh, I think it is.'

'I didn't finish telling you what happened,' Maisie continues. 'So you don't know why he's so proud.'

225

'This is absurd,' Jenny says, still snappy. I beckon her to be quiet so we can hear Maisie.

'I told you that when you ran into the building, *I ran away*, to the bridge. I went up to the fire engines, told the firemen there were people inside the school and we all pushed cars out of the way. I told you that . . . '

I remember the sound of people shouting and horns going and the smell of diesel fumes and fire reaching the bridge as if Maisie's sensory memory has somehow become mine too. No flimsy insubstantial film this time.

'While I was there, on the bridge or maybe before, when I was still running to get there, Rowena went into the school.'

'I don't understand,' Jenny says; neither do I.

'She'd seen you run in too,' continues Maisie. 'Heard you screaming for Jenny. But she didn't run away. She found a towel in the PE shed and she soaked it in water. She put it over her face. Then she went into the school to help you.'

Dear God. Rowena going into a burning building. For Jenny. For me.

'They think she must have been overcome by fumes. She was unconscious when the firemen got to her. She's not badly hurt, but they were worried she might have some kind of internal damage; they're still keeping a look-out for that.'

I never guessed she had that kind of courage, or anything like it.

Her heroism is extraordinary.

I don't think you'll completely understand, but I *know* what it's like to go in. Heat up the grill as high as you can then put your face inside the oven. Then your whole body. Add choking smoke and no oxygen. Shut the door.

Instinct and love made me run into that building and then pushed and shoved me onwards. I had the selfish desire to run away, yes, just as I told you. But I needed Jenny in my arms more than I've ever needed anything before. Ultimately more than I needed to save myself. And I discovered in that choking burning school that the reason self-preservation can't win in a mother is because part of yourself is your child.

But Rowena went in without instinct. Without love. I've barely seen her since she went to secondary school and she's never been friends with Jenny. But somehow she overcame that terror. Just her courage pushing her on. Like the knights in one of Adam's Arthurian legends, heroically selfless.

Adam.

Rowena was comforting him as I ran into the building, not pausing to even speak to him. Was it Adam's misery that prompted her?

'I didn't realise she was even missing,' Maisie says. 'When the fire engines got to the school there were so many people — parents and teachers and children and press people — and I thought she was there, among the crowd. I just assumed . . . '

'I think she was trying to make her father proud, again,' Jenny says.

'And then a fireman brought her out and she was unconscious,' Maisie continues. 'When I told Donald — '

She breaks off, distressed. Then, with effort

227

and emotion, continues. 'You shouldn't condemn someone, should you? If you love them, if they're your family, you have to try and see the good. I mean, that's what love is in some ways, isn't it? Believing in someone's goodness.'

'Does she *really* believe that?' Jenny asks.

'Yes, I think she does.'

'Jesus.'

Maisie holds my hand more tightly.

'It's funny, in one afternoon you know what you're made of. And you also discover what your child's made of. And you can feel such *shame* and such *pride* at the same time.'

But it's her father, not her mother, who Rowena wants to be proud of her. It was for him she went into the burning school. And it was in vain.

I remember the ugly hatred in Donald's voice. '*Quite the little heroine, aren't you?*' Her cry of pain as he grabbed hold of her burnt hands.

18

Sarah arrives at my bedside, looking as briskly efficient as ever and I am grateful for her competence; what good would a dinghy-on-a-duckpond person be to us now?

Maisie is sitting silently next to me, as if spent; her fingers shivering.

'Hello, Grace, me again,' Sarah says. 'It's like Piccadilly Circus in here this evening.'

'You think she can hear too?' Maisie says.

'Absolutely. I'm Sarah. Grace's sister-in-law.'

I think I see anxiety on Maisie's face. My fault. I've made Sarah out to be a dragon in the past.

'Maisie White. A friend.'

'So are you Rowena White's mother?' Sarah asks, a savvy police officer instantly recognising names.

'Yes.'

'There's a canteen open somewhere. Would you like to get a cup of tea with me? Or at least something that passes for tea?'

She isn't giving Maisie much option.

I hope to God she'll get Maisie to tell her about the domestic abuse so Sarah will add Donald to her list of suspects. But in our years of friendship Maisie's never even hinted at it. Or maybe she did and I wasn't savvy enough — or sensitive enough — to hear her.

As they leave, Sarah spots Jenny's mobile phone.

'It's Jen-Jen's,' Maisie says. 'A teacher found it outside the school. Knew she'd like it back.'

Maybe she calls her 'Jen-Jen' to show Sarah how close she is to the family, maybe to show her right to be here, and I'm touched by that; a sign of the old, more assertive Maisie.

Sarah picks up the phone and Jenny is on tenterhooks. But Sarah puts it in her pocket.

'I'll be in the garden,' Jenny says, her frustration and upset clear. 'And it's *Jenny* now. And *I* should have my phone, not Aunt Sarah.'

For some reason I'm glad of her adolescent strop; her indignant energy.

★   ★   ★

I follow Sarah and Maisie towards the cafeteria. Do you think anyone'll discover Sarah's turning their relatives' rooms and cafeterias into interview rooms?

The Palms Café is empty and the striplights turned off, but the door's open and the hot-drinks machine is working. Sarah gets styrofoam cups of something masquerading as tea and they sit together at a Formica table.

The only light now is from the corridor, making this institutional room shadowy and strange.

'I'm trying to find out a little more about what happened,' Sarah says.

'Grace told me that you're a policewoman.'

Once, Sarah would have brusquely corrected her, 'police *officer*'.

'Right now, I'm just Grace's sister-in-law and

Jenny's aunt. Would you mind telling me what you remember about yesterday afternoon?'

'Of course. But I'm not sure I can help much. I mean, I already told the police.'

'As I said, I'm just talking to you as family.'

'I'd come to pick Rowena up from school. Well, I should say work, because she's a teaching assistant, not a pupil now. I was really chuffed when she asked me to give her a lift home. I hadn't seen much of her lately, you see. You know what teenage girls are like.' She trails off. 'Sorry, this isn't important, sorry.'

Sarah smiles at her, encouraging her to continue.

'I thought she'd be out on the playing field helping with sports day. But Gracie told me she'd gone into the school with Addie, to get his cake. A trench cake that they'd made together — ' She breaks off, putting her knuckle into her mouth to bite away a sob. 'I just can't think about it, not properly, about Addie, with his mum so . . . I just can't . . . '

'That's alright. Take your time.'

Maisie stirs her tea, as if the flimsy plastic spoon gives her something to grip onto; determined to continue.

'I went to find her. When I got to the school I popped to the loo, the grown-up one. I'd just gone in, when I heard a noise, really loud, like an air-raid siren or something. Nothing like the fire alarms we had at school so it took me a few moments to realise what it was.

'I hurried out, worried about Rowena. Then I saw her coming out of the secretary's office.'

231

As she stirs, tea slops out of her cup onto the Formica table.

'Through the office window I saw Adam was safely outside by the statue. I thought everything was OK. But I didn't know about Jenny. Didn't even call for her. I didn't know to do that.'

'Which floor is the secretary's office?' Sarah asks.

'The upper ground. Just next to the main door. I told Rowena to look after Addie and I went to help the reception children. Mrs Healey thinks they're too young to be at sports day, you see. Sorry. What I mean is, I knew that they'd be in the school.'

Sarah mops up Maisie's spilt tea with her napkin, and this simple act of kindness seems to relax Maisie. Dragons don't mop up your spilt tea.

'And then?' Sarah asks.

'I went down to the lower ground floor where their classroom is. It wasn't so smoky down there and they have their own exit with a ramp leading back up to the area outside the school. Tilly — Miss Rogers — was getting all the children out. I helped her calm them down. I know them all, you see. I read with them once a week so I could help reassure them.'

Her voice is suddenly warm and I know she's thinking of those four-year-old children; their outline still fuzzy somehow, as if you'll touch their aura before you can touch the quietness of their silky hair or peachy-soft faces. Beautiful baby creatures still. I used to think she still read with them, after Rowena had grown up, because

232

she missed her own daughter being a tiny girl. But maybe, for one afternoon a week, she was trying to go back to a time before the abuse; to when she and Rowena were happy; a time when she really didn't *give a hoot*!

'Did you see anyone other than Rowena and Adam and the reception teacher?'

'No. Well, not in the school, if that's what you mean? But about five minutes later the new secretary came outside. There was a lot of smoke by then but she was smiling, like she was enjoying it, or at least she was not at all upset and she had lipstick on. Sorry. Silly.'

'It was five minutes after the alarm that she came out? You're sure?'

'No, I mean, I can't be totally sure. Never very good at timings. But we'd got the children out and lined them up, counted them at least five times. She brought Tilly the register to officially check they were all accounted for, but we knew they were.

'Just after the secretary came out, the fire got worse. There was a huge bang, and flames, and smoke was pouring out of the windows.'

'Did you see anyone else?'

'No.'

'You're sure?'

'Yes. I've been trying to remember but I really don't think I saw anyone else. But there easily could have been other people there. I mean, it's a big building.'

Sarah hasn't drunk her tea, concentrating every ounce of attention on Maisie, while not letting her feel it.

'And then?'

'A few minutes later, I think it was that, I saw Gracie running towards the school, I think she was screaming, but the fire alarm was so loud I can't be sure.'

She pauses a moment, as if she's watching me running full tilt towards the school.

'I knew she'd be so relieved when she saw Adam, and she was, and I thought that everything was alright. But then she was yelling for Jenny, over and over, and I realised that Jenny must be inside. And Gracie ran in.'

I see the pressure of tears building behind Maisie's face.

She presses her fingerpads, hard, against the skin on her temple as if it'll force the tears to stay inside.

Sarah is looking at her intently now.

'Did you know that Adam has been accused of starting the fire?' she asks.

Maisie is astonished. Is that why Sarah told her — in order to gauge her response? She must clearly see now that Maisie's astonishment is genuine.

'Oh God, that poor family.'

Tears break free and stream down her face. 'Sorry, selfish. I've no right to cry, have I, not when Gracie and Jenny . . . '

Sarah picks up Maisie's cup. 'I'll get you another?'

'Thank you.'

And this small act of kindness again seems to relax Maisie a little.

'What do you know about Silas Hyman?'

234

Sarah asks as she goes to the drinks machine.

'He's dangerous,' Maisie says immediately. 'Violent. But you'd never guess that. I mean, that he's a sham. And he gets people to love him. Young people. Exploits their feelings for him.'

I am taken aback by her vehemence, and how sure she is about him. How does she know?

'In what way is he a sham?' Sarah asks.

'I thought he was *kind*, really caring,' Maisie says. 'Wonderful, actually. When I read with the little children, I take one at a time out of their classroom up to the first floor where they have the lower school reading books, and we sit on the rug together.'

Maisie is talking to her across the shadowy expanse, as if it's a relief to talk about it, her words tumbling out.

'Mr Hyman taught in the other classroom on that floor. You'd hear his class laughing. And there was music too. He was always playing them something. I worked it out in the end. It was Mozart for Maths and jazz for getting changed for sport because it speeded them up. I once heard him telling off Robert Fleming but he didn't shout at him. He didn't need to shut the classroom door like some of the teachers in case parents overheard. And he had special names for them all. His whole focus in the school seemed to be the children. Not getting ahead in his career, or making sure there was impressive work up on the walls for parents to see. Just the children, inspiring them and making them happy. So you can see why he had me fooled, can't you? I mean, I think he fooled all of us.'

235

Sarah joins her with two new cups of tea. In all the time I've known her, Sarah has never drunk tea, only coffee, and it has to be real not instant. Maybe her police persona drinks tea because despite telling Maisie she was talking to her as a member of our family, it's the professional Sarah I'm watching.

'When did you realise you'd been fooled?' Sarah asks.

Maisie takes the tea and fusses with a little pink packet of fake sugar before she answers.

'At the school prize-giving. We give a prize, you see, every year. For Science. Rowena's going to read Science at Oxford, St Hilda's. Sorry. I mean, that's why we were there.' She pauses for a moment, as if thinking back. 'He barged in, looking so *angry*, and then he swore at the headmistress. Threatened all of us.

'But no one else took it seriously. I mean, they just found him embarrassing rather than threatening.'

'But you took him seriously?'

'Yes.'

At the prize-giving Donald was sitting pressed up next to her. Maisie knows first-hand that threats of violence can translate into the real thing. Or perhaps Donald doesn't give a warning first.

'Did you tell anyone your anxieties about him?' Sarah asks.

'Yes. I phoned Sally Healey, the head teacher, later that evening and told her she should get the police to make sure he wasn't allowed near the school again. A restraining order, I think it's called? I'm not sure. Something that meant he wasn't allowed near the children.'

'Did she?'

Maisie shook her head and I saw the upset on her face.

'You said he gets young people to love him,' Sarah continues. 'And exploits their feelings?'

But Maisie seems to have clammed up now, lost in her own thoughts.

'Maisie?' Sarah asks, but still Maisie is silent.

Sarah waits patiently, giving Maisie time.

'Grace told me that Addie adored him,' Maisie says eventually. 'But I didn't realise how much till the prize-giving.'

'What happened?'

'Has no one told you?'

'No.'

You hadn't said anything to Sarah and I wasn't close enough to her to risk this touchy subject.

'Addie stood up and defended Silas Hyman,' Maisie says. 'Told everyone that he shouldn't have been fired.'

'That was brave,' Sarah says.

I should have risked telling her.

'But it's *wrong* to make someone adore you,' Maisie says, emotion shaking her voice. 'When they're so much younger and can't properly think for themselves. That's exploitation. Wicked. And you can make them do what you want.'

Her anger is both startling and touching. I know what she's suggesting and so does Sarah. But no one could have made Addie light a fire.

I don't blame Maisie for thinking Adam easily manipulated. He's always been shy with adults, even Maisie. And after the prize-giving he'd looked so cowed, flinching from Donald's lighter.

'I should get back to my daughter,' Maisie says. 'I told her I wouldn't be long.'

'Of course,' Sarah says, standing up. 'One of my colleagues spoke to a firefighter at the scene. He told me of her bravery.'

'Yes.'

'I'd like to speak to her, if that would be alright? Just to get it all straight for myself.'

'She's upset at the moment,' Maisie says, looking fearful. 'In a bit of a state. I mean, that's understandable, isn't it, after everything that's happened. So would you mind waiting?'

Is she afraid Rowena will tell Sarah about Donald?

'Not at all,' Sarah replies. 'And you've been very kind to spare some of your time. I'll pop by tomorrow. See if she's feeling up to talking to me then.'

'I haven't told her yet,' Maisie says. 'How badly hurt they both are.'

'I understand.'

Maisie leaves and Sarah scrupulously writes up notes in the owl-covered notebook.

★   ★   ★

'So get her to give a new statement right now,' you say vehemently.

Sarah has joined you at Jenny's bedside.

'Tell Baker that someone else knew that he was violent,' you continue. 'Christ, if Maisie

238

thinks that about him, other people will too.'

'At the moment there's no point,' Sarah says patiently. 'Not unless and until his alibi is broken. And I also need to pursue other avenues at the same time.'

She makes you go for a sleep, while she takes your place at Jenny's bedside.

And I return to the garden where Jenny is waiting.

*　*　*

It's different out here in the cool of the evening. Someone has watered the flowers and filled the bird bath. If you look straight up, past the perpendicular walls on all sides, studded with glass windows, you can see the sky, that shot-silk dark blue that you get late on a summer's evening with stars punched through the fabric.

We don't feel any pain out here and I think it's because, although we're outside, the garden is in the middle of the hospital and those perpendicular walls that rise up all around us offer us protection.

My senses are so much more receptive now — I can smell the subtlest, smallest thing, as if lacking a body has left my senses exposed and quivering.

Me, who couldn't even smell when the toast was burning — *Grace, for heaven's sake, it's charcoal!*

Now the air feels softly weighted with the heavy summer perfumes of jasmine and roses and honeysuckle; strata of scents layered in the air like the coloured stripes in Adam's sand jar.

And there's another perfume. Sweeter than the others, it's igniting an emotion I shouldn't be feeling, not now — a twanging of nervousness and an expansive unlimited excitement. Time ahead of me is opening up, unbounded; a river through Grantchester then onwards away from clocks at ten to three towards London and beyond; to ever more possibilities.

It's stocks. The smell of night stocks and I am in Newnham garden, late on a warm summer evening, near to Part Ones, my mind filled with paintings and books and ideas. I'm with you. And the night-time stocks are releasing their fragrance like confetti over my love for you and my anxiety about exams and my excitement for the future.

Memories are usually like a DVD playing, not connected to the room you're in while you remember.

But I'm actually *there*, Mike. My feelings pungently real.

Love punches me in the solar plexus.

Then it's over and I'm back in this boxed piece of summer.

The loss feels cold and colourless.

But there's no time for self-indulgence. There is something significant about what's just happened, something I can use to help my children. But the thought is slipping away and I have to grab it by its coat-tails before it's gone.

It was Jenny hearing the fire alarm going off at the school. '*It was like I was back in the school, really back there.*'

I turn to her.

'When we saw Donald White with Maisie and Rowena, do you remember smelling something?'

Because I remember now the smell of Donald's aftershave and cigarettes.

'Perhaps. Yes,' Jenny replies.

'Do you think that's why you heard the fire alarm?' I ask.

'My mad person's tinnitus? It's possible, I suppose. I didn't really analyse it.'

I hear a child screaming.

Adam.

I jerk my head around. He isn't here.

'No! She's not dead. She's *not!*'

Too small a voice for such huge words.

I run to him.

★   ★   ★

He's hunched over my bed, silent. He'd never cried out his grief but I'd heard him. Mum's arms are around him.

'I'm here!' I say to him. '*Right here.* No one knows that yet but they will. And I'll wake up, my sweetie! Of course I will! I'm giving you a kiss and you can't feel it, but I'm here. Kissing you now.'

I have no voice.

Screaming in a nightmare, making no sound.

I force myself into my body but my vocal cords are still snapped and useless and my eyelids still welded shut. I try with all my might to touch him, but my arms are beams of impossible weight. In this black, vile, inert place,

241

there is nothing I can do to reach him.

And out there he's in a dark angry ocean, drowning.

Panicking, I'm breathing more quickly. I try to slow my breathing and I can! I take breaths quickly, in and out, in and out — and then deliberately slowly — surely Mum will realise I'm trying to communicate! Adam too!

I can *do* something! Maybe this means we won't need to wait for years for me to wake up!

As I take deliberate slow deep breaths I think of blowing up Adam's orange armbands before he could swim, tight around his thin white arms, and how he'd bobbed happily in the water, not feeling any fear; my breath keeping him safe.

I slip out of my body — surely Mum will be calling to a doctor, pointing out this signal from me that I am in here and Adam won't be crying any more.

But Mum is with Adam at my bedside, her face white as she tries to comfort him as he cries. Maybe I should feel angry with her. But it's tearing her apart and I know the courage it took.

Addie pulls away from her and runs. She goes after him and grabs him and they tussle. He goes limp and she puts her arms around him, like a body cushion against excruciating pain. She half carries him out of the ward and I go with them.

His face looks so pale, bruised shadows under his eyes. He's withdrawn even further into himself as if his whole body is now mute. I put my arms tightly around him.

★ ★ ★

'Next Hallowe'en, Mum, I'm going to have a <u>bath</u> in invisible ink! Then I'll be invisible.'

'I don't think it works that way.'

'Why not?'

'Well . . . '

'I'll have a glove. So that they know someone's there. I mean, otherwise, how will I get any sweets?'

Hallowe'en was four months away still. He'd have supplanted this idea with a new one by then.

'Good idea, the glove.'

'Yup.'

★　★　★

He can't see or feel my arms around him.

I will wake up. One day *I will wake up.*

★　★　★

It's dusk now. Through the glass wall abutting the garden, most of the wards are in half-light. In one of the rooms, through the uncurtained window, I see a child in bed, just a shape, with small arms. Another big shape, which I make out to be his father, smooths the child's hair and then waits. The small shape in the bed grows motionless as the child falls into sleep. The father is just standing there now, rigidly upright and alone, flapping his arms up and down, up and down, up and down as if he can fly them both away.

19

Around us, on all four sides, flickering electric lights are coming on in the windows; a man-made hospital dawn two hours after the outside natural one.

It seems impossible that only *the day before yesterday* I was putting frozen pain au chocolat into the oven. As if there's been an earthquake in time, with the fire separating the tectonic plates of our past and present irrevocably. A little high falutin', sorry, but who else can I tell? Poor Jen would probably think I was prepping her for an A-level retake in something.

★   ★   ★

As soon as I see your face, I know that no heart has been found for her. I go close to you and you tell me that there's time! It's still going to be alright! Not to be defeatist! She will get better. *Of course she will.* You don't need to speak for me to hear your burly tough optimism. Because although we no longer have a solar plexus love, we have the married kind, which means that your voice — you — are inside my mind.

Sarah arrives, her clothes crumpled, no make-up. She was doing shifts at Jenny's bedside with you last night.

'I got through to Ivo,' she says. 'He's trying to get a standby flight.'

You just nod.

You *knew* about this, Mike? You must have done for Sarah to have his number. And you thought this was *OK*? My voice clearly isn't in your head, because this is a *terrible* idea. Or perhaps my voice is in your head and you just ignored me. Yes, I'm cross. Of course I'm bloody cross!

Has Sarah told him what she looks like now?

Can anyone describe Jenny's face and body now?

Last Saturday they went to Chiswick House Park together. '*What did you do?*' I'd asked her that evening, thinking they'd gone to the café, or had a picnic, maybe read. When she didn't answer, I'd imagined all sorts of canoodling. Finally, a little embarrassed, she'd told me — they'd just looked at one another; the long sunny hours spent staring at each other's faces.

Maybe if you'd known about how they spent their afternoon, you'd have known it wasn't a good idea.

Because what will he think when he looks at her now?

And how can she bear his rejection?

I'm sorry. You think she's unconscious and will be totally unaware of him. You've no idea how badly she may be hurt by this.

Crossness and apologies. As in our old life together, our children pull us apart as frequently as they unite us; causing tensions we had no idea about when we married — although at the moment I'm the only one who's aware of them.

Sarah outlines her plan for the day — talking

to Rowena and then going to the police station — but you are going to stay put; your only mission is to guard Jenny. Despite the multitude of medical staff in ICU, you're not going to leave your post.

★ ★ ★

In the corridor Jenny is beaming.

'He's going to get a standby flight. Aunt Sarah phoned him.'

'Did she . . . ' How can I ask this?

'No. She didn't tell him what I look like now, if that's what you're worried about? But it won't matter. That sounds stupid. Of course it will matter. What I mean is, it won't change anything.'

What can I say? That only tough-as-old-boots married love could withstand this, not their fragile five-months-old romance; that 'love is not love which alters when it alteration finds' doesn't apply to teenage boys.

'*Young love*,' you used to say, smiling, and I'd want to hurl a potato at you, or whatever I was washing or peeling at the time — as if this kind of relationship could age into wrinkles and smile lines. Because what he felt for Jenny had built-in obsolescence, even without the fire.

'I thought you'd be pleased,' Jenny says, a little baffled. 'I mean, I know you don't like him much.' A very short pause, just space enough for me to argue, but I don't and she continues. 'He'll tell the police about the red paint now, won't he?'

'Yes. Of course.'

Sarah walks past us on the phone. 'This takes precedence,' Sarah says, then pauses. 'I don't know. [Pause.] No, *you* take some time off work. [Pause.] I don't have time for this right now.'

She must be talking to Roger. You try and like him out of loyalty to your sister, but I annually resent his sneering face at the Christmas table when he actually tries *to win* pulling the crackers but is the only person at the table not to wear the paper hat. Competitive about his own children, dismissive of ours; frankly, I loathe him, and perhaps that's one reason I used to dislike Sarah, for being a unit with him.

She hasn't mentioned her own family to you or her job, putting us absolutely centre stage. I'm only just discovering that how someone behaves in everyday life gives no clue how they'll be when it counts. Maybe Roger — in the right circumstances — would wear a paper hat and let Addie win the cracker. Though he's hardly shining now if Sarah's half of the conversation is anything to go by. I think I see disappointment on her face, but not surprise.

'She and Uncle Roger don't get along any more,' Jenny says to me as if reading my thoughts. So Sarah has talked to Jenny about her marriage. My God, who isn't talking to Jenny about their marriage? Perhaps a teenage daughter in the room doesn't smooth adult relationships but makes them gripe.

Sarah abruptly ends the conversation, saying she has to go.

Jenny and I go with her.

247

A nurse answers the locked door of the burns unit, surprised to see Sarah.

'Jenny's been taken to ICU, didn't anyone —?'

'Yes, actually it's Rowena White I want to see. She's been friends with Jenny since primary school, and you know how people become friends of the family too.'

She stumbles as she speaks; telling half-truths, like crumpled clothes, has never been Sarah before.

The nurse lets her in and we follow her to Rowena's side-room. A woman is wheeled past on a trolley.

'I can't do this right now, Mum,' Jenny says and I curse myself for bringing her into the burns unit. 'I'll be back in a little while, OK?'

'OK.'

She leaves.

In Rowena's side-room, a nurse is taking the dressings off Rowena's hands.

Sarah waits a little way from the open doorway for the nurse to finish. 'The burns have got damaged,' the nurse says to Rowena, surprised. 'Some of the blisters have burst . . . ?'

'Yes, I know. I'm sorry.'

'Not your fault, sweetie. But how?'

In the doorway I see Sarah listening intently to this, but the nurse and Rowena haven't seen her. I remember that Sarah did a two-year stint in the domestic violence unit.

'I told the other nurse about it yesterday,' Rowena says.

The nurse looks through Rowena's notes. 'So you did. You said you slipped . . . ?'

'Yes. I'm just so clumsy.'

I shudder at her use of Maisie's vocabulary.

'But there's damage to the top of your hands as well as the palms?' the nurse says.

Rowena is silent and doesn't meet her eye.

'Have the doctors taken a look at you?' the nurse continues.

'Yes. Does it mean I'll have to stay here longer?'

'It may do. We have to be so careful about infection. You know about all that, don't you? I think I already read you my riot act?'

'Yes, you did. Thank you.'

'I'll be back to see you in a bit.'

As the nurse leaves, Sarah comes in.

'Hello, Rowena. I'm Sarah, Jenny's aunt. Is your mother not here?'

'She's gone to get me a few things from home.'

Rowena seems at ease with Sarah so she can't know that she's been eavesdropping.

'How are you feeling?' Sarah asks.

'Fine. Getting much better now.'

'It was incredibly brave. What you did.'

Rowena looks embarrassed. 'You saw it in the paper?' she asks.

Rowena's rescue effort was hidden in the middle pages of the *Richmond Post*. I'm not sure if you read that far. It was in the mode of 'Very Small Earthquake Not Many Killed' kind of a story — 'Plain Girl Runs To Help But Doesn't Rescue Anyone And Is Slightly Hurt'. Tara wouldn't let anything detract from the main story of beautiful Jenny dying.

'I saw it, yes,' Sarah says. 'But a colleague told me too. I'm also a police officer.'

'Course. Mum told me. Stupid of me. It wasn't brave though. I mean, I didn't have time to be brave. Wasn't thinking really.'

'Well, I disagree,' Sarah says. She sits down next to her.

'Mum told me about Adam,' Rowena says. 'It's just so terrible. I mean, Adam's such a lovely boy. Well, you're his aunt, so you know what he's like.'

Her way of speaking is diffident, even when she's trying to make a forceful point. Her young face so earnest.

'You obviously know Adam?' Sarah says.

'Yes. I mean, he was only a baby really when I was at Sidley House with Jenny. But I got to know him last summer, when I was doing work experience there. I was his classroom assistant and he was just so . . . well, good. And thoughtful. Really polite. And that's pretty rare in boys his age. And it's just wrong what they're saying about him. Awful.'

I hadn't known that Rowena was courageous and neither had I seen that she's become kind and intuitive; as though paper has been put on Maisie's gentleness and Rowena is the brass-rubbing image.

'And *anyone* could have got in,' Rowena earnestly continues. 'Annette — she's the school secretary — well, she's pretty lax about security. Presses the buzzer to let people in without looking at the monitor on her desk. I don't want to get her into trouble, but it's important to tell the truth now that Adam's being blamed, isn't it?'

Sarah nods. 'Can you tell me what you remember from Wednesday?'

'Yes, but, well, which part?'

'How about from when you went to the school with Adam?'

'OK. He wanted to get his birthday cake. I knew he'd be a little embarrassed if his mum went with him. I mean, he loves his mum to bits, I know he does, but it's not cool in front of his friends, is it, to go with your mum? So I asked him if he'd like me to go with him. I had to get the medals anyway. I didn't hold his hand until we got to the road. Held it just for that bit. Sorry, that's not important, is it? Anyway, we went into the school together, and I went straight to the secretary's office and Adam went to get his cake.'

'On his own?'

'Yes. He was going to meet me again in the office, so we could walk back to sports day together. I should have gone with him, shouldn't I? If I had . . . '

She trails off, upset.

'Which floor is Adam's classroom on?' Sarah asks.

'The second. But it's the other side of the hallway from the Art room. That's where they said the fire started, isn't it? I mean, it's on the second floor too, but not close.'

She seems young and not terribly convincing as she tries to help Adam.

'So you were in the office, while Adam went to his classroom?' Sarah prompts.

'Yes. Annette was in there and she chatted to me about something silly. As per usual. And then the alarm went off. It was really loud. I went out of the office, calling for Adam. And then I heard Mum calling for me.'

'So you were with Annette in the office when the alarm went off?'

'Yes.'

Sarah must be crossing people off her list of suspects. The office is two floors beneath the Art room. Neither Rowena nor Annette could be the witness who supposedly saw Adam. And neither of them could have started the fire. Though I can't imagine Annette — let alone Rowena — as an arsonist.

'I saw Adam running out of the school,' Rowena continues. 'Mum told me to go outside with Addie and then she went to help with the reception children.'

'Do you remember if Adam was holding anything?'

'No. I'm sure he wasn't. I'd have noticed. Do you want me to tell someone that? Is it important?'

Sarah shakes her head. Presumably because DI Baker would say that Adam could easily have discarded the matches by then.

'Did you see anyone else?' Sarah asks.

'I'm not sure. I mean, I wasn't looking. I think I might have done. It was only a glimpse. I'm sorry, that's not helpful at all, but I can't remember any more.'

'If you do — '

'Yes, of course. I'll tell the police. Straight away. I am trying to remember but the more I try and think about it, the fainter it becomes until I'm not sure if I saw anyone at all and just imagined it.'

'OK,' Sarah says. 'So you went outside to join Adam. Can you tell me what happened then?'

'He was panicking, looking for Jenny. He said that she wasn't out at sports day. When I saw Annette come out, I asked her if she'd brought the office register. You know the book where you sign in and out? But she hadn't. She said it was OK because there was no one else in the building. I asked her if she was sure and she said that she was. The fire was really bad by then. I mean, there'd been this big bang, and loads more smoke and flames.' She looks upset. 'I never even thought that Jenny might still be in there.'

'Because Annette said everyone was out?'

'Not just that. I wouldn't have thought she was still up there in any case. I mean, I don't know her well, never have actually, which is silly really when we were at school together, but I'd have thought she'd gone outside. I mean, it must have been broiling up there and it was such a beautiful afternoon. Well, I don't think anyone would have expected her to sit in the medical room all afternoon in the baking heat. But she did.'

Was it because I'd implied she wasn't responsible enough to be school nurse?

'Then Adam saw his mother running into the

building shouting for Jenny,' Rowena continues. 'He tried to go after her. I had to stop him. It was awful.'

'And that's when you went in?'

She nods. Sarah seems about to say something else then sees the awkwardness in Rowena's face.

'Before you went in, when you were still outside on the gravel with Adam, do you remember how long it was until Annette came out to join you?'

'I suppose, yes, she wasn't there straight away. I mean, I remember Mum helping Tilly, the reception teacher, and I was with Addie. I suppose if I had to guess, it would be a few minutes.'

'Your mum said she had lipstick on.'

'I don't remember that. Is it important?'

'It's a little odd to put on lipstick,' Sarah says, 'in the circumstances, don't you think?'

I think she's confiding in Rowena to win her trust a little so that Rowena will confide more in return. Maybe she's sensed Rowena is keeping something from her.

'I don't know if it's odd,' Rowena says stiffly. 'And I didn't notice. I'm not much good at things like make-up, actually.'

She's so awkward and I feel for her. I bumped into her and Maisie in Westfield a couple of months ago. Her clothes were dowdy and despite being spotty she had no make-up on. I thought she was a plain girl who wasn't helping herself look prettier. I'd hoped that Maisie was going to try and get her some nice clothes or make-up. I wince as I remember how superficial I was about appearances.

'You said you were Adam's classroom assistant last summer,' Sarah says. 'Does that mean you were assisting Silas Hyman?'

'No. Addie was still in year two then. Mr Hyman teaches year three.'

'Did you get to know him?'

Rowena shakes her head. 'He wouldn't have talked to someone like me. Wouldn't have noticed me.'

'But you noticed him?'

'Well, he's very good-looking, isn't he?'

'What did you think of him?'

Rowena hesitates a moment, then looks away from Sarah. 'I thought he could be violent.'

'Was that because of what he said at the prize-giving?'

'I wasn't at the prize-giving.'

'So what made you think that?'

I think it's the years of violence by her father, which makes her more perceptive to viciousness — like bruised skin being more sensitive to touch.

'I used to watch him sometimes,' Rowena says. 'It was easy because he never looked at me so he didn't notice me watching him.'

'You saw through him?'

'I don't think it's like that, like he's hiding the real person inside. More like he's two different people.'

'One good, one bad?'

'I know it sounds strange, silly, but if you read about it, I mean literature going way back when, it's something that's been happening for centuries. You know morality tales in the Middle

255

Ages, the good angel and the devil? And the Jacobean plays with fighting for someone's soul. It's not the person's *fault* the devil is there. You have to help that person get rid of him.'

Was she talking about Silas Hyman or her father? She wasn't doing English for A level so must have scoured books looking for something to make sense of it all — to make things better. Because if there is a devil and an angel in her father, then one day the devil can be banished and the angel will win out and her dad will love her.

'You said to me that you weren't really thinking,' Sarah says. 'When you went into the school.'

'That's right.'

'You were thinking enough to get a towel and soak it in water.'

'I should have taken three, shouldn't I? And I didn't do any good. Didn't help.' She starts to cry. 'Sorry. Being a twit.'

The same word that Maisie uses about herself; a middle-aged, self-denigrating word.

'Don't say that, please don't,' I say to her. 'It's not a word that any teenager should use. Especially not you. You went into a burning building, for God's sake.'

'Mum?'

I see Jenny has come in.

'She did. And don't tell me it was all about Donald, and some wish to make her father proud.'

'OK . . . '

'You're not a victim, Rowena, you listen to me!

256

You're *gutsy* and *resourceful*. And whatever made you do it — *whatever* the reason — you're extraordinary. And I will not let your father's abuse blind me — or anyone else — to your bravery.'

'Blimey, Mum, you socked it to her. In a good way, I mean.'

'Shame she can't hear me.'

'I'm sure she will, one day. Everyone will. In stereo. I'll tell them too.'

Sarah is looking through her notes. 'If I could just go back to the secretary for a moment?' she says. 'Are you sure that she said everyone was out?'

'Yes. Definitely. Later, I mean after Jenny had been brought out, she said that Jenny had signed herself out. Said she remembered her doing it.'

'It would explain why your phone was outside,' I say to Jen.

'Maybe,' she says, her voice unusually quiet. I see that she looks pale and tense, her fingers knotting together.

'I can't remember, Mum. I can't fucking remember. Sorry. It just doesn't make sense. Why would I sign myself out, then go in again? But why would Annette lie?'

20

Sarah finds the nurse who was with Rowena earlier.

'The injuries to Rowena White's hands, do you think they were an accident?' she asks. 'I mean, the more recent damage?'

So she's guessed.

'You're Jenny's aunt, right?'

'Yes. I'm also a police officer.'

'Have you got ID?'

Sarah digs in her bag for her warrant card and shows it — Detective Sergeant McBride. 'My married name,' she says.

'OK. I don't think the injuries were accidental. At least, I can't see how she could have got them if she tripped. The blisters on the tops of her hands have been damaged too.'

I remember Donald brutally gripping hold of her bandaged hands. Rowena's quiet scream of pain.

'Do you know when the injuries happened?'

'No. But the blisters were undamaged at four thirty yesterday, because I changed her dressings myself. But then I went off shift at five.'

'Do you know who was on after you?'

'Belinda Edwards. I'll find her for you.'

★ ★ ★

Ten minutes later, Sarah is with Belinda, the briskly competent nurse who showed Donald to

Rowena's room yesterday. She carefully checks Sarah's warrant card.

'It was after her father visited,' she says.

'You're sure?'

'I'm not saying it *was* him. But I spoke to her when I arrived on my shift and she was fine, cheerful even. Her father came to see her shortly afterwards, about five fifteen. He wasn't with her long. When he'd gone, I went in to give her her usual drugs. She and her mother were distressed. Rowena was trying not to show how much pain she was in, but it had clearly increased. I took the dressings off her hands and saw that the blisters had burst on both hands.'

'She told you she tripped . . . ?' Sarah asks.

'Yes, and that she put her hands out to save herself. But that wouldn't explain the damage on the tops of her hands too. I asked a doctor to examine her and she gave him the same story.'

'Do you have Rowena's past medical record?'

'We're not computerised yet — well, not successfully, so I'll have to chase up the hard copy from records.'

'And can you get Maisie White's, her mother's?'

Belinda's eyes meet Sarah's and an unspoken accord passes between them.

'I'll chase that up for you in the same way,' she says.

'Thank you.'

'We're concerned about the infection risk,' Belinda says. 'So she'll be remaining with us for a few days yet.'

259

* * *

Sarah is going to go to the police station. Jenny and I go with her towards the exit of the hospital. I don't want Jen to go outside.

'We need to know everything in case we're the ones who have to put it all together,' I say to her. 'Can you stay here in case Donald comes back? We need to watch him too.'

Giving her a job to do, as I used to years ago — sifting the icing sugar so she wouldn't mind that it was me taking the cake tins out of the too-hot-for-children oven.

'You're *sure* it doesn't hurt you?' she asks.

'Hardly at all.'

She looks at me, unconvinced.

'Apart from colds, I'm actually very resilient.'

'I shouldn't have said that, I'm sorry. God, you went into a burning building and — '

'It's fine, Jen, really.'

She looks at me, and there's something else. I wait.

'How long d'you think it takes, from Barbados?'

'About nine hours,' I say.

She smiles a shy, happy smile and I hate Ivo for making her smile like that and for what will happen when he gets here.

* * *

I leave the hospital with Sarah, shedding the protective skin of its walls, but for a little while, maybe a minute or more, I feel alright. Then the

260

pain hits. The gravel path leading to the car park cuts into my unprotected feet. It's still early but the bright sun reflects off the cars with dazzling, migrainous intensity.

In the car Sarah talks to Roger on her hands-free, finishing their earlier argument; words starched, voices stiff. He accuses her of forgetting it was 'your son's' deadline for his course-work this week. She tells him that you need her more. He says she should start allocating her time 'more carefully'. She tells him there's a call waiting. She hangs up and blares her horn — too loud, too long — at a van hogging a box junction. She drives the rest of the way in silence.

For the first time I feel like an eavesdropper or spy.

She parks and we walk to Chiswick police station along a heat-baked concrete pavement, the road sweating tarmac. Next to the police station is the Eco shop, with its growing roof and plant-covered walls. I want to stop outside and breathe its newly made oxygen and window-shop, as I often have with Jenny, at the eclectic display.

I used to think that in the police station next door Sarah would be in her element. She was ideally suited, I thought, to a job that had uniforms and numbers and name badges and ranks clearly marked. Everyone and everything labelled; strict protocols to be followed; rules and laws to be adhered to and implemented. I'd think that if Sarah hadn't been a police officer (she drummed that word into me after my first calamitous police-*woman* mistake) then she'd have been an officer in the army in some kind of organisational role.

Because I didn't want to think her brave and driven and doing something worthwhile.

And it was easy to believe myself because up until now the police didn't seem important or connected to us. Yes, they keep criminals off the streets, but Chiswick hardly has any litter, let alone muggers or murderers on the newly widened, Bugaboo-friendly pavements. The worst vandalism we get is fly-posting for music festivals and the occasional poster for a missing cat. From newspapers and TV I thought the police were, on the whole, bolters of doors when the murderers and bombers had already done their worst and left in their stolen cars.

But now crime isn't 'out there' but exploding into my family and the police are crucial to our lives.

We go inside the police station and down a corridor with paint-peeling walls and concrete floors, which smell strongly of cleaning fluid, the same one that is used in the hospital; an archetypal institutional smell; only this institution has crime not injury as its raison d'être.

We pass offices with phones ringing for too long and loud male voices and pieces of paper pinned with seemingly no particular order onto old notice boards. Such a scruffy, chaotic place for Sarah; not the neat organised place I'd imagined.

A young woman police officer comes down the corridor. She hugs Sarah and asks her about Jenny and me. And then an older male officer

262

takes her hand as he passes her and says how sorry he is and asks if there's anything he can do. *Anything*.

★ ★ ★

We go into a main office area, which reeks of deodorant and sweat, fans overhead whirring noisily and ineffectually against the heat. And everyone in here comes up to ask after Jenny and me, to offer sympathy, to give her a hug or hold her hand for a moment. Everyone knows her. Everyone minds about her. I realise she is loved and valued here. I'd been right about this place being her element, but for the wrong reasons.

She goes into a side-office and an attractive man in his thirties, with caramel-coloured skin, virtually runs across the small space and puts his arms around her and holds her tightly. He's not wearing a uniform so must be CID. His cream cotton shirt has sweat patches under his arms. There isn't even a fan in here.

'Hi, Mohsin,' she says, as he hugs her.

'You ran the sympathy gauntlet, then?' he asks.

'Something like that.'

'Poor baby.'

Baby? Sarah? Behind them, a woman in her twenties is pretending to look at a computer monitor. A sharply cut auburn bob frames her angular face. She's the only person who hasn't offered sympathy.

'Penny?' Sarah says, and the severe-featured young woman turns to her. 'Where are we on the hate-mail investigation?'

'I'm going over the original statements now. Tony and Pete are trying to locate footage from the CCTV camera, which records the postbox where the third letter was posted. The Nationwide Building Society had it installed last year, and the postbox is next to it.'

'I think the hate mail could well be linked to the arson attack,' Sarah says.

Penny and Mohsin say nothing.

'Alright,' Sarah says, tight-lipped. 'Maybe it is just an extraordinary coincidence that Jenny was sent hate mail and then her place of work was set on fire and she was the only member of staff to be badly injured.'

'But the campaign against her had stopped, right?' Penny asks, and I hope to God that Ivo — if he actually bothers to come — will tell them about the red paint attack just a few weeks ago.

'If it turns out there is a link to the fire,' Penny continues, 'then for now that will just have to be a fortunate by-product. It can't be a focus of the malicious mail investigation.'

'We need a connection, honey,' Mohsin says. 'Something that links the hate-mail campaign with the arson attack.'

'Her oxygen may have been tampered with,' Sarah says.

Penny's eyes flick to hers. 'May?'

'It's being downplayed,' Sarah continues. 'By the hospital and by Baker. But I think someone tried to make sure they finished the job.'

'Downplayed?' Penny asks and I see the irritation on Sarah's face.

'Baker's lazy, we all know that.'

264

'But not that incompetent,' Penny retorts. She turns back to her computer screen.

'Who was this witness who supposedly saw my nephew?' Sarah asks, going closer to her.

'Detective Inspector Baker has made it absolutely clear that the witness's anonymity must be respected.'

Her harshness reminds me of Tara. But at least she wears her toughness on the outside, so gives fair warning.

Sarah turns to Mohsin.

'It's not in the file?'

'No,' responds Penny. 'DI Baker thought you might come asking for it. He's pretty astute about you.'

'Not about much else,' Sarah snaps. 'So he's hidden it?'

'He's just respecting the witness's right to privacy and anonymity.'

'How handy for him that someone comes along and does his work for him.'

Mohsin tries to put his arm round her again, but she moves away from him.

'And he's cheap. How much overtime has he signed off recently? It would be a big-budget number to do a full-scale arson and attempted murder investigation. The witness gave him a gift-wrapped package. This way he doesn't have to spend any time or money on it but gets a great clear-up rate. A model of twenty-first-century policing.'

Penny is going to the door.

'I'll tell you what Tony and Pete find out,' she says.

'Has anyone investigated Silas Hyman's alibi?' Sarah asks.

'Take that compassionate leave,' Penny says as she leaves, her personality as angular as her haircut, all sharp corners.

Sarah is alone with Mohsin.

'Jesus,' Sarah says. 'Does she always have to speak like there's a cork up her bum?'

He laughs and I'm frankly a little shocked. Sarah doesn't talk that way. And I've never seen her be so physical with someone before, apart from you, her little brother. But I can't believe she's having an affair; not *Sarah*, of all people, surely? She's just too law-abiding to break the first rule of marriage.

'Do you know who the witness is?' she asks him.

'No, I don't. You might not like Penny, but she *is* good.'

'So it was Penny who took the statement? I thought it must have been. Sod's bloody law, isn't it? The one person guaranteed not to help me.'

'True. But if the witness was dodgy in any way Penny would have been onto it. She's a bloody sniffer-dog-Rottweiler-mix that woman.'

'Can you get her to tell you who it was?'

'I can't believe you asked me that.'

'Well, can you?'

'You've never even broken a rule, let alone a law. Let alone asked someone to do that for you.'

'Mohsin . . . '

'You've never even *filed* something incorrectly before.'

She turns away from him.

'You know how the *files* sit around on that stack of trays after they've been typed up,' he continues. 'And people seem to find better things to do than put them where they're meant to be? It's woefully insecure, that area. Probably completely contravenes the data protection act. I'm sure that the anonymous witness statement isn't left so open to abuse like that. But other transcripts . . . '

'Yeah, thanks.' She lightly kisses his caramel-coloured cheek.

'So how's that husband of yours?' he asks.

She pauses a moment.

'You think that when it comes to it, when it really *matters*, that someone'll be more than they are the rest of the time. Better, somehow. You hope that someone will be like that, for you, when it counts.'

'So are you still going to wait till Mark's eighteen?'

'I don't know.'

'It was a mad idea.'

'Maybe. But neither of us wants the boys to go through a divorce. Not until they're grown-up. I told you that.'

'You breeders. So many complications.'

'You pervs. So few commitments.'

She goes to the door. 'Can I ask you a favour?' He nods.

'There's a printer's called Prescoes, which printed the school calendar for Sidley House some time before Christmas. They had their name printed on the back, but no contact number. Could you get hold of them and find out how many they printed?'

'No problem. Be careful, won't you?'

'Yup.'

'Call me. If you need to. Any time.'

'Thanks.'

So Sarah has a best mate I never knew about, who she can speak to in a language she never uses to anyone else — well, certainly not whenever I'd been with her. I'm glad for her.

I'm not sure if you know that her marriage to Roger has an end date. But I don't think you'll be surprised that it's been planned with such thought. It fits with the highly organised, practical woman I've known for so many years. And also with the kind, emotionally generous woman I've met in the last two days.

I go with her to a room where there are boxes and files of paperwork. She takes a file and tucks it under her jacket, hiding it. Her hands are shaking.

I know Sarah's done lots of dangerous things — chased armed criminals and tackled violent strangers hugely bigger than her — but I thought it was attention-seeking bravado. 'Look at me, everyone!' I didn't know about this quiet courage.

She goes into a photocopier room and starts to make copies. The door suddenly opens behind her. She starts. An older man comes in. From the pips on his shoulder he's clearly senior to her.

'Sarah? What on earth are you doing here?'

I feel dread for her.

'Haven't we given you compassionate leave?' he continues.

'Yes.'

'So stop whatever work you're doing and get off home. Or to the hospital. Work will be waiting for you when you return. You may think that it's better to bury yourself in it, but frankly it's probably not a wise thing to do.'

'No. Thank you.'

'I'm sorry. About your niece and sister-in-law.'

'Yes.'

'And your nephew. We all are.'

He leaves. She hurriedly stuffs the photocopies into her handbag, not folding them first, scrunching them. I don't know if she's managed to photocopy all the documents she needs.

She takes the file back to where she got it, holding it under the left-hand side of her jacket, pinned down with her arm. She's sweating, her hair sticking to her forehead.

With the file returned, she hurries back down the corridor.

We are almost at the exit and I am also selfishly relieved because the pain is overwhelming me now, as if I am made of it.

'Hey, you!'

A young man is hurrying towards her. I notice his fine features and grey eyes and youth, no more than his mid-twenties. He is astonishingly handsome. For some reason, he makes me think of that reading you wanted to have at our wedding — 'My lover leaping like a gazelle' from the 'Song of Songs'; lithe and beautiful. (At six months pregnant, I'd worried the congregation

269

would burst out laughing.)

'You forgot something,' he says to her.

They are alone in the institutional corridor, which smells of the cleaning fluid.

He kisses her, full on the mouth, a powerful sexual kiss that melts her bones and fills the moment because while they kiss she allows herself to be lost from the real world and enter this one. I turn away, remembering the first time I kissed you; your mouth closing onto mine and becoming an open doorway to a different, intensely physical place.

I know that while he kisses her, for these long seconds, she forgets Jenny and me and Adam and your suffering. Forgets the illegal copies stuffed into her handbag and her promise to you. A gift of a kiss.

Then she pulls away.

'We can't do this any more,' she says. 'I'm sorry.'

As she walks away I see she has kicked him harder than he's ever been kicked before and how much it hurts him. I see that despite the age difference, and that he is beautiful while she is not, that he is in love with her. I wonder if she knows.

I've never really thought through what it must have been like for Sarah when your parents died and you were still a child. I'd assumed that teenage Sarah, like the adult, was naturally responsible. But was she forced to be that way? Because inside her rule-abiding, responsible, sensible persona there's a risk-taking, life-grabbing person. Maybe it's taken to her mid-forties to let out her teenage self.

No wonder her marriage with Roger is over.

We leave the police station together and I wish I'd known her like this before. Wish we'd gone for a drink together, become friends. You always wanted me to spend more time with her, on our own, but like a recalcitrant child I resented being made to play with someone I didn't think I liked.

The truth is, I was jealous of her. I know, I never said, and you don't understand why not. Well, it's partly because I didn't dare acknowledge it, even to myself, especially to myself, only occasionally daring to sneak a look edgeways-on. But now I see it clearly. Don't worry, it's not about you. There's no weird kind of Antigone-brother thing going on (and I know you know about Antigone because I made you go to a three-hour production at the Barbican — sorry).

This jealousy thing is about Sarah's career. Because what she does *matters*. I know that fully now.

And I also know that jealousy is a shaky foundation on which to build an opinion of someone. No wonder it's collapsing.

★   ★   ★

Jenny is waiting in the goldfish-bowl vestibule.

'Are you OK?' she asks.

'Yes.'

As soon as I was back here again the pain stopped. But at the police station the floor had turned to spikes and in the car the air scorched my no-skin self.

271

I tell her about the illicit photocopies.

'Did you meet him?' Jenny asks.

'Who?' I say.

She shrugs and looks uncomfortable and I realise she means Sarah's gazelle lover.

'You know about him?' I ask.

She nods.

The surprising thing is that I don't feel jealous of Sarah being close to Jenny in that way — but of Jenny. Sarah would never confide in me about him.

We follow Sarah as she takes the corridor towards the cafeteria.

'Why isn't she going to Dad?' Jen asks.

'Probably wants to read it through for herself first.'

★ ★ ★

The Palms Café is brightly lit, but I still sense the shadow of Maisie and Sarah's conversation last night about Silas Hyman. '*Violent . . . vicious . . . But he gets people to love him.*'

Sarah takes a piece of paper out of her bag and tries to smooth out the crumples. Across the top is a border in the black-and-white chessboard pattern of the police. Underneath in whiteout letters against a black strip is 'RESTRICTED — FOR POLICE ONLY'.

21

Annette Jenks's name and occupation — school secretary — is on the cover sheet, with her contact details. Annette was with Rowena when the alarm went off; she couldn't have started it. But she was in charge of who came in.

'This is illegal, right?' Jen asks.

I nod.

As Sarah turns the page to read the transcript, a woman in a cleaner's uniform comes up. 'You eating?'

Sarah goes to buy a sandwich as rent for her table, taking the statement with her, and we wait. The cleaner sprays the table next door with some kind of pungent fluid, wiping the Formica clean.

'Did you get to know Annette Jenks?' I ask Jenny.

'My soulmate?'

You've never met Annette so you don't have an image in your head of an overly made-up twenty-two-year-old with talon-nails who looks as if she's about to go clubbing at eight twenty in the morning.

'I try to avoid her,' Jen continues. 'But she often collars me. Always has some big drama-queen number going on.'

I look at her to go on.

'Oh, you know, has a friend of a friend who's been *murdered* or has married a Mormon with seven wives already or got the bridesmaid *pregnant* at his own wedding. I'm not sure if that was the Mormon. And there's always some starring role for her.'

Does she relish what's happened to us, stirring it into her bland life like pepper sauce?

'Remember that guy in the States who pretended his child was in the runaway hot-air balloon?' Jenny says. 'If Annette had a child she'd *put him in it*.'

I smile but feel uneasy.

'She used to try and grease up to me because of Dad,' Jenny continues. 'She's desperate to get on telly. She'd entered all these auditions for reality TV shows.'

'Do you think she and Silas could be in a relationship?' I ask.

She gives me one of her withering looks.

'She's very, well, alluring,' I say. Her on-display cleavage was something of a standing joke amongst us buttoned-up mothers. 'And you said yourself that he was unhappy in his marriage.'

'Even if he was having an affair, I expect he'd want at least a scattering of brain cells. Anyway he'd left before she started working there.'

'Yes, but — '

I stop as Sarah returns with her sandwich. She turns over the cover page. At the top is a key: PP stands for Detective Sergeant Penny Pierson. I think of the sharp-featured young woman I'd just seen at the police station. AJ stands for Annette Jenks.

The time of the statement is 6.00 p.m. on Wednesday.

'They didn't hang about before interviewing people,' Jenny says. 'But why talk to Annette so quickly?'

'Probably because she lets people into the school.'

I also want to know who she let in on Wednesday afternoon.

And whether she's telling the truth about Jenny signing herself out.

We read the document with Sarah.

PP: Can you outline for me your duties at the school?

AJ: Yes, I'm the secretary, so I sort out the mail, take phone calls, that kind of thing. Couriers leave things in my office, I sign for them, you know, the usual. I also get the registers and send out the letters for Mrs Healey. And I buzz people in through the gate, though in the mornings a teacher sometimes stands by the gate, kind of a welcoming thing, and it means I don't need to do it, which is lucky because it's in the mornings that parents come in here asking for all sorts of things, like I don't have enough to do.

PP: Anything else?

[AJ shakes head.]

Elizabeth Fisher had been the school nurse as well as the secretary. Why didn't Annette Jenks have that role too? If she had, Jenny wouldn't have been up in that sick-room. She wouldn't have been hurt.

Yes, it would have been Annette. Yes, I would

rather it had been her than Jenny. Anyone other than Jenny, apart from Adam. Motherhood isn't soft and cosy and sweet, it's selfish ferocity; red in tooth and claw.

PP: I'd like to ask you about who you let in earlier today.

AJ: You think it was deliberate? I mean, like arson? It's a bit weird, isn't it? To suddenly get a fire, like, out of nowhere? I mean, yeah, it's hot. But it's not hot like Australia, is it? I mean, we don't get bush fires, stuff like that. Not in a building.

'I told you,' Jenny says, seeing my expression. 'I bet she loved this, being interviewed by the police.'

The drama queen finally gets her stage.

PP: If we could return to who you let in?

AJ: Just the usual. I mean, no one I didn't know.

PP: I'll ask you for a list a little later. This afternoon, during sports day, who did you let in?

AJ: There were a couple of children who needed to use the toilets and Mrs Banks, the year-two teacher, was with them. We have to call people Mr and Mrs at school. It's very stuck up. But they weren't here long. There were a couple more teachers who'd forgotten something or other. Not for long either. Then there was Adam Covey and Rowena White, and then her mum.

She's always very polite, Mrs White, waves a thank-you at the camera so I see it on the screen. Hardly anyone does that.

PP: Anybody else?

AJ: No.

PP: You're sure?

AJ: Yeah.

PP: You said you have a screen.

AJ: Yeah, it's linked up to a camera on the gate so I can see who it is before pressing the buzzer.

PP: Do you always look at it before pushing the buzzer?

AJ: Yeah, not much point having it if I don't, is there?

PP: But it must be tempting when you're busy just to push the button and let them in.

AJ: Course I look at the bloody screen. Sorry. It's stress. I mean it's just so tragic, isn't it? What's happened. Tragic.

'That's bollocks,' Jen says. 'I've *seen* her press the buzzer and not look at the screen. She's done it while she's talked to me, for Christ's sake. Doesn't she get how important this is?'

It's what Rowena had said too, in a milder way.

I look again at the word 'tragic'. It's as if Annette had thought about it for a while and found the appropriately dramatic label.

PP: What about earlier in the day?

AJ: You mean like somebody came and hid?

PP: Could you please answer the question?

AJ: No, just the usual. People who are a part of the school. One or two suppliers, bringing things in.

PP: Do you know these suppliers?

AJ: Yeah, a caterer and a cleaning guy. They go round to the side entrance into the school, the building, I mean. Everyone has to come in through the main gate.

PP: Do you think it's possible that someone could have got in?

AJ: Dunno. But if they did, it wasn't me who let them in.

PP: I'd now like to talk about the immediate events around the time of the fire. Where were you when the fire alarm sounded?

AJ: In the office. As per usual.

PP: On your own?

AJ: No. Rowena White was with me. She'd come into the office to get the medals for sports day.

PP: You're sure Rowena White was with you?

AJ: Yeah. I was telling her about a friend of mine's problems when the alarm went off. Christ, it made a din.

Like Sarah earlier, Penny was presumably crossing suspects off a list.

PP: You said that as part of your job, you keep the registers. Can you explain how that works?

AJ: Well, yeah, at eight forty and again after lunch the teachers tick off all the kids in their class against the class register. Any kid

278

who isn't there is marked as absent. The register is brought to me in the office — a kid usually does it, like a treat. Anyways, if a kid arrives after the register's taken they have to sign in a different register that I keep on a shelf in my office. Anyone leaving before the end of the school day has to sign themselves out in that too.

PP: Anyone being who?

AJ: Kids, mainly, leaving early because they've got to get to the dentist's or whatever. But adults too, sometimes, like parent readers.

PP: And teachers?

AJ: Yeah, but hardly ever. I mean, they get in before me and leave later. Mrs Healey makes them work like dogs. But teaching assistants, well, they're different. I mean, it's like me. An eight-thirty-to-five deal and any excuse to leave early. So they sign themselves out.

PP: What did you do after the fire alarm went off?

AJ: I went outside.

She hasn't told Penny that she waited for five minutes before going outside. Nor what she was doing in that time. Presumably Penny didn't know to ask her.

AJ: I gave Tilly Rogers, that's the reception teacher, the register for her class, but there wasn't any need. I mean, she knew all the kids were there. Then I saw a boy getting hysterical. By that statue. Rowena was

279

trying to calm him down, but he was just getting more wound up.

PP: Do you know the child's name?

AJ: Now I know, I mean, I realise now why he was like that. Anyways, Rowena asked me if I'd seen Jenny. I said not to worry, that I knew she wasn't inside. I knew, OK. Everyone gives me that look, but I knew.

PP: How did you know?

AJ: Because she'd signed herself out. In the register I was telling you about. The one in my office. Look at it yourself if you don't believe me.

PP: You think a paper register survived the fire?

It doesn't give a tone of voice but I imagine Penny's was contemptuous. Wooden window frames and plaster and carpets didn't survive the fire, so how the hell would paper?

AJ: She signed herself out, right? In the register. I remember her doing it.

PP: What time was that?

AJ: Around three, I suppose. I didn't check the time.

PP: Didn't she write the time in the register?

AJ: I watched her sign out but I didn't go and check what she'd written. Why should I?

PP: Why didn't you bring the register out?

AJ: I didn't think it mattered. I just thought the reception-class one mattered.

PP: Surely the whole point of that register is to know who's in the building in case of fire?

AJ: Look, I'm new, OK? Only been here a term.

They had a fire practice a few weeks back but I was off sick. Even if I had brought the register out it wouldn't have made no difference, right? It would have said Jenny was out of the building. Shown her bloody signature. Proved what I am telling you now. That she signed herself out.

I glance at Jen, enough to know that she still can't remember and that it's tearing her up.

'Perhaps she just doesn't want everyone to think it was her fault,' I say.

Because why on earth would Jenny go in again?

PP: When did you realise that Jennifer Covey was still in the building?
AJ: I saw her mother running in, yelling for her. And then that daft cow went in too.
PP: Do you mean Rowena White?
AJ: Yeah. There were fire engines coming up the road by then. She should have left it up to them, not made their job even harder for them. They ended up having to rescue her too. Not sure what she was trying to prove. She must have wanted the attention.

I hear Annette Jenks's jealousy without needing to listen to her voice. Because when it came down to it, the drama queen failed to do anything remotely deserving of attention. I can almost taste the bitterness of her words. She'll be seething now about Rowena's small mention in the *Richmond Post*.

281

[Detective Sergeant Baker asks PP out of the room. After three minutes PP returns.]
PP: Do you know Silas Hyman?

I remember Sarah telling you that the head teacher or a governor would have given the police information on anyone who could have a grudge against the school, *'straight off the bat'*. So someone, presumably Sally Healey, had told the police about Silas Hyman.

Perfect recall and logic and they think I'm a cabbage.

AJ: I've no idea who Silas Hyman is. What kind of a name is Silas anyways?
PP: He was a teacher at the school, who left in April.
AJ: I wouldn't know him then, would I? Only started working there in May.
PP: You've never heard of him?
AJ: As I said, only started at the place in May.
PP: Nobody gossiped about him?
AJ: No.
PP: A teacher who'd been fired only a few weeks before and there was no gossip?
[AJ shakes head.]
PP: I must say that I find it hard to believe.

My respect for the harsh-faced PP goes up a notch.

'You see,' Jenny says. 'Silas and Annette didn't even know each other. Let alone have an affair.'

Sarah gets another crumpled statement out of her bag.

282

Her mobile rings and she starts, as if someone has seen her. I go closer and hear Mohsin's voice at the other end.

'Prescoes, that printing company, they printed three hundred copies of the Sidley House calendar. Does that help at all?'

'Three hundred people knew that it was Adam's birthday on Wednesday. And also that it was sports day so the school would be virtually empty. What about the witness?'

'Sorry, honey, Penny won't budge on that, and no one else is talking to me either. They probably don't trust me. Fuck knows why.'

She thanks him and hangs up. Then she smooths out the next crumpled statement.

The key this time is SH for Sally Healey. The interviewer is AB — Detective Inspector Baker. The time it started was 5.55 p.m. The interviews were almost concurrent.

22

I remember Sally Healey on telly the evening of the fire — her pink linen shirt and cream trousers and assembly voice and immaculate make-up. And how the carefully assembled frontage had started to fall apart.

AB: Can you tell me who you knew to be in the building at the time of the fire?

SH: Yes. There was one reception class. Our other reception class was at the zoo. All their names are in the register I gave you. There was also Annette Jenks, the school secretary; Tilly Rogers, a reception teacher; and, of course, Jennifer Covey, who's a temporary classroom assistant.

AB: Was every other member of staff out of the building?

SH: Yes, at sports day. We needed all of them. We are ambitious in the number of activities and it would be chaotic unless there were enough staff to run things smoothly.

'Christ,' Jenny says. 'Even now she's trying to promote the school.'

AB: Did you see any members of staff return to the building?

SH: Yes, Rowena White. Or, at least, I didn't see

her but I was told she'd gone to get the medals.

AB: Anyone else?

SH: No.

AB: I know one of my officers asked you about this at the scene of the fire, but if you'd bear with me, I need to go over the same territory again.

SH: Of course.

AB: How easy is it for people to get into the school?

SH: We have one entrance to the school, which is a locked gate. It has a numerical keypad. Only members of staff know the code. Everyone else needs to be buzzed in from the office. Unfortunately, there have been instances in the past where parents have been irresponsible and held open the gate for someone, without checking. We had an incident when a complete stranger got into the school because a parent inadvertently held the gate open for him. Since then we have had a monitor installed and our school secretary has to watch exactly who she is letting in.

AB: So you think your school is secure?

SH: Absolutely. Security for the children is our top priority.

'Like Annette can be bothered to watch the monitor,' Jenny says scathingly.

'Mrs Healey must know what she's like, surely?'

'Yes. I don't suppose she did when she hired her.'

285

'And she knows that parents and some children know the code?'

'Gets really annoyed about it.'

If she's lying about the security on the gate, what else might she be lying about?

AB: Do you know of anyone who has a grudge against the school?

SH: No, of course not.

AB: I have to tell you that it looks, at this stage, as if the fire was arson. So can you please think if there is anyone who may have a grudge against the school?

[SH is silent.]

AB: Mrs Healey?

SH: How could someone do this?

There are no stage directions for her mood at this point — misery? fury? panic?

AB: Can you answer the question, please.

SH: I cannot think of anyone who would want to do this.

AB: Perhaps a member of staff who —

[SH interrupts.]

SH: No one would do this.

AB: Have any members of staff left the school recently? Say, in the last six months to a year?

SH: But that's nothing to do with the fire.

AB: Please answer the question.

SH: Yes. Two. Elizabeth Fisher, our former school secretary. And Silas Hyman, a year-three teacher.

AB: What were the circumstances?

SH: Elizabeth Fisher was getting too old to be able to do the job. So sadly I had to let her go. There were no hard feelings. Though I know she misses the children a great deal.

AB: I'll need her contact details, if that's possible?

SH: Yes. I have her number and address in my palmtop.

AB: You also said Silas Hyman, a year-three teacher?

SH: Yes. Circumstances there were more unfortunate. There was an accident in the playground when he was on duty.

AB: When was this?

SH: The last week of March. I had to ask him to leave. As I said, health and safety is our top priority.

AB: You actually said security was your top priority.

SH: It all lumps in together, in the end, doesn't it? Keeping the children safe from physical or criminal harm.

The words 'or both' must have hung in the air but weren't recorded.

AB: Are Silas Hyman's contact details also in your palmtop?

SH: Yes. I haven't updated it.

AB: Can you write them down for me.

SH: Now?

AB: Yes.

[SH writes down Silas Hyman's details.]

287

AB: If you could please excuse me one moment.
[AB leaves the room and returns six minutes
later.]

Baker must have gone to tell Penny about Silas
Hyman. Presumably he also sent someone to
find him — he'd told you the police had spoken
to Silas Hyman that evening.

AB: We were talking about school security. Can
you tell me about the fire regulations at the
school?

SH: We have appropriate fire-fighting equipment — extinguishers both foam and
water, as well as fire blankets and sand
buckets on every floor and in vulnerable
areas such as the kitchen. The walking
distance to the nearest extinguisher does
not exceed thirty metres. Staff are trained in
the use of appropriate equipment. We have
signed exits, both pictorially and in writing,
in every classroom and in rooms such as
the Art room, dining room and kitchen. We
also routinely practise evacuating the
building. We have certified smoke detectors
and heat detectors, which are linked directly
through to the fire station. We have
quarterly, yearly and three-yearly mainte-
nance and testing by a qualified engineer as
required by BS 5839.

'It sounds like she's memorised it all,' Jen says,
and I agree with her, but why?

AB: You have all those facts to hand?

So AB noticed this too.

SH: I am the head teacher of a primary school. As I just told you, safety is my number-one concern. I delegated myself as the fire safety manager. So yes, I have the facts to hand.

AB: Firefighters reported that windows at the top of the school were wide open. Can you comment on that?

SH: No. That's not possible. We have window locks to prevent them being opened more than ten centimetres.

AB: Where are the keys to the window locks kept?

SH: In the teacher's desk. But surely . . .

She must have trailed off at this point. I imagine again that figure going to the top of the school, but now more was required before he could fling open the windows and let the breeze suck the fire upwards.

AB: You said your staff were trained to put out fires?

SH Yes. Clearly containment, alongside evacuation, is the best method of minimising the impact of a fire.

AB: But the staff were all out at sports day? Apart from the three you told me about?

[SH nods.]

AB: Why was Jennifer Covey inside the school

and not at sports day too?

SH: She was in charge of the medical room. For minor injuries.

AB: Where is the medical room?

SH: On the third floor.

AB: At the top of the building?

SH: Yes. We used to use the secretary's office. Elizabeth was a qualified nurse. There was a sofa in there and we had a blanket. Just to hold the fort until a parent arrived to take the child home. But the new secretary isn't medically trained in any way so there was no point keeping it there. Mr Davidson, our head of upper school, has it on his floor. He's our trained first-aider but he was needed at sports day.

AB: How long had you known that Jennifer Covey would be the nurse this afternoon?

SH: Nurse is a little grand for the title. Clearly I didn't expect a girl that age to deal with anything remotely serious.

'I did a St John Ambulance training, you witch,' Jenny says as she reads it and I'm glad she's focused on Sally Healey's answer and not Baker's question. Because right at the beginning he'd suspected the fire was aimed at her. I suppose he'd have put her name in the computer and the hate-mail case would have come up instantly.

AB: If you could answer my question. How long had you known that Jennifer Covey would be the nurse this afternoon?

290

SH: I announced it at the Thursday staff meeting last week. It wasn't my original plan but I decided that in view of Jennifer's consistently inappropriate clothes during the hot weather it would be better if she wasn't in view of the parents.

'She *is* a witch, Mum,' Jenny says.

AB: Original plan?
SH: Initially I'd allocated the job to Rowena White. Rowena has done a St John Ambulance course. She was upset about the change but I felt it was appropriate.

Jenny turns to me. 'Do you think Rowena could have told her father she was going to be nurse, to make him proud, same old, but then didn't tell him when I replaced her?'
'Maybe,' I say.
Was the wrong girl hurt?

AB: Who was at the Thursday staff meeting when you announced the change?
SH: The senior management team. Then they disseminate the information to all the other members of staff.
[SH is silent.]
AB: Mrs Healey?
SH: Jenny, is she going to die?
[SH cries.]

It didn't say for how long.

★ ★ ★

Sarah takes the final photocopy out of her bag.
I'd hoped it would be a transcript of Silas
Hyman's interview but it's Tilly Rogers's, that
archetype of a reception teacher — pink cheeks
and long fair hair and smiling face with white,
pearly teeth. A healthy, clean-living, nice girl
who'll do this job for a few years before marrying
and having a family of her own. Children in her
class love her, fathers feel wistful, mothers
maternal.

I can't imagine she has anything to do with the
fire.

Tilly's interview started at 6.30, so after Mrs
Healey's. It was AB, Inspector Baker, who
interviewed her.

I skim-read it, just getting the basics. She was
with her class doing circle time when the alarm
went off. Maisie White helped evacuate the
children, who all knew her already as a volunteer
reader. She didn't mention a delay before
Annette brought her the register, maybe because
she didn't notice or because she didn't think it
was important. Nobody had noticed and asked
her. It's two pages before I see a question that
seems relevant.

AB: Do you know Silas Hyman?
TR: Yes. He was a year-three teacher at Sidley
House. Up until April that is. But I didn't
exactly know him. We taught on different
floors. I'm right at the bottom — well, you
know that already. And the reception

292

classes don't integrate with the rest of the school, not until they reach year one.

Is she telling the truth about not really knowing Silas Hyman? Is it possible that she's his accomplice? Did the fresh-faced, floral-frocked Tilly Rogers leave her class with their storybooks and Listening-Teddy to go upstairs and find the keys to the windows and open them for him? Pour out white spirit and find a match?

Once I'd have said that it was impossible to imagine. But nothing is impossible to imagine any more.

But I can't see how she could have got back to her classroom in time. Because if she'd started the fire, surely Maisie would have arrived to help with the evacuation and found her missing.

AB: Is there anything else you think may be relevant?

TR: Rowena White. I don't know if it's relevant but it was extraordinary.

AB: Go on.

TR: I was outside the school with the children but most of their mothers had got there by then, so I was able to look around. I saw Rowena running into the PE shed and coming out with a towel. A big, blue swimming one. The children leave them in there sometimes. There were two bottles of water on the gravel at the side of the school, by the kitchen entrance. You know, the really large four-litre ones? And she poured water on the towel. Then I saw her going into the school. As she got to the door, I saw her putting the towel over her face. It was just so brave.

Sarah leaves to find you. Jenny and I wait a moment, both quiet with disappointment. No magic sentence to free Adam from guilt.

'Maybe Aunt Sarah will see something we haven't,' I say. 'Or it will at least give her a lead.'

'Yes.'

★ ★ ★

A little while later, we join you and Sarah in the corridor of ICU. You're looking through the glass at Jenny, holding a transcript.

Jenny is standing a little distance away, so that she can't see herself through the glass.

'Do you think it's like my mobile?' she asks. 'An infection risk?'

'Must be.'

But I wonder if the photocopied transcripts really are an infection risk or if Sarah is trying to be as discreet as possible, avoiding Jenny's highly staffed bedside.

You're holding Annette Jenks's transcript. I hope I'll now hear Sarah's take on it, which I could only guess at before.

'But how the hell can Jen have signed herself out?' you say as you read it. 'I don't understand.'

'I'm not convinced yet that she did,' Sarah says. 'It could be that Annette Jenks just wanted to stop people from blaming her. A hit-and-run mentality.'

'So there's nothing useful from it.'

'I wouldn't say that. It's clear from her statement that she didn't actually light the fire. She says she was with Rowena White in the office when the alarm went off and Rowena told me the same thing earlier. The office is on the upper-ground level; the Art room on the second floor. So neither of them could have started the fire.'

'Could she have let Hyman in?'

'She claims not to know him, or even have heard of him, but I find it strange that she didn't hear any gossip about him at all. She strikes me as a gossipy kind of girl. So, for some reason, I think she's probably lying. And we know from both Maisie and Rowena White that she waited a few minutes before coming outside. In here she makes no mention of that. We have to find out what she was doing.'

As I expected, Sarah is bang on the button.

You read through Sally Healey's transcript, pausing when you get to the fire regulations she had in place.

'It's like she's memorised the manual,' you say to Sarah.

'I agree. And Baker picked up on it too. I think Sally Healey was worried about the real possibility of a fire. Almost as if she *knew* it was going to happen and was trying to minimise the consequences.' She catches your expression. 'No fire regulations would have stood a chance against an accelerant and open windows and an old building.'

'Maybe she knew that?'

'I can't see why she'd burn down her own school. But something's not right. As well as having all this down pat, she said there were no hard feelings when Elizabeth Fisher, the old secretary, left. But on Elizabeth's side, there clearly are.'

'Is that relevant?' you ask, sounding a little impatient.

'I don't know yet.'

I feel sick as I reread the head teacher's statement. Because this time her telling Baker that the medical room is *on the third floor*, right at the top of the building, leaps out at me. So too does her *announcement* that Jenny would be nurse, and that the information would be *disseminated* to *all* the other members of staff.

Everyone at the school knew Jenny would be up on the top floor, on her own, in a virtually deserted building.

'Is this all you've got?' you ask.

'Yes. I'm afraid so.'

'Can't you — '

'I was only able to get copies because the paperwork was temporarily in an insecure area. Everything will be securely filed by now.'

'But you *will* talk to Silas Hyman?'

'Yes. And I've already set up a meeting with the head teacher and Elizabeth Fisher. And while I'm doing that, you can go home and see Addie.'

You are silent.

'ICU is heavily staffed, Mike. If you're still worried, I could get Mohsin to sit with her.'

You are still silent and she doesn't understand.

'Addie's only got you right now, Mike. He needs you to be with him.'

You shake your head.

Her grey-blue eyes look deeply into your matching ones, as if searching for an answer there. Because you are a loving father; not a man who would ignore his eight-year-old child, especially not now. Surely, in there somewhere behind the hard expression on your face, is the boy she's known all his life.

You look away from Sarah as you speak so she can't read your face any more; can't see the man inside.

'They told me Jenny has three weeks to live unless she gets a heart transplant. A day less now.'

'Oh God, Mike . . . '

'I can't leave her.'

'No.'

'She *will* get a heart transplant . . . ' you begin, but I am looking at Jenny's face as she hears a car speeding towards her. Death isn't quiet but loud, deafening, getting closer. A joyriding grim reaper mounting the pavement, directly at her, and there's nowhere to run.

She leaves the room and I hurry after her.

'Jen, please . . . '

In the corridor, she stops and turns to me. 'You should have told me.' Her face is white and her voice shaking. 'I had a right to know.'

I want to tell her that I was trying to protect her, that I knitted a shawl of untruths to wrap her up; that I believe in your hope for her.

297

'I'm not a child any more. Your daughter, yes. Always. But — '

'Jen — '

'Can't you get it, Mum? Please? I'm an adult now. You can't run my life for me. What's left of it. I have my own life. My own death.'

23

I see her at six in a pink and orange flowery swimming costume, diving underwater before popping up with a beaming wave, *our little fish!* And I am watching her, my eye beams a rope around her, because I will jump in — *splash!* — and rescue her the moment she's in difficulty. And then she's twelve years old, self-conscious in a modest navy sports swimsuit, checking everything's in place as she swims; and then a metallic silver bikini over a perfect teenage body that makes everyone stare at her and she feels their gazes like sunshine on her skin, enjoying her beauty.

But she's still the little girl in the pink and orange flowery swimming costume to me and I still have my invisible rope around her waist.

'You can have my heart,' I say.

She looks at me a moment and smiles and I see in her smile that I'm forgiven.

'Oh for heaven's sakes,' she says.

'If no one else's turns up.'

' 'Turns up'?'

She's teasing me.

'We're the same tissue type,' I say.

I'd thought us both the *wrong* tissue type before; our bone marrow equally useless to help my father survive Kahler's disease.

'It's really kind,' she says. 'That's a huge understatement. But there are a few snags in the plan. You're *alive*, for a start. And even if Dad and Aunt Sarah let them, which they won't, they're not going to stop giving you food and water for ages.'

'Then I'll just have to find a way of doing it myself.'

'How, exactly?'

All these smiles! Now, of all times! I was wrong earlier, she hasn't taken in the reality of how desperate the situation is at all. I used to wish that she took life 'a little more seriously'.

⋆ ⋆ ⋆

'Walking out of an A-level paper isn't funny.'

'It's not that I'm laughing at.'

'So what is it?'

'No one ever tells you when you're doing all that course work and revision and timed essays and study skills that it's an option.'

'But it isn't an option.'

'It is, because I just took it.'

And she found it funny, as if she'd been released from prison rather than slammed the door shut on her future.

⋆ ⋆ ⋆

I had despaired of this trait she has of hiding behind humour rather than facing the truth. Now, I'm glad.

But her question about how I actually intend to commit suicide is fair enough. I can't open my eyelids or move a single finger so how can I

300

organise an overdose or jump under a train? (A selfish option, I've always thought — those poor drivers.) Ironically, you need to be reasonably fit to commit suicide.

Sarah walks past us and you are with her, for the first time leaving your post.

'They'll get her a heart in time,' you say. 'She will live.'

But your words are harder to hear now. Your vigorous hope weakening by the time it gets to me.

I try to grip onto it again, searching for a handhold.

'Of course she will, Mikey,' Sarah says.

Sarah's voice adds to yours, a doubling of belief, and my grip is firm again. Somehow, she will get better. She has to. '*Of course she will.*'

★ ★ ★

You return to the ward and Sarah walks on towards the exit of the hospital.

'You go with Aunt Sarah,' Jenny says. 'I'll wait here, in case Donald White comes back.'

'I'll stay with you.'

'But you said we need to know everything, in case we're the ones who have to put it all together.'

She *wants* me to go with Sarah.

She wants to be on her own.

I used to hate that — the closed bedroom door, the little walk away from me when she was on her mobile. I still hate that. I don't want her to want to be on her own.

'We have to let her make her own mistakes,' you said, a few weeks ago. 'Spread her wings. It's natural for her to do that.'

'Bubonic plague is 'natural',' I snapped back. 'Doesn't mean it's good for you.'

You put your arm around me. 'You have to let go, Gracie.'

But I can't let go of my rope around her. Not yet. I've been spooling it out as her legs got longer and her figure curvier and stares lingered, but I'll keep on holding it until she can safely swim out of her depth, without drowning, from the shore of childhood to that of adulthood.

Until then I won't let go.

★   ★   ★

I walk with Sarah along the gravel path to the car park but the stones are no longer needle-sharp and the harsh midday sun doesn't scald me yet, as if I'm building up some kind of protective covering for myself.

Sarah stays bang on the speed limits, sticking to one small law as she drives to break large ones.

My nanny voice tells me that my swimming image is 'totally out of date!' Jenny has told me to 'cut my rope; she's grown up! She doesn't want it any more!'

I retort that underneath she still needs me as much as ever, especially now. All teenagers have to make an escape attempt from childhood, just to keep face to themselves, but I think that most, like Jen, hope to be caught before they've gone too far.

'She didn't come to you about the red paint, did she?' my nanny voice says, rapping me harshly over the knuckles with a hard-edged fact. 'She didn't turn to you then; didn't need you then.'

Maybe I was out all day.

It was the tenth of May. You know that date.

It was Adam's class trip and although I'd cleared my diary for it, I hadn't been allowed to go.

'*You've already been on three trips this year, Mrs Covey, better give another mother a chance.*' Like there were mothers queuing up with compasses in their Prada handbags to go orienteering in the pouring rain, rather than mean Miss Madden not wanting me around. (I glared at her when she shouted at them at the V&A.)

So I stayed at home and worried about Adam not finding due north and being partnerless. Not worrying about Jenny. Because we thought the hate mail had stopped.

I was at home all day.

Jenny came back that evening, later than she'd said, her long hair cut into a bob. She'd seemed anxious and I thought it was about her new haircut. I'd tried to reassure her that it suited her.

Even for Jen, she spent an absurdly long time on the phone and although I didn't hear what she was saying (her door was closed), her tone sounded fraught.

If she'd come to me, I'd have washed her hair, got the paint out for her somehow and she

303

wouldn't have had to have it cut.

I'd have taken her coat to that really good but expensive dry-cleaner's in Richmond that can get almost anything out.

If she'd come to me, I'd have reported the attack to the police and maybe she wouldn't be in hospital now.

She still needs my rope around her, even if she doesn't realise it.

'What is it with this drowning thing?' Nanny Voice demands. 'Adam and his armbands, Jenny and the rope?' Well, maybe it's because swimming is the only thing in careful modern life you allow your children to do, on a regular Saturday basis, which is potentially life-threatening. Psychoanalysts put sexual content into water imagery; mothers imagine danger.

And then I imagine them safe.

Snared in thoughts about Jenny and arguments with myself, I'm shocked to see we're driving up to the school. I'm afraid of seeing the site of the fire; nauseous with anxiety.

Sarah turns off along the small road towards the playing field and parks next to it.

★   ★   ★

There are three Portakabins on the playing field now. They make it look so different from sports day and I'm relieved. I don't want to remember. But as we leave the car I see the painted white lines are still here, reflecting in the harsh overhead sun; I hurriedly look away.

I can smell grass; the heated air shot through

with the scent of it, and I am being pulled back inside Wednesday afternoon, with teachers' whistles glinting in the sun and little legs pounding the ground and Adam hurrying towards me, beaming.

Can you get a summer snow-globe instead of a winter one with green grass and flowering azalea bushes and blue sky? Because I'm here; inside it. If you shake it, perhaps it fills with black smoke, not swirling snowflakes.

Sarah knocks on a Portakabin door and the sound jolts me out of the memory snow-globe.

Mrs Healey answers the door. Her normally foundationed face is flushed; her linen skirt creased and covered in dust.

'Detective Sergeant McBride,' Sarah says, holding out her hand — disguising by default that she is related to us. I never understood why she didn't keep her maiden name, but I think now it's because she wants a public self — responsible, grown-up Detective Sergeant McBride, married to sensible stolid Roger — to keep teenage Sarah Covey safely hidden inside.

We go into the stifling Portakabin. Stale particles of Mrs Healey's perfume, Chanel 19, float like scum in the hotly humid air.

'On Monday we are getting ten more Portakabins plus toilet facilities,' Mrs Healey says, her voice quick with uncharacteristic nervous energy. 'The council have given us a temporary emergency licence. The children will need to bring packed lunches but I'm sure parents will understand that. Fortunately we use cloud computing so we've got a back-up of

305

everything on the internet — contact details, lesson planning, children's reports.'

'That's very organised.'

Sarah sounds politely interested, but I wonder if there's a tougher reason for her observation.

'One of the fathers is the CEO of a computing giant; he did it for us last term. Parents like to do things to help. It's a godsend now. I've already been able to print out address labels for every family. They'll all have a letter tomorrow morning outlining what's happening and giving reassurances.'

A printer whirs, spitting out more letters. On the floor is a pile of addressed envelopes.

'Wouldn't it be easier just to email the parents?' Sarah asks.

'It looks better to send out a proper letter on decent paper. It's a demonstration that we are on top of what's happened. Will this take long? I have a huge amount to do, as you can see, and I have already spoken to the police.'

'We can talk and you can carry on, if you like,' Sarah says, as if benignly. But I remember washing up Sunday lunch with her once and her saying that she wished she could do the washing-up with a suspect — she'd wash, he'd dry — and he'd be far more likely to talk and tell the truth while occupied with a task. At the time I'd worried what she wanted out of me.

'You were told Adam Covey was accused of starting the fire?' Sarah says.

'Yes. My decision not to press charges, or take it any further, has the full backing of the governors. From what I understand it was a

306

prank that went wrong and poor Adam has been punished more than enough already. He must feel desperately guilty.'

'Do you know him well?'

'No. I'd recognise him, of course. But I don't really know him. Head teachers are more like chief executives than teachers nowadays so, sadly, I don't get to know very many of my pupils.'

When Jenny was at Sidley House, Mrs Healey's door was always open with children wandering in and out of her office; she taught each class once a week herself to keep in touch. But Adam barely saw her.

'You don't think it odd that an-eight-year-old — just eight — could commit arson?' Sarah asks.

'Apparently it happens relatively frequently. From my time as a teacher, with children this age, I am not surprised. It's horrifying what children are capable of.'

I think of Robert Fleming.

'Adam isn't that kind of child,' Sarah says.

'He didn't do it?' asks Mrs Healey.

'You seem concerned.'

'Alright, yes. I am. I need this to be over with. Sorted out. So that we can all move on. For his sake though, I'm glad, of course. So is that why you're here?'

'I have some questions. I'm sorry if you have to go over old ground.'

Mrs Healey nods an acknowledgement. She's folding the letters now and putting them into the envelopes; her paper folds neatly sharp.

'Where were you when the fire started?' Sarah asks.

'I was at sports day, running the sack race for our year-two children. As soon as I knew what was happening, I made sure that the children I was in charge of were delegated to a form teacher, then made my way as quickly as I could to the school. By the time I arrived all the reception children had been safely evacuated.'

'And Jennifer Covey?'

She folds a piece of paper hurriedly; no neat ridged lines.

'She hadn't followed our procedure. She had signed herself out of the school but not signed herself back in. There was no way anyone could have known she was still in the building.'

'Did you see the register in which she signed herself out?'

'No.'

'So how did you know that she had?'

'Our school secretary, Annette Jenks, told me.'

'And you believed her?'

'I am not a policewoman but a head teacher. I tend to trust what people tell me.'

Her moment of antagonism is met with Sarah's.

'Why didn't you tell us about Silas Hyman at the prize-giving?'

Mrs Healey looks thrown by this abrupt change of subject. Or is it Silas Hyman's name?

'Why didn't you tell the police that Silas Hyman had threatened revenge on the school?'

'Because he didn't mean it.'

'A school burns down, two people are left critically injured and a man has threatened revenge but — '

'I *know* that he didn't mean it.'

'Have you any evidence for that?'

She's silent. One of her fingers has a paper cut and each white Conqueror Weave envelope has a thin line of red.

'Did a parent phone you after the prize-giving?'

'Yes.'

'Did they ask you to inform the police and get a restraining order or injunction against him to make sure he couldn't come near the school again?'

'You mean, Maisie White?'

'Just answer the question.'

'Yes.'

'So why didn't you do as she asked?'

'Because her husband phoned me an hour later and said his wife was overwrought and that there was no need to contact the police. Like me, and the rest of the staff and parents, he knew Silas was all hot air and bluster, that he didn't mean any of it.'

Why had Donald countermanded Maisie? Why would he protect Silas Hyman?

'So you didn't even report it?'

'No.'

'You weren't worried, at *all*?'

'Yes. I was. But not about Silas doing something violent. I'd spent months, *months*, building up a good reputation for Sidley House after the playground fiasco and I thought that in five minutes of drunken idiocy he could have destroyed it. But apart from Mrs White, nobody took him seriously. He'd made an idiotic spectacle of himself, that was all.'

'Can you tell me about that 'playground fiasco'?'

'A child was seriously injured when he fell from the fire escape. He broke both his legs. We were lucky it wasn't worse. Silas Hyman was meant to be supervising the playground but he wasn't.'

'So you fired him?'

'I didn't have any alternative.'

'Did you fire him before or after the article about the incident in the *Richmond Post*?'

'Clearly the article increased the pressure from parents.' She pauses a moment as if pained by the memory. 'I had to fire him three days later. Without the article he could have stayed in post till the end of that term.'

'Do you have a system of warnings?'

'I'd already given him one warning when he called a child 'wicked'. Naturally, the parents complained. His language and attitude towards the child were unacceptable.'

I think of Robert Fleming's callous cruelty.

'Do you know how the *Richmond Post* found out about the playground incident?'

'No.'

'Was it from someone at the school?'

'I really don't know who told the press.'

'Did Silas have any enemies at the school?'

'None that I know of, no.'

'What effect did this playground accident have on the school?'

'It was very hard for a while. I don't deny that. Parents put their children into our care and one

310

of them was badly injured. I understood their anger and upset about that. I could completely understand why a few parents wanted to withdraw their children. I spoke to all the parents, class by class at special meetings. If parents were still anxious I met with them individually and gave personal reassurances and guarantees that it would never happen again. And we weathered the storm, no parents took their children away — not a single one. On sports day there were two hundred and seventy nine children in school. There is just one place free in a year-three class because a family relocated to Canada at the end of last term.'

I know she's telling the truth. At sports day every class each had twenty children, the maximum Sidley House allows.

'What is your own opinion of Silas Hyman?' Sarah asks.

'A brilliant teacher. Gifted. The best I've come across in my career. But too unorthodox for a private school.'

'And as a man?'

'I didn't get to know him socially.'

'Was he having a relationship with anyone at the school?'

She hesitates a moment. 'Not that I know of.'
A careful answer.

'Was there any gossip?'

'I don't listen to gossip. I try and discourage it by example.'

'Can you tell me what the code was on the gate on Wednesday?'

'Seven-seven-two-three,' she replies. I think

she looks wary of Sarah now. 'I told another officer that already.'

'I wanted to confirm it for myself,' Sarah says coolly, and for the moment Mrs Healey is pacified. But surely she'll suspect something as this illegal interview continues. That ice Sarah told you about seems perilously thin.

'Why did you get rid of Elizabeth Fisher?'

Sally Healey looks startled and tries to hide it. She is silent as Sarah looks at her and the sound of the printer is loud in the Portakabin, spewing another letter out onto the dusty floor.

'Mrs Healey?'

24

Mrs Healey's normally powder-dry face is sweating profusely now, the sweat glistening in the too-bright Portakabin.

'She was too old to do the job. I already told the police that.'

Mrs Healey is kneeling on the floor, but has stopped putting the letters into envelopes — is it because she can't multitask with lying?

'She seemed competent to me,' Sarah says.

'We have a policy of retirement at sixty for all support staff.'

'But you waited seven years to enforce it.'

'I was being kind. But the school is not a charity.'

'No, it's a business, isn't it?'

Sally Healey doesn't reply.

'Is Annette Jenks an improvement?' Sarah asks, seemingly without irony.

'The governors and I made an error of judgment when we hired Annette Jenks.'

'The governors hire staff?'

'They sit on the interview panel, yes.'

'I noticed how meticulous all your fire precautions were,' Sarah says, again abruptly switching tack. Maybe it's deliberate, to unsettle the other person into spilling out more than they want.

'As I told your colleague, safety of the children is my number-one priority.'

313

'So you fulfilled all the legal requirements?'

'*More* than the legal requirements.'

She wipes her sweaty face with her hand. 'But with old buildings it's impossible to prevent a fire spreading. We've all learnt that to our cost. And how can anyone plan for an individual's act of destruction? When that person starts the fire in the worst possible place in the school with virtually no staff on hand to contain it? How can we possibly plan for that?'

'When did this start?' Sarah asks, unmoved. 'This 'more than' fulfilling of the legal requirements?'

'We had a governors' meeting just before half-term. At the end of May. One of the points on the agenda was to examine and update our fire safety. We all agreed it and I took charge of implementation.'

'This meeting was after the prize-giving?'

'Yes. But it's not connected. Like all schools, we regularly look at ways to update and improve our safety systems.'

'Just six weeks later there's a catastrophic fire. It looks as if you expected it?'

'We *planned* for it. Yes. We have to plan for terrible scenarios. We plan for what to do with the children if London comes under a terrorist attack or there's a dirty bomb; we plan for a madman coming in with a gun and getting through our security. We plan for these things. We have to. But for God's sake it doesn't mean that we thought something would actually happen.'

'There's one thing I find a little surprising,'

314

Sarah says, again unmoved by her speech. 'You made sure all the fire precautions were in place — correct signage and fire extinguishers and no combustible artworks hung in the corridors. You have all these sensible precautions?'

'Yes.'

'So why do you let children bring *matches* into the school?'

For a moment Mrs Healey doesn't reply. Then she stands, trying to brush the dust off her skirt, but her hands are too sweaty and the dust leaves dark marks on the fine linen.

'It's just on a birthday. And the matches are handed directly over to the class teacher for safekeeping.'

'Which they keep in a cupboard?'

'Yes. Clearly on sports day a teacher should make some provision . . . ' She scowls at the dirty marks on her skirt. 'Unfortunately, human errors do occur. His teacher should have made sure the matches were safely stored.'

I doubted Miss Madden was aware of this responsibility.

'Presumably, the building is insured?' Sarah asks.

'Of course.'

'And the insurance company will want to know that all the fire precautions have been met before they'll pay out?'

'I have already spoken to the insurers about the matches and fortunately it doesn't invalidate our claim. It was one member of staff's error of judgment, a human error. All our systems were in place. Besides, you're telling me now that it wasn't Adam Covey who started the fire. So

presumably the matches are no longer significant.'

'You said earlier that the stricter fire regulations were decided at a governors' meeting?'

'Yes.'

'Do the governors have a financial stake in the
school?'

'Yes, they own it.'

'So the governors are also the shareholders?'

'Yes.'

'Unelected?'

'Yes. It's a completely different system to a state
school. Or one with a charitable foundation.'

'Do you have any shares?'

'I was given a shareholding when I took the
job of head teacher. A perk of starting with a new
school. But my shareholding is relatively small.
Only five per cent.'

'In a business worth, presumably, several
million, that is a sizeable amount.'

'What are you insinuating? My God, people
were *hurt*. Terribly hurt.'

'But even so, you must be relieved that the
insurance money can't be contested because of
your impeccable fire precautions.'

'Yes, I am relieved, but only in as much as I
can continue to run a school of excellence. A
school that nurtures and educates children to the
highest possible standard and instils a sense of
self-worth alongside academic achievement.'

She sounds impassioned and I remember her
as the ardent educationalist she'd been when
Jenny joined the school. She gestures around the
Portakabin.

'This is clearly a temporary and unsatisfactory solution, but during the summer holidays I will find alternative accommodation and be ready to start on September the eighth for our new academic year. What was burnt down was a *building*, not a *school*. The teachers, the children, the ethos, the parents are what make a school and we will simply relocate and pick up from where we left off as best we can. And we *will do it*.'

'Can I have the names of the governors?'

I see suspicion hardening Sally Healey's face. 'I already gave them to the police.'

It wasn't in her transcript. Perhaps it had been during a phone call, someone tying up a few loose ends. The ice thins beneath Sarah but she affects not to notice.

'Of course. I'll confer with my colleagues,' Sarah says.

'And I've already been asked all about the shareholders as governors.'

'Yes,' Sarah says, going to the door. 'Thank you for your time.'

She leaves the Portakabin.

Sally Healey watches her as she walks away; the ice creaking under her.

★   ★   ★

On the edge of the playing field, next to Sarah's Polo, Mrs Healey's black sports car gleams like a giant, lacquered cockroach. The woman I'd met all those years ago when Jenny started at Sidley House bicycled to school. '*Can't mess up the*

317

planet for the children, can we?' she'd said with a bicycle clip around her trousers.

With only sixty children then, the school had been such a nurturing place. When Adam joined, nine years later, I hadn't wanted to see the change. But Jenny had seen the school as a business. And you'd annually fumed about the ever-increasing fees and vowed that the children would go to a secondary school that wasn't privately owned and which had a board of independent governors to complain to. At Sidley House we didn't even know the governors' names. Even if we had, as investors they were hardly likely to take the parents' side and vote themselves a smaller profit.

As I see the ugly, boastful sports car I know my image of the school is as outdated as Sally Healey with a bicycle clip. That nurturing school solidified into rigid staff hierarchies and rules, concerned with the uniform rather than the child inside it, as the pupils turned into a living business prospectus.

I turn away from the polished sports car and all that it signals. The azalea bushes edging the playing field have wilted in the heat, their once-bright blossom lying brown on the ground.

I know that there's a memory globe of that afternoon and inside I am still hugging Adam, his 'I am 8!' badge digging into me; still looking around for Jenny; still thinking she'll be out to join us soon. The sky is summer-blue, the azalea bushes are bright as jewels.

★   ★   ★

318

Sarah drives away from the playing field and the school. She's silent, probably thinking over her interview with Sally Healey. Jenny's conversation pulls at me again.

She asked me, clearly, to see her as a grown-up. But how can I? When she didn't tell us about the paint attack because she still wanted to go out in the evenings? Too young to realise that we wouldn't have 'grounded' her but protected her. Not seeing the whole picture, not *understanding*.

And what about Ivo? She'd want me to see him as grown-up too. But he didn't tell us when she'd been attacked with red paint or persuade her go to the police. So how can I see him as a man? As anything other than an immature and irresponsible boy? In every way the opposite of you.

And it's not just the red paint, it's the not finishing a History essay because she'd rather go to a party, and spending too long with her friends instead of revising for exams. It's living so much in the present, not thinking of the future, and that is the joy of children, yes, because they haven't yet grown up.

You don't agree with me, I know. You take Jenny's side, as I often take Adam's, our family splitting down the familiar fault line.

* * *

'You know what would really stop the world having wars?' Adam asked. He'd just finished reading Give Peas A Chance *but wasn't convinced that a worldwide boycotting of vegetables*

319

by children would stop global warfare.

'What?' I asked, peeling potatoes, hopeful they would now be eaten.

'An alien invasion from space. Then everyone in the world would band together.'

'True,' I said.

'But drastic,' you said, coming in.

'Imaginative,' I corrected.

Do I always correct you with Adam?

'Like the testudo,' you said to him.

Adam smiled at you, then saw my blank expression.

'Roman soldiers held up their shields over their heads to make a shell around the whole group,' he said. 'So no one could get hurt.'

''Testudo' is Latin for tortoise,' you said, enjoying — infuriatingly — that you were being erudite over me.

*　*　*

My flow of thought about testudos and aliens is brought to an abrupt halt as Sarah parks on a fast busy road in Hammersmith, her car half straddling the meagre pavement.

I follow her to a small terraced house, the bricks stained black by exhaust fumes.

Sarah rings the doorbell. A moment later Elizabeth Fisher calls through the door, without opening it.

'If you're from any religion or an energy company I'm already sorted out on both fronts.'

I'd forgotten how funny and stern she could be at the same time. But it strikes me that she's also nervous, afraid even; not opening the door. She's on her own in a rough neighbourhood. I'm struck, again, by the financial discrepancy between the staff and the parents at Sidley House.

'It's Sarah Covey. Grace's sister-in-law. Can I come in?'

'Wait one moment.'

From inside is the sound of her unbolting the door and the chain being taken off.

She opens the door, dressed in smart trousers and ironed shirt as she was every day at Sidley House; her posture rigorously straight. But her smart trousers are a little shiny on the knees where the cloth has worn.

'Has anything happened?' she asks, worried.

'No change,' Sarah replies. 'Would it be OK if I asked you some questions?'

'Of course. But as I said before, I really don't think I can help.'

She leads Sarah into her tiny sitting room. Outside the traffic thunders past, shivering the walls.

'Can you tell me what your duties were at the school?'

Mrs Fisher looks a little taken aback, but nods.

'Certainly. I did all the basic secretarial ones, such as answer the phone and type up letters. I was also responsible for the registers. I was the first point of contact for potential new families, sending out prospectuses and organising invitations to open days; then getting the paperwork ready for all the new children. I was also the

321

school nurse, the part of my job I enjoyed the most actually, really just putting on ice-packs and sometimes using an epi-pen. I'd tuck the child under a blanket on my sofa and then wait with them for Mum or a nanny to arrive. We only ever had one serious incident. The one I told you about.'

Her job had so many more responsibilities than Annette Jenks's. And she did it well. So why did Mrs Healey really get rid of her?

If she'd still been there — still been school nurse — everything would have been different.

'What about the gate?' Sarah asks.

'Yes, I'd buzz people in. There was an intercom and I always made sure they identified themselves first, by name.'

'Did you have a screen monitor?'

'Good God, no. I just spoke to them. It seemed quite adequate. You get to know voices as well as faces after a while. But in fact, it was pretty shoddy security. Half the children and most of the parents got to know the code. They weren't meant to, of course.'

'Do you have a copy of your job description?' Sarah asks.

'Yes. It's in my contract.'

She rummages in a bureau and takes out a document, which has clearly been much thumbed, encased in a plastic wallet.

'The part about retirement age is on page four,' Elizabeth says, handing it to Sarah.

'Thank you. Do you have a school calendar?'

Elizabeth sits down, clearly in her customary chair. She gestures to the wall opposite, the one she'd see most clearly. The Sidley House School calendar is hanging there.

'All the staff are given them at the end of the Christmas term. I look at it quite frequently . . . '

I see how much she misses the children. She always put them first; making adults wait if a child was in her office needing a grazed knee tending, or with a piece of artwork or writing or Hama-bead creation to show her.

'Do you know what the code on the gate is?' Sarah asks.

'It was seven-seven-two-three when I was there. They've probably changed it by now.'

But it was the same. I remember Sally Healey telling Sarah.

It dawns on me that Sarah might think Elizabeth Fisher is the culprit. But surely she can't do? The idea is ridiculous. These must just be standard questions. Because Elizabeth may know the code to the gate and have a calendar with Adam's birthday and sports day on it, and feel wronged by being sent packing, but there is no way on earth Elizabeth Fisher set fire to the school.

* * *

The pain took about an hour to kick in this time and I am now racing back to the hospital, the gravel tearing at my feet. Too late, I see Jenny watching me from inside — I must be grimacing in pain.

She hurries up to me, anxious.

'Mum?'

323

'I'm fine, really.'

And I am, because the moment I'm back here the whiteness of the walls again soothes my scorched skin and the cool shiny floor heals the cuts on the soles of my feet.

'I'm sorry,' she says. 'I shouldn't have bossed you into going. It hurt you too, didn't it?'

'Not really.'

'You're a terrible liar.'

'OK, a bit. Nothing more. And it's gone now.'

'Is it your way of trying to commit suicide?'

'What?' I am at a loss.

'If you experience that amount of pain for long enough — '

I interrupt her. 'No. Really not. Your body didn't change a jot when you went outside that time with Granny G and Adam, did it?'

She nods in agreement.

'Anyway, us cabbages are pretty tough.'

'Mum!' she says, shocked but smiling at me.

★ ★ ★

We follow Sarah as she makes her way to ICU.

'So are you going to tell me what happened, then?' Jenny asks. 'No, don't tell me. You've discovered it was *Mrs Healey* having the affair with Silas?' She sees my expression. 'It was a joke.'

But is it so comically ridiculous? Mrs Healey is only in her late forties. There's no difference in the age gap between her and Silas Hyman than between Sarah and her beautiful gazelle policeman. But Jen's right. It's an absurd idea. It

324

was Mrs Healey who fired Silas; Mrs Healey who brought his career crashing to the ground. And even if that hadn't been the case, Mrs Healey is far too professional to have an affair with a junior colleague.

Yes, I'd once have thought that of Sarah.

I outline our meeting with Mrs Healey to Jen. Listen to me — '*our meeting*', as if I was an active participant rather than eavesdropper. But, weird as this must sound, I do feel a little like Sarah's silent partner.

'The thing I find strangest,' I say, 'is Donald phoning Mrs Healey the night of the prize-giving, and counter-manding Maisie. Why would he protect Silas Hyman like that?'

'Maybe because he was *there*, Mum, like you were, and didn't find Silas threatening at all. Just like you didn't. Not until this happened and blame started being thrown around the place.'

I find her innocent certainty about Silas Hyman, a man more than a decade older than her, another reason to still see her as not yet an adult.

'Maybe Mrs Healey wasn't *worried* there was going to be a fire,' Jenny continues. 'But *planned* to start it herself and wanted to make sure the fire precautions were in place so the insurance paid out. She banged on about her bloody precautions on TV, the night of the fire. Even then she wanted to make sure everyone knew.'

I remember Mrs Healey's pink linen shirt and assembly voice.

'*I can reassure you that we had <u>every</u> fire precaution in place.*'

'She knew the fire precautions wouldn't make any difference,' Jenny continues, 'because the building was old and the fire was so intense.'

She must have been thinking about this; working it all out.

'But Mrs Healey was at sports day,' I say. 'People would have noticed if she'd left.'

'She's a mini-dictator. Nearly all the teachers are on short-term contracts, which she can choose not to renew. And if they're chucked out by her they're still dependent on a reference from her to get another job. She could have blackmailed someone into it.'

Jenny is so keen for this to be the scenario; for her terrible injuries to have been an accident, not deliberate. Right from the beginning she'd thought — hoped — that it was something to do with the school as a business; an insurance fraud.

'She'd choose sports day,' Jenny continues, 'because there'd be virtually no staff to try and put it out. I mean, Annette would be next to useless and I wouldn't be much better, and that only leaves. Tilly, who'd have her hands too full of young children to try and do anything to stop it spreading.'

I agree with her about sports day being a deliberate choice of date. It also meant there was hardly anyone there beforehand to see the arsonist open the windows; pour out the white spirit.

'But what good would it do her?' I say, gently.

'She's a part-owner, right? So she'd get her share of the insurance money.'

'But why would she want to burn down a

successful business? She's already trying to find premises to get the school going again. There won't be any financial benefit. She'll just use the insurance money to rebuild.'

I can't yet see Jenny as an adult, but I am trying to be more straightforward with her.

We move onto Elizabeth Fisher, who Jenny has always liked. Like me, she knows Elizabeth would have had nothing to do with it.

★   ★   ★

We still haven't spoken about the three weeks, less a day, left to her. My grip on your optimism isn't strong enough to confront the ticking clock, the speeding car, with spoken words. And I think Jenny is deliberately turning her back on it too. It's as if looking at it properly, even peeking, would turns us to stone, terrorised and mute. But the fact is there, huge and monstrous. And we are playing grandmother's footsteps with a gorgon.

As we arrive on ICU, you see Sarah. And you run. Literally run. I see the urgency in your body with *big news* to tell her. A heart must have been found! The monstrous fact smashed to pieces.

Then I see your face.

25

'Mike?' Sarah asks.

'He was here. Watching her through the glass. I *saw him* watching her through the glass.'

'Who was it?'

'I don't know. He had a hood up, and there was a trolley in the way so I couldn't see his face.'

'How did you know he was dangerous?'

'He was still.'

Sarah looks at you, waiting for more.

'*Totally still*,' you say. 'No one is totally still. Everybody's moving. No one just stands there, watching. He was waiting for her to be alone. For me to leave her.'

I think of that figure on the edge of the playing field; the figure I noticed because of his stillness.

'He wants to kill her,' you say.

'Did you see anything else?' Sarah asks.

'He turned away, when he saw me looking, and I just saw the coat, that's all. A blue coat with a hood.'

'That's it?' Jen says. 'Some guy in a coat was a bit *still*?'

But I see that she's afraid.

'I'll be in the garden.'

'OK.'

She leaves, turning her back on this.

'It could have been Hyman,' you're saying to Sarah. 'If Jen saw him at the school, or

328

something which incriminated him.'

You've said this before, and it's as if repetition gives increased validity to your suspicion.

'Or the hate-mailer has become more dangerous than we realised,' Sarah says, and again I wish to God I could tell her about the red-paint attack.

'When they stop having to sedate Jenny so heavily, she'll be able to tell us if she saw something,' you say.

But neither Sarah nor I share your confidence. Sarah, because she's not sure that Jenny will ever get well enough for the doctors to stop sedating her; and me, because I know that at the moment she can't remember anything past texting Ivo at two thirty.

'I'll phone the station,' Sarah says. She leaves ICU to make the call.

I hug you, resting my face against your shirt, feeling your heart beating.

I feel so close to you now, my darling.

We are the only people who know the man in the blue coat is real. Sarah takes it on trust from you, but you and I *know*. And we are totally united against the threat to our daughter. We are Earth battling the aliens; a testudo of a family.

And although you don't make Jen finish her homework or revise, or tell her that she ought to do retakes, you guard her ferociously and devotedly when a hate-mailer sends her vicious letters; when a maniac is out to kill her.

And when a doctor says she has three weeks to live without a transplant, you tell her that she *will* get one.

You say you won't let her die. And I wish to God I could believe that.

A momentary swish of air as a young man on a ventilator, unconscious and totally still, is wheeled quickly past us. He can't be more than twenty. His mother is with him. We both watch him.

Sarah rejoins us.

'Can you stay with Jen?' you ask. 'Till the police get here? I need to be with Addie, just for a bit, and — '

She puts a hand on your shoulder.

'There's nobody coming. I'm sorry.'

Like Jenny, the police were hardly going to find someone *standing still* cause for alarm. The trail of trust in your suspicion ends with Sarah.

'I'll go and see Silas Hyman, find out where he's been this morning,' she says. 'And I'll talk to the *Richmond Post*, and see who told them about the fire.'

'But first, I need to see Addie and — '

Sarah interrupts you. 'If someone is trying to kill Jenny, we need to find out who it is *as soon as possible*. And that will help Addie too. Because I don't want him to spend another day being accused of this.'

You nod; perhaps remembering all those police statistics Sarah's quoted at us over the years; the number of cases solved decreasing exponentially with the amount of time that elapses — trails *going cold;* witnesses missed who then became *untraceable;* door-to-door enquiries not done *in time*.

You stay by her bed but I know that you again feel the pain of being torn in half.

* * *

I go to Jenny in the garden. The sun is directly overhead, the shadows tiny silhouettes of what make them, offering no shade.

Jen is sitting with her arms around her knees.

'I'm going with Aunt Sarah,' I say.

She turns to me. 'You know when you last saw Addie?'

I nod, flinching at the memory. Mum had told Adam I wasn't going to wake up again and I'd tried to comfort him but he couldn't hear me.

'Just before,' Jenny continues, 'you asked me if a scent could have made me hear the fire alarm at school. You know my mad person's tinnitus?'

'Donald had just gone into Rowena's room,' I say. 'I thought it could have been his aftershave, or cigarettes.'

'Like a sensory teleporter?' she says, caught with the idea. '*Beam me up, Scotty!*'

A you and Adam catchphrase. I smile at her. 'Something like that.'

'Do you think a smell could make me remember more of the fire?'

I think of the night stocks in this garden and the grass-scented air at the playing field today, and how each time I was captured by the past, for a few moments actually there. Her sensory teleporter isn't so off the mark.

'It might do,' I say.

But being back in that fire, even for a few moments, would be terrifying.

'It's *before* the fire that I need to remember,'

331

she says, seeing my anxiety. 'When the person was lighting it.'

'I'm not sure you can control your memory like that.'

'I have to do something to help Addie.'

I remember his small face as Mum led him away, the bruised shadows of grief under his eyes, how his whole body seemed mute.

'You go with Aunt Sarah and I'll go on a scratch-and-sniff tour of the hospital,' she continues.

I nod, because I'm not worried about her remembering anything too close to the fire — there's nothing in the hospital that smells remotely like a fire, or even like the school.

'You're *sure* it doesn't hurt you to go outside?' she asks.

'Absolutely.' Fingers crossed behind my back.

This time I don't think she's getting rid of me. But I do think there's another reason she wants to stay in the hospital.

'Flights this time of year get really booked up,' I say. 'It might take him quite a while to get a standby.'

She turns away from me, as if caught out; a little embarrassed. 'Yeah.'

★   ★   ★

I leave the hospital with Sarah.

As we drive I think about the young man I saw in ICU. I'd wondered if he would die or if he was brain-dead already and just being kept alive. I'd wondered if he was the right tissue type for Jenny. I'd hoped that he was.

332

Then I'd seen his mother; her suffering. And I felt ashamed. Because I *still hope* that he's the right match for Jenny; and that he's dead. The hope is ugly inside me, tarnishing the person I once was.

I think you feel the same.

It's not always good things that unite people, is it?

Sarah pulls up outside Silas Hyman's house. The pain still hasn't kicked in. I'm building up greater stamina.

★   ★   ★

Natalia opens the door, looking hot and flushed and furious.

'Yes?'

Her voice is aggressive, ambient rage surrounding her like a heat haze.

'Detective Sergeant McBride,' Sarah says, her voice cool. 'Can I come in?'

'Like I get a choice?' she says, but there's fear on her face.

Sarah doesn't answer her question, but follows her into the flat.

'Is your husband home?'

'No.'

She volunteers nothing more.

It's sweltering in here. The walls of the flat probably ooze damp in the winter but now trap the heat. A toddler, grimy and hot, is screaming, his nappy sagging heavily.

Natalia ignores him, going into a bathroom. Sarah follows.

'Do you know where he is?' Sarah asks her.

'A building site. Been there since first thing this morning.'

He was in the hospital the last time he'd told her he was at a building site.

Two little boys are in the bath fighting, one of them swishing the scummy water over the edge of the bath onto the chipped tiled floor. They have sunburnt necks and faces.

'Do you know which building site?' Sarah asks.

'Maybe the same as yesterday's. A big development in Paddington. But he didn't know if they'd want him again. Get out of the bath, Jason. *Now!*'

Building sites are a pretty good alibi.

'Early for bath-time?' Sarah says, and I think she means to be friendly but it comes out as a criticism.

Natalia glares. 'I'll be too knackered to do it later.'

The youngest one is still screaming, more desperately, his nappy almost at his knees with the weight of urine. Natalia sees Sarah looking at him.

'You know how much they cost? Nappies? Do you know that?'

Through her eyes I see Sarah for a moment. I used to think that she was judgmental too.

'Do you know when he'll be home?' Sarah asks.

'No clue. He was out till past ten yesterday. Didn't stop working till it got dark.'

Natalia grabs one of the boys and pinions him

in a towel as he struggles to get free. The red sunburnt marks are livid red stripes.

No wonder her exotic beauty is fading so fast. Three boys under four in a small flat with no patience to expand the walls.

'On Wednesday afternoon, you said Silas was with you?'

'Yeah. We went to Chiswick House Park for a picnic. Set off from here 'bout eleven, got back around five.'

'A long picnic?'

'Would you stay in here? The park's free. Suncream isn't. How are you meant to put it on as often as you're supposed to? Silas played with them. Let him ride on his back, that kind of stuff. He could do it till the cows came home. Bores me mental.'

'Does Silas know Donald White?'

She wants to know why Donald phoned Mrs Healey the night of the prize-giving, counter-manding Maisie's request for a restraining order. Why did Donald protect him?

'Who?' Natalia says and looks genuinely blank; or maybe she's a proficient actress.

'Would it be alright if I wait for Silas in the sitting room?'

'Suit yourself.'

Sarah leaves.

I look back to the bathroom, the tension impregnating the steam and dampness. And it seems so sad that bath-time is fraught and hostile.

I remember Jenny at three hiding under a towel after the bath.

'Magic rock, magic rock,' I had to say.

'Yes!' From under the towel.

'Will you give me a little girl of three with fair hair called Jenny, please?'

Towel is thrown off. 'Here!'

I'd pick up her warm, still-damp body and put my arms around her.

Magic.

★   ★   ★

In the hallway Sarah passes the open doorway to the kitchen and goes in. She's noticed the school calendar hanging on the wall: 11 July — Adam's birthday and sports day — ringed in red like a curse.

She goes into the sitting room and quietly rummages through a pile of papers and post in an untidy heap on a table. I don't know quite *how* illegal this is, what will happen to Sarah if she's found out, but she continues, quickly and methodically with that quiet courage of hers that I've only just discovered.

At the bottom of the heap, in an envelope, are birthday cake candles. Pastel blue. Eight of them.

Natalia comes into the room behind Sarah, silently. Her movements, like her eyes, are feline. I shout a warning, loud as I can, but Sarah can't hear me.

'Silas said he found them on the mat yesterday morning,' Natalia says and Sarah starts.

'Weird thing to do, isn't it? Why would someone post us fucking birthday cake candles?'

I remember Jenny talking about the arsonist

and her mobile phone. '*Perhaps he wanted some kind of trophy.*'

Was that what Silas Hyman had done? And then pretended someone had sent them?

Two of the little boys, trailing water, run into the room; one is screaming, the other hitting him, their commotion not filling the silence between the adults.

Sarah goes towards the front door.

'You're not waiting for Silas, then?' Natalia asks.

'No.'

So we won't, yet, find out where he was this afternoon.

I think Sarah has been jolted by something. Perhaps it's just hit her how many laws she's breaking by coming to their house and going through their things.

Perhaps it's the candles.

Natalia yells at the children to shut up. Then she blocks the door to Sarah. She looks hostile and sweaty and plain.

'I didn't used to be this way,' she says, as if seeing herself through Sarah's eyes.

No, I think, you were exotically beautiful and poised not that long ago, when Silas was still in work and when you only had one child.

'You didn't used to be this way?' Sarah asks, and there's *fury* in her voice. 'Jenny didn't used to be this way either,' she continues. 'And Grace used to be able to talk. Smile. Look after her children. Count yourself lucky your children are healthy and you can be a mother to them. Count yourself *lucky*.'

Natalia stands aside as if Sarah's blast of words have shoved her, and Sarah leaves.

I hadn't thought to envy Natalia Hyman. Now I realise there's every reason in the world why I should.

★ ★ ★

We drive towards the *Richmond Post*. I watch Sarah as she drives.

'*You're being over-sensitive, Grace,*' you said; use of my proper name, bad sign. '*Sarah likes you, how many more times?*'

'She <u>tolerates</u> me.'

'*Well, I don't know how these women-things work.*'

No, I thought, because men don't spend time in the kitchen thinking that being in proximity to food or washing up means two people will bond. Even women with high-flying careers still do the 'Can I give you a hand in the kitchen?' thing. Sarah and I had done that countless times over the years, but had remained like toddlers, parallel playing.

And all this time we could have been friends.

'You *say that*, my nanny voice interjects, 'but would she have wanted to be friends *with you?*'

I wish she'd hang out with some positive nanny voices, the ones who've been made kind by years of cognitive therapy, but she continues relentlessly. 'You don't have *anything* in common, do you?'

And I have to agree that, family aside, we have nothing in common.

I'd hoped when Sarah had a baby, a year after Jenny was born, that we might bond in some way. Or, more accurately, that she would show a flaw or two. But she was brilliant at motherhood, just as she was brilliant at her career, with a baby who slept through the night and a toddler who smiled on his way to nursery and a child who could count to ten and read long before the end of reception, while Jenny as a baby screamed the house down at four every morning and clung to me at the playgroup gates and saw letters as impossible hieroglyphs.

And Sarah was back at work and being promoted! Still on her fast-track career. I told you before I was jealous of her; well, sometimes I loathed her. There, said it. Terrible. I'm sorry.

The truth is, loathing her was easier than not liking myself.

I did the whole baking muffins for cake sales and going on trips and being there to do home-work and inviting friends round. All of that. But I didn't know how to do what was important.

'Magic rock, magic rock, give me a confident teenager with ambition and self-confidence and the A-level grades to get into university with a boyfriend who is worthy of her. Give me an eight-year-old boy who is happy at playtime and isn't bullied and believes he's not stupid.'

I was meant to be their magic rock, but I failed.

And I have no excuses.

26

We arrive at the offices of the *Richmond Post*.

It's been an age since I was here, preferring to send in my monthly page by email. As we go in, I'm embarrassed that Sarah will discover that I'm not loved here as she is at her police station. Frankly, I'm probably no more valued than the out-of-date yucca plant in the corner of what passes for reception.

Sarah must have phoned ahead because Tara arrives almost immediately, pink cheeks glowing. Sarah looks less than thrilled to see her.

'I spoke to one of your colleagues,' Sarah says curtly. 'Geoff Bagshot.'

'Yes, I recognised the name, Detective Sergeant McBride,' she says. 'You chucked me out of the hospital.'

I remember Sarah's uniform-and-truncheon voice as she virtually pushed Tara away from you. But Tara only knows her as a police officer; not as a member of our family.

'Geoff's left it for me to handle.'

I see Sarah stiffen at Tara's 'handling' of her.

'There's an office we can use this way,' Tara says, her stride quick and determined; she's always enjoyed a spat.

'When I met you, you said you were friends with Grace?' Sarah says.

'I was trying to gain access to her ward, so I stretched the truth a little. It's what you have to do sometimes in journalism. Clearly I don't have much in common with a thirty-nine-year-old mother of two.'

'Nor she with you. Clearly.'

Thank you, Sarah.

Tara escorts her into Geoff's office; she must have turfed him out. It looks like the set for a film about journalists — old mugs with the dregs of cold coffee in them and illegal ashtrays brimming with butts. I've only been here once or twice a year, and it's been mineral water, no smoking and a digestive biscuit if you're lucky. Maybe Tara's taken over décor.

'What time did you arrive at Sidley House School on the day of the fire?' Sarah asks, wasting no time on preliminaries.

'Three fifteen p.m. I already told your buddy.'

'That was extremely fast?'

'What is this? Interviews in duplicate?' She's enjoying herself.

'Who told you?' Sarah asks.

Tara is silent.

'You arrive barely fifteen minutes after a fire started which has left two people critically ill and I need to know who told you.'

'I can't reveal my source.'

'Your tip-off was hardly from Deep Throat. And this,' she says, gesturing around the crummy office, 'isn't exactly the *Washington Post*.'

She must have heard me joking to Jenny about Tara; remembered it. Unlike me, she's said it to her face.

'Can we do a deal?' Tara asks.

341

'Excuse me?'

'I'll tell you in return for information that you will only give to my paper.'

Sarah is silent.

'You don't think the kid did it any more?' Tara says. 'You can't do or you wouldn't still be investigating.'

Sarah says nothing, which Tara takes as an affirmative. She glows with satisfaction. The cat that got the cream with a side order of pilchards.

'So are you going to investigate Silas Hyman properly this time?' she says.

Again, Sarah says nothing.

'I need something back if I'm going to play ball here,' Tara continues.

'Adam Covey isn't responsible for the fire,' Sarah says. 'And in a few minutes we'll discuss Silas Hyman.'

Tara almost purrs with self-satisfaction.

'It was Annette Jenks,' she says. 'The secretary at the school, who phoned us. At a minute or so past three. She had to shout above the sound of the fire alarm.'

'Why did she call your paper?'

'I've been thinking about that. We did a photo and article a few weeks back when the school raised money for a charity. You know the whole giant-cheque-and-smug-rich-kids-holding-it routine? Sidley House were keen to get publicity for it and we obliged. She'd have our number from that.'

'Did she phone any other papers?'

'I don't know. But she did phone a TV station. Their reporters and cameramen arrived about half an hour after us.'

I remember again the TV news playing while you were hurrying through the hospital to find Jenny.

'She wanted us to take her picture,' Tara continues. 'I think Dave, our photographer, took a few to keep her quiet. But once the TV mob arrived she was all over them.'

I remember Maisie talking to Sarah in the shadowy cafeteria. ' . . . *There was a lot of smoke by then but she was smiling, like she was enjoying it, or at least she was not at all upset and she had lipstick on.*'

The idea of someone getting a kick out of this — an ego-driven high — is horrible. But is it anything more than that? Could her need to take centre stage be extreme enough to *create* the stage; making reality TV so that she could be in it? I remember Jenny talking about the hot-air balloon: '*If Annette had a child she'd put him in it.*'

'Going back to Silas Hyman,' Sarah says. 'You published a story about him a few months ago. After the incident in the playground.'

'Yes.'

'How did you find out about that?'

'An anonymous text message was sent to the landline here. It was read out by one of those weird electronic voices.'

'Do you know who it was?'

'Like I just said, anonymous.'

'Yes. But do you know who it was?'

Irritation hardens Tara's face.

'No. Couldn't trace it. It was from a

343

payphone. But it wasn't Annette Jenks, if that's what you're thinking, because she wasn't working there then. It was still that old cow of a secretary. Took me ten minutes before she'd let me speak to the head to confirm the story.'

'So you published your article. Front page.'

Tara tosses her silky hair as an answer.

'You had quotes from outraged parents. Did you tell parents about the incident, or did they come to you?'

'I really don't remember.'

'I am sure you do.'

'Alright, I phoned around a few families; got a couple of quotes in response to what I told them. So what do the police have on him then?'

'Nothing.'

Tara looks at Sarah, coldly furious. She turns off her iPhone, which has been covertly recording this; not wanting her humiliation on record.

'You said you'd do a trade,' she says, petulantly. Her parents really should have made her play Monopoly and lose once in a while.

'No,' Sarah says coolly. 'That's what you inferred.'

★   ★   ★

As we walk to the car, I glance back at the *Richmond Post* offices and, in a fit of self-indulgence, think of my dreams being filed away in an ugly grey filing cabinet.

Because following Sarah, seeing her talent and commitment, has made me see that any promise

344

I once had hasn't been kept. She's made me remember what I so hoped for — longed for — once for myself. It wasn't to review art and books, but *to be* the artist or the writer. It was absurd to think I could bash out *Anna Karenina* or a Hockney between school drop-off and pick-up while still fitting in a trip to Sainsbury's. Although people do. And a mediocre book or painting would be fine. Just something; to *try to create* something.

I used to make excuses to myself: when I had more *time*; when Jenny was older; when Adam started school. But somehow, without realising it or even really noticing, I stopped making excuses because I'd given up.

★ ★ ★

In the car, Sarah phones Mohsin on hands-free. She turns off the air-conditioning so she can hear him.

'Hi, Mohsin.'

'Hey, baby, you hanging in there?'

'Has Penny got anything on the hate-mailer?'

'No, not yet.'

'Until she does, I'm going to work on the assumption that Jenny saw either the arsonist or someone connected to the arsonist, which is why he wants to kill her now.'

Mohsin is silent.

'You did hear about the attacker?'

'Yes.'

He doesn't say anything more and the sound of his silence fills the hot car.

I see the effect on Sarah, a slight sagging of the shoulders, and I wish I could tell her I am with her, supporting her.

'It was the secretary, Annette Jenks, who tipped off the *Richmond Post* about the fire,' Sarah says. 'But there was another tip-off, four months ago, about Silas Hyman not supervising the playground. Someone wanted him out of the school.'

Mohsin is quiet. I hear a noise, maybe a biro point being clicked in and out.

'What if the witness is right, Sarah?'

'You're not an uncle, are you?' she says.

'Not yet, though my sister's working on it.'

'I *know* Adam. Who he really is, the bedrock of him, if you like, because he is a part of Michael. And therefore a part of me. And he didn't do this.'

Silence seems to ratchet up the heat in the car.

'Silas Hyman had birthday cake candles,' Sarah says. 'Eight blue ones, like the ones that must have been on Adam's cake. And he has the school calendar with Adam's birthday ringed. And his wife, I know she's lying. Or hiding something at least. I'm sure she is.'

'You went to his house?' He sounds horrified.

'No one else is doing anything, are they?' she snaps. 'Not now everyone's decided that my gentle little nephew is an arsonist.'

'For fuck's sake, Sarah, you can't just go to someone's house.'

She says nothing. The sound of a pen tapping hard now in the background, or maybe a foot.

'I'm worried about you, darling, what'll

happen if someone finds out and — '

Sarah interrupts, her tone weary now. 'I know. Actually from a getting-into-hot-water angle, it's a lot worse.'

'How?'

'His wife was bathing their kids and I just didn't clock it. I'm a mother, an aunt; bathing children is just so normal and . . . '

She breaks off. So that's what rattled her. She'd been pretending to be on police business when children were naked.

'I left once I realised,' Sarah continues. 'But it made me so angry that I was in this position. And then I felt so angry about everything. And then this bloody woman was feeling sorry for herself, *sorry for herself!*'

'Do you think she'll report you?'

'If she finds out I didn't have any authorisation to go round there, then yes. Most probably.'

'Well, I'm kind of impressed, actually,' Mohsin says. 'I always knew you had a subversive streak but never had you down as an out-and-out rebel.'

'Thanks. So will you help?'

We both wait for the sound of Mohsin's voice in the car. Nothing.

'You told me the files wouldn't be securely stored,' Sarah ventures.

'I know. Totally out of line. Baker will bust my guts for that if he finds out.' The sound of the clicking biro again. 'What do you need?'

Sarah's relief is an exhaled breath, changing the atmosphere in her car.

'The names of the investors in Sidley House.'

'Penny told me that fraud was ruled out almost straight away,' Mohsin says. 'They're comfortably in the black, according to the bank.'

'Yes, and they're starting the school up again in September. There's no reason for fraud that I can see. But I need to check all of it. And when I spoke to the head teacher she didn't like talking about the investors and I want to know why not.'

'You spoke to her too?'

Sarah was silent.

'Jesus, honey.'

'I also need to know if we've got anything on a man called Donald White. I'm pretty sure he's abusive to his daughter, possibly his wife.'

'OK. I'll do what I can,' he says. 'I'm doing an extra shift tonight. So I'll meet you for breakfast tomorrow morning. Is that grim hospital café still going?'

*   *   *

We arrive back at the hospital car park and the residual heat in the early evening air scalds me. I hurry ahead of Sarah towards the building. This time I can't see Jenny waiting for me.

Once inside the hospital's protective skin the pain again vanishes, and for a moment the state of not-being-in-pain makes me feel euphoric.

I follow Sarah towards ICU. Jenny is leaning against a wall in the corridor.

'I tried, you know, the scratch-and-sniff memory thing,' she says. 'But it's no good. A school doesn't smell like a hospital. At least Sidley House didn't.'

348

It's what I'd been banking on. Sidley House smelt of polish and hoovered carpets and cut flowers, not strong disinfectant and antiseptic and lino.

A little ahead of us, Sarah is scrolling through her texts and emails; the last point before ICU where mobiles are still allowed. We look over her shoulder. Nosiness and eavesdropping are becoming second nature.

Among her texts is one from Ivo. He's got a standby flight from Barbados, an overnight, and will be here in the morning. I look at Jen, expecting to see her beamy-happy, but her face looks tight with anxiety; almost fear. Maybe she's started to see their relationship for what it is. And perhaps that's better now, than when he actually arrives.

'Jen — ' I begin, but she cuts me off.

'I was about to go in,' she says, pointing at a door behind her.

It's the entrance to the hospital chapel, which I've never noticed before. The chapel is the one place in the hospital that won't smell of disinfectant and antiseptic.

We go in together. But I'm not worried, because surely it won't smell anything like a fire in here. In any case, I'll be with her.

Wooden pews and a carpet, threadbare but a carpet nonetheless. Even lilies, like the ones Mrs Healey always has in the small waiting area outside her office; their smell pungent in the room.

The combination of scents transports me momentarily into Sidley House; as if the gateway to a memory has a keypad and the right sensory code is punched in.

Looking at Jenny, I know that she feels it too.

'I was near Mrs Healey's office,' she says. 'And the lilies smelt really strong, you could smell the water a little too. I can remember that.'

She pauses a moment and I wait. She's going further into the memory. Should I stop her?

'I'm feeling happy. And I'm going down the stairs.'

Behind us, the door closes. An elderly woman has come in. It's broken the sensory thread to the past.

'You were going *down* the stairs?' I ask. 'Are you sure?'

'Yeah. I must have already got to the upper ground floor because that's where Mrs Healey has those lilies.'

Maybe Annette Jenks was telling the truth after all about Jenny signing herself out.

Jenny closes her eyes again, and again I don't know whether to let her continue with this. But how else are we going to help Addie?

Her face relaxes. It's all OK. She's back in a summer's afternoon at school.

She screams.

'Jenny — ?'

She's running out of the chapel.

At the back, the elderly woman has lit a candle, the smoke no more than a charcoal line in the air. But enough.

I catch up with her.

'I'm sorry, I should never have — '

'It wasn't your fault.'

350

I put my arm around her and she's shaking.

'I'm fine now, Mum. I wasn't actually back in the fire, just close.'

We walk to the garden together.

I'd thought memories were kept behind a gateway, wrought-iron, I'd visualised, with spaces to glimpse through and sometimes opening for a short time to let you actually wander in again.

But I see a corridor, now, like a long hospital corridor, and behind each set of swing doors is another memory leading inexorably to the fire. I don't think you can control how far you go along it, or know what lies behind the next set of doors. And I dread her reaching the end and the full horror of that afternoon.

★   ★   ★

Out here in the garden, the shadows are lengthening into soothing darkness.

'It was a good idea,' I say. 'To think of the chapel.'

The one place in the hospital that smelt like the school; that even had candles and matches.

'That wasn't why I was there,' she says.

She turns a little away from me, her face half hidden in darkness.

'I was hoping to suck up to God. A last minute dot com search for a place in heaven.'

Anxieties hidden in sleeves and pockets and fears stuffed up jumpers, but my God, Mike, I didn't expect this.

'I'm not that scared actually,' she says. 'I mean, this whole thing, whatever we are now,

351

does make it likely there's a heaven, some kind of an afterlife, doesn't it? It *proves* that the physical world and the physical body isn't all there is.'

I've imagined talking to her about so many things: drugs, abortion, STDs, tattoos, piercings, internet safety. Some of these we have actually discussed and I had all my research to hand. But I've never researched this conversation. Never imagined it.

I thought we were so liberal, bringing up our children without God in the house — no church-going, no grace before food, no prayers at bedtime. I secretly thought we were more honest than our church-going friends, who I assumed used going to church as a means of getting their children into high-achieving free St Swithun's. No, I'd let my children *make up their own minds*, when they were older. In the meantime, we'd sleep in on Sunday morning and go to a garden centre, not church.

But my lazy lack of faith, my in-vogue atheism, has taken away the safety net hanging beneath our children's lives.

I just didn't think it through; never thought what it would be like facing death with no knowledge of a heaven or a father-figure God to go to.

Maybe in the old days, when children died so frequently, people were more religious because they had to know where their dead children were. And if a child was dying they needed to tell her where she was going next. That it would all be alright. And to believe that. No wonder they all flocked to church. Did antibiotics kill off the devout in us? Penicillin replacing faith?

I'm talking too much, my thoughts jabbering away; like Maisie trying to hide the jagged truth with a swirl of words; trying to drown out the ticking clock, the speeding car, the sound death makes.

'Do Christians believe that you go to purgatory if you're not baptised?' Jenny asks.

She's facing this.

'You won't go to purgatory,' I snap, furious. 'There's *no such thing* as purgatory.'

How dare any God send my daughter to purgatory? As if I could walk into the head teacher's study and say that it's *absolutely unjust* for her to have a detention and I am taking her home right now.

Still talking too much.

I have to join her. Face this too.

I turn to look at the gorgon.

And death isn't a clock ticking or a car speeding towards her.

I see a girl falling overboard from life and no one is able to reach her.

Exposed and alone.

Three weeks less a day until she drowns.

Maybe it has been there all the time; this girl-alone-in-an-ocean silence; that ghastly vast expanse of it which I didn't want to hear.

'So that was what this drowning thing was really about,' Nanny Voice says. 'All along it was really this.'

Perhaps. Yes.

But she's not going to drown. I won't let her.

My certainty startles me. And there's fear in it;

353

the nervous, jittery-as-hell kind. But anything else is simply unthinkable.

Jenny dying before August the twentieth, *an actual date* on our calendar in the kitchen, and all those days afterwards that won't contain her is ludicrous. Unbearable.

And I'm not clinging onto your hope now but believing it — knowing it — for myself.

Jenny living is my only truth.

Because your child staying alive trumps everything.

'You're going to live,' I say to Jenny. 'You don't need to think about any of this. *Because you're going to live.*'

I have my rope around her.

27

Saturday morning. The radio should be going and I should be drinking coffee in bed, which you brought me half an hour ago, but didn't wake me so it's tepid now, but I'm glad of it. I should smell bacon and sausages frying downstairs as you prepare your *monster* breakfast for you and Addie and I'm hoping you've remembered to open the kitchen window so our neurotic, overly sensitive heat detector won't blast out the neighbours and make the guinea pigs bolt around their hutch. Jenny is still slumbering deeply, not hearing the bleeping of a text on her mobile, which has been going off since about eight — clearly a wrong number because none of Jenny's friends will be up yet either. But soon she'll arrive, sleepy-eyed, and sit on the end of my bed, bemoaning you not bringing her tea.

'*Tea's more effort than coffee, Jen.*'

'*Tea-bag tea 'ud be fine.*'

'*You still have to soak it and then take it out, put it in the bin. Then put in the milk. Dad only does one-step morning drinks.*'

She leans back against the pillows, next to me, and tells me who she's meeting up with this morning and it seems only a blink ago that it was me spending Saturday with friends in preparation for the main event of the evening. How can it be possible that I wake up each morning to find myself *a thirty-nine-year-old mother of two*?

Even before Tara earlier, I sometimes think of myself in tabloid descriptions. I prefer it to be along the lines of 'Daring bank robbery by thirty-nine-year-old mother of two!' variety than anything more maudlin.

Jen gives me a kiss and goes '*to make my own tea*'.

★ ★ ★

Dr Sandhu tells you Jenny is getting weaker; slowly deteriorating, as they'd predicted.

'Can she still have a transplant?' you ask.

'Yes. She's still strong enough for that. But we don't know how much longer that will be the case.'

Jenny is waiting for me outside ICU. She doesn't ask if a heart has been found. Like me, she can now read an expression at ten paces and interpret a silence. Before, I thought the only crushing silence was the one after 'I love you . . .'

'Aunt Sarah's gone to meet Belinda, that nurse,' Jenny says.

'Right.'

'And she got a text from someone to meet in the cafeteria in half an hour. She looked really pleased. Do you think it could be her man?'

Last time I was jealous of Jen's closeness to Sarah, but now it's the other way around. Jen and I don't talk about this kind of thing at all. I say *this kind of thing* because even the language is a minefield. For example, 'sexy' is old-fashioned and shows I don't have a clue, but 'hot' is embarrassing for someone as old as me (*a thirty-nine-year-old mother of two*). Actually no, it isn't a minefield to be negotiated, the entire area is off-limits; each generation linguistically roping it off for themselves. But somehow Sarah's been allowed in.

But that doesn't mean I see having sex as a rite of passage to becoming an adult. If anything, I think it's sometimes the reverse. You tease me for being a hypocrite. It's me who wants to use the creative 'making love' term rather than the acquisitive 'having sex'. But I have to break off this little cul-de-sac of a conversation because we've caught up with Sarah who's striding briskly down the corridor.

★   ★   ★

Belinda, spruce in her nurse's uniform, goes through Maisie's notes with Sarah.

'She had a cracked wrist, last winter,' Belinda says. 'She said she slipped over on an icy doorstep.'

'Any reason for the doctors or nurses looking after her to be suspicious?'

'No. A&E gets filled with broken arms and legs when it's icy. And then at the beginning of March this year there's this.'

I read, with Sarah, the notes about Maisie being admitted unconscious to hospital with two broken ribs and a fractured skull. She'd said she'd fallen down the stairs. After being discharged from hospital two weeks later she had failed to keep any of her outpatient appointments.

I'd tried to ring her during that time, but had only got her voicemail. Later she said Donald had treated her to a spa break. I'd thought it an odd thing for her to do and when I'd asked her about it she'd seemed embarrassed. I'd thought it hadn't been a success.

There's nothing else in Maisie's records. She hadn't shown any doctors her bruised cheek, nor the bruises on her arm the day of the fire, hidden under her long FUN sleeves.

Belinda gets out Rowena's notes, but it's clear she's already read them; her normally smiley face is upset.

'She had a significant burn to her leg last year. She said she dropped an iron on it and the burn mark suggested an iron.'

I remember Donald's lighted cigarette and Adam cowering away.

Was Rowena's scar the reason she was wearing long trousers on sports day? I'd thought she was just being more sensibly dressed than Jenny.

'Anything else?' Sarah asks.

'No. Unless they went to another hospital. It sometimes happens. Communication between hospitals isn't as efficient as it should be.'

'I'd like you to tell me if Donald White comes to visit again,' Sarah says. 'I don't want him to have unsupervised access.'

Belinda nods. She meets Sarah's eye.

'There's nothing I can do until one of them reports it,' Sarah says with frustration.

'You'll encourage them to?'

'Let's get them both to a state where that's an option. Get Rowena back on her feet and out of here first. I don't want to ask them to do anything while they're so vulnerable. For a start,

358

if you get that kind of decision now they could well go back on it.'

★ ★ ★

Sarah joins Mohsin in the hospital cafeteria. His caramel-coloured face is tired; shadows under his eyes.

'Is that him?' Jenny asks.

'No. Her lover's younger and more gorgeous,' I say.

She doesn't even flinch when I say the embarrassing word 'lover', but instead smiles.

'Good for her.'

Sarah and Mohsin's heads are bent close together; old confidantes. We go to join them.

'It looks like domestic abuse to both mum and daughter,' Sarah is saying.

'We've got nothing on him,' Mohsin says. 'One speeding ticket, issued last year, sum total.'

'According to the head teacher's transcript, Rowena White was going to be the school nurse on sports day,' Sarah says. 'They only changed their mind and swapped to Jenny last Thursday.'

'You think he was trying to hurt his daughter?' Mohsin asks, clearly thinking along the same lines as Jenny had earlier.

'It's possible,' Sarah replies. 'Maybe he believed Rowena was still the school nurse. Maybe no one told him about the substitution. Can you find Maisie and Rowena White's medical notes at other hospitals? See if there was anything we've missed?'

He nods.

'What about the investors at Sidley House?' she asks.

'There are a couple of small fry. Venture capitalists who invested in a number of similar projects; legit business people. Another investor, the largest one, is the Whitehall Park Road Trust Company.'

'Do you know who that's owned by?'

He shakes his head. 'It could be one case of nasty domestic violence,' he says, carefully. 'And another case of malicious mail. And another of arson. All three completely separate.'

'There's a connection. I'm sure there is.'

'Go into any institution — including a school — and you'd probably find an instance of domestic violence. And another of bullying, not to the malicious-mail level like Jenny had, but you'd find something cruel going on in the classroom or staffroom or cyber-bullying.'

'And Jenny being attacked?'

Mohsin turns fractionally away.

'You still don't believe it?' Sarah asks.

Mohsin is silent. Sarah studies him.

'So what do you think?'

'I think I need to set your mind at rest.'

'Well, that's more than anyone else is doing, so thank you.'

They are not used to this awkwardness.

He takes her hand, gives it a squeeze.

'Poor Tim's grieving for you.'

'It wasn't — ' She hesitates. 'Appropriate, any more. I should get back to Mike.'

Almost before they've gone the cleaner sprays the table with something pungent.

Can you be homesick for a table? Because I'm overwhelmed with yearning for our old wooden table in the kitchen at home, with Adam's knight figures at one end, yesterday's newspaper at the other, someone's jacket or jumper draped over a chair. I know, I used to get irritated by '*the mess!*' and demand people '*tidy up after themselves!*' Now I long for a messy life, not one devastated and transferred to an overly organised world of slick shiny surfaces.

I see that Jenny's eyes are closed, that she's very still.

The cleaning fluid is still pungent on the Formica table.

'I went into the school kitchen,' she says. 'They'd cleaned it all up. And it was steamy because the dishwashers had been running.'

In here there's steam from newly washed cups and saucers being placed on a rack by the coffee machine.

'I was feeling kind of excited,' Jenny continues, 'about going outside.'

I'm monitoring this closely, I won't let her get too far along the memory corridor; won't let her go through the last set of doors — or anywhere near them.

'I got two bottles of water out of the kitchen,' Jenny continues. 'The really big heavy bottles with the carry handles? It was my job to bring out extra water at the end of sports day in case they didn't have enough. The plastic handles are too narrow and they dig into my hands. I take them up those narrow steps, you know, the exit by the kitchen?'

Then she stops and shakes her head.

'That's it. I was going out of the school, definitely *out*. But I don't know what happened then.'

'The water bottles were outside at the side of the school, on that gravelly bit by the kitchen exit,' I say, remembering that Rowena had used one to soak her towel before going in.

'But why did I go back inside again?' Jenny asks.

'Maybe to help?'

'But the reception children all got out fine, didn't they? And Tilly? Everyone got out.'

I don't know what to say.

'Maybe that's when I lost my phone,' she says. 'When I bent to put the water down. It was in that little pocket at the top of my red skirt. It's fallen out before.'

'Yes.'

'You should go and see what Aunt Sarah's up to,' she says. 'I'll stay here if that's OK. It's the only place that's halfway normal.'

'You won't try to remember any more, will you?'

'Mum . . . '

'Not without me. Please.'

'OK.'

★ ★ ★

I leave Jenny in the cafeteria and go to ICU.

Ivo is standing in the corridor. Just seeing his narrow back-view and trendy haircut brings vivid memories of Jenny, a whole dimension of her that has been left behind since the fire — the exuberant, energetic teenager with joie de vivre and passionate good humour; Jenny walking on air. And a kind of helplessness as she fell in love, so trusting of Ivo to catch her.

He hasn't gone to her bedside but neither has he run away.

I go closer. His face is white as he looks at her through the glass wall; tremors are coursing through his body and I see a boy lying on a pavement being beaten and kicked and punched.

I feel overwhelming pity for him.

Sarah is with him.

'I spoke to her on Wednesday,' he says. 'And she sounded just like usual. Happy. And then we texted each other. The last one, from me, she must have got at just after three, her time.'

He turns away from looking at Jenny. 'Will you tell me what's happening?'

'She's very badly injured. Her heart failed yesterday. She needs a transplant to stay alive. Without one, she'll only live for a few more weeks.'

Sarah's words kick him over and over again.

'I'm sorry,' Sarah says.

I think he'll ask if she'll be disfigured; if Sarah will tell him that we don't know yet. He's silent.

'It was arson,' she says. 'We don't know if someone deliberately targeted Jenny. Possibly it's connected to the malicious mail. Do you know anything?'

'No. She hadn't got any idea who it was.'

His voice is quiet and shaken.

I see you leaving Jenny's bedside and coming

363

out into the corridor, but they haven't yet seen you.

'Someone threw red paint at her,' Ivo says. 'She phoned me. Said she'd had to get a friend to cut her hair. The paint wouldn't come out. She was crying.'

Sarah jumps on this. 'Did she see who it was?'

'No. It was from behind.'

'Any description at all?'

'No.'

'When was this, Ivo?'

'About eight weeks ago.'

'Do you know where it happened?'

'In Hammersmith shopping arcade, just by Primark. She thought he must have run into a shop or a side exit to the street straight afterwards. She said a woman was screaming because she thought it was blood on her.'

I see you grappling with the information, no corner of your mind free to store anything else, but it's forcing its way inside.

'I should have made her go to the police,' Ivo says. 'If I had — '

'*I'm* the police, Ivo,' Sarah says. 'No, look at me. Please. She should have felt that she could come to me. I'm her aunt and I love her. But she didn't. And that's my responsibility. Not yours.'

'She said her parents would be so upset if they found out. She didn't want to worry them. Maybe that was true for you too.'

'Yes. I'd like you to give a statement at the police station to a colleague of mine. I'll get a car to pick you up and drop you back again so it should be as quick as possible.'

Ivo nods.

Sarah gives him Jenny's mobile. 'Can you look through this, see if there are any contacts you don't recognise? Or messages that seem strange to you? I've looked, but I can't see anything odd.'

He takes it, fingers tightening around it.

'Shall I look at the phone now?' Ivo asks. 'While I wait?'

Like you, he wants to be *doing* something.

'Yes.'

Sarah sees you. 'There was red paint, Mike — '

'I heard.'

Maybe she expects you to be angry with Ivo. But you aren't. Is it because you hadn't gone to the police about the hate mail for two weeks? Your whole body seems caved in and your face gaunt.

'Why don't you go and see Adam?' Sarah says. 'I can stay here with Jenny for a while now.'

I think Sarah's realised how much you need Adam, as well as him needing you.

'Ivo has to give his statement,' she continues. 'And I've got a few things to read through which I can do here. I'll call you immediately if there's anything.'

Ivo comes up, interrupting.

'I'm not sure if it means anything, but the last text I sent her on Wednesday afternoon has been deleted.'

'She could have done that,' Sarah suggests.

'It was a poem. Not that bad. Even if it was, she wouldn't have deleted it.'

'Jenny's phone was found on the gravel just

365

outside the school,' Sarah says. 'Anyone could have tampered with it.'

'But why would someone want to delete my message?' Ivo asks.

'I don't know,' Sarah says.

'Have you found out yet why it was outside?' you ask.

'No. Not yet. And we couldn't get prints because it's been handled by the reception teacher and Maisie.'

'Should I wait here for the ride to the police station, or down in the foyer bit?' Ivo asks.

He still hasn't gone to Jenny's bedside.

I think he's relieved for the opportunity to be away from her.

★ ★ ★

I find Jenny in the goldfish-bowl atrium, people swarming past her. Does she feel like she has a stronger handhold on life to be amongst so much of it? Or perhaps she's waiting for Ivo, not knowing he's already here and in ICU. '*You should have told me. I had a right to know.*'

'Ivo's here.' I say. 'He's in ICU with Dad and Aunt Sarah.'

'I don't want to see him,' she says, her voice quiet.

Yesterday she wasn't excited about him coming. Perhaps she's realised that their relationship is based on physical beauty. She's so vulnerable and I'm glad she's protecting herself from rejection and further hurt.

I don't tell her that he stared at her through

366

the glass and was tortured by what he saw.

I don't tell her that he didn't go any nearer.

'He's told Aunt Sarah about the red paint,' I say instead. 'He also said that he sent you a text at three, but it's deleted.'

'But I never delete his texts.'

'Maybe someone did that after you dropped your phone.'

'But why?'

'I don't know. He's going to the police station to give a statement.'

'So he'll come through here?' Her voice is panicked. She turns and hurries away from the atrium.

I go after her.

'How many people know your mobile number, Jen?'

'Loads.'

'I don't mean friends, I mean, well, people at the school, for example?'

'Everyone. It was written up on a notice board in the staffroom for teachers to put into their own mobiles. They were meant to call me if they needed anything from the sick-room during sports day.'

She hurries on, fleeing from the possibility of seeing Ivo.

But I stand still a moment, feeling frustration as a physical force. *I have to talk to Sarah.*

She needs to know that Jenny was *outside the school*, but then went back in. Something or someone must have persuaded her; or made her. Could it have been a text? And could the person who sent it have deleted it, and deleted Ivo's too in their haste?

28

I join you as you leave the hospital, desperate to see you and Addie together. The only time you've been with Addie since the fire, he pushed you away from Silas Hyman. But now, alone together, it will surely be different.

Our car has been too long in the shadeless car park and inside the air is heavy with heat; the metal clasp of the seat-belts stingingly hot. But you don't open the windows or switch on the air-con.

As you drive, I don't think of us going out to dinner with friends but feel as if we're somewhere wild and lawless and blisteringly exposed; more akin to a lion pair in the Serengeti, protecting their cubs against poachers, than any neighbours in W4 with their safe, smooth lives.

Adam told me a few weeks ago that he and Jenny made you and me blood relatives, because in them we share the same blood. Is that why we're pulled so viscerally and fiercely together now? To make sure Jenny lives. To prove our son is innocent.

You left Sarah at Jenny's bedside with the illegal transcripts, her incongruous owl notebook and Elizabeth Fisher's contract. Sarah must have read those transcripts a dozen times already and goodness knows what she'll get from Elizabeth's contract. Yes, I know. I'm hardly a trained

368

detective and am in no position to comment. Besides, I trust Sarah. If she thinks something is worth doing then it must be.

As we near home, I think of the first journey we ever made from the hospital to home. Adam was four hours old; me on a cushion in the back, staring at him: so perfect and vulnerable. With Jenny nine years earlier, going home to our old tiny flat, my nanny voice had told me it was *terrifying* I was just allowed to take a baby home with *absolutely no clue* what I was doing. *Something awful* could happen. I was too young, too immature, too *downright silly* to be in charge of a baby. How would a knowledge of Florentine frescoes or the difference between Coleridge and Johnson as literary critics help me look after her? I'd felt more akin to animals in a wild and dangerous place then too, unequipped to prevent terrible things from happening to my baby.

But Jenny turned us into parents. With Adam we knew how to put in a backward-facing babyseat to avoid crushing by air bags; and sterilise bottles to avoid nasty bugs; and purée first food without salt that could collapse tiny kidneys; and when to apply eye ointment and nappy cream and Calpol; and immunisations against terrible diseases were routine. I put nine years of experience, the NHS and John Lewis's nursery department between my baby and the dangerous wilds of the Serengeti.

You carried our blanket-wrapped boy, asleep in his car seat, up the front doorsteps. Safe.

★ ★ ★

369

You park the car and you don't get out straight away. But I hurry inside.

In Addie's bedroom, Mum is drawing the curtains against the too-bright sun. He's in bed and she's got the portable air-conditioner going, the white noise soporifically calming.

'You're exhausted, poppet,' she's saying to him. 'And it'll just be a nap. I'll sit with you.'

He believes, from her, that I'll never wake up; that I'm the same as dead.

It wasn't only Jenny's dying that I'd seen as drowning, but also Adam's grief. I still do.

A small boy out in a dark angry ocean where I can't reach him.

I long to go to him, but I know he won't feel me and I don't think I can bear that now; so instead I watch Mum.

She sits down next to him in the darkened room. She takes his hand and I see his face relax a little. She used to sit with me when I was a child, and it was so comforting — Mum there with me and the curtains drawn while it was still light outside.

As I look at them I can imagine what will happen to him if I never wake up again. It's just for a moment, but enough time to punch a window out of my dread into a vista of new thoughts. His armbands can be puffed full of my mother's breath and Sarah's and Jenny's. And yours — most of all yours. Maybe other people's love will keep him afloat.

I hear the front door closing and your footsteps in the hall. And I almost hear you yell, 'I'm home!' up the stairs and feel Adam leaping out of bed and away from the book I'm reading and yelling, 'Daddy!'

'*A Railway Children moment every day,*' you said once, not even trying for an ironic tone.

But then you'd had to go away more frequently and for longer; and even when you were working in London, got home later. Your *Railway Children* moments with Addie had become few and far between.

Adam sits upright, his whole body tensed.

Mum goes downstairs to find you. Away from Addie, her face looks terrified.

'Has anything happened?' she asks.

'All the same.'

'Addie's in bed, but he's awake.'

She doesn't say that she's told him I'll never wake up. Is that an oversight, or deliberate? One hell of an oversight, but then everything is out of whack and disproportionate now. And she looks so sad, so vulnerable without her mask for Addie in place.

Your footsteps sound heavy on the stairs, weighted down.

You knock on Addie's door. He doesn't answer.

'Ads?' you say.

No response.

'Addie, open the door, please.'

Silence.

I see your hurt.

'He hates me,' you say quietly, and I think Mum must be there, but it's just me. Did you really say it? Or do I just know you so well that I know what you are thinking?

It's not just the thing with Silas Hyman, is it? It's the fire.

You think that as a father you should have stopped it from happening. A father doesn't let your mother and sister be horrifically injured. A father *protects your family.*

Do you think this is why he hates you?

Why he's not opening his door to you?

The other side of the closed door, Adam is curled up on top of his bed, as if unable to move as well as speak.

For God's sake, Mike, just go in there right now and tell him you know he didn't start the fire.

But you say nothing.

You think he already knows.

The closed door between you, with its peeling white paint on one side and Peter Pan cut-out on the other, shuts off my vista of hope.

★　★　★

We drive back to the hospital and I don't think about bringing Adam home, but the journey ten hours earlier, with each contraction pushing me beyond the perimeter of normal and imaginable and bearable.

★　★　★

When we arrive back, I think I see Jenny amongst the tawdry group of smokers outside the hospital, but when I look again I can't see her. I must have been wrong.

Outside the ICU, Sarah is on her mobile. I go closer to listen. She's finishing a conversation with Roger, sounding snappy and disappointed. She hangs up, then phones Mohsin straight afterwards,

'Hi, me. I've got five minutes while Jenny's having some tests done. Dr Sandhu promised he wouldn't leave her for a second.'

'Her boyfriend's giving a statement to Davies, right now,' Mohsin says. 'Jesus, honey, why didn't they tell anyone?'

'They didn't want to worry us. What's happening with the hate-mail investigation?'

'It's turned into stalking and assault, so the enquiry's upped several gears. Penny's going to widen the DNA search and she's got people sweating blood over the CCTV footage. She'd already narrowed it down to a three-hour time frame when the letter must have been posted. Her team's weeding out anyone over sixty or under fifteen and then she'll get stills of those remaining. From those mugshots she's hoping to get an ID.'

'Is anyone connecting it to the arson attack?'

'Not yet.'

'You?'

She tenses as she waits for his reply.

'I think that knowing someone must have been tracking Jenny, and then physically assaulting her, changes how we should look at the fire. I think that a stalker means it's far more likely the fire was aimed at her. I think that it's more than possible now that the witness, whoever they are, was lying.'

'And the attack in the hospital?'

'I just don't know.'

She waits a moment but he doesn't say anything else.

'I think you must have been right about Donald White,' she says. 'It must be a separate thing.' She pauses a moment. 'Has Ivo told you about his missing text?'

'Lord Byron? Thank God there wasn't texting when I was a teenager.'

'If he really sent his poem at just after three, the fire had already taken hold. She wouldn't have been deleting poems. Can we get the techno guys to check it out?'

'Sure. Though I don't know what we're checking for.'

'I have to get back to Jenny now.'

★ ★ ★

You come to my bed and pull the curtains around and we are surrounded by ugly brown geometric squares.

'He doesn't want to see me.'

'Of course he does. He loves you. And he needs you. And — '

'I don't blame him. I've been a bloody useless father. Not just this. Just . . . Christ. But before, bloody useless before too.'

'That's not true.'

'No wonder he turned to Silas Hyman. I was never there, was I?'

'You were earning the money so — '

'But even when I was with him I got it wrong.

374

He's never wanted me in a crisis. Always you. And now . . . '

'I've just been there. That's all. And he's never actually had a crisis before this; just unhappy times. If he had it would have been you he turned to, because look at you — being so bloody strong for everyone.'

'You do this, not me, and *I don't know how*.'

'Of course you do! You just need to be with him, that's all. Talk to him.'

But you can't hear me. Your insecurity about Adam blocks out what I am telling you as much as my lack of a voice.

And your loss of confidence with Addie is my fault.

I was always putting you straight and telling you off and pointing out what you should be doing with Adam, never letting you just do it your way, never trusting you as a father to want the best for him too. So many small things — what kind of birthday present; what to write in his homework diary if he hadn't finished his Maths so that he wouldn't get into trouble. '*Let him get into trouble*,' you'd said and I'd thought you cruel. But maybe if he had got into trouble, he'd have realised it wasn't so awful. Maybe other kids would have liked him more too. And perhaps I *should* have risked being late to school with him, as you wanted and I'd thought insensitive. He might have seen that the world didn't collapse when he was late and then maybe he'd have stopped worrying.

And even if you were wrong, what right had I to say I knew better? Knew Adam better?

And I'm sorry that I said you didn't stand up for him at the prize-giving, weren't proud of him, as if you were always that way. Because a few months later, you demanded a meeting with Mrs Healey and you made sure Robert Fleming wouldn't come back the next academic year. And it was nothing to do with you being a man or your celebrity status causing 'a smellier stink'. I think Mrs Healey just realised that she was no match for you when you were protecting your son. And I remember that later that night, when I quizzed you, you told me she'd got Robert Fleming and his parents in too, probably hoping to outnumber you. But instead you'd been *glad* to publicly say that it was all down to Robert, nothing to do with Adam; and you told them you were proud of the way Adam is. What did they make of you, this big, tough man, famous for presenting a macho survival series, having pride in his small bullied son?

But the memory faded too fast; maybe because we didn't speak about it again. You didn't want Adam to find out about your meeting, worried about him feeling even more powerless, while I was anxious he might feel guilty for Robert being made to leave. But I think you should tell him now; so he knows that you'll always look out for him; protect him. That you're there for him when it counts. That you're proud of him.

You are still silent.

'You *can do this*, Mike.'

Dr Bailstrom pulls the curtains back.

'It's important to observe your wife at all

376

times,' she says curtly.

'To prove that you're right and there's fuck all to observe?' you snap back at her as you leave, and only I see the falter in your step.

   ★   ★   ★

You arrive at Jenny's bedside, where Sarah is sitting guard. She has Elizabeth's contract open.

'Is there anything you can remember about when Elizabeth Fisher left?' she asks you.

'Who?'

'The old secretary at the school.'

'No,' you say impatiently. You catch your sister's expression. 'I think Grace organised some flowers for her. Her husband was dying. She'd been there since the school started.'

'Actually, her husband left her,' Sarah says.

   ★   ★   ★

I leave with Sarah. I still haven't seen Jenny, and I wish I knew *where on earth she's got to.* And the feeling of being irritated is comforting because it's so familiar — we're again the Push-me-Pull-you Doctor Dolittle creation that a mother and teenage daughter make; her pushing me away and me pulling her back.

As I get to the atrium with Sarah, I catch a glimpse of Jen outside, screened by a knot of smokers. It is definitely her. I hurry out. She's flinching as the gravel cuts into her soft feet; the sun scaldingly hot.

I'm worried that she's waiting for Ivo to come

back from the police station.

She sees me.

'I need to remember,' she says. 'I know you told me not to, without you, but I need to know the reason I went back into the school. For Addie. There's gravel by the kitchen exit. And the sound of it — the feel — I thought would help.' She pauses a moment, upset. 'But it hasn't done any good. So far anyway.'

I'm relieved that she hasn't remembered anything on her own — thank God cigarette smoke smells nothing like a fire. I'm relieved too that she's not waiting for Ivo.

A smoker strikes a match, cupping it in his hands to light his cigarette. The smoke from a match is flimsy, weaker than candle smoke and unable to push open a memory door.

Then Sarah walks past us on her way to the car park. The sound of her footsteps crunching gravel and the sun overhead joins with the faintest of smoke trails from the match.

'The fire alarm was going off,' Jenny says. She pauses a moment as the memory comes into focus. How many times has she done this? Waited for someone to strike a match and for someone to crunch the gravel?

'I thought it was a mistake,' she continues. 'Or a practice and Annette wouldn't have a clue what to do. I thought it would be mean to leave her on her own, so I put the water bottles down on the gravel and I went back in. And then I smelt smoke. And I knew it wasn't a practice.'

She stops, frustrated.

'That's it. That's where I get to.' She's upset

378

and in pain. 'I'd thought I went in because I saw something, you know, something wrong. A person doing something. The arsonist. But it was just to make sure Annette was OK. Nothing else. Christ.'

I put my arm around her to comfort her.

But why, if she went in just to help Annette, wasn't she able to leave again? Annette had time to phone the *Richmond Post* and a television station and put on lipstick and still get out with no problem.

If there really is a deleted text, then maybe it wasn't to get her into the school — her kindness towards Annette did that — but *to keep her there*. And maybe it was the reason she was at the top of the school. Because she was *two floors above* Annette's office when I found her.

She's shaking, her face knotted in pain. She hasn't built up any tolerance to this.

'Go inside, sweetheart,' I urge her, and she does as I ask.

She hasn't said anything about Ivo, and I don't press her on it.

I catch up with Sarah by her car.

* * *

Twenty minutes later we're again outside Elizabeth Fisher's exhaust-stained house; Sarah's Polo half straddling the narrow pavement. In the harsh sunshine an oil spill on the road reflects black, deformed rainbows.

Elizabeth looks pleased to see Sarah. She leads her hospitably into her tiny sitting room.

'I heard the parents at Sidley House sent you flowers when you left?' Sarah says.

'Delphiniums and some freesia bulbs; with a lovely letter. Mrs White and Mrs Covey organised it.'

'They thought your husband was dying.'

Elizabeth turns away and she looks ashamed. 'Somehow they got the wrong end of the stick.'

'Didn't you put them straight?'

'How could I? After those beautiful flowers and their kind letter. How could I say that my husband had left me and that I'd been fired for being too old?'

The pollution from the road has seeped into the room, exhaust fumes heavy in the hot air. Sarah gets out Elizabeth Fisher's contract.

'I have a query I want you to help me with,' Sarah says. 'Your job description has a chunk about new admissions — sending out prospectuses and welcome packs, sorting out the forms?'

I remember that Elizabeth had also told Sarah this on her last visit.

'Yes. It was quite an onerous task.'

'Your successor, Annette Jenks, doesn't have admissions as part of her job description.'

I remembered Annette Jenks's transcript. At the time, I'd only noticed that she wasn't the school nurse.

'No, well, I suppose the new girl wouldn't have to do admissions, or at least — ' She breaks off.

She looks suddenly older and frailer.

'After the accident in the playground,' Sarah says, 'were there fewer new admissions?'

Elizabeth nods, her voice is quiet.

'The admissions didn't fall off straight away. It was after the *Richmond Post* published that article about the accident. I just didn't put it together. Why the hell didn't I put it together?'

'Could you just tell me what happened?' Sarah asks.

'New parents stopped phoning us. Before that I'd get two to three phone calls a week from prospective parents. Some of the mums had only just given birth. One family even tried to reserve a place when the mother was still pregnant.

'But after they printed that nonsense about Silas we didn't have any new enquiries. Why choose Sidley House when there are two other private schools in the area with good results and no children almost being killed in the playground?'

'How many new children were coming to Sidley House in September?'

'At the time I was booted out, we were down to six in the two reception classes for the next academic year. Most of the parents phoned to cancel. They wanted their deposit back. The rest didn't even call us, too rich or too rude to bother.'

When Adam went to Sidley House, both reception classes were full with another fifteen children on a waiting list if a place became vacant.

'Who knew about this?' Sarah asks.

'Sally Healey. And the governors, I imagine. But she didn't want to worry the other staff; said she'd be able to sort it all out.'

Elizabeth's posture is hunched now.

'Thank you. You've been very helpful.'

'I believed her. When she said she could sort it all out. She'd done it with the existing parents, got them all to stay. I believed her . . . '

She falters for a moment and tries to regain her composure.

'She didn't want anyone to find out,' she says. 'That's why she fired me, isn't it?'

★   ★   ★

I get in the car with Sarah. Almost immediately the incar phone rings.

'Sarah?'

Mohsin's voice sounds different. And he almost never calls her Sarah, always 'darling' or 'baby'.

'I was about to call you,' she says and she's buzzing. 'I just saw the old secretary. The one Annette Jenks replaced.'

'You mustn't — '

'I know. Shouldn't have done that. But listen. Annette Jenks didn't have admissions as part of her job, but it was a big part of Elizabeth Fisher's job description. That's the reason Sally Healey got rid of Elizabeth and why she deliberately hired someone as brainless as Annette — '

'Sarah, please. Listen to me. Baker's had Sally Healey checking up on you. He's talking about disciplinary procedures.'

'Right. Well. You'd better not be caught fraternising with the enemy then.'

'Darling — '

382

She hangs up. The phone rings again but she doesn't answer it.

*   *   *

After three days of intense heat, the grass is parched and balding; the azalea flowers, once blooming up to chest-height, lie desiccated on the ground.

Sally Healey's Portakabin door is open. Her face is shining with sweat and her hair clinging to her scalp.

Sarah knocks on the open door. Sally Healey is visibly startled to see her.

'I know that you made a complaint about me. And I understand that. It's fair enough. But I'm here now as Jenny's aunt and Grace's sister-in-law.'

Sally Healey looks shocked. 'I didn't know.'

'If you want me to leave, just say so.'

Sally Healey says nothing and barely moves. The hot humid air seems to weigh us all down in the small space.

'Shall we walk and talk?' Sarah says, stepping out of the Portakabin.

Sally Healey waits a moment then joins Sarah outside.

There's a faint breeze and carried on it is the distant echo of whistles and children's voices and small feet pounding the ground.

They start walking around the large playing field and I follow.

'You told me that your school was full on sports day,' Sarah says. 'And how hard you'd worked to achieve that.'

'Yes, and we will start again; just as I said. Over the summer I'm looking at properties; we'll be ready to start again on September the eighth just as in the school calendar and — '

'But in September there are only a handful of new children joining reception, isn't that right? Possibly none the year after that or the year after that?'

'I can get those children back. I can get new children to join. I'm going to offer bursaries and scholarship schemes. Target families who wouldn't normally go to private schools.'

But as she speaks her voice is limp, wrung out by the energy needed for such optimism.

'Do the other investors share your confidence?' Sarah asks.

Sally Healey is silent.

'I imagine,' continues Sarah, 'they only saw the school facing financial ruin. Which would become apparent to everyone in September. Presumably the rest of the school would start to fall apart too. No one wants their child in a school that's going down the tubes. Was it you — or someone else — who decided to get rid of the member of staff in charge of admissions? To keep things quiet.'

'She was too old to do the job any more. I told you that.'

'That's bollocks, isn't it?'

Sally Healey's stride has become jerky. She doesn't reply.

'Was it you who made up the story of Elizabeth Fisher's husband dying?'

Mrs Healey says nothing. Sarah is now leading them on towards the edge of the playing field.

'You must have known her husband had left her, for your ploy to work.'

'I'd heard he'd left her, yes.'

'Though you don't listen to gossip?'

'A member of staff, Tilly Rogers, told me when she found out I was making Mrs Fisher redundant, in the hope that I would reconsider my decision.'

'But instead you used that personal vulnerable information against her.'

Mrs Healey turns to Sarah. 'I didn't want her to contact parents and tell them about the fall in admissions.'

'So you made sure she'd be too embarrassed to do that.'

'We just couldn't afford any more negativity. I'm not proud of what I did. But it was necessary.'

'You then replaced her with an unintelligent young secretary who could be relied on not to notice that no new families were signing up.'

'That's not how it was.'

'I think that's exactly how it was.'

We've reached the edge of the playing field now. Through the branches of the horse-chestnuts, lining the driveway, you can just glimpse the black cadaver of a school.

'And this?' Sarah says. She turns to Mrs Healey, her eyes blazing. '*Whose idea was this?*'

'I had nothing to do with it,' Sally Healey says. 'Nothing! I spent years building up a school to be proud of.'

'So was it an investor who wanted a fire?'

'Nobody wanted a fire. *Nobody!*'

'Wasn't that why you wanted those fire precautions in place, so that the insurance would pay out?'

'No!'

'And no one gives a damn about Jenny and Grace. Just *fucking money.*'

She's here as your sister and she can swear if she wants to.

Mrs Healey is just staring at her school.

'I heard that some of the children have already been given places in other schools,' she says, her voice very quiet now. 'And who's going to give me a job? When I allowed my school to burn down, when one of my teaching assistants is so badly hurt?'

'A colleague of mine will interview you formally,' Sarah says, curtly.

Tears mix with the sweat on Mrs Healey's cheeks.

'We were never going to come back from this, were we? Whatever I did.'

29

On her car phone Sarah tells Mohsin about the ticking financial time bomb at Sidley House. As she speaks, I remember Paul Prezzner, the *Telegraph* journalist, talking to Tara. '*The point is that it's a <u>business</u>. A <u>multi-million-pound business</u>. And it's gone up in smoke. That's what you should be investigating.*'

Jenny had thought so too.

'I'm sorry,' Mohsin says when Sarah finishes. 'We'll get people onto it straight away. Talk to the head teacher, get the background on the investors. The whole shebang.'

'Thanks.'

'I leave you alone for an hour,' he says, his voice affectionate, 'and you create a whole new line of enquiry. New suspect. New motive.'

'Yup.'

Adam is *so close* now to being cleared. And surely that will help him; surely that will mean he can talk again.

Mohsin is quiet; on speaker phone we can hear him take a couple of breaths.

'Baker's getting Davies to contact you about the disciplinary meeting. He wants you to come in at three today. But this may make him drop it.'

'I doubt that, somehow. I do mind, you know, even if I don't show it, about losing my job.'

'It won't come to that.'

'It may come to much worse than that. The

thing is, I've just got too much to worry about to really notice that I'm worrying about that too. Has Ivo left?'

'About twenty minutes ago. He should be there by now.'

★ ★ ★

We arrive back at the hospital, but I can't see Jenny.

I follow Sarah to ICU.

You and Ivo are standing next to each other in the corridor. You're looking at Jenny through the glass, but Ivo isn't. Have you noticed that?

No, that isn't a criticism of him, because none of us can bear to look at her; but we are her parents, so we have no choice.

'I'm pretty sure it was fraud, Mike,' Sarah says to you.

You stare at Jenny, not turning to Sarah.

'Do you know who?'

'Not yet. We're checking it all out, making sure the paper trail's there.'

She doesn't tell you about her disciplinary meeting with Baker; that the ice has given way beneath her now.

'Does it matter?' Ivo says, speaking for the first time. 'Who did this or why?'

I understand why to him it doesn't matter. Will the who or the why mend her body, heal her face? How can anything matter compared with that?

No one's yet told him that Adam's been accused, that he's the reason it matters.

388

Ivo turns away and leaves. The doors of ICU bang shut behind him.

Where is Jenny?

I go after him, calling out, 'No. Don't go. Please.'

He hurries on, me at his side.

'She doesn't mean it, saying she doesn't want to see you. She's just trying to feel that way, to protect herself, but it won't last. She wants to see you desperately. I know her so well, you see. And she adores you.'

He's reached the escalator.

'She'll come to find you. Soon. Because she won't be able to keep this up much longer. And she'll need you to be at her side.'

He walks quickly along the ground-floor corridor towards the exit, not hearing me.

'*You have to be with her.*'

He doesn't turn.

I yell at him, '*Don't do this to her!*'

He gets to the glass wall that abuts the garden. He stops.

In the garden, Jenny is sitting on the wrought-iron seat.

He looks at her through the glass, totally still now. People swarming past him.

How does he know she's there? How?

He looks for the door and finds it.

As he's about to go out, a security guard comes up to him.

'That garden's not for use. It's just for looking at.'

'I have to go out there.'

From the security guard's point of view Ivo

389

must look a little mad — shaky, his face white but with eyes oddly glowing.

'If it's outside you're after, go out of our main exit, sir, walk along the road and follow the signs to the park.'

Ivo doesn't move.

The security guard waits a moment, decides he can't be bothered to do much about this and walks away. I wonder if he'll call Psychiatry and check that all their in-patients are accounted for.

I think things like this so I won't feel Ivo's emotion that seems to shatter the glass between them. Not a hormonal tide, as I'd once patronisingly assumed, made of an overflow of teenage glands, but something finer and lighter and purer — love that is young.

I was wrong about him too. Horribly so. I distrusted him because he was so different to you. And because I'd rather feel itchy distrust and scepticism than flesh-wounding jealousy.

When Jenny told me about her and Ivo staring at each other's faces in Chiswick Park, I tried to bury missing the way you once looked at me: *'Our eye-beams twisted, and did thread/Our eyes, upon one double string.'*

But at some point — how long ago? Was it sudden or gradual? — the double string turned into a washing line of domesticity.

Who's going to stare at my thirty-nine-year-old face for an entire afternoon?

Deep down, I must have always known that this was about me not him.

That looking at Ivo, with Jenny, was looking at what I'd lost.

'Oh grow up!' says my nanny voice. 'Stop whining! For goodness sake, you're a thirty-nine-year-old mother of two, what do you expect?' She's right. I'm sorry.

Ivo goes into the forbidden garden.

He goes towards Jenny.

But she hurriedly leaves.

'Jenny . . . ?' I say.

'I want him to leave me alone.'

I look at her, not understanding.

'I don't want to see him! I told you that!'

She walks quickly away from the garden and Ivo.

He looks around, as if searching for her. Then he leaves too, confused and hurt. As if he knows he's lost her.

And perhaps I have too, in a small way.

Because I don't understand her, Mike.

I don't know her and I thought I did.

Ivo waits by the garden, hoping she'll return. And I wait too. But there's no sign of her.

★ ★ ★

I'm not sure how long we've been here now, and still no sign of Jenny, but I've just spotted Mohsin hurrying along an upper walkway.

When I catch up with him, he's meeting Sarah.

'I tried to get you on your mobile, but it's switched off,' he says.

'Not allowed near ICU.'

'The fraud line plays out. The head teacher is giving a statement backing up what you said and

Davies has been looking more closely at the investors. The Whitehall Park Road Trust Company put two million pounds into Sidley House School thirteen years ago.' He pauses a moment. 'It's owned by Donald White.'

The fraud has a face now; one that had seemed warmly avuncular and then became harsh under the hospital lights and closer scrutiny.

'It fits with what you suspect,' Mohsin continues. 'If he's capable of domestic violence then I think he'd be capable of arson.'

He puts his arm around Sarah.

'Baker's 'reassessing' the witness report against Adam. Which is code for he fucked up. He now thinks — we all do — that this was fraud. And that Adam played no part in the arson attack.'

Relief feels like a cool wind; a balm. And I see that Sarah feels it too. I long for her to run to you, right now, and tell you.

'Donald White could have attacked Jenny that first night,' Sarah says. 'When her oxygen was tampered with. His daughter was in the burns unit too. If he'd been discovered no one would have questioned him being there.'

'Baker's brought him in for questioning,' Mohsin says. 'I'm going to talk to Rowena and Maisie White now. See if they can shed any light on what Dad's been up to.'

Sarah kisses Mohsin lightly on the cheek. 'I'll tell Mike.'

* * *

I go with Mohsin into the burns unit and towards Rowena's room.

Maisie is with her, unpacking some toiletries from a floral washbag.

'. . . and I've brought your Clinique soap as well as the nice bath one — ' She sees Mohsin and stops talking. I think she seems afraid.

'Maisie White?' He holds out his hand and she takes it. 'I'm Detective Sergeant Farouk.' He turns to Rowena. 'And you're Rowena White?'

'Yes.'

'I'd like to ask both of you a few questions.'

Maisie steps towards Rowena.

'She's not really in a state to — '

'That's why I've come to talk to you here, rather than ask you to come to the police station.'

Rowena rests her bandaged hand lightly on her mother's.

'Mummy, I'm fine. Really.'

'I gather that Mr White was an investor in Sidley House School?' Mohsin asks.

'Yes,' Maisie says, her voice oddly terse.

'Why didn't he use his name?'

'We wanted to keep it private,' Maisie says. She looks anxious. 'Why do you want to know about it?'

'If you could answer my questions. You were saying that you want to keep the investment private?'

'Yes. I mean, we didn't want Rowena to be different to other children when she was at the school. Didn't want anyone thinking she was getting special treatment or anything. And I, well, I had one or two really good friends there. I

393

didn't want them to watch what they said about the school. Using a trust name, not ours, made it feel not so much to do with us. And pretty quickly that's what it felt like. I mean, Donald invested the money and then we all sort of forgot about it.'

'Forgot about a two-million-pound investment?' Mohsin asks.

'Mum didn't mean it like that,' Rowena says. 'It was more that we dissociated the school with the financial investment Daddy had made.'

Maisie is blushing and I think she feels *a twit!* And I feel sorry for her because I do believe her. I think she shoved it under the carpet and got on with being just a normal parent at the school.

'But it must have generated an income?' Mohsin asks.

'It didn't for ages,' Maisie says. 'It's only been quite recently that it's been paying anything.'

'It's been our only source of income actually,' Rowena says. 'Dad's other businesses didn't weather the recession very well.'

'Did you know that you were about to lose all of that money and the income it generated?'

'Yes,' Rowena says immediately. 'We discussed it as a family,' she continues. She's trying to be the adult; mature.

'It wasn't that big a thing,' Maisie says. 'I know that sounds silly. But money isn't everything, is it? And we'll be alright. I mean, we're going to have to sell the house. Get somewhere smaller or rent. But in the great scheme of things, well, that's not what happiness is about, is it? Where you live? And Rowena's finished at school now, so there are no more school fees. That would have been the only really hard thing to change, if she'd had to leave her school.'

'And how does your husband feel about this?'

'He's disappointed,' Maisie says, quietly. 'He wanted to give Rowena everything. In her second year at Oxford she has to live out of college and Donald had planned to buy her a little flat of her own. We didn't want her in some student house that could be miles from her lectures and not very safe. And it would be an investment, too, we thought. But clearly . . . well, that's not possible. Poor Rowena, it was a big blow.'

But I think there might be a more sinister reason for Donald wanting to buy Rowena a flat. Did he want to continue controlling her, under the guise of indulgent father?

'I don't mind not having the flat,' Rowena says. 'Really. Not a bit.'

'And she'll have to get a student loan and a job while she's at university,' Maisie says. 'And that's hard. I mean, when you're studying as well. I don't mind for me. I mean, I've always rather wanted a job, actually.'

'Mummy, the police officer doesn't want to hear all of this.'

'Do you think your father was just disappointed?' Mohsin asks Rowena.

Maisie quickly answers for her. 'He was also upset, of course he was. But there was nothing anyone could do about it.'

'I have to tell you that your husband has been brought into Chiswick police station for questioning.'

'I don't understand.'

Rowena is pale. 'The fire, Mummy. They must think it's fraud.'

'But that's just ridiculous!' Maisie says. 'He once joked that he'd burn the place down, but it was just a *joke*. You don't joke about something like that if you're actually going to do it, do you?'

'I'd like to talk to you in private later, Mrs White, but for now I want to ask Rowena a few questions.'

'She has nothing to tell you. Nothing.'

'Rowena? Do you want to talk to me without . . .'

I see Rowena's eyes meet Maisie's.

'I'd like Mum to stay.'

Gently, thoughtfully, Mohsin probes Rowena about Donald. But each avenue of questioning is blocked off by Rowena's loyalty. No, he's never lost his temper. No! He'd *never* hurt her in any way at all. He's a devoted father.

As I listen to Rowena's earnest voice I think how different she is to Jenny. Not just her seriousness and what she's had to contend with during her life, but even the words she uses. None of them would be found in that dictionary Jenny made for me. I wonder how often she chats to her contemporaries; if she has any friends.

'You've got it all wrong!' she finally bursts out. 'Daddy didn't do anything. He wouldn't hurt anyone. You've got it *all wrong*.'

As Rowena cries, Maisie puts her arms protectively around her.

She and Maisie have both covered for him

over the years, and surely they're covering for him now.

Jenny thought Rowena ran into the burning building to make Donald proud, but was it to protect him again, by trying to limit the harm he'd done?

I'd thought that you needed love to push you into that burning school. Maybe it was love for her father, however little he deserved it, that had made her go in.

Mohsin, clearly frustrated, winds up his interview. Maisie is going to the police station, despite Mohsin telling her she won't be allowed to see Donald. I don't understand her loyalty to him. Not with Rowena being hurt too. I just don't understand.

But it doesn't matter. The hows and whys don't matter.

Adam is cleared.

*   *   *

You are at my bedside, silent. I'm not sure what I expected, hoped for, not a smile on your face, but a relaxation in your body now that Adam is exonerated. But your muscles are wound so tight that your body looks unnaturally stiff; like a marionette.

Where's the man in the Cambridge tea shop who was going to climb and abseil and white-water raft through life?

When I reach the bed you tell me about the insurance fraud; that Adam won't be blamed any more. 'About bloody time too!' And for a moment

397

there's an energy in your voice, but that's as much relief as you have. Because no heart has been found for Jenny and I am still in a coma.

Then you tell me that a heart *will* be found for Jen, and that I *will* wake up. And that man is right here by my bedside. Not a marionette but a climber. How absurd I was to think you could relax at all now; how insensitive and *stupid*. Every fibre of your strength is needed to carry us both up that mountain of hope; our weight is the weight of your love for us; an almost impossible burden.

I'm so sorry for what I said about Ivo earlier. Because we do love each other, I know that. Not with that intensely perfect young love we once had, but with something stronger and more durable. Our love has aged with us; less beautiful, yes — but more muscular and robust. Married love, which is built to last.

★ ★ ★

I return with you to ICU for yours and Sarah's changing of the guard at Jenny's bedside. Despite Donald being in custody, you've refused to stop guarding her.

'*Not till the bastard's admitted it. Not till we're totally sure.*' Maybe you're finding it hard to let go of your suspicion of Silas Hyman, despite the evidence against Donald. You need a written confession; something tangible before you'll desert your post.

Like me, I think that each time you leave her ward and then return you allow yourself to hope that a heart has been found for her. And that somehow not being there will make it more likely; a watched-pot-never-boils on a life-and-death scale.

Nothing has changed.

* * *

Jenny is outside ICU.

'No heart?' she says and waits a moment. 'Sounds like a bid in bridge.'

'Jen . . . '

'Yeah. Gallows. Sorry. Aunt Sarah's phoning Addie and Granny G.' Her face crumples. 'He's in the clear, Mum.' Her relief is expressed in tears. Her love for Addie is one copper-bottomed fact about her that never changes.

'About Ivo, Jen — '

She pulls sharply away from me. 'Lay off the interrogation. Please.'

She walks quickly away and I watch her go.

I think I glimpse someone in a blue coat, getting out of the lift. I hurry towards him.

Is that him, turning a corner towards ICU? God I wish you were here.

I race to catch up.

A group of doctors are going into ICU and I can't see anyone in a dark coat.

Maybe that's him, hurrying away, half obscured by a porter wheeling a patient.

But there's no way they would have let Donald go already. Surely?

Nothing now. The corridors empty, just two nurses in the lift.

I can't be sure I saw him. I'm probaby just jumping at shadows.

★ ★ ★

In the car park Mohsin is waiting for Sarah.

'It's really not good form to be late for your own disciplinary meeting,' he says, teasing her. But she doesn't smile.

'Addie still isn't talking,' she says.

But surely now everyone knows he's innocent, he'll be feeling a little better? Surely he can now at least turn away from the burning building?

'I just spoke to Georgina,' Sarah says. 'I thought that when he knew he was cleared it would change things for him, but . . . '

She's always spoken neatly before, correctly finishing her sentences, but nothing is neat about this.

'Give him a little more time,' Mohsin says. 'Maybe it hasn't really sunk in yet.' Both Sarah and I hold onto his words.

He drives her to the police station. The car is fogged with heat, the air-con uselessly blowing hot air back in. The heat-haze on the tarmac gives a mirage. For a while Sarah is silent.

'They say that Grace has no brain function,' she says abruptly.

'But you said — '

'I was a coward.'

I want to shout out that I'm here, as if they'll suddenly discover me and be embarrassed.

'I've argued with them. Said they were talking bollocks. Because I can't bear Mike to lose her.

400

Can't bear for him to go through that.'

Mohsin puts his hand on hers as he drives, reminding me of you.

'When Mum and Dad died I promised him that nothing awful would happen again.'

'And you were what?' Mohsin asks. 'Eighteen?'

'Yeah. But I still kept thinking that. Until Wednesday, I thought that because he'd already been through something terrible, nothing else bad would happen to him. As if terrible things, losing people you love, are doled out equally. God, as a police officer I should have known better. And now, it's too much for him. And I can't make it better. *I can't make it better for him*.'

I realise, fully, that she loves you as a mother; as I love Jenny and Adam.

* * *

In the police station, jackets are discarded, belts loosened against the heat. Sarah goes into DI Baker's office, closing the door behind her. There's no need for me to shadow her any more, not now that we know the arsonist, and Adam is no longer blamed, but I want to be with her when she's hauled over the coals.

I just want to be with her.

DI Baker's doughy face is shiny with sweat, his too-tight clothes clinging to his paunchy body. The stagnant air is sticky with body odour.

He glances up as she comes in, his voice is curt.

'Take a seat.'

He gestures to a plastic chair but Sarah remains standing. She goes closer to him.

'Is it *clear* to you now that it isn't a case of a little boy playing with matches?' Her anger startles me and DI Baker.

'Detective Sergeant McBride, you are here to — '

'You owe Adam a formal and public apology.'

Her pent-up, furious energy reminds me of you.

'This meeting is about *your conduct*. It is about — '

'Are you going to prosecute your supposed 'witness' for what he or she has done to Adam?'

Has Sarah already written off her career? Is that why she's come into this room all guns blazing, because she has nothing to lose?

'This is not a meeting to discuss the case, or what you have found out through your illegal methods. Ends *do not justify* means, Detective Sergeant. Even before PACE, what you did would have been seen as beyond the pale. I understand the emotional strain you must be under but there are *no excuses*. All the reforms of the last twenty-five years have made the police investigate cases *by the book*. And rightly.'

'But you just flipped to the end of the book — decided on an ending, to use your analogy — not bothering to do any work at all to get there. Not bothering to investigate at all. Because of your laziness and crass stupidity, a child could have been blamed for this for the rest of his life and the real culprit not be punished.'

'Are you asking for a mutual pact of silence

402

— in effect, trying to blackmail me, Detective Sergeant?'

What I see as nothing to lose he sees as blackmail.

'Fortunately,' he continues, his voice icy in the hot room, 'the person who made the complaint against you withdrew it just over an hour ago.'

Perhaps Mrs Healey felt compassion for Sarah once she knew she was Jenny's aunt and my sister-in-law. Or maybe she thought the police would go easier on her if she'd been kind to a fellow police officer.

'But that doesn't detract from the *seriousness* of your misconduct — ' Baker continues, but a knock on the door interrupts him. The sharp-featured Penny Pierson comes into the room.

'What is it?' Baker snaps.

'Silas Hyman gave a sample of DNA on Wednesday night when we questioned him about the fire. His DNA didn't match anything at the site of the fire but it went into our database.'

'So?' asks Baker, impatient.

Penny turns to face Sarah. I think I see a flicker of an apology on her face.

'Silas Hyman's DNA matches the semen in the condom sent to Jennifer.'

30

'We are now certain that Silas Hyman is Jennifer Covey's hate-mailer,' Penny continues. 'The condom was a part of his malicious-mail campaign. We think it must be Silas Hyman who also attacked Jennifer Covey with red paint. We therefore need to *seriously consider* whether he also tampered with her oxygen. It could have been an escalation of his previous assault with paint.'

I was totally wrong when I thought Silas Hyman too intelligent, too subtle a personality, to cut out letters and stick them onto A4, let alone to post a used condom and dog mess through the letterbox.

And I remember him flirting with the pretty nurse. A smile and flowers, that was all it took, to get through the door of a supposedly secure ward.

'You need to send someone to guard Jenny straight away,' Sarah says.

Maybe I wasn't jumping at shadows.

Baker shifts in his sweaty seat. 'There is no evidence that she needs guarding. It was a faulty connection. It happens.'

'Because otherwise your incompetence left her exposed?' Sarah says to him. 'Because if you hadn't been duped into thinking it was an eight-year-old — '

'That's enough!'

He's shouted at her and I think Sarah is glad of it. I think she wants shouting in here.

He turns to Penny. 'You will arrest Silas Hyman in relation to the malicious mail and question him about the assault against Jennifer Covey with paint.' He looks at Sarah, 'I will decide in due course what steps should be taken against you.'

'And the guard?' Penny asks, winning my respect, but Baker is clearly infuriated by two women confronting him.

'I have already told you my decision. There is no evidence of any tampering. If you choose to persist in your paranoia, I can remind you that the intensive care unit has a very high ratio of medical staff to patients; Donald White is in custody for the arson attack. And Silas Hyman will shortly be arrested and put in custody for the malicious mail and possibly the paint attack.'

'If we can find him,' Penny says.

* * *

Sarah phones to check that Jenny is OK and to tell you about Silas Hyman. I don't hear your response.

She joins Penny in the police station car park.

'I checked with Sally Healey,' Penny says. 'Jennifer was a teaching assistant with Silas Hyman last summer. That's when they must have got to know each other.'

I don't want to hear this, but know it will continue. Because Jenny is now connected, forensically connected, to Silas Hyman.

I remember he confided in Jenny about his failing marriage last summer — or a marriage he'd made out to be failing. Confiding in a sixteen-year-old when he was thirty. I'd thought it was shabby of him but nothing more; because surely she was far too young to think it anything more.

I remember Jenny standing up for 'Silas', even when I'd joined you in my suspicion of him. But she's naturally fair-minded and open to people; one of her charms and strengths.

Each time I edge near a sight of a relationship between them, I pull myself away.

But I don't know her well enough any more to say for definite no, not possible.

I thought she loved Ivo. I thought she was desperate to see him. And I was wrong.

I don't know her as I think I did.

So I skate around the circumference of a denial of a relationship between Jen and Silas Hyman, unable to state it for definite — however much I want to.

Sarah gets in the car next to Penny — an unspoken agreement that Sarah should be there when Silas Hyman is arrested.

'You still think that Donald White is the arsonist?' Sarah asks Penny as they drive.

'Yes. After your one-woman investigation,' Penny says with a faint smile. 'We are working on the assumption that it was fraud.'

'So we're still working on two separate cases.'

I'm glad she uses 'we' for police; maybe Baker won't force her out.

'Yeah. Jenny's hate-mailer, now identified as

Silas Hyman, who must also have thrown the red paint. And Donald White as the arsonist to get the insurance money.'

'Let's see how Mohsin is doing with that,' Sarah says. She phones him.

'Hi, baby. I heard what happened with Baker,' he says. 'We all did. Like the All Blacks rugby scrum outside his door while you were in there.'

'Yeah.'

'The consensus is that he'll drop it.'

'Maybe. Have you got anything from Donald White?'

'Nothing. He's keeping quiet; waiting for his expensive lawyer. But his wife is kicking up a fuss. Very *gently and politely* kicking up a fuss. She says that he was in Scotland the afternoon of the fire.'

'She'd say anything he wanted her to,' Sarah says.

'Yeah. The technical guys have been looking at Jenny's mobile. They think that two messages were wiped. They're trying to retrieve them but aren't sure it's going to be possible.'

'Right.'

'We'll all pop by the hospital and see her,' Mohsin says. 'Make social calls. With a rota.'

He's offering Jenny police protection on the sly.

'They don't allow unauthorised visitors,' Sarah says. 'Infection risk. It would have to be official. But Mike's with her.'

She thanks him and hangs up.

'Why did Silas Hyman volunteer his DNA, do you think?' Sarah asks Penny. 'He must have known we'd trace it.'

'Maybe he didn't know that we cross-reference cases, that it's just one database. Or he just assumed that the hate-mail investigation was over or that we wouldn't pull out all the stops. But without the DNA we wouldn't have got him. The CCTV footage didn't have anything. Baker'll probably roast my hide for wasting police resources on that.'

'Probably. How many hours, *exactly*, did you spend on the CCTV?' Sarah asks, teasing.

'Too many,' Penny responds, smiling. But it's a strained kind of banter between them, a pretence at camaraderie that they can't quite pull off.

We drive in silence; the police radio and the air-con hissing at different pitches. I see tension on Sarah's face.

'Can you tell me who the witness is who saw Adam?' she asks.

'Not yet. I'm sorry. Baker would — '

'Yeah.'

'I will once it's authorised.'

I wonder if anyone will ever inspire enough love in Penny for her to break the rules, let alone risk her career — jettison it — as Sarah has for Adam. I can't imagine it. But then once I couldn't have imagined it of Sarah.

★ ★ ★

At Silas Hyman's house, another police car draws up behind us. A young uniformed officer, the archetype of a fresh-faced bobby, gets out and enthusiastically half jogs up to Silas

408

Hyman's door and rings the bell. Penny follows more slowly.

Natalia is opening the door and I feel the claustrophobia of the stifling flat oozing into the street. She looked furious and tired.

'Where's your husband?' the young bobby asks.

'A building site. Why?'

'Which one?'

She's looking at the two police cars outside her house.

'What is this?'

Penny is walking slowly towards them, staring at Natalia.

Natalia holds Penny's eye as she gets close to her.

'It was you,' Penny says to Natalia. 'Not your husband. You.'

Natalia steps away from her. 'What you going on about?'

'I've got you on CCTV,' Penny said. 'Posting one of your nasty little letters.'

'Posting a letter is a crime, is it?'

But she's backing into the house.

Penny puts a hand on her shoulder, preventing her from retreating any further.

'I'm arresting you under the malicious communications act. You do not have to say anything, but it may harm your defence if you do not say something now which you later rely on in court.'

I remember the Postman Pat comic in Silas's car that day in the hospital underground car park. Were some of the words red and cheerful before she dismembered them into letters and rearranged them into hatred?

And the dog mess, did she go out with a shovel and a parcel-box? Their house is only three streets from us. Easy to hand-deliver and get home again.

Other times she'd posted her disgust from places all over London — was it to make her seem omnipresent? Or to muddy the geography of where she really lived?

I don't think about the condom. Not yet. Not yet.

But I think about the red paint down Jenny's long fair hair. A woman's touch.

And who'd notice a harassed mother with children in a shopping arcade? She'd have blended in and disappeared.

Gradually I edge towards the figure in the blue coat, bending over Jenny, tampering with her oxygen supply; trying to kill her. The figure could have been a woman. I only saw the back view and from a distance. But how could Natalia have got into a locked ward? And did her hatred really extend to murder?

★ ★ ★

Natalia is in the back of Penny's car. Sarah next to her.

For a little while no one speaks, Natalia picking at a thread in her seat-belt. Then Penny turns off the air-conditioner and, without the drone, the car is suddenly hushed.

'So why did you do it?' Penny asks.

Natalia is silent, still picking at the thread, and

410

I think she's itching to talk.

The car starts to heat up, as if silence has its own temperature.

I remember Sarah telling a rapt dinner table that the best time 'to get info out of a suspect' is when you first arrest them, before they've reached the police station; before they've had time to think or take stock.

'You love him, do you?' Sarah asks, a note of sarcasm cutting through her words.

'He's a little shit. Weak. Useless. Fucked up my life.'

Her words seem to mix with the heat in the car, fugging it up with loathing.

'So why bother with the hate mail then?' asks Penny. 'If you don't even like him?'

'Because the little shit belongs to me, right?' Natalia snaps.

I remember her stressing *my* in 'my husband'. Not loyalty but possessiveness.

I remember Jenny saying, '*She told him he was a loser. That she was embarrassed by him . . . But she won't get divorced.*'

Silas Hyman was telling her the truth.

'The head teacher, Sally Healey, told me I should keep my husband on a tighter leash,' Natalia continues.

'Mrs Hyman — '

'Tighter leash. Like he was a dog. A fucking cocker spaniel. She'd got his measure. I asked what she meant, pretended I didn't know. I have some pride, right? She said flirting with teaching assistants wasn't acceptable. Flirting, not fucking. She's very refined, Mrs Healey. But clever.

411

She delegated him to me to deal with. I admire her for that. Shows some spunk.'

'But you punished Jennifer Covey, not your husband?' Penny says.

'The stupid bitch made me a fool.'

I lift my hands to cover my face as if her words are spit, but they get through.

'I saw them, her all long legs and short skirt and long blonde hair, a tart; fuck knows why they let her dress like that. He was flirting his pants off at her. Mrs Healey didn't need to tell me to get a leash.'

'And the red paint?' Penny asks.

'The tart had to get her hair cut.'

'Why send the condom? When you knew it would be traceable?'

'I never thought ... ' Natalia begins, and I hear her picking at the thread again. 'I wanted her to know that we were still having sex. He was fucking her, but he was making love to me.'

★ ★ ★

We reach the police station. Penny takes Natalia to be questioned. Sarah is going straight back to the hospital. As she gets out to swap into the driver's seat, Mohsin comes up.

Sarah meets his quizzical gaze. The question he didn't ask earlier — that Penny didn't ask — is now too large and loud to be ignored.

'Jenny wasn't having an affair with Silas Hyman,' Sarah says. 'She'd have told me.'

I am envious she has such faith in how well she knows Jenny, which I lost only a little while ago and now feel its absence terribly. Is there a moment for every parent when you realise that your child has outgrown your knowledge of them? A moment when you can't keep up?

For some reason I think of her shoes.

Knitted bootees becoming tiny soft shoes, then small sandals with width fittings for summer and black school shoes for winter, all the time incrementally getting a little bigger until she was into small adult sizes and the decision in the shoe shop took longer — until one day she went on her own and came back with boots; but I didn't see that she was starting to stride away from me with boots that didn't come in width fittings on her long adult legs.

It's not the fledgling birds that are thrown out of the nest by their parents and made to fly; it's the parents who are made to get the hell out of the cosy family nest by their teenage offspring. It's we who are made to be independent of them, crash-landing if we don't manage it.

⋆　⋆　⋆

You and Sarah are in the corridor of ICU, Jenny listening. I can't hear what you're saying, but can tell from your posture that you're furious. I go closer.

'For Christ's sake, his wife made a mistake.'

'I know that, Mike,' Sarah says patiently. 'I just wanted to tell you.'

'It's *bloody ridiculous*. The man's *thirty years old* and *married*, for God's sake!'

Jenny turns to me, bemused.

'His wife thought I was having an *affair* with him?'

I nod. Then summon up my courage. 'Were you?'

'No. He flirted with me, he flirts with everyone, but nothing more.'

And I believe her; of course I do.

She smiles at me. 'But thank you for asking.'

She means it.

I don't ask her about Ivo, who I saw sitting in the corridor by the garden, a shoal of people separating briefly to pass him.

Guessing — hoping — that she wouldn't have had an affair with Silas Hyman, and trusting her to tell the truth, doesn't mean that I have full knowledge of our daughter again.

'Dr Sandhu's here,' Jenny says.

I turn to see him, with Jenny's cardiologist, the young Miss Logan.

'We'll be taking Jennifer for an MRI and CAT scan later today,' Miss Logan says. 'To check that she's still a candidate for transplant.'

'You think it's likely then,' you say, grabbing at her words.

'The time frame is extremely narrow. We are simply following protocol.'

'Remember we talked about the two kinds of burns?' Dr Sandhu says. 'We now know that Jenny's burns are superficial second-degree partial thickness burns. Which means that the blood supply is intact and her skin will heal.

There will be no scarring.'

But he sounds defeated rather than pleased.

'That's fantastic!' you say, refusing to be defeated too.

They go into the ward, to Jenny's bed.

Jenny stays in the corridor with me.

'Dead but not scarred,' Jenny says. 'Well, that's comforting.'

'Jen . . . '

'Yeah, well, sometimes only gallows humour cuts it.'

'You're not going to — '

'So you keep saying.'

'Because it's the truth. You're going to live.'

'So why didn't Dr. Sandhu or Miss Logan say so? I need a walk.'

'Jenny — '

She starts walking away from me.

'They've found you a heart.'

She doesn't turn.

'I'm too old for fairy stories, Mum.'

31

Sarah is waiting in the cafeteria, fingers tapping as yours do when you are impatient. She has her owl notebook out and has been reading through it. I sense increased energy in her exhausted face. She stops tapping as she sees Mohsin and Penny arrive.

'Natalia Hyman's been charged under the malicious communications act and for assault,' Penny says. 'She's admitted to all the incidents of hate mail and to the paint attack.'

Her sharp features are softened with satisfaction at a job well done.

'Silas Hyman had *nothing* to do with his wife's malicious hate-mail campaign,' she continues. 'He didn't even know it was happening.'

'And the tampering with Jenny's oxygen?' Sarah asks.

'Natalia swears blind it wasn't her,' Penny says. 'And I believe her. She's our hate-mailer, but I really don't think she's the saboteur.'

'And Donald White?' Sarah asks Mohsin.

'His alibi checks out,' Mohsin replies. 'He was on a BMI flight at three on Wednesday, halfway between Gatwick and Aberdeen. But we still think you were right about the arson for fraud. He must have had an accomplice.'

'His smart lawyer is trying to spring him,' Penny says. 'But Baker's not having it, not yet anyway.'

416

'Or the arsonist was Silas Hyman,' Sarah says. Mohsin and Penny are taken aback.

'I think my brother might have been right from the beginning,' Sarah continues.

I want her to stop, right now. I don't have the emotional capacity or the mental energy for this. We have it *sorted out*. Done and dusted. Donald White burnt the school down to get the insurance money. Possibly Jenny saw something that incriminated him, which is why he may be the person who tried to kill her. Natalia Hyman was getting misplaced revenge on Jenny. Maybe, just a possibility, it was Natalia who attacked her in the hospital. That's it. These two people make sense of it all. Not a nice neat parcel of facts, but an ugly, vile dossier of the foulness in people. But known. Done.

'Don't you want the truth?' Nanny Voice snaps at me. 'Don't you want Adam unequivocally cleared and Jenny safe? Isn't that what you want?'

Of course it is, I'm sorry.

'But we've found out about the fraud,' Mohsin says to Sarah. 'Rather, you found out.'

Is he also frustrated and tired by this now?

'I found a motive, yes,' Sarah says. 'But I now think the arsonist could equally well be Silas Hyman.'

'Taking revenge on the school?' Mohsin asks.

'Yes.'

'I never bought that Silas Hyman could be the arsonist,' Penny says sharply. 'Even first time around.'

'I think we were too quick to dismiss him,' Sarah says.

'But what about his wife giving him an alibi?' Mohsin asks. 'She clearly loathes him, so she'd hardly lie for him, would she?'

'If he gets sent down, she'll be a single mother with three children and no income,' Sarah says. 'It's in her own interests to lie for him. In any case, I think she still has feelings for him, in her own weird and perverted way.'

I agree, because sitting next to Natalia in the car, beneath her spat-out furious words, her passionate viciousness, I glimpsed something fragile and wounded. *'He was fucking her, but he was making love to me.'*

'Give me ten minutes?' Sarah asks and before they can reply she leaves, holding her owl notebook. Mohsin looks perplexed, Penny irritated.

'I'll call the station,' Penny says, annoyed. She leaves. Mohsin goes to the counter to get another cup of tea.

★ ★ ★

Alone, I think about Jenny. *'I'm too old for fairy stories, Mum.'*

I remember you reading to her every night: your big hands, the knuckles with dark hair, rough and masculine, around a sparkly covered book. Her favourites were the old ones, the ones that begin 'Once upon a time' and so, as convention dictates, must end 'happily ever after'.

But that happily ever after was hard won. Those beautiful princesses and girls with pure white skin and defenceless children were pitted

418

against vicious cruelty. A witch keeps children caged, fattening them up to eat; a stepmother abandons children in a forest to die; another demands a woodcutter kills her beautiful step-daughter and brings her the heart for supper.

Inside the sparkly covers was a world of good against evil; snow-white innocence against dark violence.

But despite the wickedness, the children and the wronged beautiful girls and the blameless princesses won through. They survived — always — into a happy-ever-after ending.

And I believe in fairy stories now, did I tell you that? Because I've gone through the looking glass; stepped through the back of the wardrobe. The young girl will get her prince, the children will be reunited with their loving father, and Jen will live.

She *will live*.

*   *   *

Mohsin finishes his cup of tea as Sarah comes back into the cafeteria, Penny just behind her. And I must think about dark wickedness again — the who and the why of our story. Unlike those fairy tales, the narrative isn't neatly linear but looping back on itself to Silas Hyman.

'OK, let's run with your idea of Silas Hyman as arsonist then,' Penny says to Sarah, with a note of derision in her voice. 'Let's say he did want to torch the place. Even if he knew the code on the gate — let's actually get him inside — how would he have walked through the school

419

up to the second floor, unnoticed?'

'I've thought about that,' Sarah responds calmly. 'Although most of the staff were at sports day, there were still three members of staff in the building and it would have been risky.'

'Exactly. So — '

'So he had an accomplice. Someone who made sure the coast was clear for him.'

Penny looks even more annoyed and impatient. I hope her children are intelligent and fast or homework time will be a nightmare in her house.

'What if it was Rowena White who was helping him?' Sarah asks. 'What if she kept lookout? Possibly made sure the secretary was distracted while he got in?'

'And why on earth would she do that?' Penny asks.

'Because I think that Silas Hyman was having an affair with someone at the school. A teaching assistant. But it wasn't Jenny. It was Rowena.'

I am startled. Rowena?

'That's absurd,' Penny says. 'I understand why you don't want your niece to have been having an affair with him. But Natalia Hyman was *clear* it was Jenny. She *saw them* together.'

'Saw her husband flirting with Jen, yes,' Sarah says. 'But he flirted with every female at the school. Elizabeth Fisher called him a cockerel in the hen-house. I think he flirted with Rowena White too. That it went further.'

They've reached Mohsin now, who's listening intently.

'What about the head teacher and the leash

thing?' Penny asks. 'Sally Healey knew it was Jennifer.'

'She just said it was a teaching assistant,' Sarah replies. 'It was Natalia who drew her own conclusions from that. And if you put the two girls side by side it's easy to see why you'd pick Jenny.'

'OK, I need to get brutal here,' Penny says. 'Jennifer — long legs, long blonde hair, beautiful face. Jenny, I buy.'

She sees Sarah react on 'beautiful face', and Mohsin glaring at her.

'Sorry. But why ugly, dumpy Rowena White when he has Natalia at home?'

'Because Natalia is the kind of woman who shoves shit through letterboxes?' hazards Mohsin.

'And Rowena's extremely intelligent,' Sarah says. 'Reading Science at Oxford. Maybe he's attracted to that. Or maybe he knew he could seduce her because she's vulnerable. Or she's seventeen and that's beauty enough. I don't know his reason.'

'Because there isn't one,' Penny says.

'There's more,' Sarah said, rummaging in her bag. 'I've got my notes here from when I spoke to Maisie White.'

Penny watches her, alarmed.

'Who the fuck *didn't* you speak to? Does DI Baker know about this?'

You arrive, interrupting.

'Is Jenny on her own?' Sarah asks, her anxiety clear. Because if it's Silas Hyman, as she thinks, he's out there somewhere and a threat.

'Ivo's with her,' you say. 'And a whole load of

doctors. About Rowena White. After we spoke I remembered something.'

Penny and Mohsin both look awkward with you here. Penny even blushes a little. It's affecting to be physically close to someone who is emotionally stripped raw.

'When I spoke to Silas Hyman's wife,' you say, 'she accused me of getting her husband sacked. Of 'wanting him out'.'

I remember Natalia following you to the car; her hostility like a strong cheap perfume around her.

'I thought she meant me as a parent,' you continue. 'Just a generic parent at the school. But I think she meant me *personally*. She thought *I'd* got him fired — presumably because she thought he was having an affair with my daughter.'

Sarah nods and I see the allegiance between the two of you.

'She got the wrong girl so she blamed the wrong father,' you say.

Penny is silent. Presumably it's not good police practice to argue with a father whose daughter is in ICU; nor cast aspersions about said daughter's morals to her distraught dad. And now I realise why you're here; why instead of waiting for Sarah to come to you, you've interrupted this meeting with her colleagues.

You'd said the idea of Jenny and Silas Hyman having a relationship was '*bloody ridiculous*'. You don't want lies being told about Jenny, something you'd see as a slur on her — an affair with a married older man.

422

When you leave, there's a pause before anyone speaks again.

'I think Mike's right about that interpretation,' Sarah says. 'And it makes sense if the red-paint attack was to punish Jenny for getting Silas the sack. It would explain the escalation of violence. She just got the wrong girl.'

'You said you spoke to Maisie White . . . ?' Mohsin asks.

'Yes.'

She opens her owl notebook. As she does so, I remember the shadowy empty cafeteria and Sarah writing up her notes, the moment that Maisie had left to join Rowena.

'I spoke to Maisie White on Thursday July the twelfth, the day after the fire, at nine p.m.'

Sarah concentrates on her notebook, but must be aware of Penny's disapproval.

'She told me, 'It's wrong to make someone adore you, when they're so much younger and can't think for themselves.' I thought she was talking about Adam. But I think now that she was referring to her teenage daughter.

'She said that Silas got people to love him because no one realised he was a sham. She said that he 'exploited' people, and emphasised that word.'

Penny is silent now; like Mohsin, listening intently.

'I asked her when she'd changed her mind about Silas Hyman. From my notes she didn't answer immediately.'

I remember Maisie fussing with a little pink packet of fake sugar, not answering for a while.

423

'She then said it was at the prize-giving,' continues Sarah. 'But I think it was before then — when she found out about Silas and her daughter.'

I remember Maisie's pale face at the prize-giving. How unlike her it was to hate someone. I remember her saying, '*That man should never have been allowed near our children.*'

Silas Hyman wasn't at the school when Rowena was a pupil there. But he was there last summer when Rowena was a sixteen-year-old teaching assistant. Why didn't I realise she meant Rowena? And why hadn't she told me — and later Sarah — the truth?

I think it's probably because, like you, she thinks it's a slur on her daughter. She thinks Silas has already exploited Rowena and she doesn't want to damage her any further by making it public. Even to a friend.

And she's used to keeping secrets.

'When I spoke to Rowena the next day,' Sarah says, 'she told me that Silas was violent.'

'You have your notes on that interview too?' Mohsin asks.

Is he teasing her? No. It is standard procedure to write contemporaneous notes.

She nods and gives him the notebook.

I've never really understood the police's obsession with procedure and note-taking and bureaucratic attention to detail; which Sarah has always excelled at. Now I do.

'The good angel and the devil thing, that's interesting,' Mohsin says as he reads.

'If she'd helped him with the arson attack,' Penny says, 'it would explain why she ran back in. Maybe she hadn't realised that people would get hurt.'

'Let's talk to her,' Mohsin says, getting up.

'I'll call the station,' Penny says. 'Get them to find Silas Hyman urgently.'

★　★　★

I follow Mohsin and Sarah, thinking about Ivo standing guard at Jenny's bedside while you came to talk to Sarah and her colleagues. I'm glad you trust him enough to let him stand guard in your place; glad that you're not as prejudiced against him as I was.

★　★　★

We arrive at the burns unit and I look through the glass wall into Rowena's side-room. As I said before, she doesn't look plain or ugly to me any more — how can anyone with an undamaged face ever look even plain to me now — but I do understand Penny's harsh honesty about her.

But she was beautiful as a little girl. Like a fairy child, with her enormous eyes and elfin face and silky honey-blonde hair. Remember that bronze statue that Mrs Healey commissioned to mark the first year at Sidley House? We weren't meant to know which child it had been modelled on, but we all guessed it was Rowena. But at six her tiny white perfect teeth had been replaced by uneven gappy ones that looked too big and

425

discoloured next to the remaining pearly milk teeth. Her eyes seemed to shrink as her face grew and her shiny fair hair turned dull matt brown. You think it's odd that I noticed these things? At school you watch children grow and change, and you can't help but notice. I felt for her. It must have been so hard to have been so gloriously pretty and then to lose that. She'd cried at the dentist's, Maisie told me, demanding her old teeth back, as if she knew, even while it was happening, that she was losing her little-girl beauty. I used to wonder if that was what made her so competitive; as if she was trying to prove herself in other ways.

Jenny did the opposite: our gawky duckling growing into a beautiful teenager, while Rowena suffered the adolecent blight of acne. Growing up must have been fraught for Rowena, even without her father's physical abuse. I doubt she's had many romantic bids from boys her own age.

Did all of this — feeling plain, ugly even, and being cruelly treated by her father — did this make her vulnerable to a man like Silas Hyman?

Sarah and Mohsin go into her room.

'Hello, Rowena,' Mohsin says. 'I'd like to ask you a few more questions.'

Rowena nods, but she's looking at Sarah.

'As you're under eighteen,' Mohsin says, 'you should have an adult with you to — '

'Can Jenny's aunt stay with me?'

'Yes, if that's what you'd like.'

Mohsin looks at Sarah and some kind of communication passes between them.

Sarah sits in the chair next to Rowena's bed.

'Last time we spoke,' she says, 'you said that Silas Hyman was very good-looking?'

Rowena turns away from Sarah, embarrassed.

'You said you used to watch him . . . ?'

Rowena looks so acutely self-conscious that I feel uncomfortable too.

'Did you find him attractive?' Sarah asks, kindly.

Rowena is silent.

'Rowena?'

'I had a crush on him from the moment I saw him.'

She turns away so that she can't see Mohsin, as if she doesn't like him being there, and he steps further back towards the door.

'I knew he'd never look at someone like me,' she continues to Sarah. 'Men like him never do. You know, the handsome ones.'

She stops talking. Sarah doesn't butt into the silence, waiting for Rowena. 'If I could swap being clever for pretty,' Rowena says quietly, 'I'd do it.'

'You also told me you thought he could be violent.'

It's as if Sarah has slapped her.

'I shouldn't have said that,' she says. 'It wasn't right to say that.'

'Maybe it was honest?'

'No. It was stupid. I really don't see him that way at all. I mean, I just guessed that he could be. But we all could be, couldn't we? I mean, anyone has the capacity for it, don't they?'

'Why did you have a crush on him if you thought he might be violent?'

427

Rowena doesn't reply.

'Was he ever violent to you?' Mohsin asks.

'No! He never touched me. I mean, not in that way. Not in a bad way.'

'But he did touch you,' Sarah says.

Rowena nods.

'Were you having a relationship with Silas?' Mohsin asks.

Rowena looks at Sarah, seemingly torn.

'I'm a police officer asking you a question,' Mohsin continues. 'And you have to tell me the truth. Doesn't matter what promises you've made.'

'Yes,' Rowena says.

'But you said he didn't look at you?' Sarah asks gently.

'He didn't. I mean, not to start with. It was Jenny he wanted. He was besotted with her; flirted with her all the time. She didn't flirt back, got a little irritated I think. But I was always there. And finally he noticed me.'

'How did that make you feel?' Sarah asks.

'Unbelievably lucky.'

For a moment she looks happy and proud.

'Going back, Rowena,' Sarah says. 'You said he'd never touched you in a bad way?'

She nods.

'Has he *ever* hurt you? Maybe accidentally? Or . . . ?'

Rowena turns away.

'Rowena?'

She doesn't reply.

'You said to me that someone can have the angel and the devil inside them?' Sarah says, coaxing. 'And that your job is to get rid of the devil?'

Rowena turns to face her.

'It sounds medieval, I know. You could put it a different way, go twenty-first century and talk about multiple personalities, but the cure's the same, I think. Just love. Loving someone can cast out the devil or make a person mentally well again. If you love them enough.'

'Has Silas been to visit you here?' Mohsin asks.

'No. It's over between us. A while ago, actually. But even if we were still together, well, he wouldn't want Mum to see him with me.'

'Your mum doesn't like him?' Sarah asks.

'No. She wanted me to break it off.'

'And did you?'

'Yes. I mean, I didn't want to upset Mum so much. I don't think he understood though.'

'Was it your parents who told the *Richmond Post* about Silas, after the playground accident?' Mohsin asks.

'It was just Mum. Daddy said it wasn't fair to try and get someone the sack. Not for personal reasons. Said it wasn't right. But Mummy hates Silas. So she phoned the paper.'

Good for Maisie. Vestiges of the friend I used to know remain intact when it counts. She might not have left Donald but she stood up for her daughter with Silas.

I'm not sure if she knew that her phone call would lead to the bankruptcy of her family. But I think even if she did, she would still have gone ahead.

'How old were you last summer, when it started?' Sarah asks.

'Sixteen. But my birthday's in August, so I was almost seventeen.'

'You must have missed him, after you had to break it off?'

Rowena nods, upset.

'Did he try and get in touch with you again?'

She nods, tears spilling now.

'Did he ever ask you to do something for him? Something that you knew was wrong?'

'No, of course not. I mean, Silas wouldn't do something like that to me. He's always been kind to me.'

She's a terrible liar.

A nurse comes in. 'I need to change her dressings and give her her antibiotics.'

Mohsin stands up. 'We'll see you a little later, Rowena, OK?'

★ ★ ★

Mohsin and Sarah leave.

'So it's textbook — abused child goes for abusive partner?' Mohsin asks.

'Could stick it up on PowerPoint at the next domestic violence seminar,' Sarah replies. 'Some experts think it's because the abused girl hopes that she can make the abusive partner love her and be kind to her. And that will somehow make amends for her father. She'll be making her father love her by proxy.'

'Sounds like bullshit to me,' Mohsin says. 'I'll call the station and get someone down here with

430

the recording equipment. We'll do it all by Baker's bloody *book*.'

Sarah nods.

'Do you think Silas Hyman asked her to start the fire?' Mohsin asks.

'I don't know. It's possible but I think it's more likely that she enabled him to do it. She's clearly vulnerable to him and I think he'd exploit that. But the same is true of her father. I think both Silas Hyman and Donald White would exploit Rowena for their own ends.'

Penny is hurrying down the corridor towards them.

'Donald White has been released without charge,' she says. She sees Sarah's expression. 'He has an alibi and a good lawyer. There was nothing we could do to legitimately keep him any longer.'

'Do you know where he's gone?' Sarah asks.

'No.'

'And Silas Hyman?'

'We're looking at the building sites. Nothing yet.'

So both Donald White and Silas Hyman could be here in the hospital.

★ ★ ★

I follow Sarah along a glassed-in walkway towards ICU. As I look down to the parched, too-hot garden beneath, I can see Jenny's blonde head and, beside her, Ivo. From above I watch him move closer towards her. She bends her body towards his.

32

You are in the corridor of ICU with Sarah, keeping watch on Jenny through the glass.

'But there must be some way they can find him?' you say, incredulous; furious.

'We don't even know if he's actually working on a building site, or if that's a line he spun his wife. We'll keep looking for him. And Donald White.'

'I only spoke to Donald at school things. And it was years ago. But I don't think he's the type of bloke to do this.'

'There isn't really a type,' Sarah says. 'Have you spoken to Ads?'

Emotion tenses your face. You shake your head. 'I'll go and see him as soon as you've found them both.'

Sarah nods. 'Maybe when the arsonist is locked up it'll be different for Addie,' she says.

Will he speak then? Surely he will.

Ivo walks past you and into Jenny's ward. But only I see that Jenny is with him. They go up to her bed.

This is the first time she has seen herself since right after the fire. Her face looks worse than it did then, more swollen and blistered. Even though she knows she won't be scarred, I dread what she must feel as she sees her burnt face; her plastic-encased body.

I make myself look at her.

Her tears are falling onto Ivo's face and he wipes them away as his own.

I think she was afraid of his rejection before and she was protecting herself. And now she doesn't have to. It's his love that gives her the strength to look at herself.

Sarah comes up to Ivo, moved by his distress.

'She's not going to scar,' she says to him.

'Yes, her dad said.'

But I know it's not her appearance that distresses him. It's what she must have suffered.

You tell Sarah and Ivo that you need to see me for a little while. Sarah wants to catch up with the police, but there's now Ivo as a member of the guard rota at her bedside. And I trust him, as you do.

Jenny and Ivo stay at her bedside together.

I join her.

'Dad's got Ivo guarding me now?'

'Yes.'

For the first time she doesn't argue that there's no need for a guard; doesn't say it's *ridiculous*. Maybe now Ivo's here she can face this fear, as she's facing her body.

★   ★   ★

You reach my bed and hold my hand. My fingers look pale after being out of the sun for nearly four days; my ring mark is disappearing. But your fingers, with the dark hairs and square-cut nails, still look strongly capable.

'Ivo's with Jenny, darling,' you say to me. 'I think that's what she wants.'

433

'Yes.'

Because I was right about Jenny after all — she does love him. But I was right too when I said I don't know her; not all of her. Just as I can't physically pick her up any more, she is no longer entirely knowable by me.

'You think she's too young for something to be so serious,' you say. 'But . . . '

'She's nearly grown up now,' I finish off. 'And I ought to see that.'

She's become an adult; a young adult, yes, but still an adult with spaces that are hers alone.

'I know she'll always be little Jen too, to us,' you say.

'Yes.'

'But we have to kind of disguise that. For her sake.'

You understand.

'I don't think any parent really ever lets go,' I say to you.

'Some parents are just better at pretending,' you say.

As we talk, with only me hearing both of us, but you intuiting my words, I remember, again, that we have spoken every day since we first met. Nineteen years of talking to each other.

When you were away filming, we spoke long distance, the words between us hissing and fading in and out, but I still painted a picture of my day, and you — well, I was going to say you framed it, neat and pat, but it's not that. Because we might not have young love, or find each other beautiful in that eyebeams-threading way any more, but you give me the canvas to paint on tomorrow.

And it's only now, right now, that I properly appreciate you sitting with me and still talking to me. Every chance you get, whenever Sarah and now Ivo can guard Jenny, you come to me.

Do you remember Sarah's reading at our wedding?

At the time I didn't take much notice. We were only in the church to please my father ('*It'll mean so much to him*' and I'd wanted to make up for being a pregnant bride) and we'd gone for the usual off-the-shelf ready-made-for-weddings reading from Corinthians.

'*Love is patient and kind,*' Sarah read out, standing in the pulpit. But I felt far from patient or kind as she read, *so bloody slowly!* My shoes were much too high, Mum had been right about that, and my toes were pinched. How come the guests were allowed to sit down but we weren't?

'*Love bears all things, believes all things, hopes all things, endures all things.*'

Apart from killer-heels on a hard church floor.

But I do remember the ending of her reading.

' . . . *now faith, hope and love abide, these three; and the greatest of these is love.*'

And I think that you loving me still takes faith.

And your faith that I can hear you now takes love.

★　★　★

Again a watched-pot hope as we return to Jenny's bedside together.

She isn't here.

A nurse sees your panic and tells you she's just

been taken to the MRI suite and her boyfriend and a doctor from ICU have gone with her.

You hurry out.

ICU is secure with its locked door and high ratio of medical staff but out here danger prowls the corridors and jostles into the crowded lifts and maybe a murderer is striding towards our vulnerable daughter.

I try and still my panic. Ivo is with her. And there's a doctor with her too. They won't let anything happen to her. Besides, surely both Donald and Silas are too intelligent to risk another attack.

I slow my pace to a walk while you race on.

I pass the chapel door and hear a low, animal keening sound. I go in.

She's kneeling at the front of the church. Her crying is the sound of despair; a scream fragmenting into tears.

Every nerve in me jangles into a run to her. I put my arms around her.

'I didn't want to be with him, Mum.'

'But he loves you. I saw that. He's only left you now so that he could go to the MRI suite, because Dad was with me. He hasn't rejected you, if that's what you — '

'I know he loves me. I've always known that.'

She turns to me and I can hardly bear to look at the anguish on her face. As bad as looking at her burnt face. Blistering with pain in front of me.

'I knew that if I saw him I'd want to live too much.'

'Jenny-wren — '

'I don't want to die,' she shouts; and her shout echoes around the chapel until it's a sonic boom of emotion that breaks bones.

'*I don't want to die!*'

'Jen, listen — '

Her face is starting to shimmer. She's getting too bright to look at. When this happened before her heart had stopped.

This can't happen. Not now. Please.

This can't happen.

And I'm running to the MRI suite, down corridors, through swing doors, passing too many people, their faces so harsh in the barred overhead lights.

She needs a heart. Right now. Right this moment. The surgeons need to be taking her old damaged one out and putting in one that will keep her alive.

I race to the lifts and get in as the doors close.

But Miss Logan had told you, rammed it home, that she had to be stable first. Not dying. Not this.

I think of that awful sound in the chapel.

She's been so frightened as she faced death. Terrified. But all along standing tall and sheltering me with her humour.

Sheltering me.

I'd discovered she'd grown up, but I hadn't seen her courage.

The lift is going too slowly. Too bloody slowly.

I think about the red paint. '*She said her parents would be so upset, she didn't want to worry them . . .* ' But I hadn't paused to hear her words.

How long has she been protecting us? And I called her immature.

I remember Sarah hadn't looked surprised.

The lift stops, *stops!* People politely waiting to get in. I run to the stairs.

I think of the gravel cutting into her feet and the sun scorching her as she made herself remember back to the fire, to help Adam. Because she loves him and is courageous in her love for him.

I reach the ground floor, and hurry to the MRI suite.

I think of the times that I've been tactless and insensitive and patronising and she's just teased me; her generosity of spirit.

Nearly there. Nearly there.

Why haven't I seen this before? *Seen Jenny?* The extraordinary person that she has grown into.

No longer a child; an astonishing adult.

'*But your daughter, yes. Always.*'

There's a cubicle and medical staff are hurrying towards it.

I go in.

★   ★   ★

Doctors surround her and their machinery makes inhuman noises and you are there and I think of the river Styx and Jenny being rowed towards the underworld. But the doctors are trying to reach her, throwing ropes with grappling hooks over the side of the boat, and they're pulling it, pulling her, back to the land of the living.

You are staring at the monitor.

It has a trace.

It has a trace!

I feel euphoric.

★   ★   ★

'Her physical condition has drastically deterio-
rated,' Miss Logan tells you and Sarah at Jenny's
bedside. 'We can keep her stable for two, maybe
three, days.'

'And then . . . ?' you ask.

'We've run out of options. I have to tell you
that the chance of finding a donor heart in the
time frame left to her is non-existent.'

I feel your exhaustion. The boulder of love
you've been carrying up that mountain has
slipped all the way down to the bottom. And you
have to start that Herculean task all over again.

*'You've got it wrong, Mum!' Addie told me.
'The boulder wasn't Hercules. Hercules had to
kill loads of monsters, the really awful ones, you
know, like Cerberus? Although he did have to
clean out a cow-shed too.'*

'That sounds easier.'

*'No, cos the cattle were special god-cattle and
they made huge amounts of poo and he had to
divert a river. It was <u>Sisyphus</u> who had to push
the boulder.'*

'Poor Sisyphus.'

*'I'd rather push a boulder than fight a mon-
ster.'*

★   ★   ★

Mohsin arrives in the ward.

'I'm sorry, but I thought you ought to know straight away. It was deliberate. Just now, while she was in the MRI suite, someone disconnected her respirator.'

★   ★   ★

In the parched garden, I sit with Jenny.

'They'll give you proper protection now,' I say. 'Apparently Baker's sending half of Chiswick police station down here. And Penny's already started taking statements.'

'Bolting the stable door and all that . . . '

'Yes.'

Then we talk, properly; privately.

It wouldn't be right to tell you our conversation, that's up to Jenny — one day; if she can remember. But I can tell you I apologise to her. And that I'm now going to tell her my shoe analogy because I think she'll like it.

She looks at me with amusement.

'So I was soft little bootees until one day I was boots striding away from you?'

'Sort of. Actually I was quite proud of the analogy. Thought it said quite a lot — size getting bigger, with the subtlety of width fittings; supervised shopping versus independence.'

She smiles at me.

'Really,' I say. 'It's a sad day when there's no longer width fitting. A milestone.'

It makes her smile more.

'You bought me the sparkly sandals, didn't you, Mum?' she says.

440

'Yes.'

'I love them.'

Maybe I shouldn't get so hung up on growing up as a loss.

I expect my nanny voice to say something cutting. She usually does when I venture a new thought. Nothing.

Maybe I've grown up too and finally managed to evict her.

'When will the transplant happen?' Jenny asks.

'Tomorrow morning. First thing.'

★   ★   ★

Penny is in the small institutional office where Baker once accused Adam. With her is an ashen-faced doctor. Ivo is waiting outside.

'And you're *sure* you were next to her, *all the time?*' Penny asks.

'Yes, like I said. Right next to her.' The doctor pauses as Sarah and Mohsin come in, but Penny gestures at him to carry on.

'Someone must have walked past and quickly tugged out the endotracheal tube. It must have been quickly because I didn't see. I mean, I didn't take my eye off her for long. I was just looking at her chart and checking the details for her scan. I didn't expect anyone to . . . Then I heard the alarm go off, the device that alerts us to a cardiac failure. And I was dealing with that. It was only when other people came to help that I saw the tube to the portable respirator. Saw it had been disconnected.'

'Thank you,' Penny says. 'Could you wait in

441

the corridor and a colleague will come to take a full statement.'

When he's left the room, Penny turns to Sarah and Mohsin.

'The MRI suite has four scanning rooms and a waiting room, with changing rooms and lockers. It has a secure door, but it's far busier than ICU. There's administrative staff as well as medical personnel — not only doctors and nurses who work with the MRI machines, but also porters bringing patients into the suite, and out-patients, some of whom bring a partner with them. I've got Connor interviewing the reception staff, and I'm hoping her boyfriend might have something.'

'Have you got pics of Donald White and Silas Hyman to show?' Mohsin asks.

'We're trying to organise it but it's not easy to get mug shots when we don't know the whereabouts of either man. And neither wife is being helpful.'

She calls Ivo in.

It had once seemed to me as if he was lying on the pavement being punched by facts. But now he walks in determinedly tall.

'She's not going to die,' he says.

He reminds me of you. Not the denial in the face of the facts, that bullish optimism, but the strength it takes to walk upright. So she's gone for a man like her father after all.

All these revelations; all so quickly. No wonder Nanny Voice left, the landscape of my mind can't feel like home any more.

'Can you tell me what you saw?' Penny asks.

'Nothing. I didn't see anything.'

He is furious with himself.

'If you could just tell me — '

'They wouldn't let me in with her. Other patients had partners with them, I saw them going in, but I wasn't allowed to.'

His voice so furious still, this time with other people. Because older adults had discounted Ivo as I once had — just a teenage girl's boyfriend; a world away from married adults.

'I told her father I'd look after her. I said I'd be with her. So he could be with his wife for a little bit.'

'I'll explain and he'll understand,' Sarah said.

'How can he? I can't.'

'Did you wait for her?' Penny asks.

'Yes. Outside the MRI bit. In the corridor.'

'Did you see anyone?'

'No one I noticed. Just what you'd expect. Doctors, nurses. Porters. And patients, some in normal clothes so I suppose they're not staying in the hospital.'

Ivo leaves to return to Jenny. Penny answers her phone.

'She was already dying for crying out loud,' Sarah says to Mohsin. '*Already dying*. Why shorten her life any more? Why do that to her?'

'Maybe Donald White or Silas Hyman — whoever did this — doesn't know she's dying,' Mohsin says. 'When you've spoken about it, it's been about her needing a transplant. Maybe that's what he has heard too.'

'But the transplant was never really going to happen. Not really. We just wanted to . . . It was a million-to-one shot . . . in the time that she

443

had left. And now . . . '

Mohsin takes her hand.

'Perhaps he didn't know that,' he says. 'Perhaps he was worried about her getting a transplant.'

'I was here, all the time, I was *fucking here* and I didn't stop it. Didn't look after her. Right *here*.'

She breaks down. Mohsin holds her.

'Darling . . . '

'How can I help Mike?' Sarah says. 'How?'

A father's voice now, wanting to *do* something; because she's been a father as well as a mother to you and I'd never thought about that before.

She abruptly pulls away from Mohsin, furiously blows her nose.

'We need to find the bastard.'

'Are you sure you — '

'His daughter is dying and his wife is dead in all but name and there's nothing I can do to help. All I can do for him now is what I am trained to do. And he won't care at all about justice now — what difference will it make to him, for fuck's sake? But maybe in time, years, it will be one thing that was done right. Just one thing. Besides, it's all I can do for him.'

Penny gets off the phone. 'Baker wants us to wait for him before talking to Rowena White. Fifteen minutes. This time, we'll get the truth out of her.'

★ ★ ★

You're at my bedside. You're silent, but I am used to that now; as if you can tell when I'm actually with you.

Ivo is with Jenny and I'm glad you're demonstrating your trust in him by letting him guard her again.

I reach you and put my arms around you.

You tell me the doctors have said she will only live another two days.

'Just *two days*, Gracie.'

And as you tell me the truth of it hits you. That open green prairie of your mind, with its stockade of hope, is flooded with terror for her. You can't hope any longer.

I want you to tell me about the person *who did this!* I want you to vow vengeance, I want you to be Maximus Decimus Meridius.

But if your anger is still there you don't notice it.

I think of the tsunami on Christmas Eve and the film of a woman in labour clinging high in the branches of a tree, too overwhelmed by childbirth to look at the violent destruction around her. Only she and the life of her child could matter.

You hold my hand and I feel you shaking and I can't help you.

A nurse and a porter arrive to take me for a scan. The one where you need to pretend to hit a ball for 'yes', to light up a part of your brain for their monitors.

The porter unclips the wheels of my bed, like I'm in a buggy.

'Hit it for yes, Gracie,' you say. 'Hard as you can. Please.'

I remember telling Mum that I was going to be Roger-fucking-Federer.

The porter wheels me out of the ward, a nurse at my side.

But I stay with you, holding your hand.

I'm sorry.

33

Rowena and Maisie are waiting in an office, with a young police officer I don't recognise.

Sarah is with Mohsin and Penny just outside.

'Baker's on a call. He won't be long,' Mohsin says. 'I'm still not sure about allowing Maisie White to be present at this.'

'We'll be able to watch her reaction too,' Penny replies. 'And questioning Rowena might tip Mum finally into telling us the truth. If it doesn't work, Jacobs is finding a social worker to act as a competent adult.'

Baker arrives. I see him meet Penny's eye and something is communicated between them, but I can't interpret it. Perhaps it's the closest Baker gets to shame.

'Has Maisie White told us yet where her husband is?' Sarah asks.

'Claims she has no idea,' Penny says. 'The stupid bitch is lying again for him.'

I am shocked by the ugliness of her epithet for Maisie. Odd that language can still have the power to shock me. They go in, while Sarah waits outside.

★ ★ ★

The air is thick with heat, the plastic stacking chairs sticking together. The nylon fibres in the carpet-tiles glint in the harsh light.

Rowena looks frail in her nightdress and dressing gown, her damaged hands still bandaged. Maisie fusses around her, sorting out her drip stand.

Mohsin formally introduces everyone in the room while the young police officer records it.

'Are you sure you're comfortable?' Mohsin asks Rowena.

'I'm fine. Yes. Thank you.'

Maisie rests her hand on Rowena's arm, unable to hold her hand. She's again wearing a long-sleeved shirt, no sign of the bruises underneath.

'Your father has an alibi for the time of the fire,' Mohsin says, his voice matter-of-fact; but I see him studying Rowena's face intently. Penny is watching Maisie.

'Yes,' Rowena says, barely reacting. 'Daddy was in Scotland on Wednesday.'

'Did your father ask you to light the fire, Rowena?' Mohsin asks, still matter-of-fact.

'Of course he didn't,' Maisie says, her voice too high. A vein is flickering in her temple.

'What about Silas Hyman?' Mohsin says to Rowena, his voice sterner. 'I asked you before — '

'No, I told you,' Rowena says, distressed. 'He didn't ask me to do anything.'

'An hour ago someone tried to kill Jennifer Covey,' Baker says. 'We don't have the time or patience for you to protect the man who did it.'

I hear a sharp intake of breath. Maisie has gone white. She looks clammy as if she might vomit.

Rowena is silent, struggling. She turns to her mother.

'I think it's best if you left.'

'But I have to be with you.'

'We can find another competent adult to be with Rowena,' Baker says.

'Is that what you'd like?' Mohsin asks Rowena. She nods.

Maisie leaves the room. I don't see her face. But I see her stumble as she's rejected.

The door closes behind her.

'If you just give me a little while,' Penny says to Rowena. 'We need to find someone — '

'I have to tell you the truth now. Because of Jenny. I have to. It wasn't Dad. It wasn't anything to do with him.'

I think of Silas Hyman flirting with Jenny then moving onto Rowena. I think of him swearing and raging at the prize-giving. I think of the flowers he gave to the nurse and the door to ICU opening.

'It was Mummy,' Rowena says.

Maisie?

I see her loving face and feel her encompassing hugs.

I think of her that day at the sports field, handing me a *little something* for Adam, beautifully wrapped, a spot-on present inside.

She'd known it was his birthday.

Of course she had! She'd known him since he was born. And *three hundred* other people knew it was his birthday.

She went to the school just before the fire.

To *find* Rowena. To give her a lift. Because the tubes were up the spout. *'Chauffeur-Mum to the fore!'*

The spool of our friendship stretches back through the years we've known one another and won't unravel.

'Mummy's afraid of being poor,' Rowena quietly continues. 'She's always had lots of money. My grandparents were rich and she's never had to work.'

But Maisie said it wouldn't matter to her being poor and she didn't mind working. *'I've always rather wanted a job, actually.'*

'She went into Sidley House to read,' Rowena continues, 'so that she could keep a check on what was happening after I'd left. Sally Healey didn't tell anyone that there were no new admissions. Even Dad. Well, not for ages. But Mum found out from Elizabeth Fisher that no one was phoning any more.'

But she didn't go in to spy! She went in to read because she loves being around young children.

I *feel* our friendship. So heavily substantial and Aga-warm; so many years invested in it, each one adding to its weight.

'Did she ever leave your room?' Mohsin asks.

'Well, yes, she goes and gets things to eat. She went home to get me a clean nightie and my washbag. She goes out to use the phone, too. You're not allowed a mobile in here.'

'An hour or so ago, when we left you with your mother,' Mohsin says, 'did she leave your room again then?'

Rowena's voice is so quiet that I have to strain to hear it.

'Yes. Almost right away.'

There is no way, *no way*, that Maisie tried to kill Jenny. Everyone's got this *wrong*.

'Thank you, Rowena. We need to interview you again, formally, with what's known as a competent adult present with you.'

* * *

Outside the office, Baker turns to the young policeman.

'Chase up that social worker. I'm not going to give a defence lawyer any rope on this one.'

'Maisie White must have seen Jenny being taken out of ICU and followed her,' Mohsin says. 'Got lucky with the MRI suite. Security's not as tight.'

Sarah nods. 'When Jenny's ventilator was tampered with the first time, it was in the burns unit. Maisie was staying in Rowena's room just down the corridor. No one would have questioned her being there.'

'So you think it was Maisie, not Natalia Hyman?' Mohsin asks.

'Yes.'

I'd only seen a back view and hadn't got close — but it couldn't have been Maisie. *It couldn't have been.*

'Jenny must have seen her at the school,' Sarah says.

'And she had Jenny's mobile,' Mohsin says. 'If there was anything incriminating on it, she'd have had plenty of time to delete it.'

As they speak it's as if a painting-by-numbers portrait is being filled in, one colour at a time.

451

But I won't look at their vicious portrait of my friend.

Because Maisie's known Jenny since she was a little girl of four. She's heard me talk about her and Adam, all the time. *All the time.* She knows how much I love them.

She's my friend and I *trust her.*

I can't add this to what has happened.

I can't.

So I turn away from their picture of Maisie.

'What about the domestic abuse?' Mohsin asks.

'God knows what's been going on in that family,' Sarah says.

'Find Maisie White,' DI Baker says to Penny. 'And arrest her for the arson attack and attempted murder of Jennifer Covey.'

'She's in Rowena's room,' Sarah says. 'I saw her there a few minutes ago.'

Sarah's been keeping tabs on her, I realise.

★   ★   ★

Penny goes to arrest Maisie. I don't go to watch, but instead follow Sarah back into the stifling office.

'OK, Rowena, we're waiting for a social worker. In the meantime — '

'Will Mummy be taken away?' Rowena asks.

'I'm sorry, yes.'

Rowena says nothing, staring at the floor. Sarah waits.

'She didn't think I'd tell anyone,' Rowena says, and she looks ashamed.

452

'But she told you?' Sarah says.

Rowena is silent.

'You don't have to say anything. This isn't an interview. Just a chat. If you'd like it.'

I don't think Sarah is seizing an opportunity. I think she's just being kind to Rowena. Or perhaps she just needs to know right now, unable to wait.

'Mummy feels terrible. Really guilty. It's been awful for her,' Rowena says. 'She needed to tell someone. And maybe because I got hurt . . . maybe she felt she owed me something.' She starts to weep. 'She'll hate me now.'

Sarah sits down next to her.

'This is awful, but I was glad that she told me,' Rowena continues. 'I mean, that she confided in me. She doesn't do that. Never has. Everyone thinks we're close, but we're not. I'm her 'little disappointment'.'

But Maisie *adores* her.

'When I was little I was pretty, you see,' Rowena continues. 'She was proud of me then. But as I got older, well, I stopped being pretty. And she stopped loving me.'

Argue with her, I urge Sarah. Tell her that mothers *don't do that*. They don't stop loving their children.

'I know this sounds silly, but it was my teeth to begin with,' Rowena says. 'She made me go to an orthodontist because they were so crooked, but they were yellow too. Something to do with an antibiotic I'd had as a baby. Mummy tried everything, had me bleaching them at home every night, even though the dentist said it

453

wouldn't work with that kind of staining. And then it was the usual, you know, blonde hair goes mousey brown and my eyebrows got all big and my face got larger but my eyes didn't. So I turned ugly. Cinderella in reverse, I suppose. I wasn't the kind of daughter she wanted any more.'

And still Sarah says nothing. But surely to God, if there is *one thing* about Maisie that I am absolutely convinced of, it's that *she loves Rowena*.

'It's hard, you know,' Rowena says. 'Not being pretty. I mean, at school the popular girls are the ones with the pretty faces and long hair who are good at music and English and Art. Not the clever girls with bad skin. Not me. A cliché really, isn't it, for a clever girl to be ugly? And then you go home and it's the same.'

'You're going to Oxford, aren't you?' Sarah asks.

'To read Natural Sciences. She doesn't tell people that bit. Pretends I'm off to May balls and parties and handsome undergraduates, not a Science lab and an all-girls' college.

'You know that Shakespeare sonnet, about love not being love which alters not when it alteration finds? I think it's about a mother with her child growing up. But not mine.'

But all I can think is how proud Maisie is of Rowena's reading: '*Even Shakespeare, when she's doing Science A levels. My little bookworm!*'

Her pride in Rowena. Her love for her. How can these not be real? Her true colours. Because they are what make Maisie who she is.

'I thought she'd be pleased about Silas,' Rowena says, and I hear grief in her voice. 'I mean, he's handsome, isn't he? I thought it was like proving to her that I could be like a pretty girl too.'

'But he's *married* for crying out loud,' I say to her. 'And he's thirty. Of course your mother didn't want him to be your boyfriend; of course she wanted something better for you.'

'She went to see him,' Rowena continues, her voice halting. 'It was Valentine's Day and he'd sent me a card. She went to his house. Told him he had to stop our relationship.'

The hate mail from Natalia stopped the day after Valentine's Day. Maisie's talk with Silas worked.

And I'd do the same for Jenny. If she was sixteen and was with Silas Hyman, I'd do the same. Because this is nothing like Jenny's relationship with Ivo, nothing like it at all.

'I loved him,' Rowena says quietly. 'I still do. I thought he'd fight for me. But he didn't.

'And then Mum got him fired. She phoned the newspaper, not thinking what would happen to the school, just wanting to get him out; punish him too. And she told me she sent him candles, eight blue ones, like the ones on Addie's cake. She said she wanted him to know that if he ever started anything again with me, she'd make his life hell. That she has that power.'

The Maisie I've known for thirteen years is warm and vibrant and ran in the mums' race every year and always came last by a mile and *didn't give a hoot!* I've also learnt that she is

455

fragile and vulnerable and bruised. Both these Maisies have been assimilated into my picture of her.

But not this.

A nurse knocks and comes in. It's Belinda, the nice smiley nurse.

'There's a ward round and the doctors need to take a look at her. It'll take about twenty minutes.'

Sarah stands up. 'Of course.'

★   ★   ★

It's cooler up here in my ward, the open windows and white linoleum at least visually lowering the temperature. A porter is wheeling a trolley, with my comatose body on it, back towards the bed. My scan must be finished.

You are waiting.

Dr Bailstrom's shoes click across the linoleum towards you, black today but Louboutins, the red flashing on the underside like a warning.

She tells you that their scan shows I have no cognitive function. No brain activity beyond the basics of swallowing, gagging and breathing.

I wasn't out on a grassy tennis court, warm under my toes, running for a ball, racket outstretched, and thwacking it over the net. I was with Sarah as she spoke to Rowena.

I have never been near my body when they've done their scans.

No wonder they think I'm not there.

You ask to be alone with me.

You take my hand in yours.

456

You say you understand.

And I am amazed by you.

You pull the curtain around my bed.

You lay your head down next to me, so that our faces are close, my hair falling across your cheek. United by almost twenty years of loving each other and seventeen years of loving our child.

The essence of our marriage is distilled in this moment.

Jenny is standing in the doorway.

'Jen, come in.'

But she shakes her head. 'I didn't know,' she says and leaves.

And I didn't know either; that our tough-as-old-boots-strong married love contains this delicate intensity at its heart.

I think about speaking to each other every day for nineteen years. Nineteen years times three hundred and sixty five days times however many conversations per day — how many words does that make between us?

An uncountable number.

My hair is still falling across your cheek but I move away from you.

It will help you, my darling, if you think I'm not here. It will make this easier. And I want to make this easier for you.

I leave the room.

★   ★   ★

Outside the office on the ground floor, everyone is gathering for another interview with Rowena.

457

The social worker is already in there and now people start filing into the office. The corridor has got hotter, faces are sweating. DI Baker's shirt is untucked and his hands leave clammy marks around the file he's holding.

I'm thinking of you.

Of when you'll realise I'm no longer there with you.

Only Penny and Sarah now remain out in the corridor.

'There's something you should know,' Penny says, not meeting Sarah's eye. 'You probably should have been told before.'

'Yes?'

'Maisie White was the witness who said she saw Adam coming out of the Art room, holding matches.'

I have never known her.

34

'I never thought Maisie White was involved in the fire directly,' Penny tells Sarah. She's keeping everyone waiting in the office, but she has to tell Sarah; owes her this.

'She seemed *genuinely* distressed by what had happened to Jenny and Grace,' Penny continues. 'And was *reluctant* to tell me it was Adam. I thought I was having to force it out of her.'

'If I'd known — ' Sarah begins.

'Yes. I'm sorry. Since we found out about the fraud — *you* found out — we've been questioning the validity of her witness statement, but have been working under the assumption that she was protecting her husband. In retrospect she was playing us. I'm sorry.'

'I told Maisie that a witness had seen Adam,' Sarah says. 'And she was surprised. I thought it meant she had no idea.'

'A good actress?' suggests Penny.

Sarah thinks a moment then shakes her head. 'It's because I'm a police officer. She thought I would *already know* it was her who was the witness. She'd have assumed I'd been told. It was my ignorance that surprised her.'

No wonder Maisie had initially seemed so nervous of Sarah that evening in the cafeteria.

Penny goes into the office.

★　★　★

459

There are so many people in here, making Rowena seem smaller. She is staring at the shiny carpet-tiles, not looking up.

'You told one of my officers earlier that your mother knew you were going to go bankrupt?' Baker says.

'Yes.'

'Why did your mother say she saw Adam coming out of the Art room?' Penny asks, and DI Baker looks irritated.

'She wanted a child to be blamed,' Rowena says quietly. 'So that no one would suspect fraud. It was just chance that it was Adam's birthday that day.'

'Sports day?'

'Yes. She didn't want anyone hurt.'

'And there'd be no staff to put it out?'

Rowena is silent.

'So who actually started the fire?'

Rowena is silent.

'Was it you?' Mohsin asks. 'Did your mother ask you to do that?'

She doesn't reply.

'You said that you need to tell the truth?' Mohsin reminds her.

'I didn't know what she was going to do. Not till too late. And it's only been in here that she's told me everything. She thought she could trust me. Oh God.'

'So it was your mother?' DI Baker asks.

She shakes her head.

'She made Adam do it.'

But no one could make Adam do that. He's too good, too thoughtful.

'She told Adam that Mr Hyman had left him a birthday present in the Art room,' Rowena continues. 'She told him it was a volcano. They'd done that in year three — you know, with the vinegar and the baking soda, making an eruption?

'She told Adam it was a different kind of volcano and he needed to light it. She said he could use the matches from his birthday cake, which she'd fetched for him.

'She said the pathetic little wimp didn't want anything to do with the matches.'

There's a vocabulary that goes with this person I don't know. Thinking about her words, not what she's done. Because I can't, yet, think about what she's done.

'She said she had to lay it on thick then,' Rowena continues. 'Told him Mr Hyman had brought the volcano present to the school *himself*, even though he'd get into terrible trouble if he was found there.'

It's making a ghastly kind of sense now: a volcano, not a fire, for Mr Hyman, his beloved teacher.

'She told Addie that Mr Hyman was waiting to say happy birthday to him. That he'd be back any minute. And that he'd be really disappointed if Addie wasn't playing with the birthday surprise.'

So Silas Hyman is directly linked to the fire — but as a phantom presence; a motivating force, blameless of what was being done in his name.

'And Adam lit the volcano,' Rowena says, her voice quiet.

'What was in this volcano?' Penny asks.

461

'She said it was white spirit and another accelerant. She'd also put cans of spray mount around it. She told me Adam must have been chicken and thrown the match from a distance away, otherwise it would have blown up in his face.'

'Did she intend to kill him?'

'No. Of course not.'

'You just said it would have blown up in his face, if he'd got closer, as he was clearly meant to have done.'

'She *can't* have meant to kill him.' But her voice shakes, no scaffolding of conviction to sustain it.

'Is there anything else?'

Rowena nods, unable to look at another person's face, her own cloaked in misery and shame. 'She came up to Addie, when his mother had run in to find Jenny. She said, 'You weren't meant to actually do it, for goodness sake, Addie!''

Rowena mimicked her mother's voice with unnerving accuracy. I flinch from her and Rowena herself seems disturbed. She continues, quietly now. 'She told him it was a knight's test, and he'd failed it. That it was all his fault.'

And Adam believed her.

Because Adam believes in quests and tests of courage and honour.

Because in his eight-year-old imagination he was Sir Gawain.

Because at eight you really can think you're a knight who's been found wanting.

But instead of the giant nicking the side of

462

your neck, your mother and sister are trapped in a burning building in front of you while you're told that you are to blame.

I have to run to him now and tell him it isn't his fault. *It isn't!*

But my vocal cords no longer make sounds.

And Adam, too, is mute. The one thing that DI Baker got right is that Adam's guilt silenced him.

'That's why I went in,' Rowena says quietly. 'After what she'd said to Addie.'

She pauses a moment, upset.

'I'd really like to see him, tell him it wasn't his fault at all,' Rowena says. 'I mean, he probably won't want to see me, but I'd really like to.'

Her voice peters out for a moment.

'It was partly my fault,' she continues. '*I* told Mummy about the volcano experiment. I was in Adam's class as a teaching assistant, last summer term. And *I* told her how good Adam is. I thought it was so sweet the way he liked books about knights; how he almost saw himself as one — or at least wanted to be like one — and *I* told her.'

But I'd already told Maisie that, countless times — and that his goodness makes me worried for him. That I wished, for his sake, he was good at football instead.

Rowena is miserably silent. I want one of them to tell her it wasn't her fault either, but they are police officers in that room, with a job. The 'touchy-feely' stuff, as Sarah called it once, would come later. I used to think it meant that she didn't value empathy.

'Do you know why your mother wanted to harm Jenny?' Penny asks.

'She didn't mean to. It wasn't till Grace ran in, shouting for her, that I knew she was in there. And Mum was the same, I'm sure. She wouldn't have hurt Grace or Jenny. I know she wouldn't. It was a terrible mistake.'

She's shaking violently now. Mohsin looks at her with concern.

'I don't think she's up to any more,' he says to DI Baker.

'Do you think your father knew what your mother intended?' DI Baker asks.

'No.' She pauses a moment. 'But he blames me for not stopping her in time. I mean, I was there. I should have stopped her.'

Penny escorts Rowena out of the room and back to the burns unit.

★ ★ ★

I go to my ward. The curtains are drawn around my bed.

Inside, you're lying with me, pressing yourself against me, sobbing so hard that your body judders the bed.

Crying because you know I'm not there.

I long to go to you but it will make it harder; so much harder.

Then Sarah comes in and runs to you and puts her arms around you and I'm so grateful to her.

She tells you about Maisie, but you hardly listen.

464

Then she tells you that Adam was tricked into lighting the fire; that he was told it was his fault.

For the first time you turn from me.

'Oh Christ, poor Ads.'

'You'll go and see him?' Sarah asks.

You nod. 'As soon as I've seen Grace's doctors.'

★ ★ ★

You've asked for the meeting with my doctors to be at my bedside, as if you need to see my comatose body right here in front of you to do this.

I am at the far side of the ward. Any closer and I'm afraid you'll sense me and this will be too hard for you.

A nurse is wheeling a drugs trolley from bed to bed, and the noise she makes as she unloads her cargo disguises the lower, subtler sounds of your conversation.

You've asked Dr Sandhu to be here too and it's his kind face I look at, not yours. I can't bear to look at yours. I was wrong about him a couple of days ago. He didn't arrive where he is now through a series of coincidence and chances, this was a vocational straight-as-the-crow-flies journey to a family like ours.

The nurse with the drugs trolley has stopped at a bed for longer, and in the silence your voice carries across the ward to me.

You tell them that you know now that I won't wake up.

That I am not 'in there' any more.

465

You tell them that Dad had Kahler's disease and that Jenny and I were tested to see if we were suitable donors for bone marrow.

You tell them that Jenny and I are a tissue match.

You ask them to donate my heart.

I love you.

The squeaky trolley starts up again, and the nurse is chatting to someone and I can't hear the rest of your conversation. But I know what it will be because I have already been down this seemingly logical path with Jenny.

Across the ward, I strain to listen, catching at words that make the sentences I expect.

Dr Bailstrom's high voice carries furthest. She tells you I am breathing unaided. It will be at least a year, probably longer, before they'll even *contemplate* getting a court order to withdraw food and fluid.

You faced my living-death out of love for Jenny and you think nothing has come of it. Now you're only left with the brutal fact.

Dr Sandhu suggests a 'Do Not Resuscitate' document. I imagine that it's pretty standard procedure in these circumstances. But, as Dr Bailstrom points out, standard procedure or not, there is no reason why I should collapse and need resuscitating. My body, ironically, is healthy.

I think Dr Sandhu is trying to give you a little kindness, a little hope. Because if my body does collapse, instead of being resuscitated, it would be kept oxygenated until my organs could be transplanted.

In Dr Sandhu's office you sign the DNR form. Jenny comes in and watches.

'You can't do this, Mum.'

'Of course I can and you — '

'I've changed my mind.'

'It's too late to change your mind, sweetie.'

'This isn't custard instead of cream on my pudding, for fuck's sake!'

I laugh. She's furious.

'I shouldn't have said yes. I can't believe I did. You got me at a really bad — '

'I am never going to wake up again, Jen, but you can get better. So logically — '

'Logically what? You're turning into Jeremy Bentham now?'

'You've read him?'

'Mum!'

'I'm impressed, that's all.'

'No, you're changing the subject. And you can't. It's too big to change. If you go ahead with this, I refuse to get back into my body. Ever.'

'Jenny, you want to live. You — '

'But not by killing you.'

'Jen — '

'I refuse!'

She means it.

And yet she longs overwhelmingly to live.

* * *

You're going home to see Adam and I go with you. As we walk down the corridor, you lean a

467

little towards me, as if you know I'm with you. Maybe now you no longer think I'm in my body you can sense me with you in other places.

As we pass the garden, the shadows lengthening into evening, Jenny is joining Ivo. Before, I'd marvelled at him knowing where she was, amazed at the connection between them, which I saw as an almost spiritual thing. But looking at them now, I just want her to be in his world, the real world — for him to be able to *physically touch her*.

As I long to touch you.

★ ★ ★

In our car, I fantasise once more, just for a minute or so, that we're back in our old life and we're going out to dinner with a bottle of wine in the boot. I wish, absurdly, that it could be me driving. (*That's a decent Burgundy in the boot, Gracie! So go gently on the bends!*)

I even fantasise a row, let's make this a bit more realistic.

'You were heavy on the indicator there,' you say.

'*Heavy* on an indicator? How can you be *heavy* on an *indicator?*'

I'm quite enjoying this, a mixture of teasing and arguing and flirting.

'The stick, you need to be . . . '

I either laugh at you for being ridiculous in a mock row, or start a real row about you patronising me. We nearly always opt for the mock version. So I laugh at you and you hear what I am not saying. I continue to drive and five minutes later you don't mention my illegal right turn.

The little fantasy shatters as I see our house.

The curtains are drawn in Adam's room. It's seven thirty now. Bed-time.

You turn to me, as if you've caught a glimpse of my face. Am I a ghost to you now? Haunting you?

You go into our house but I wait a little while before following you. Our windowboxes of geraniums have shrivelled and browned in the heat; but Adam's two pots of carrots and his tomato growbags have been watered. I am strangely satisfied by that.

Is this what ghosts are? Are ghouls and ghosties actually sitting in cars fantasising mock rows with their husbands and checking on their growbags and windowboxes?

You're with my mother in the kitchen. A little afraid, bracing herself, she says she told Adam after that first big meeting with my doctors that I wasn't going to wake up; that I was dead.

But you are grateful.

And I think that, like me, you see Mum's courage. The only one of us to take the body blow of what the doctors said first time.

You tell her about your failed attempt to donate my heart.

She says she hopes by some miracle it can happen.

'I couldn't bear it, for her to live when her child is dead. To suffer that.'

You put your arm around her.

'And you, Georgina?'

'Oh, you don't need to worry about me. I'm a tough old bird. I won't fall apart. Not till Adam's left for university and I'm in the nursing home. I'll fall apart then.'

'Fall apart' is one of my expressions from my twenties that Mum picked up. 'Tough old bird' is one of hers. I love the legacy of language. How much of what I say has gone into Jen's and Adam's vocabularies? And when they use those words they'll think of me; feel me in a more than language-deep way.

'Adam's been talking about the great rain at the beginning of the world,' Mum tells you.

You're moved. 'He thought of that?'

'Yes. She doesn't just go, Mike. Everything Gracie is, it can't just go.'

'No.'

You go up the stairs to Adam's room.

I look in at the open doorway of our bedroom. Someone has made our bed but our things are exactly as we left them; my bedside table a stilled frame of a moment in my life. Before Jenny, crammed on a smaller bedside table, was a novel — a big classic with tiny print; a packet of Marlboro Lights and a glass of red wine taken up to bed with me. You were horrified by how unhealthy I was and I took no notice of your nagging. With Jenny the classic novel, cigarettes and wine were shoved aside for dummies and cloth books; nowadays I have reading glasses and novels again, newly published, with bright shiny covers and grabbing shoutlines.

You're outside Adam's bedroom door.

'It's Dad.'

The door remains closed.

'Addie . . . ?'

You wait. Silence the other side.

Open the door, I think, just bloody well open it!

My God, I've become my nanny voice. I'm sorry. Perhaps you're right to wait for Addie to come to you; showing him you respect him. I'd have just barged in there, but that's not the only way to do this.

'I know you think you're to blame, my lovely boy,' you say. 'But you're not.'

You've never called him my lovely boy before. A whole phrase of mine you've adopted already and I'm glowing about that.

'Let me in, please?'

The door is still shut between you.

I'd have my arms around him by now, and I'd —

'OK, here's how it is,' you say. 'I love you. Whatever you think you did I love you. Nothing — absolutely nothing — can ever change that.'

'It *is* my fault, Daddy.'

The first words he's spoken since the fire. Words so huge they've been smothering speech.

'Addie, no — '

'It didn't really look like a volcano. Just a bucket, with some orange tissue paper on the top and something inside it. She said I was supposed to light it. But really it was a test. I wasn't meant to do it.'

'Addie — '

'I don't like matches. They scare me. And I

471

know I'm not meant to use them. You and Mum and Jenny are always telling me that. I mean, when we have a fire and you light it, I'm not allowed to. Not till I'm twelve. So I *knew it was wrong*.'

'Please, listen to me — '

'Mr Hyman said Sir Covey would pass the test with flying colours. Sir Covey is me. He thought I was like a knight. But I'm not.'

'Mr Hyman was *never there*, Addie. He cares about you and he'd never, ever ask you to do something like that. You're still Sir Covey.'

'No, you don't understand — '

'She made it all up. About Mr Hyman. The present for you. All of it. She made it up to get you to do something for her. The police have arrested her. Everyone knows it wasn't your fault.'

'But it is. I *shouldn't have done it*, Dad! Whatever she said to me. Sirens and the green giant's beautiful wife tempted people but the good people didn't do what they said. The strong knights didn't do it. But I did.'

'They were grown men, Addie, and you're eight. And a very brave eight-year-old.'

Silence the other side of the door.

'What about the time you stood up for Mr Hyman? That was really brave. Not many adults would have the courage to do that. I should have told you that before. I'm sorry I didn't. Because I am really proud of you.'

Still silence from Addie's room; but what more can you say to him?

'It's not just that,' he says.

You wait and the silence is awful.

'I didn't go and help them, Daddy.'

His voice, so full of shame, punches a hole in both of us.

'Thank God,' you say.

Addie opens the door and the barrier between you is gone.

'I couldn't bear it if I'd lost you too,' you say.

You put your arms around him and something floods through his body, relaxing his taut limbs and frightened face.

'Mum's never going to wake up. Granny G told me.'

'Yes,' you say.

'She's dead.'

'Yes. She . . . '

I think you're going to say something more, perhaps the difference between 'no cognitive function' and being dead, but Adam is eight and you can't talk to him about the details of why he has no mother now.

He starts to cry and you hold him as tightly as you can.

Silence expands between you, a blown soap bubble around the emotion it contains, then breaks.

'You have me,' you say.

And your arms around Adam aren't trying to hug him now, but clinging onto him.

'And I have you.'

35

Five hours have gone past and it's nearly midnight now. Jenny's fairy stories were down on this time of night — coaches turning into pumpkins and dancing princesses needing to be back in their beds — but the stories Adam enjoys give a more positive spin: the witching hour when moonlight is bright and the world is silent and everyone is asleep apart from the little girl and the BFG, blowing his dreams into bedrooms.

I can see *The BFG* on the second shelf. You are on the top bunk, Adam on the bottom, Aslan tucked in next to him.

My dancing shoes, if I had any, would smell of antiseptic.

I've been to the hospital and I need to tell you what happened.

* * *

I watched as you sat with Adam, holding his hand, grateful that I'd built up enough tolerance to the pain of being away from the hospital so I could be with him as he slept.

I thought how lovely it was that the children call Mum 'Granny G', to differentiate her from your mother, Granny Annabel; because although she died before they were born she's still their grandmother too.

You found Addie's old night-light, then you moved up to the top bunk, your hand stretching down in case he needed you.

Mum came in, wanting to go and see Jen for a little while now that you were looking after Addie.

I went with her.

* * *

I'm not sure if I've told you this, but once Mum found out I was no longer in my body she started talking to me all the time, in all sorts of places. *'A scattergun approach, Grace, poppet, sometimes you'll be there to hear me. I'm sure.'*

She drove her ancient Renault Clio furiously fast along the almost empty dark roads towards the hospital.

'I watered Adam's carrots and tomatoes,' she said.

'Thanks.'

'Should have given your windowboxes a proper soak. They get dehydrated so fast when it's hot.'

'Maybe you can re-plant. I'd really like it if you did.'

She was silent for a little while, her face so much older now. She jumped a red light but there was hardly any traffic to notice or care.

'I'll put in something which doesn't mind drought so much. Lavender would be pretty.'

'Lavender would be perfect.'

* * *

475

We arrived at the hospital. The goldfish-bowl atrium was almost deserted, just a few straggling patients, their foot-steps echoing in the empti-ness; a single doctor hurrying. Lights from cars flashed through the glass of the window from the darkness outside.

I thought about Mr Hyman and how afraid I'd been of him when he came to the hospital. '*Get away from my children, get away!*' Is that what happens in the aftermath of a terrible crime? All the ugliness and cruelty of it spilling out onto the people around; an oil slick lapping ashore, indiscriminately blackening what it touches. He's deeply flawed, yes, but not guilty of any sin. A fallible man but not a wicked one. Blameless of any crime. Addie was right to trust him. And I'm so glad you told Addie that Mr Hyman cares about him; that he'd never do anything cruel to him; glad that you called him Mr Hyman again.

Mum went to Jenny's bedside. In the corridor, I saw Jenny waiting for me.

'I need to know,' she said. 'Why I went back to the school, and why I went up to the top again, and my mobile phone thing. I need to know all of it.'

We had the big picture then, the huge facts, but not the details.

'The police will find out when they question Maisie tomorrow,' I said.

'But I might not have that long,' she said and we were talking about something else entirely.

'Of course you do.'

'No. I told you, Mum, I'm not going through

476

with your plan. And I'm *not going to change my mind.*'

I didn't argue with her, not then. Because as well as courage, our daughter has also inherited your infuriating stubbornness. '*Independence of mind!*' you'd correct. '*Strength of character!*' Well, all I know is that whereas other little girls at nursery were on the good-biddable-weedy scale of character, Jenny was up the other end as stubborn-wilful-strong-minded depending on your vantage point.

And yes, I'm proud.

I always was, secretly.

But I didn't share her need to know. I only ever wanted to find the truth to clear Adam, nothing beyond that. And I also knew that she had plenty of time, because that's what I would give her. I *would win* that argument.

'I need to remember it all, Mum,' she said. 'Because if I don't, it's like a part of my life didn't happen. The part of it that changed everything.'

I understood why she needed to know and I had to respect it. And I would be ready to protect her if she got too close to the fire.

We went towards Rowena's room, because Jen had had her 'mad person's tinnitus' memory there. At the time, we'd thought it was the smell of Donald, not Maisie, that had prompted it.

As we walked, we pieced together what Jenny had remembered of Wednesday afternoon so far. We knew that she'd taken two large bottles of water from the school kitchens and gone outside, using the side entrance. She'd heard the fire

477

alarm and thought it was a mistake or a practice. She'd been worried Annette wouldn't know what to do, so she'd put the bottles of water down by the kitchen entrance, and gone back in. Inside she'd smelt smoke and known it wasn't a practice.

We reached Rowena's room. Jenny closed her eyes. I wondered which of the scents in the room had prompted her memory last time — perhaps Maisie wore perfume that I hadn't consciously noticed before. Her cardigan was still draped over a chair. She must have left it behind when she was arrested.

I waited with Jenny for a few minutes; three or four maybe.

I braced myself to face the stranger that my friend had become.

'I'm taking water out of the kitchen,' Jenny said. 'I get outside. The fire alarm is making a hell of a din. I think Annette won't know what to do. So I put the water down and go back in. Bloody hell, it really is a fire.'

She broke off. We'd got to this point before. The only new thing was that we thought her mobile phone had fallen out of her pocket when she put the water down.

Jenny took my hand.

'I was afraid to do this alone,' she said. 'I mean, go any further.'

But I already knew that was why she had waited for me first.

She closed her eyes again.

'The smoke isn't that bad,' she said. 'You can smell it, but no worse really than when there's

478

something in the oven that's caught. I'm not frightened, just working out what I should do. I think that actually Annette won't be worried at all, she'll be loving this! Finally she has her drama.'

I saw Jenny struggling as she reached the final doors in the memory corridor.

I thought of Sarah's 'retrograde amnesia' — fire doors, I imagined, thick and heavy, protecting her from what lay beyond them.

I think it's knowing she is so loved by Ivo — and also by me and you and Adam and Sarah — which gave her the strength to push at those doors to make them open; to re-enter the horror of that afternoon.

'And then I see Maisie,' she said.

Her body had gone rigid.

★　★　★

Mum is back in our spare room now, and I'm sitting on Adam's bed, holding his small soft hand as he sleeps. Jenny's memory has been playing in my mind like a film, which I can't switch off; looping over and over again. I'm hoping that telling you what I see will make it finally stop.

★　★　★

The fire siren screeches into the summer's afternoon. Jenny puts down her bottles of water and goes back into the school, using the kitchen entrance. She smells smoke, but isn't frightened.

She's thinking about Annette, that she'll be loving this.

She goes up the stairs towards the upper ground floor. Then she sees Maisie, in her long-sleeved FUN shirt.

Maisie is crying.

'I saw Adam coming out of the Art room,' she says. 'Oh God, what have you done, Ro?'

Rowena, in her sensible linen trousers, is facing her, blazing with anger.

'You saw Adam, and you blame *me*?'

'No, of course not. I'm sorry I — '

Rowena slaps Maisie's face, brutally hard. I hear the sound of her palm slamming against Maisie's wet cheek and in that sound the fictions disintegrate.

'Shut up, hog.'

'You sent me a text,' Maisie says. 'I thought you'd — '

'Forgiven you?'

'I just wanted what was best — '

'You take away my lover and then you bankrupt us. Stunning, Mummy. Fucking stunning.'

Maisie rallies for a moment. 'He was too old for you. He was exploiting you and — '

'He's a pathetic piece of shit. Spineless. And you are an interfering bitch.'

Shouting at her, whipping her with words.

'I should go and help,' Maisie says. Then she turns to Rowena, finding courage.

'Did you make Addie do it, Ro?'

'You decide, Mummy.'

She wipes the tears off Maisie's face; the red mark visible from where she slapped her.

480

'You need to wash your face,' she says. Then she pulls down Maisie's trouser zip. 'And dress properly, for fuck's sake.'

Maisie leaves to help with the reception children. She hasn't seen Jenny.

But Rowena sees her.

She sees Jenny and knows she's heard everything.

★   ★   ★

Jenny remembered that at that moment the fire didn't seem important. She knew there was virtually no one in the school and everyone could easily get out. All she could think about was Rowena hitting her mother, hurting her.

'Adam's gone to look for you,' Rowena said to her. 'Up in the medical room.'

And everything changed.

The school was on fire and *Adam was at the top of the school.*

Jen ran to find him.

★   ★   ★

And Addie? Where was he, really? I need to rewind a little now so he can feature in this ghastly film too.

I watch him leave sports day with Rowena, who's suggested she takes him to get his cake. So carefully planned.

She's wearing sensible clothes, in contrast to Jenny, and I think she looks so grown-up now.

They reach the edge of the playing field. By

the chest-height jewel-coloured azalea bushes I think they pause a minute, while Rowena tells him about the birthday present Mr Hyman has left for him. And Addie is really pleased that Mr Hyman has got him a present.

Because I think that still figure I saw on the edge of the playing field was Rowena, with Adam next to her; but he was too small to be seen above the azalea bushes.

They walk on towards the school.

Rowena goes with Addie up to his classroom to get his cake. She takes the matches out of Miss Madden's cupboard. She tells him that Mr Hyman's present is in the Art room. It's a different kind of volcano. He has to light it. He can use his birthday-cake matches.

But Adam doesn't want to, surprising Rowena, because she underestimated him; thought him wet. So she tells him Mr Hyman brought the volcano present to the school *himself*, even though he'll get into terrible trouble if he's found there. She tells him Mr Hyman will be coming up to the Art room soon and will be so disappointed if Addie isn't playing with his present. So Addie reluctantly agrees.

Rowena leaves and goes down the stairs to the office.

Addie goes to the Art room. He trusts Mr Hyman, loves him even. But he's afraid of matches and he's never lit one before, isn't sure how to do it.

Rowena has time to listen to Annette's inane chatter, hardening her alibi.

Adam gets a match to light. He stands well

back and throws it at the volcano because he's afraid of fire, even a sparkler.

And the bucket, full of accelerant, pauses a second, as the flame catches, and then it explodes, flames leaping out. Addie is terrified and runs.

I know, darling, I want to have been with him then too. Made it alright for him too.

Maisie is coming out of the ladies' toilets, the alarm sounding, and she sees him as he runs from the Art room.

Adam dashes down the stairs, past the secretary's office, and out of the main exit.

And the two films collide now because Maisie sees Rowena.

'I saw Adam coming out of the Art room,' she says. 'Oh God, what have you done, Ro?'

And Jenny hears their argument; sees Rowena hit Maisie.

So Rowena tells her that Adam is looking for her up in the medical room.

A single sentence and our family is destroyed.

Because Jenny goes up to the third floor, looking for Addie.

She smells smoke, but it's not too bad, not yet, and maybe she hears flames, but nothing yet to see.

She doesn't know that the fire is travelling through the wall cavities and ceiling spaces and through vents.

Outside, on the gravel, Rowena has her arm around Adam. Next to them is the statue of herself as a child.

And I think it's now that Rowena texts Jenny. I think she tells Jenny that Adam is still in the school; to keep her in there. I see her fingers quickly pressing the pads on her mobile.

By the side of the school, near the discarded water bottles, Jenny's mobile bleeps with a message.

But no one hears.

Because the fire explodes. Flames ricochet along walls; heat tunnels along corridors and through ceiling cavities, punching through into rooms and blowing out the windows and the school is drowning in choking smoke.

On the playing field I see the thick black smoke and start running.

Next to the bronze child Rowena tells Addie that it's all his fault.

★　★　★

Jenny had opened that fire door into her memory, and it was terrifying. She was shaking violently.

'I'm in the fire. Addie must be here too. And it's everywhere, the fire, burning, and . . .'

I put my arms around her and told her that she was safe now. I helped her to come back to me.

Rowena was still sleeping.

We left her room, neither of us could bear to be near to her now. But we could still see her through the glass in the door.

Her sleeping face looked like the blank slate of a person's character.

'Addie was outside all the time, wasn't he?' Jenny said. 'I mean, that's what Annette's statement said, and Rowena's, that he was outside straight away.'

'Yes.'

They'd *both been outside*; for a minute, maybe two, *both had been safe*.

But Jenny had been by the kitchen exit, at the side of the school.

And then she'd gone back in.

Behind us, the doors to the burns unit opened and there was a sudden frenzy of noise and activity as a trolley with a patient was wheeled in surrounded by medical staff. The lights were up full now and you couldn't tell if it was night or day. I remembered Jenny being brought here, that first afternoon; the horror of it.

The noise disturbed Rowena. She stirred in her sleep.

'She planned to kill Addie,' Jenny said. 'Must have done.'

I remembered Rowena describing the white spirit and accelerant in the 'volcano', and the cans of spray mount stacked up behind. Brilliant at Science, Rowena would know which chemicals explode and burn and poison.

'It was meant to blow up in his face,' Jenny said. 'She must have been terrified when he was OK — then thought it was bloody Christmas when he couldn't speak.'

'Yes.'

'She only had one injury, the burn from an iron. It *was* an accident, just like she said.'

Jen needed to see this picture in its entirety while I wanted to turn away, but I made myself look at it too.

'I don't think her dad ever hurt her before,' Jenny continued. 'Just that one time. Because he

485

knew what she'd done to us.'

I remembered back to that scene in Rowena's room. I remembered Donald grabbing her hands, because he knew. *He knew.*

'He realised she'd only gone in to the fire to look good,' Jenny said.

I remembered Rowena walking towards Donald and his look of hatred and fury. '*You disgust me,*' he'd said.

'She probably just went as far as the vestibule,' Jenny continued. 'Then lay down knowing the firemen were coming. She wanted to make sure no one suspected her.'

'*Quite the little heroine, aren't you?*' Donald had said and his fury was shocking.

I remembered another time, and Maisie's voice; the sadness in it.

'*You shouldn't condemn someone, should you? If you love them, if they're your family, you have to try and see the good. I mean, that's what love is in some ways, isn't it? Believing in someone's goodness*'.

It was her daughter, not her husband, she'd been protecting all this time.

Had Rowena planned, from the start, to blame her mother?

'*She texted me a little while ago, said the tubes were up the spout. So Chauffeur-Mum to the fore!*'

I don't suppose there was anything wrong with the tubes.

Through the glass, I watched Rowena getting out of bed.

'You need to get better, Jen,' I said. 'And then you can tell everyone what you heard and saw.'

She half smiled at me.

'Good try, Mum. But Addie will tell everyone it was Rowena who made him do it, without any help from me.'

'But — '

'It's just a fluke that Dad still thinks it's Maisie, not Rowena. But Adam will tell him properly.'

'Yes, and Dad will believe him. And so will Aunty Sarah, but no one else will. Maisie will have given a full confession by now.'

'*You know I'd do anything for Rowena,*' she'd said quietly. '*Don't you, Gracie?*'

'And if Donald was going to say anything he'd have done so by now.'

'But the police might still believe Addie,' Jenny said.

'They're not going to believe an eight-year-old against adults. Maybe they might have listened to him at the start. Not now though, when it's taken him so long.'

'But they *might*,' she insisted.

'Oh God.'

'Mum?'

Thoughts were circling around something so horrible that I couldn't bear to look at it; but they were getting inexorably closer.

'Rowena will think that too; that the police might believe him.'

The circling thoughts spiralled downwards into a single memory.

'*I'd really like to see him, tell him it wasn't his fault,*' Rowena had said. '*I mean, he probably won't want to see me, but I'd really like to.*'

Jen shook her head as I told her, as if that would stop it from being true. But she knew that it was.

'You need to get better,' I said to her. 'To make sure Adam is safe.'

And I hated blackmailing her like that. But it was the only way. As I said, the life of your child trumps everything.

'You can do that,' she said.

'I can't because — '

'Mum — '

'Let me finish. Please. OK, let's say that by some miracle I can speak. Let's just play that one out — what could I say? I didn't hear the conversation you heard. I was still at sports day. I can hardly say that we chatted like this, can I? What judge will believe that? I have no proof at all that it was Rowena, not Maisie.

'But there won't be any miracles. I believe in a lot of things now that I didn't before. Fairy stories, ghosts, angels. I think they're all real now. But I don't believe I'll get better.

'I have no cognitive function, Jen. I'll never recover from that.'

I didn't know if that was a white lie or not. I still don't.

'I can't protect him,' I said. 'But you can. You can live and give him an adult's voice.'

In her room, Rowena was disconnecting her drip.

'Angels, Mum?' Jenny asked, trying to smile. 'You think that's what we are now?'

'Possibly. Maybe angels aren't really good or special, just ordinary, like us.'

'And the wings?'

'What about them?'

'Wings and a halo. Basic kit for an angel.'

'The earliest painting of a Christian angel, which is in the Catacomb of Priscilla, third century, doesn't have wings.'

'Only you could say something like that at a time like this,' she said.

And then her voice was quiet and ashamed.

'I want to live so much.'

'I know.'

'I will never love anyone the way you love me.'

'You stayed looking for Addie in the fire. You didn't get the text, but you stayed anyway.'

★ ★ ★

Rowena left her room and went out into the corridor towards the exit. A nurse saw her.

'Just going for a cigarette,' Rowena said.

'Didn't think you were the type.'

Rowena smiled at her. 'No.'

Jenny and I followed her out of the burns unit.

So quiet out in those midnight corridors.

★ ★ ★

We followed her as she went to ICU.

Inside, the lights were full on, the ward as busy as ever; no day — night rhythm here.

She rang on the buzzer.

A nurse answered the door.

Rowena's voice sounded fragile. She drew her dark blue, hooded dressing gown around herself.

'I'm a friend of Jenny's. Is she alright? I can't sleep for worrying.'

'She's very ill.'

'Will she die?'

The nurse was silent and sad.

Tears welled in Rowena's eyes. 'I thought you'd say that.'

So she'd come to make sure.

I couldn't bear to look at her face.

But Jenny did.

'I am going to live,' Jenny said and her voice was loud with hope; a promise.

But Rowena turned, as if she'd heard a whispered threat.

★　★　★

Mum left the hospital and I went with her. The night was still heavy with heat. In the block of flats opposite the hospital, I saw people sleeping outside on their tiny balconies. That film of Wednesday afternoon kept playing, looping, over and over again, with me powerless to change anything that happened.

As I watched it, I knew that I should have *looked* at that police painting-by-numbers portrait of Maisie. I should have found the courage to do that. Because if I had, I would have seen the spaces they hadn't filled in with criminal suspicions; the ones which were already coloured in with livid bruises.

And then I would have overlaid their suspicions with strong colours of knowledge from the years of knowing my friend.

But I had no doubts with Rowena. It was shocking it was her, not only because she's a teenage girl, but also because it was so transparently and quickly the truth. Search and replace 'Maisie' with 'Rowena' and the story revealed is vile but clear. Her acting wasn't that remarkable. She knew how to play the part of victim, who carries on loving her abuser, from years of watching her mother.

Rowena makes sense of it all, she connects to everything — to Silas and to the school and to the fraud and to domestic violence; but in none of the ways I'd imagined.

But I don't think she's entirely evil; wicked even.

She went into a burning building to rescue me and Jenny.

Jenny thinks she did it to appear courageous and deflect suspicion. But I don't think that. I don't want to think that.

I hold onto this one action as hugely courageous and honourable. I choose to see it as dramatic contrition; whatever went before or comes afterwards.

Because I need to believe she has some goodness; one bright colour in the acrid smoke.

Rowena herself talked about the angel and devil in a person. We'd thought she meant Silas Hyman or her father, but I think she was describing herself.

I don't believe in grey any more. I think black and white, good and evil, co-exist but don't mingle together; a world not of nanny voices but of devils and angels.

As the film loops again, and I watch her running into the burning building, I imagine that her angel is yelling at her loudly enough to drown out the devil. Really. *An angel.* Not one with a frilly dress and silver wings like the one at the top of the Christmas tree, but a muscular Old Testament one, a Raphael or Michael — a bold, strong angel as the good in her takes a shape and finds a voice.

Because I cannot leave this world thinking there is nothing redemptive in a teenage girl. I do not want to have hatred inside me when I die.

★   ★   ★

We arrived home. Mum went to bed, exhausted, and I was the only one awake. It was almost the witching hour, the house silent, everyone asleep. The last time I'd been up on my own like this was when Adam was a young baby.

I went to Jenny's bedroom. I'd left her with Ivo in the garden, promising I'd see her again in the morning. No goodbyes yet.

'What's it like to have a teenage daughter?' a mum at school asked me once, whose eldest child is the same age as Adam.

'There are always boys in the house. Huge great boys with huge trainers in the hallway,' I said, because I always trip over them. 'You're always out of food in the fridge because the same boys are always hungry. The girls eat nothing and then you worry about anorexia, and even if your daughter seems fine and eats fine you worry about bulimia.'

'Does she borrow your clothes?'

I laughed. As if. 'It's the contrast that's hard,' I said. 'Her skin glows. Mine is wrinkling. Even my legs look wrinkled next to hers.'

The school mum pulled a face, thinking it wouldn't happen to her, not realising that it probably already had, but without a teenage daughter for comparison she wouldn't know.

'The main thing,' I continued, warming to my theme, 'is sex. It's everywhere when you've got a teenager.'

'You mean they . . . in your house?' She sounded horrified.

'No, not exactly,' I said, wondering how to explain that sex comes into the house and takes it over; wafting through the corridors and loafing on the stairs, hormones funnelling out of the windows.

The scent of it lingered there, in Jenny's room.

Not sex or hormones, I realised, but great quantities of life still to be lived.

I sat at her desk and saw that there were virtually no books, but a whole shelf of Ordnance Survey maps for hiking and climbing. As far as I could tell, her desk had mainly been used to paint her nails. I could see little smudges of shiny red on it.

Did I tell you that a few weeks before her A levels she said she'd rather '*live my life now, than revise for a future one*'? So different to me at that age, desperate to get to university; swotting the whole way through sixth form.

I thought university would be wonderful for her too. I thought she'd do the full three years and love every moment of it. I was going to make certain she didn't get pregnant at the end of year two.

It wasn't that I wanted her to live out the unlived part of my life, but that I thought what made me happy would make her happy too.

And I was cross with you when you didn't try and stop her from going climbing in the Cairngorms instead of doing that revision course, or when she swapped a French exchange visit for canoeing in Wales with Ivo. I was so sure that she was being childish, not *thinking of the future* — not realising that she was living a life-choice right there in front of me. An outdoorsy girl, like you, my darling, who prefers canoeing and climbing to Dryden and Chaucer.

I should have looked at her life from her perspective; climbed up a mountain with her and seen the surrounding landscape of other ways to achieve fulfilment and happiness.

Or just come in here and properly looked around.

★　★　★

I'm lying next to you on Adam's top bunk — a new perspective on his so-familiar room. From up here, I can see that the top of his globe lampshade needs dusting; Iceland is just a smudge. '*A tidy house is a sign of a wasted life*,' Maisie once told me, kindly, knowing my antipathy to housework, and that's good, because from up here mine's clearly been very profitably spent.

I'm actually really proud of my mothering

now, of both Jenny and Adam, if I had any hand in the making of the people they've become.

And I have no regrets about my choices, even the default ones. Other people can write the great book, paint the wonderful painting, because I don't need a work of art to speak for me after I've gone; my family will do that. There is no need to throw something into the void, because it is full of people I love.

I go down to Addie's bunk.

I've always known how much you love him. But until the fire, I didn't know how much he was loved by Jenny and Mum and Sarah too. Between you, there's enough love to inflate a lifeboat for him.

And look at you. You survived both your parents dying — more than survived it: you grew up to be this wonderful confident man. And Adam can too.

I hold his hand.

I walk into his dreams and I tell him how special he is.

'The most special boy in the whole world,' I say.

'The galaxy?'

'The universe.'

'If there's life out there.'

'I'm sure there is.'

'There's probably another me out there, exactly the same.'

'No one could be exactly the same as you.'

'In a good way?'

'Yes.'

36

Another oven-hot day; the sky a sadistic cloudless blue.

I return to my ward.

The windows are open but there's no breeze, heat from outside seeping in. Nurses are sweating; wisps of hair sticking to their foreheads.

No sign of Dr Bailstrom's clicking red heels and I'm grateful that I won't be distracted by fashion in what should surely be a serious, high-minded moment.

I take a last look at shiny linoleum and nasty metal lockers and ugly curtains. We twenty-first-century people really don't know how to do death properly at all. I remember the ending of the film about J.M. Barrie, when he wheeled his dying lover into a magical Peter Pan set he'd secretly constructed in the garden. No brown geometric curtains for her. But they'll have to do.

I fight my way back into my body, through layers of flesh and muscle and bone, until I am inside.

I am trapped, as I knew I would be, under the hull of a vast ship wrecked on the ocean floor.

My eyelids welded shut; my eardrums broken; my vocal cords snapped off.

Pitch dark and silent and so heavy in here; a mile of black water above me.

All I can do is breathe.

* * *

I remember that the Latin word for breath and spirit is the same.

* * *

I hold my breath.

* * *

When Jenny faced her death in that chapel and looked for a heaven, I faced mine too. Properly. Fully. I told you then that I wouldn't let her die.

I knew that my child staying alive trumps everything. Adam's grief. And yours. My fear. Everything.

* * *

I must not breathe.

* * *

But I still hoped it would be someone else. Somebody else's mother and daughter and wife. Someone else's life.

My hope was desperate and ugly and futile. Because it was never really going to be someone else. And maybe that's fair. We keep our child but lose me. A balance.

* * *

I must not breathe.

★ ★ ★

But she's an adult, not a child, and I know that now; a lesson learnt.

I think, underneath, I knew it already. I was just afraid that when she was an adult she wouldn't need me any more.

I was afraid she wouldn't love me so much.

Not realising that she'd already grown up.

That she still loves me so much.

★ ★ ★

I must not breathe.

★ ★ ★

Instinct is fighting back; a riptide of selfish desire for life against every pulse of energy in me. But I have become far stronger over the last few days. And although it wasn't the reason I left the hospital's protective skin, it does mean I have the stamina to do this.

★ ★ ★

I must not breathe.

★ ★ ★

When I was twenty weeks pregnant with Jenny, I found out that her ovaries were already formed.

Inside our unborn baby daughter were our potential grandchildren (or at least the part of us that would be a part of them). I felt the future curled up inside me; my body a Russian doll of time.

★　★　★

I must not breathe.

★　★　★

I think of Adam far above me, up there on the surface in his inflatable lifeboat made out of other people's breath.

I think of Jenny reaching the shore of adulthood.

I think that the fear of my children drowning showed me how I could do this.

★　★　★

So little air in my lungs now.

★　★　★

Will you read Addie 'The Little Mermaid'? It's in his *Stories for Six-year-olds* on the bottom shelf of his bookcase. He'll say he hasn't read those stories *for years, Dad,* and in any case it's *too girly,* but you'll insist. You'll put your arm around him, and he'll turn the pages for you.

You'll read to him about the pain the little

mermaid felt when she left the water, walking on knives, because she loved her prince so. Because I want him to know that when I left my body in the hospital, when I went too far away for their scans, I was walking on knives because I couldn't bear for him to be accused of this terrible crime. Because I believed in him. Because I love him. Tell him that the hardest thing in this world is leaving him.

★   ★   ★

I don't have to try to hold my breath any more.

★   ★   ★

I slip out of the wrecked ship of my body into the mile-deep dark ocean.

You told me once that the last of the senses to go is hearing. But you're wrong. The last of the senses to go is love.

★   ★   ★

I am floating up to the surface, and with no effort I am slipping out of my body.

★   ★   ★

An alarm is going off, shuddering the air, and a doctor is running towards me.

A trolley loaded with equipment is being speeded across the lino, as if it's on skates, a frightened nurse at the helm.

My heart has stopped.
I hear clicking red heels.
Dr Bailstrom says there's a DNR order.
They talk of transplant.
They will keep my body functioning until my heart can be given to Jenny.

* * *

I watch their machinery as my inert body has oxygen artificially pumped through it. You are ushered hurriedly into a room to sign a consent form.

I shouldn't really be here, surely, hanging around like this. Shouldn't I be going to the next place now? A guest still at the table when the hosts are washing up in the kitchen.

And I'm still talking to you!

Last weekend, sitting at our kitchen table in our old life, I read in the paper about 'sticky air'. A futurologist predicts that people will be able to leave messages for each other suspended in the ether. So you never know but maybe, one day, you'll hear what I've been saying to you. Because surely as I talked to you the molecules in the air around me were changed; the air charged with words.

It must be when my heart is taken out and the machinery switched off that I will finally leave.

I remember that at the end of 'The Little Mermaid' she doesn't get a prince but a soul.

* * *

I go to ICU where Jenny is being prepared for the transplant. She's watching herself, Sarah bending over her body. I was jealous of Sarah's closeness to Jenny once, but I'm now outrageously grateful.

Jenny sees me and I take her hand.

'So much for becoming independent from me,' I say. 'I'll always be with you now.'

'Mum, that's macabre.'

'Beating away.'

'Please!'

'Seriously,' I say, 'it's just a pump.'

'*Your* pump.'

'You have far more use for it.'

We don't know what to say. Neither of us has talked about whether she'll remember this. Remember me.

'You'll get better,' Sarah says to Jenny, filling the silence. 'And you'll do a great job looking after Adam. But *other people are going to look after him too.*'

I glimpse you coming out of the doctor's office.

'So be a girl, Jen, not a woman too early,' Sarah continues.

'You're bloody *marvellous*,' I say to Sarah who, of course, can't hear, but Jenny smiles.

I tell Jenny it's time to get back into her body now.

She hugs me and I want to hug her longer, hang onto her, but I make myself pull back.

'Ivo and Dad and Aunt Sarah and Adam are waiting for you,' I say, and she goes back into her body.

Surely there should be a dramatic storm; the

pent-up compressed heat of the last four days released into thunderous drenching rain.

Through the window of the ward the sky remains relentlessly blue, a heat haze fuzzing the edges, but I feel cool.

I see you coming towards Jenny's bed.

I remember dragging Jenny down the stairs and thinking of love as white and quiet and cold.

You look at me. And in that moment you see me.

This is what love looks like an uncountable number of words later.

I go to you and kiss your face.

★　★　★

I watch you go with Jenny as she is wheeled towards the operating theatre. I think about angels. Not the fierce, strong Old Testament angels this time, but the angels of Fra Angelico, with their shining jewel-coloured robes, long wings down their backs; Giotto's hovering above Earth like larks, their shimmering gold halos pinpricks of light; Chagal's blue angel with her sad pale face. I think of Raphael's angels and Michelangelo's and the angels of Hieronymus Bosch and Klee.

I think that beneath each angel — just out of sight of the painting — are their children they were forced to leave behind.

But the heavenly afterlife isn't where I am, not yet.

I am sitting on the bottom step of our stairs packing Adam's bag with his uniform, which he'll need to change into after sports. I am knotting his tie so that all he has to do is slip it on and pull the skinny part because he still hasn't got the hang of tying his tie and I hope you know to do this for him.

And I'm in the sitting room, searching for a Lego piece down the back of the sofa, and you come up to me and hug me, 'Beautiful wife,' you say, and upstairs I hear Jenny on the phone to Ivo and Adam is reading on the rug and I am suffocated with need for you all.

★   ★   ★

They are taking my heart out.

All the light and colour and warmth in my body is leaving it now and coming into me — into whatever I am.

My soul is being born.

And Jenny is right, it is *beautiful*, but I rage against this birth of light. I want to see my grandchildren or just touch you once more and call to Jenny, 'Nearly supper, OK?'; or to Adam, 'I'm coming!'; to everyone waiting for me in the car, 'Two minutes, alright?'

Just a little more life.

But then the anger leaves and I am left without fear or regrets.

I am a sliver-thin light, diamond-sharp, that can slip through gaps in the world that we know. I will come into your dreams and speak soft words when you think of me.

There is no happy ever after — but there is an afterwards.

This isn't our ending.

Acknowledgements

My thanks go once again to the gifted Emma Beswetherick, without whom this book could not have been written. My huge thanks also to Joanne Dickinson for her conviction, enthusiasm and commitment. I'd also like to thank Ursula Mackenzie, David Shelley, Paola Ehrlich, Lucy Icke, Sara Talbot, Darren Turpin and the rest of the team at Piatkus and Little, Brown.

I want to thank Felicity Blunt at Curtis Brown for being the best agent a writer could have. My thanks also to Kate Cooper and Tally Garner, also at Curtis Brown.

Thank you Anne Calabresi who told me that her parents were the roof which had sheltered her, which I used in this story.

My friends and family made writing this book possible. So thank you again to my parents for their continuing support and to my sister Tora Orde-Powlett who is always my first and best reader. I also want to thank Sandra Leonard who read the ending before I'd written the beginning and encouraged me to carry on; to Michele Matthews for her generosity of time; to Trixie Rawlinson, Kelly Martin, Livia Firth and Lynne Gagliano who saw me often while my head was buried in the story and were so practically supportive. And to my old friends whose emails kept me going — Anne-Marie Casey, Nina Calabresi, Katy Gardner, Katie London, Anna

Joynt, Alison Clements and Amanda Jobbins.

I'd like to thank Richard Betts, and all the teachers like him, whose classrooms are safe, happy and inspiring and where children can fly.

Last, but most of all, to my husband Martin, who says he doesn't need thanking.

We do hope that you have enjoyed reading this large print book.

Did you know that all of our titles are available for purchase?

We publish a wide range of high quality large print books including:
Romances, Mysteries, Classics
General Fiction
Non Fiction and Westerns

Special interest titles available in large print are:
The Little Oxford Dictionary
Music Book
Song Book
Hymn Book
Service Book

Also available from us courtesy of Oxford University Press:
Young Readers' Dictionary
(large print edition)
Young Readers' Thesaurus
(large print edition)

For further information or a free brochure, please contact us at:
Ulverscroft Large Print Books Ltd.,
The Green, Bradgate Road, Anstey,
Leicester, LE7 7FU, England.
Tel: (00 44) 0116 236 4325
Fax: (00 44) 0116 234 0205

SISTER

Rosamund Lupton

When Beatrice hears that her little sister, Tess, is missing, she returns home to London on the first flight available. But Bee is unprepared for the terrifying truths she must face about her younger sibling when Tess' broken body is discovered in the snow. The police, Bee's friends, her fiance and even their mother accept the fact that Tess committed suicide. But Bee is convinced that something more sinister is responsible for Tess' untimely death. So she embarks on a dangerous journey to discover the truth, no matter the cost . . .

A DANCE OF GHOSTS

Kevin Brooks

PI John Craine struggles with the past. Seventeen years ago his wife, Stacy, was brutally murdered. Craine found her body in their bed. And since then, to escape the pain and the unanswered questions, he has buried himself in work by day, and whisky by night. But then the mother of a missing young woman, Anna Gerrish, calls on his services. Craine soon finds himself at the centre of a sinister web of corruption and lies that lead back into the murky waters of the past — and to the night that Craine has spent years trying to forget. As he delves deeper and deeper into the case everything gets increasingly, terrifyingly personal. And it's down to Craine to stop history from repeating itself . . .

SCREAM

Nigel McCrery

DCI Mark Lapslie's anonymous email bears a strange subject line: 'You Need To Listen To This.' He hears a woman scream — she screams twenty-seven times before her final death rattle is heard . . . Lapslie investigates and discovers that the message was sent from the hospital where his new girlfriend works and where he's undergoing treatment for his synaesthesia — a neurological condition that confuses his senses so he tastes sound. Who is screaming? And why? Meanwhile a murder victim has been brutally tortured and dumped on an island in the Thames Estuary. Then, a case is brought against him after questioning a minor and he's taken off the investigation. Unable to work, Lapslie must sit around, while the killer comes far too close to home . . .